A Wing and a Prayer

By Steve Semler

I0671261

Venture City books by Steve Semler

A WING AND A PRAYER (April 2015)

A STRONG, STRONG WIND (May 2015)

ALL FORESTS ARE ONE (Summer 2015)

Misplaced Powers

The huntress moved with a determined grace into the frozen yard.

She strode up to Sheena, ignoring the men. Towering more than a full head over her, the woman looked down at Sheena as if she was a bug she was thinking about crushing. The huntress sneered, "Sheena, huh? A game warden? Really?"

Sheena blushed and managed to stammer, "My… my parents liked the show. And I…."

"Never mind that!" the archer interrupted. "I paid Ankh a lot of money to acquire Shanikali's legacy. And I waited a long time for him to find the stone with the right power. Power that got into you by accident! And mark my words, I'll figure out some way to get it *out* of you and get the power I deserve!"

Sheena's thoughts reeled as she tried to find some way to escape. The woman turned to consider the house and then glanced at the men, still frozen to the ground. She casually drew another arrow from her hunting quiver. Over her shoulder, she said to Sheena, "You need to stay alive until I can make arrangements to wring that power out of you. Your friends are under no such restriction, however."

The huntress nocked the arrow and drew back her bowstring. She gave Sheena an evil smirk. She pointed the arrow at each of the men in turn. "Who gets it first? The suit? The government shaman? Your cute nerdy husband, maybe? Oh, choices, choices!"

Table of Contents

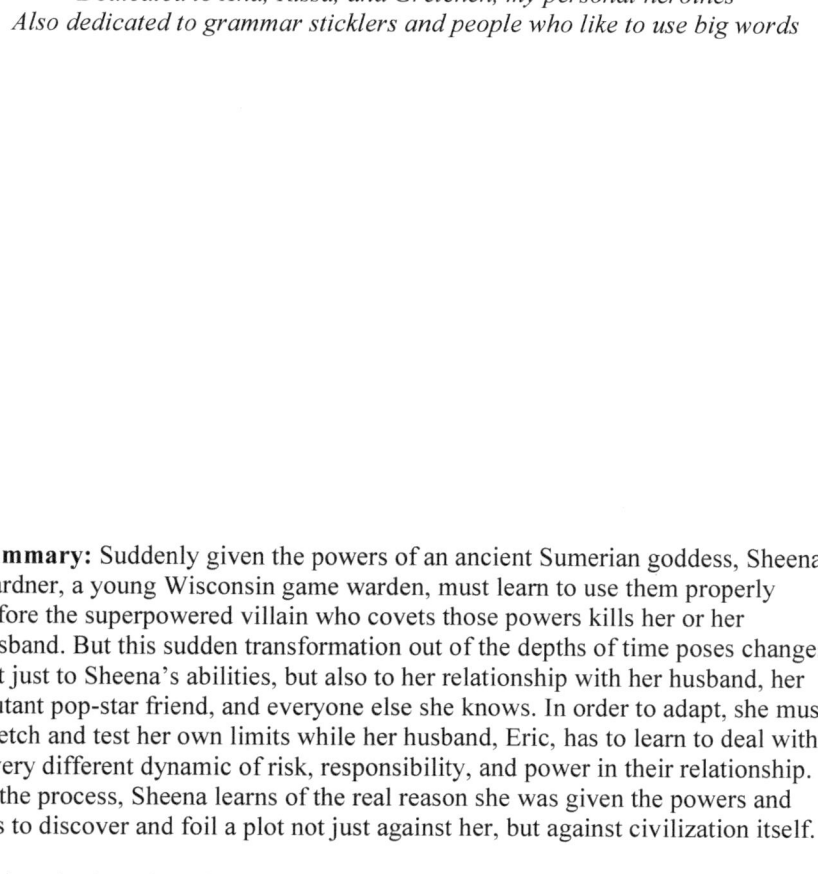

Dedicated to Ana, Rissa, and Gretchen, my personal heroines
Also dedicated to grammar sticklers and people who like to use big words

Summary: Suddenly given the powers of an ancient Sumerian goddess, Sheena Gardner, a young Wisconsin game warden, must learn to use them properly before the superpowered villain who covets those powers kills her or her husband. But this sudden transformation out of the depths of time poses changes not just to Sheena's abilities, but also to her relationship with her husband, her mutant pop-star friend, and everyone else she knows. In order to adapt, she must stretch and test her own limits while her husband, Eric, has to learn to deal with a very different dynamic of risk, responsibility, and power in their relationship. In the process, Sheena learns of the real reason she was given the powers and has to discover and foil a plot not just against her, but against civilization itself.

Written in the spirit of the *City of Heroes* MMORPG, *The Secret World Chronicles*, *Arrow*, *The Flash*, *The Avengers*, *Iron Man*, and many other works of comic book-based heroic science fiction.

Chapter 1 – Stakeout at the Cabin

"Officer Gardner, you can watch from over here, behind the car," the agent told her. "The Federal Bureau of Superpowered Affairs appreciates your assistance and professionalism, but we don't want you in harm's way for this, if anything happens."

Sheena nodded and crouched on the gravel beside the sedan. Game wardens seldom carried firearms, but she would have been more comfortable if she had been armed. Still, Sheena thought, it probably wouldn't do any good against what they were up against. They were after a metahuman artifact thief, and she was along as a local guide. She watched the FBI agents don their lightweight body armor in the last glow of twilight. Specially equipped by the FBSA, they would go in to make the arrests. They had tanglers and some sort of high tech rifle that could stop even a supervillain in his tracks for a short time. At least, that was the theory. Sheena had taken as much extra law enforcement training as the Wisconsin Department of Natural Resources would allow, but this stakeout was in another league entirely.

The young officer pulled her hat firmly down over her long mane of blonde hair and fumbled her prescription sunglasses into a shirt pocket, replacing them with her regular glasses. The frames for the thick lenses were several years out of style, but Sheena wasn't particularly interested in trying to keep up with the latest fashion. She considered herself more of a nerd, actually. Whatever happened tonight, she didn't want to miss any of it.

"Hey, Sheena," a smooth Spanish-accented voice said behind her with a hint of amusement, "you don't need to take cover just yet!" The other FBSA agent, Special Agent Felix Calderón, grinned at her. He was a well-built man in his mid-forties wearing the same dark suit and glasses outfit as his partner. Where his partner, Special Agent Thomas Schauer, was the classic "Man in Black"—a walking stereotype with short cropped brown hair, dark suit, dark glasses, discreet earpiece, and a bland expression—Calderón's collar was open and he wore a beaded bone choker around his neck. His dark wavy hair was longer and greying at the temples.

"No? Aren't we ready to go?" She glanced across the four-acre corn field at the cabin they were watching. There wasn't much to see through the trees surrounding the well-kept vacation home at the end of the gravel road. The opposite side of the cabin from the corn field was on a hill looking out over the lake. The forest around the property wasn't too thick to walk through, but it did a fine job of screening the cabin from view from any direction but straight out on the lake. The nearest other cabin was almost one hundred meters down the lakeshore.

"Sí, but Doctor Ankh isn't here yet with his stolen goods, and he is the guest of honor!" Calderón leaned his elbows casually on the roof of the sedan.

The corner of Sheena's mouth tilted up and she shook her head. "You're saying I should relax, aren't you?"

"You won't miss the excitement, I promise you." The FBSA agent had a very calming voice. Despite being up among the pine trees of the Wisconsin north woods, he was obviously not feeling out of his own comfort zone.

Sheena shivered and nodded. "This is way out of my usual routine, Agent Calderón. I guess I'm a little nervous."

"That is understandable. What is your normal routine? I do not know much about what game wardens really do. Check fishing and hunting licenses?"

She chuckled. "It's way more than that! Stopping poachers, giving classes on firearms safety and hunting regulations, investigating environmental violations, working with other law enforcement groups, like you guys...." She smiled wryly to herself. "This job has so much variety that it's hard to tell what I'll be doing from one day to the next. That's part of what I like about it."

"What's the other part?" He was watching the cabin as the light faded from the sky, but she could tell he was paying attention to what she said.

"Well, for me, it's the opportunity to protect animals, nature, and people. You know, keeping the balance. People should be able to use the land, to hunt and fish, to boat and swim. They just have to keep it safe and sustainable."

"No superpowered criminals out here?"

"Hah! No metahumans at all, as far as I know! Occasional drug smugglers and drunk hunters, but no supervillains."

"Sounds quiet."

"I suppose it depends on what you're used to." She paused thoughtfully as she watched the cabin. "I met a metahuman in high school, but I don't think I've ever run into any others."

"Really?" She could tell Calderón was curious. "Who was that?"

"Her name was Gayle." Sheena laughed. Calderón raised an eyebrow over the rim of his dark sunglasses. At the agent's questioning glance, she explained, "It was funny because Gayle had a breeze blowing around her all the time, and this was back in a town called Breezy Point, near Milwaukee."

"Ah. I see," he responded with a slight smile. Sheena couldn't read anything into that.

"She was a mutant. You could tell how she was feeling by the scent in the air. If it was burnt leaves, she was angry. If it was citrus or some kind of fruity smell, she was feeling good. I accidentally startled her really bad once and all of a sudden there was this sour milk smell. Weird." Sheena thought back to high school. Gayle had been a junior when she was a sophomore. She met Gayle in the high school music department where they both played in the school band. Gayle was an avid musician and played the saxophone like a pro. She sang and played the guitar and other instruments, as well. She could also do some pretty impressive tricks to control the wind, too, but that was the sort of thing Gayle had tried to keep hidden. They weren't exactly close friends, but they got along well and Sheena had stood up for Gayle several times when other students tried to bully her or set her up for cruel jokes.

Calderón ventured a guess. "Gayle. That would be the daughter of the superhero, Aspen, right?"

"Yeah," Sheena sighed. "That was so sad. No one knew that was her mom until the K'rk'ti attacked and Aspen died saving Milwaukee from the aliens."

"I heard that Gayle didn't handle it very well." His tone was neutral, but Sheena looked over sharply.

"Well, no... but what do you expect? She was seventeen, always getting hassled by kids at school, had already had to switch high schools twice because she was 'a distraction,' and then her mom dies stopping a swarm of aliens attacking the city!"

"That would be hard."

"Yeah. It was." Sheena remembered the trouble. It was Memorial Day when the K'rk'ti attacked the earth. While Aspen had saved Milwaukee, Gayle had gone through a very rough time after that and there wasn't a lot Sheena could do to help. She had tried to be supportive, but Gayle went through dramatic mood swings and distanced herself from her friends. She turned into a hard-partying "bad girl." The next year, Gayle barely managed to graduate.

"Were you very good friends?" Calderón asked.

Sheena shook her head. "I didn't think so at the time, but I guess I was to her. She probably didn't really have many real friends, being so different and all."

"Probably not. Do you still keep in touch?"

"Yeah, a bit. She moved out east to Venture City and became a hero, like her mother. And a rock star, too. Gayle sent me an autographed CD when she released *Nature Lover*." The gift had also included a long personal apology letter, but Sheena didn't tell him that. Gayle's letter asked Sheena to forgive her for pushing her away and thanked her for standing up for her back in high school. Both the disc and the letter were among Sheena's prized possessions.

The agent didn't seem surprised to hear any of this. Maybe he knew Gayle. She asked, "Has Gayle ever worked with the FBSA on superhero cases?"

Calderón chuckled softly. "Sí, Sheena, she has. My partner there, Tom, has worked with her, but I have never had the pleasure."

Over by the FBI van, Agent Schauer raised his hand to his earpiece. He looked over at Calderón and nodded.

"Ah," Calderón said. "There is the signal. Time to catch a crook. If you will excuse me?" Sheena nodded and he adjusted his jacket and joined the FBI agents as they prepared to go. According to the agents, the villain, Doctor Ankh, had been using this cabin as a hideout and a place to stash the magical artifacts he and his minions had stolen from all over the world. The FBI had received a credible tip that Doctor Ankh would be returning tonight with more stolen goods.

The agents moved out through the cornfield as the moon rose in the east. The cornfield sloped gently down toward the cabin from the gravel road where they had parked their vehicles. At this point in the season, the corn was only shoulder-high. Sheena put on her night vision goggles to watch the action. She blinked in surprise. She lowered the device and looked out at the disappearing backs of the agents, then tilted the goggles back into place. Whatever they were wearing was nearly invisible to her goggles. Nothing to see, that way, she guessed. She sighed and relaxed against the car. The metal was starting to get cold.

She looked over at Calderón's partner, Agent Schauer. He was standing in the shadows watching the cabin impassively through his dark glasses. Sheena mentally shrugged and turned her gaze back in the direction of the cabin. She wondered what it was like working with superpowered heroes and villains. Everybody knew that there were strange and fantastic things in the world, like magic and mutants and superadvanced technology, but most people spent their lives without ever actually meeting a metahuman in person. Some places seemed to attract more than their fair share of superpowered attention, like Venture City, Massachusetts, or New York City and San Francisco. Cities like Chicago, Milwaukee, and Minneapolis had some well-known heroes, as well.

The Federal Bureau of Superpowered Affairs, or FBSA, had been created in the 1950's to try to manage the whole spectrum of superpowered criminals and crime fighters. From what Sheena remembered from her law enforcement history classes, it had always worked closely with the FBI. Sometimes, like in the last decade, it also served as a liaison to United Nations groups, like the Vanguard. Whether the threat was a small-time bank robber with a freeze ray or a full-scale alien invasion from another dimension, the FBSA tried to coordinate an appropriate government response. Their efforts were also meant to show people that there was some truth to the claim that their government was doing something to protect them. The FBSA worked with and through dozens of other groups—from local law enforcement to international coalitions of superheroes. It was probably a difficult and relatively thankless job, Sheena guessed.

After what seemed like hours but was probably only twenty minutes, Agent Schauer tapped her twice on the arm and pointed toward the cabin. Sheena adjusted the magnification on her goggles. Above the tree line Sheena saw something flying in from over the lake. It was a man, in view for just a few seconds before dropping below the trees. No parachute or jet pack or anything—just flying under whatever superpower carried him. Sheena whispered to the FBSA agent, "That's him?"

Schauer nodded. He kept his gaze locked on the target. Sheena guessed that the agent had his own kind of micro-display unit tucked into those glasses. Probably with some sort of communications link to the team, too. He whispered back to her, "They're recording. We'll get the whole thing for evidence. Standard part of the procedure. Ready to go now. Stay alert."

Sheena watched the little bit of the cabin she could see over the rows of corn. She could barely make out its porch, even with magnification. She saw shadows moving rapidly near the cabin, and then a bright burst of light—one of the agents' flash grenades. It was followed quickly by another, and the door from the porch into the cabin was open and dark shapes were moving inside. Sheena held her breath.

A bold reddish light streamed from the cabin windows and doors, painting the nearby trees with a blood-red glare like a Fourth of July firework. Something unnatural was happening inside. Sheena could hear… something… howling and shrieking. Even two hundred meters away, the sound hurt her ears. Not because of its volume, but because of something alien that the sound carried. Almost like fingernails on a blackboard, but low, not shrill. She shuddered.

The eerie glow faded, but sounds of fighting mixed with the troubling shrieks reached her ears. Sheena watched and waited, trying to follow what was going on. Then, a different flash of light burst forth and an explosion rocked the night. Sheena watched in wonder as several glowing objects spiraled away from the cabin like Roman candles gone astray. In the blink of an eye, she realized that one was headed right toward them. Sheena dropped behind the car and shouted, "Duck!"

The glowing object skimmed wildly back and forth over the cornfield and then shot quickly over the car, stopping in midair a few feet from Sheena and the FBSA agent. It was like four brilliant golden balls rotating around each other inside a transparent balloon. The thing lit up the little roadside clearing like a stadium lamp. Both Sheena and Agent Schauer turned their heads and narrowed their eyes against the glare. It bobbed in place silently for a few seconds. Sheena got the sudden impression that it was examining her. The object made a noise like a set of wind chimes, and seemed to collapse in on itself. As it did so, the light and sound flowed out of the strange glowing thing like a river of energy— straight into Sheena.

It was like nothing she had ever experienced. Sheena felt filled with energy and life; exhilarated and frightened, all at once. She shivered uncontrollably for several seconds as she felt a liquid warmth and a frosty chill run through her at the same time. Flashes of things she had never seen or even imagined danced through her mind, like someone else's memories. Some seemed fresh and recent. Others felt very, very old. As soon as one vision faded, another flashed before her eyes. Sheena couldn't remember any of them consciously, but the same golden light was present in everything. The visions passed and she could see her surroundings again. Schauer was standing with his mouth agape staring at her. Sheena felt a twitch in her back. Then another twitch, accompanied by an uncomfortable pinching. She was confused. The pinching got worse. What was going on?

"Ow!" Sheena yelled and arched her back, jerking her shoulders around to try to stop the stabbing pain. A brief flash of the golden light was accompanied by the sound of tearing cloth. Suddenly, she felt much better. She rolled her shoulders, trying to loosen her shirt. What remained of her shirt. She tried to free her wings. Sheena stopped still, her eyes wide. Her wings? She looked slowly over one shoulder, then the other. Unbelieving, she extended her left wing, and then her right wing. Growing from between her shoulder blades were two mighty golden eagle's wings, a couple of shades darker than her own blonde hair. Her uniform shirt still constricted her arms and wings. She unbuttoned the last couple of buttons that remained and freed herself from the torn garment, heedless of Agent Schauer or the fact that the golden light illuminating the clearing was now coming from her. She felt stronger, better than she ever had, almost, but very confused.

Sheena heard the sound of someone running through the cornfield. She turned in that direction to see who it was. A big bald-headed man in a flannel shirt and torn jeans skidded to a halt at the side of the road. He was carrying a worn canvas backpack bulging with something. "Aw, crap!" he wheezed. "A cape! Ankh didn't say nothing about no capes!"

Before Sheena or Agent Schauer could react, the crook sprinted back into the cornfield. Without conscious thought, Sheena thrust her left arm after him, fingers splayed, and growled, "Stop him!" Out of nowhere, a large wolf appeared and ran off after the fleeing man with a hunting howl. Her right arm shot up to the night sky and then flashed down in a launching gesture. From the air, an eagle appeared out of thin air and swooped down at the crook. It caught up with him as he fled. The hunting bird flapped and clawed at the man's head. He raised his arms and ducked to try to fend off the bird's attacks. That gave the wolf enough time to leap at the man, knocking him to the ground in the corn.

Sheena gasped, "Did *I* do that? *How* did I do that?"

Agent Schauer readjusted his dark glasses and cleared his throat, reluctantly tearing his eyes away from Sheena. He drew his gun and followed the path the fleeing man had made into the cornfield. Sheena blinked away her surprise and followed him, still glowing brightly, her night vision goggles and hat forgotten by the car.

A dozen rows into the cornfield, Schauer came upon the crook. The wolf Sheena had summoned was holding him immobile on the ground. The big man whimpered. Every time he began to move, the wolf dug its teeth excruciatingly into his ankle. Schauer raised his eyebrows and glanced at Sheena. "Is this yours?" he asked. The wolf growled a warning and the agent quickly backed up a step.

"Yes, I...," Sheena began. She frowned in confusion. Was the wolf hers? How did she know how to do that? What was it she had actually done? "I... I don't know! What is happening to me?"

Two of the FBI agents who had assaulted the cabin came through the corn and stopped short in amazement, glancing first at the wolf pinning their quarry, then at Sheena's glowing form. Schauer didn't answer her, but gestured to the man on the ground and told the agents, "Take him into custody. I think we'll find evidence of Doctor Ankh's thefts in that backpack he was carrying." He snorted. "And stop staring. You're supposed to be professionals."

As the FBI agents sidled around the crook, the wolf opened its jaws and stood up. With a canine smile, it dissolved into mist and disappeared. Sheena realized that the eagle had done the same thing after it had done its job. The golden light she had been giving off was fading rapidly, but she still had wings. She realized that she could see as well in the moonlight as she could in the daytime, even without the glow. She shivered and repeated her question to Agent Schauer, "What was that? What is happening to me?"

Schauer straightened his tie. "Officer Gardner, I would have to say that you have acquired some form of metahuman abilities. On behalf of the FBSA, welcome to the club."

Chapter 2 – More than Human

While the FBI agents took Doctor Ankh and his minions into custody, Sheena tried to make sense of what had just happened. She went to her own SUV and pulled a spare shirt from her emergency supplies, but try as she might, there was no way to get it over her wings. She had to settle for changing out of her bra and into a bikini top from her swimsuit. It offered no more coverage, but at least it wasn't underwear. Agent Schauer tactfully kept his back to her while he made calls on his cell phone.

Agent Calderón walked up to the car carrying three smooth cloth bags. He nodded to Schauer and lifted his cargo up onto the hood of the agents' sedan. Each bag was embroidered with some sort of silvery writing and there was something about the size of a softball inside. Sheena thought she saw a slight glow from whatever was inside two of the bags. Unconsciously, she took a wary step back.

"Three of these things… escaped," Calderón reported in his smooth Spanish accent. "You know what happened to one." He nodded at Sheena who listened with a worried crease between her eyebrows. "These others deactivated themselves, as far as I can tell. They were out in the woods. Not too hard to find. I picked up the spent one that affected Sheena from the ground by the car. I bagged them all with silk so they wouldn't be able to 'leak' out any extra magic."

"Or so goes the theory," Schauer commented. "Are those the things we were looking for from the tip-off about Doctor Ankh? And, did he say anything?"

Agent Calderón shrugged. "No, Ankh asked for a lawyer and then clammed up. I would have to check the paperwork to know if these were tagged. They sure qualify as magical artifacts. Don't know whether they were stolen, or what they're supposed to do. If we can't match them to the list we've already got, I suggest we contact ART for analysis and identification."

Schauer hesitated. "All right. Just as long as we don't let ART hold onto them. You know how effective they are at guarding valuable magic." Both agents chuckled. It sounded like there was a sarcastic tone to it.

Sheena wondered what they meant. "What's ART? Can he… they… figure out what's happened to me?"

Schauer turned to Sheena and answered, "Officer Gardner, let's get back to the sheriff's office and see what we can find out. ART is the Arcane Research and Tactics group, a division of the FBSA. Their nearest office is in Chicago. Because the, um, effect that you encountered was of magical nature, ART would be the logical place to start looking for answers. But, I have a few field tests that might help you that we can do locally. I just need a safe and lighted place to do them."

Sheena blinked and realized that she was seeing as easily by moonlight as she could by the light of the sun. She looked over at her SUV and said, "Okay, but…." She looked back over her shoulders. How was she ever going to fit into her vehicle well enough to drive safely? She tried flapping her wings, but just managed to make them twitch and flutter. She felt stupid doing it and stopped.

"I can drive," Calderón said. "Come on. Let's pick up your things, and then I'll help you get settled inside."

Agent Schauer nodded. "Good. I'll make sure that the FBI team has preserved the evidence we need. I don't think they'll need us for anything else tonight. I'll meet up with you at the sheriff's office."

With Calderón's help, Sheena managed to get into the passenger side of her SUV. It was normally very roomy, but even when folded back her new wings almost brushed the ceiling of the cab. With a little experimentation and lots of patient help from Agent Calderón, Sheena was able to sit comfortably, her wings tucked to either side of the seat.

"Don't worry about it," the agent offered in a casual tone. "People can get used to different shapes and all sorts of superpowers that seem inconvenient at first. If this is a permanent sort of thing, you'll be able to figure out how to work with it."

She nodded numbly and gave him the keys. During the trip back to the sheriff's office that was serving as the headquarters for this operation, Agent Calderón tried to make light conversation, asking questions about the local area. Sheena barely heard him, and couldn't concentrate to answer him. Calderón eventually lapsed into silence but didn't seem put off by her unresponsiveness.

"What will Eric think?" Sheena asked out of the blue.

"Eric?" the agent asked.

"My husband. When he sees me like this!"

Calderón glanced at her briefly, then back to the road. "I am sure he will be surprised. Even shocked. But, he will adapt." He didn't say what was on his mind, however. *A man's wife, who was very pretty to begin with, has turned into a winged goddess? He would be crazy to be upset!*

They arrived at the county sheriff's office. Sheena managed to get out of the SUV without too much difficulty and made her way inside. "Oh, wait," she said to Agent Calderón. "I should call in to my boss."

"Go ahead. He is probably worried," he replied. "I suggest that you just say that the operation was successful, and that there are some details that will take you a few days to sort out with the FBSA. Probably best to leave out anything too strange until we get a better sense for what's happened."

Sheena nodded. That made sense. She called her supervisor, the district manager. He had been waiting for her call. He was very glad that everything had gone smoothly. Sheena managed to convince him that she would fill him in on all of the details as soon as she could, but that the government agents wanted her to make detailed reports of the whole operation, which might take a while. She let out a sigh of relief as she finished the call.

Sheriff Thompson walked into the briefing room and did a double take. "Sheena?!?"

"Hi, Dave." She shrugged and her wings flexed, spreading out the feathers smoothly, then relaxing again. She gestured at herself. "Some weird floating thing from that suspect's cabin went off, and it decided to zap me. This is what it did, I guess."

The sheriff looked at her wings, then looked the rest of her over again. He shook his head in admiring disbelief. "Heck, I... Wow. Really!"

She narrowed her eyes. "What?"

"You look awesome!" he stammered. He made a quick excuse and stepped into his office.

"Be right back," Sheena muttered to Calderón. She went down the hall to the ladies' room and looked at herself in the mirror. Her jaw dropped. She kept herself in pretty good shape, but now her muscles were firmer and perfectly toned. Her skin was smoother. It looked like she had lost a couple of inches from her waist and firmed up her chest and hips. Her hair was softer and more lustrous, and still long and full. She was still herself, but looking like the best she could be; in perfect physical shape. She looked herself over in amazement.

"Wow," she echoed Sheriff Thompson's stunned comment.

When she emerged from the ladies' room, Calderón chuckled softly to himself at her bemused expression. Agent Schauer and the lead FBI investigator had just arrived, as well. They spent the next half hour going over what had happened at the cabin in detail, recording it for the official report. Sheena knew that everything could end up as evidence in the trial, and any detail could be important, so she did her best to recall everything exactly as she remembered it. This also helped take her mind off her own situation for a while, so that when they had finished, she was ready for Agent Schauer's next question.

"Well, that takes care of the routine recordkeeping. Are you ready to go over the special powers information?" When she nodded, Schauer thanked the FBI agent and looked over at Calderón.

His partner nodded. "We'll use the sheriff's office for this."

Sheriff Thompson was just locking up. Agent Schauer pulled him aside and asked if they could use his office to debrief Sheena. With another quick glance at her, the sheriff nodded. The agents sat down in the sheriff's own office as the sheriff left for the night. Agent Schauer pulled up some files on his tablet computer and set it down on the desk. He gestured for Sheena to sit down. "Just a checklist," he said.

"You haven't done this before?" Sheena asked as she tried to make herself fit into a chair.

He shook his head. "No. It's not every day an individual has a supernormal encounter right in front of me and gains some sort of powers from it."

"First time for everything," joked Calderón. He pulled out his own tablet and started working. "I'll see what I can find out about those magic artifacts."

"But, this sort of thing has happened often enough that the FBSA has a checklist of things to go over when a new event occurs," Schauer continued. He glanced down at his list. "First off, we should address the privacy concerns. It is our policy not to release any information to news media. All information about this event, the nature and scope of any powers you display, and your own comments and reactions will be recorded for analysis. This will become part of your law enforcement record, but accessible only through the FBSA, and on a need-to-know basis. Everything else will be kept strictly confidential."

"Why is that?" Sheena asked.

Schauer spread out his hands in an apologetic gesture. "Privacy. But, it only goes so far. If you turn into a super-powered criminal, we need to know everything possible so that we can apprehend you and take you into appropriate protective custody with minimal risk to civilians and law enforcement personnel. I don't expect that to happen in this case, but we just don't know."

Sheena nodded slowly. "I suppose."

"If the subject has experienced any special trauma, or if the situation seems unstable, we are advised to take the person into protective custody for several days of observation. This is to make sure that the person is not in any danger and does not pose a threat to self or others. This also gives the subject access to specially-trained medical and psychological staff." He looked up from the tablet at her. "In this case, because magic was involved, I would recommend working with ART, as I mentioned earlier. Let's assess the situation. How do you feel?"

Sheena considered. "Actually, I feel really good. Energetic, but pretty much calm, which makes me nervous. How can I be so calm and feel so good when all this has happened to me?"

"I can't say, exactly, but I would guess that whatever happened here was a beneficial effect. Let's hope that bears out. That would be much easier for you than if you had to fight it in some way." Schauer glanced at his checklist. "Any voices speaking to you? Urges to do things that would not normally occur to you? Anything you feel that is unusually important?"

Sheena shook her head. "No, there were no voices. Visions, yes, like I explained, but I can't specifically remember any details from those at all. No voices in my head, or urges, or anything." She concentrated for a minute, trying to sift through what she was feeling. "No, nothing pushing or pulling me in any direction. I really want to call Eric, my husband, but I know that can wait for a bit, still."

"Good, good." Schauer made notes on his tablet. "Let's go through a list of things that might be relevant abilities. They've got hints and 'what to look for' text for each of these. Frankly, I think that what you did with the bird and the wolf are pretty key, and the wings and physical 'makeover' are probably linked to that in some way. Magic has a way of getting done what it wants to get done. I would guess that what happened here has something to do with the purpose of that glowing thing."

"But, what is that purpose? And why me?"

Schauer replied, "We may never know everything, but Agent Calderón is working on finding more information about those things that flew out of the cabin with the explosion. That should get us close. In the meantime, take a look at this questionnaire and see what you can fill in."

Sheena scrolled and tapped her way through the FBSA diagnostic. There was also a lot of information and advice about understanding superpowers and adapting to the various changes that they might cause in a person's life. By the time she had finished the first set of questions and the supporting material, it was well after midnight. Her phone vibrated once with an incoming text message.

"Oh, it's Eric!" Sheena said. "It's getting really late. Should I reply? Is it safe to go home? What happens next?"

"We can drive you home, with your car. I have a message in to our regional Director explaining the situation. Let's plan on getting together in the morning, say at ten o'clock, and we can continue through the information and adjustment material," Schauer suggested.

Calderón added, "How about we continue that work at her residence, until we get more detailed instructions? People will be talking, already, but Sheena has to decide when she wants to go out in public."

"Good point," Schauer nodded. He asked Sheena, "Will that work?"

"Yeah, I think so," she replied. "I don't see why not. I'll text Eric and let him know I'm fine and we're almost done here."

Sheena and her husband, Eric, lived in a spacious two-story farmhouse built in the early 1950's. It was sturdy, comfortable, and had weathered the years well with a little maintenance and a few minor renovations. The place was on a partially wooded 20-acre property on the north side of the lake. The previous owner was the local veterinarian. When he and his wife retired to Arizona a few years ago, he had not only offered to sell Eric his medical practice, but his home, too. Since the property came with a barn, a clinic building, an extra garage, and a kennel, it was perfect for the sort of veterinary medicine Eric wanted to practice. He worked on a mix of livestock and pets. Periodically, he would take in a wild animal or bird rescued by Sheena or other area residents and do what he could to rehabilitate the injured animal so it could return to the wild.

Eric was waiting at the door when they pulled into the driveway, a lanky and earnest-looking 28-year old with a tousled head of light brown hair and deep blue eyes. He usually worked in a plain white t-shirt and long sleeve cotton shirt with the sleeves rolled up, jeans, and work boots during the summer, and even this late at night, he hadn't changed. He stepped out onto the front step. When she opened the car door, he caught a first glimpse of his wife clad in her dark blue bikini top and some sort of cloak and he frowned with concern. Her wings spread slightly for balance as she hopped down from the big SUV. Eric exclaimed, "Honey! What happened to your glasses? And your shirt?" Then, he realized what he was actually seeing and he froze in surprise. He took another deep breath, closed his eyes, and opened them again. She was still there, with wings, standing in the moonlight.

Sheena tried to pre-empt the flood of questions she could see building up. "It's okay, really, Eric! I stayed back out of it, where I was supposed to, but some magic thing escaped from Doctor Ankh's cabin and... 'zapped' me. Remember, 'Open mind...?'" She used the mantra the two of them had used to deal with unpleasant surprises and shocks since shortly after they had met in college.

"…open mind, open mind, open mind. Yeah," Eric breathed. He prided himself on keeping an open mind to whatever life threw at him. This was going to stretch that resolve far beyond anything he had experienced before. He looked at the FBSA agents. "What happened?"

Schauer answered smoothly, "We successfully apprehended Doctor Ankh, the criminal. Your wife was affected by a stray magical effect. She experienced a physical transformation and displayed unusual powers as a result. At this time, the full extent of the effects and whether or not they are permanent is unknown. She is, however, doing extremely well and is in no apparent danger."

Sheena came up the steps to her husband into the porch light. She smiled at him nervously. "Well? What do you think?"

Eric blinked in amazement as he looked at her closely. She stood before him like a nervous schoolgirl, hoping for his approval. "Wow! You… you're gorgeous! I mean, even more than usual!"

"Good recovery," muttered Calderón. Schauer smiled politely behind his dark glasses.

"And wings?" Eric asked. "You've got real live wings?" He rubbed the bridge of his nose and shook his head. But, maybe this wasn't as hard to believe as it seemed. After all, she had gone to help the feds catch a supervillain. These kinds of things happened in the world, somewhere, sometimes. When she nodded, he said, "Turn around and let me see those things. No, wait! Come inside where the light is better and let me see. Do they work?"

"I don't know. I can't do anything with them, yet." Sheena went into their house as he held the door for her.

"Are you guys coming in?" Eric asked the agents.

"No, Doctor Gardner," Agent Schauer replied. "We'll be by again at ten o'clock if everything goes as planned. We should have more information for your wife by then from researchers who are familiar with this kind of thing."

"All right. I'll make a hole in my clinic schedule and hope no one has any emergencies with their animals. I want to hear what you find out."

The FBSA agents nodded and left in Schauer's sedan.

"Oh! My! God!" Eric said as he looked at her. He reached out hesitantly to touch one of her wings. It was real. He could barely believe it.

Sheena smiled self-consciously and twirled a strand of hair around one finger. "You like it? Really?"

Her husband just looked at her and nodded with an amazed, slack-jawed expression.

"I guess I don't need the glasses or the acne lotion anymore, either," she ventured.

"Honey, have you looked in a mirror? It's amazing! You're amazing!"

Sheena turned around in a circle so he could see all of her. "I looked in the restroom mirror at the sheriff's office, but…." She shrugged and hesitated, pursing her lips. "I was afraid you'd be freaked out. Heck, I don't even know what to think!"

"How did this happen?" Eric asked. After Sheena explained the details, he shook his head in amazement. "Man, this is the kind of thing you just read about in stories or comic books or something. Who'd think this would happen in real life?"

"I know, right?" she sighed. Sheena took a deep breath and let it out slowly as she tried to relax. She took another deep breath, and then giggled as she noticed how it drew her husband's attention. "Distracted, doctor?"

Eric blushed. "Um, yeah, a bit."

She smiled. "I feel like I should be crying and having a panic attack or something, but I just feel too calm. It just seems like this is a good thing. Or, that I'm just so healthy that I can't feel sad about it, or whatever."

"Well, that's good, right? I mean, you've got this upgraded body and some magical powers to go with it. If there's a purpose for it all, maybe it's not a bad thing!"

Sheena hugged herself, and her wings wrapped around her body, as well. She laughed. "I think I'm getting the hang of these things, maybe!" At Eric's raised eyebrow, she explained, "I don't know how the wings work, but I'm starting to get a sense for it, and they're starting to do what I want them to do."

"Maybe you have to kind of grow into them a bit?" he offered. "They shouldn't work at all, from a physiological perspective."

"Well, yeah.... It's magic!"

Eric chuckled. "You can say that again, whatever it means!"

Sheena looked at herself in the hall mirror. "I wonder how I'm going to sleep with these things growing out of my back."

"Hmm...." Eric stepped closer to get a good look at her wings. He gently felt the muscles of one wing, and then the other. He spread them out and studied the movements of the wings and their connection to Sheena's upper back. Then he had her fold and unfold her wings and flap them lightly. She was able to control her wings well enough to do that. He put his left hand on her upper back where the wing connected and his right hand on her chest over her pectoral muscle and had her pull and push her wing against his hand. After a bit he shook his head. "Again, according to physiology, this should be impossible. But, you do have a flexible anchor and a wrap-around to your chest muscles. You can move the wing almost directly out to your side. When you pull on the wing, most of the tension is going into the wing muscle itself, with a much smaller portion into the anchor muscle and the pectoral."

"So, it works, then?"

"Yeah, somehow. I don't know if it will really support flight, but that would be magic, too, so all bets are off on that." He moved his right hand lower. "And this feels good, too!"

She laughed softly. "Yes, it does! Come on and help me get undressed. I'm tired after all this excitement."

"Tired?"

"Well, not *too* tired!" She grinned slyly at him. She took her husband by his hand and led him upstairs to their bedroom.

Chapter 3 – An Infusion of Power

Sheena handed Agent Schauer a tall glass of iced tea and another one to Eric. The ice cubes clinked as they settled. The Gardners' back porch was well shaded and the breeze blew in from the lake, but the day was still hot. Sheena tucked her wings to either side of her chair and sat down. She took a long sip from her own glass. "It seems to get a little bit hotter here each summer. Global warming, go figure."

Schauer nodded politely. "I just got a message from Agent Calderón. He should be here shortly. He's found some information on those magical artifacts." Despite the ninety-degree weather, he wasn't sweating. Sheena wondered if his black suit was internally cooled. Or, maybe he wasn't really human.

"Do you think that will tell us what happened to Sheena?" Eric asked. "I mean, why it happened, and…," he gestured aimlessly trying to find the right words. "…what we should expect?"

Schauer nodded again, slightly. "More information is always helpful. My partner seemed to think he had some useful answers for us. While we wait, Officer Gardner, I suggest that you try looking within yourself for some answers, as well. I have a concentration exercise that you may find productive. It is intended to 'unlock one's internal magic,' according to the ART advisor I talked with this morning. It is simple enough. Would you like to try it?"

Sheena shrugged. She had found a light blue tank top with a low back that kept her wings free. She had been able to step into it and pull it up, slipping the straps over her shoulders, but regular shirts were going to be out of the question with those wings in the way. A simple pair of white shorts and some sneakers were cool enough for the heat outside. "Let me know if there are any safety steps I should take, but, sure, let's give it a try."

The FBSA agent consulted his tablet and explained the exercise. Sheena followed along with his explanation and then began to apply it. She slowed and deepened her breathing to relax and repeated the strange words Agent Schauer had taught her. She thought of water—the look and the sound and the feel of it. When she felt that it was "right," Sheena asked herself, as if she were talking to the magic, "What is this power within me?"

Eric and Agent Schauer looked on; Schauer impassively and Eric with a skeptical expression, but both silently. Sheena had closed her eyes. She looked thoughtful. After a short while, she said, "Hmm…," and began glowing like she had the night before.

Eric caught his breath and stared, trying not to disturb her.

Sheena muttered, softly, "I'm in a place. A forest with big cedar trees. There are spirits in the mist. Animals. Trees. Peace. Water. Stepping without breaking a twig or bending a branch." She paused, as if looking around. She was still emitting a soft golden glow. "It seems not solid, but real. Time is a moving stream. Hunting along the side of the stream. Stepping in it. Carried by it. Making it flow backward and forward."

Sheena's eyes were still closed and she watched whatever she was seeing in her mind. Agent Calderón walked up the driveway and around to the back porch. "Ah, I thought I'd find you here. Feels like power brewing."

Eric gave him a confused look, but Schauer just nodded. He said, "She's trying the contact exercise."

"Ah, good," Calderón said. "It's working, I see." Sheena continued to speak softly to herself. Eric listened again, trying to catch everything he could hear.

To his partner, Calderón said, "Here's what we know. The thing that dumped its power into Sheena was a source stone of the goddess Shanikali, the hunter of time, a contemporary of Ishtar and Pazuzu. Presumably winged, though I did not find any clear pictures in my quick search." Schauer looked impressed.

Sheena startled them by saying, much louder than before, "Yes, Shanikali. The hunter of evil. The spirits of the Beastlands heed her call. Her gift is to come again when Dark Ones threaten the forest."

"What?" Eric asked. "What forest?"

Sheena broke from her reverie and looked around. "Wha… what?" she asked, confused.

Her husband repeated what she had said. "You're glowing. You have been saying things as you've been doing that meditation."

"Oh." She considered for a moment, then tried to remember what she had seen. "The forest of spirits, I think. The place where… I don't know. Something might happen." She looked up at the others. "That's all I can find. It's hard to explain."

"That explains the stone that affected Officer Gardner, at least," Schauer said. "And the other two?"

Calderón replied, "Source stones. All three of them seem to be of the same general origin."

"Source stones? Like sorcery?" Sheena asked.

"Close, but *source*-ery would be more correct," Calderón corrected, putting the emphasis on the word *source*. "A powerful being puts its power into a special vessel so it can be a source of power for the future. Then, when it is needed, the magic wakes up and makes the power available. Some sort of very powerful spirit magic." He shrugged and grinned slightly. "I found a few different examples of this sort of thing. Most often, the source stone has enough intelligence to find a person who meets the original maker's criteria, and it gives that person its power. Sometimes, the power goes to the one who does a ritual. Or, sometimes, all a person has to do is rub the lamp, so to speak. Like with genie powers."

"Do you think… Do you think it *chose* me, somehow?" Sheena asked.

Schauer looked at Calderón, who nodded confidently. "I'm sure that was what happened. The conditions were right and you matched what the stone was waiting for."

"But, what is it? Is there something I'm supposed to do?"

"Probably," the agent replied. "The three stones were taken together by Doctor Ankh. They were not reported as stolen in any database I could find, which suggests that they were either uncovered from a place they had been hidden for many years, or that they were in the possession of a special collector who doesn't want to alert the authorities."

"Or, who doesn't know they are missing, yet," added Schauer. "Ankh just returned last night and there were a lot of artifacts in that haul. These are just a small part of what we recovered."

Calderón nodded. "It's also possible that the previous owner knows about the theft, but is confident that he can get the stones back without involving law enforcement."

"What's the connection between the different stones?" Eric asked.

"All three were source stones for gods of the same pantheon," Calderón explained. "Shanikali was a female hunter in an ancient pre-agricultural culture. She was exceptional because women in that culture were just beginning to plant crops and the men were the tribal hunters. The other stones belonged to Erismus and Horgan. Erismus was known as a wise judge, able to see within a person and tell truth from lies. Horgan was a god of rain and storms. Pleasing him would bring the good rains. Angering him would cause him to make storms."

"So, do I have this ancient goddess telling me what to do?" Sheena frowned at the thought.

"It does not appear to be a case of possession, no," Calderón answered. "Instead, you can think of it as if you opened up a can of 'Goddess Lite' and drank it to get the powers. And the frosty refreshment, for what it's worth."

Sheena laughed. Eric frowned. Agent Schauer merely smiled politely again.

Sheena spent the rest of the morning trying to call forth different powers. She managed to summon a wolf and an eagle. She had the impression from her shadowy memories that there were others she could call on, but she would have to rediscover their names. They were not real creatures, it seemed, but the spirits of creatures that had been real at one time. Looking at them very closely, she could see that they were slightly transparent. Each time she called on them, they appeared and did what she wanted them to do. When she had no task for them to do, they waited. When she felt no need of them, they dissolved into mist.

She also gained better control of her wings, but she still felt clumsy with them. She was better when she wasn't thinking about them, actually. Sheena figured that she was probably getting in her own way. But, if she didn't learn to use them consciously, she wouldn't really know what they could do. She did manage to flutter off the ground for a few seconds. Not enough to count as flying, maybe, but enough to know that she probably could fly with more practice. She wasn't sure how she felt about that, but the possibility certainly was exciting.

Eric talked with the agents a while longer. Every now and then they would turn and look at her, but Sheena tried to ignore it. She could hear what they were saying if she concentrated on listening. Her hearing was far better now than it used to be. Mostly, Agent Schauer was briefing her husband on things that could change when a family member suddenly developed super powers. To Sheena, Eric seemed nervous, but about the situation, not about her.

She fluttered over to the men. It was a struggle, but she managed to stay about six inches off the ground as she crossed the yard behind the animal clinic. With a satisfied smile she dropped to the ground and gasped for breath. "How was that?"

"Amazing!" Eric said.

Agent Calderón was about to say something when a pale arrow plunged down into the earth between the four of them. It burst into a super-cooled wave of ice. The cold was intense and the ice formed around each of them in a heartbeat, freezing them so they couldn't move.

From the trees nearby, a woman's voice rang out scornfully, "Those powers you are struggling to comprehend were supposed to be mine! You've stolen my power!"

She was tall and willowy with a pale face that would have been breathtakingly beautiful if it wasn't so hardened with disdain. Her blood-red hair was tied back into a long ponytail to show off sharply pointed ears. She was wearing a red leather tunic with black trim and carried a bow of some dark wood almost as tall as she was. The bow was inscribed with silver runes that seemed to float over the surface of the wood. Leggings of a sheer black material hugged her legs and descended into elegantly tooled red leather boots that matched her tunic and forearm guards. The huntress moved with a determined grace into the frozen yard.

She strode up to Sheena, ignoring the men. Towering more than a full head over her, the woman looked down at Sheena as if she was a bug she was thinking about crushing. The huntress sneered, "Sheena, huh? A game warden? Really?"

Sheena blushed and managed to stammer, "My... my parents liked the show. And I...."

"Never mind that!" the archer interrupted. "I paid Ankh a lot of money to acquire Shanikali's legacy. And I waited a long time for him to find the stone with the right power. Power that got into you by accident! And mark my words, I'll figure out some way to get it *out* of you and get the power I deserve!"

Sheena's thoughts reeled as she tried to find some way to escape. The woman turned to consider the house and then glanced at the men, still frozen to the ground. She casually drew another arrow from her hunting quiver. Over her shoulder, she said to Sheena, "You need to stay alive until I can make arrangements to wring that power out of you. Your friends are under no such restriction, however."

The huntress nocked the arrow and drew back her bowstring. She gave Sheena an evil smirk. She pointed the arrow at each of the men in turn. "Who gets it first? The suit? The government shaman? Your cute nerdy husband, maybe? Oh, choices, choices!"

"No!" Sheena cried. She yanked at something she couldn't see and she was free of the ice. Then, her eagle screeched and swooped in to attack the huntress. Sheena flung her arms wide at the villain. A flock of black birds appeared out of nowhere and swarmed around the woman.

"Ack!" The woman batted at the birds and tried to protect her head.

Sheena desperately called for the wolf. While it was appearing, the huntress scowled and made a complex gesture with her free hand. A writhing inky presence surrounded her. Tendrils of darkness cloaked her and reached out for the harassing birds. The birds disappeared and the villain raised her bow again.

"Maybe a little something to remember me by, then!" she snarled. She drew and loosed her arrow with a single smooth motion, almost too quick to follow. The arrow jumped from her bow and crashed through the window into the clinic building, where it burst into an expanding ball of fire.

"Sic her!" Sheena shouted. The wolf leaped for the woman's arm. Sheena prepared to call another eagle. She didn't know how to do much, yet, but she would keep calling the animal spirits as long as she could.

The ice was melting from the FBSA agents and Eric. Schauer drew a shiny black pistol from beneath his suit coat. Eric lost his balance as feeling returned to his legs and he fell to the ground.

The huntress sneered and flicked the wolf off of her with a wave of inky darkness from her open hand. "It's getting a little hot around here. Don't worry, kid, I'll get you, and your little dog, too! But, later. And you might want to rescue that sheriff of yours before he dies of heat stroke. He can be very talkative, with the right persuasion." With an intricate hand gesture, she conjured a circle of blackness hanging like a doorway in midair. She stepped through and was gone, the circle disappearing as she did.

"Eric! The animals!" Sheena realized that the clinic was on fire. All of the animals Eric was boarding or treating inside the clinic were in danger.

"I'll get the hose! See what you can do! But be careful!" her husband yelled. He picked himself up and ran around to the hose attached to the back of the house.

Schauer flicked his wrist and popped open the chamber on his weapon. He deftly plucked the cartridge and replaced it with a different one from somewhere inside his suit pocket. With another flick of the wrist, he closed the chamber and readied the weapon for action.

"Rain coming," Calderón called out. "Tom, you got the extinguisher?"

Schauer nodded and moved to where he could get a good shot at the fire. He raised his weapon and pulled the trigger. An expanding glob of foam sprayed over the fire. A low rumble of thunder crashed overhead and raindrops started to fall as Calderón held his arms to the sky and chanted.

Sheena wished there was something else she could do to fight the fire, but getting the animals out was enough. The panicked sounds of the dogs and cats were difficult to hear. Three of them had been injured in the blast. Sheena ferried them out to the yard as the others struggled to contain and put out the fire. She was glowing brightly again. Without knowing just what she was doing, or why, Sheena waved her hand over the wounded animals and their injuries disappeared as if they had never been hurt. She blinked in surprise. "Wow!"

"What?" asked Eric.

"I just healed the animals!"

"What?!?" he repeated.

"I waved my hand over them and they weren't hurt anymore! The wounds just went away!"

Eric said nothing, but just shook his head and kept spraying the remaining patches of fire.

Within another few minutes, the fire was out. The clinic was in shambles, but not completely destroyed. The fire had not reached the house or the other outbuildings. The yard was a smoky, muddy mess. Eric and Sheena moved the animals to the kennel and the barn for safety.

While the Gardners worked, Schauer looked at his partner meaningfully. "According to the villain database, that was Elf Shot."

Calderón shrugged. "What, the archer woman? If you say so. I don't recognize her."

"She's trouble."

"So I can see," Calderón snorted.

"She's persistent."

"Oh." He paused and thought it over. "So much for a peaceful life in the woods?"

"Yes."

Calderón sighed. "I was afraid of that." He paused. "Wait, what about the sheriff?"

"We need to find him. One minute, I'll do a GPS locator on him, if he's still got his phone or radio nearby." Agent Schauer pulled another device from his suit coat pocket and fiddled with it calmly. Calderón looked over at the Gardners and shook his head. It was a shame that they couldn't have lived with the power peacefully for at least a little while. Now, they were already deep in super powered conflict with threats against their lives.

Willing or not, the spirits were moving them.

Chapter 4 – This Changes Things

They found Sheriff Thompson stuffed in the trunk of his patrol car a couple of miles down the main road from the Gardner's house. He was almost unconscious from the heat. Elf Shot had forced him to tell her what had happened to Doctor Ankh. Of course, she looked normal when she first approached the sheriff, he explained. She had claimed to be a reporter. Somehow, she had convinced the sheriff to drive her to a quiet place where they could talk privately. Schauer and Calderón had exchanged knowing glances when the sheriff said that.

"A glamor," Schauer said, more a statement than a question. Calderón nodded.

It was only when he had realized that he was telling the strange woman details about Sheena—what she looked like, where she lived—that Sheriff Thompson had been able to stop himself. That's when she had suddenly dropped the pleasant disguise and turned into a menacing villain. Elf Shot easily overpowered the sheriff and forced him to tell her the rest. Then, she restrained him with his own handcuffs and stuffed him into the trunk. She left him there parked by the side of the road sweltering in the sun-fired oven of the car's trunk. It must have been soon after that when she found and threatened Sheena and the others.

Sheena got the sheriff into the ambulance she had called and waved to the deputies as they pulled out to escort the ambulance to the local medical center. She turned back to Eric and the FBSA agents and shook her head. The stories were going to be flying fast throughout the county now. With the onlookers, the paramedics, and the rest of the sheriff's staff, she wasn't going to be able to keep her transformation a secret; even if she had wanted to. Sheena wasn't sure what she wanted. The whole experience was becoming a blur.

"Okay, what now?" she asked Agent Schauer.

"I suggest that we get you and Doctor Gardner home again. This changes things somewhat." At her worried expression he added smoothly, "But not very much, perhaps."

Eric grumbled, "So, what then? We wait for that crazy woman to come back and kill us?" He threw his hands up in the air. "C'mon, guys! I'm a veterinarian! Sheena's a game warden! We're out here in the country by choice! Weird stuff like this happens in the cities, not here! The most we should have to worry about is dodging hunters with bad aim. She might get shot at by drug smugglers sometimes, but that's normal. This… this is definitely not normal!"

"You're right, Doctor Gardner," Calderón agreed. "This is *not* normal. And it won't ever be normal again."

"Huh?" Eric was taken aback.

"It happened. Sheena was given supernatural powers. She didn't ask for them. You didn't ask for this, either. But now, you and your wife have to deal with it. We'll give you all the tools and protection we can, but you're the ones who have to figure out what you will do with this situation you find yourselves in."

"Will she really come after us? After me? To take these powers out of me?" Sheena asked.

Schauer replied calmly, "Yes, Officer Gardner. Elf Shot is a credible threat. She is ruthless, and will stop at nothing to get what she wants. She will eventually find a way to get those powers out of you. Theoretically, it can be done. Unfortunately, that probably means killing you in the process."

Eric burst out, "No! Not Sheena! This can't be happening! We have to do something! We...," he tried to think, then grasped upon an idea. "We'll move so she can't find us!"

"You can," Calderón replied calmly, "but she will eventually find you. Even if Sheena didn't stand out so much." He nodded at her. She wrapped her arms and her wings around herself, wishing she could disappear.

In a hopeless tone, Eric said, "So, what, then? What *can* we do?"

Sheena's eyes lit up and she lifted her head. Her wings spread out and folded behind her again. With a voice of realization, she said, "Gayle."

"What?" Eric asked.

"Gayle! She would know what to do. She's been through this kind of thing a lot. For years, even, and she's made it through. She's even doing fine!"

Eric opened his mouth, a frustrated look on his face. He clamped his jaw shut without saying anything.

Schauer asked, "Who is Gayle?"

Sheena explained. "Gayle Magnuson! Or, Gayle Force, now. She was my friend in high school. I still say hi to her now and then online. She gave me an autographed copy of her first CD!"

"Aw, come on, Sheena! You only talk to Gayle maybe twice a year! She's a big time hero. Is she going to have time to help us?" Eric objected.

"You don't know her, Eric," Sheena protested. "She *will* help. And she probably knows what to do about something like this, too."

"Actually, that is an excellent idea," Agent Schauer remarked. "Gayle Force is a powerful and experienced hero. She may even be able to help you learn to use your powers."

Calderón nodded and added, "Yes, she has been helpful to the FBSA. Always friendly and cheerful with the public, too. A good role model, despite some of the early... um," he faltered. Sheena thought he was blushing behind his dark glasses.

Schauer continued for his partner. "Yes. Gayle Force has been through a lot. She has resisted the dark side of fame and power. Not everyone can do that. A lot of villains would like to see her dead, but she has managed to stay ahead of them all. I think she could help you do the same."

"You mean, make Sheena a sidekick?" Eric said skeptically.

Agent Calderón shrugged. "If that is the path your wife decides to take, maybe. But, first, we need to make sure you are both safe."

Gayle Magnuson brushed back a stray wisp of hair from her face. She kept her strawberry blonde hair cut fairly short in a light shag kind of hairstyle. With the constant breeze flowing around her, wearing her hair any longer would have been a nuisance. Here at home in her skyrise Venture City luxury apartment suite, she let the breezes blow freely. Occasionally, she would forget and leave something light out on a table or countertop, and she would find it wedged into a corner where the air currents deposited it later. Mostly, though, Gayle was used to holding papers and things down with paperweights or whatever else was at hand.

She leaned back in her chair and stretched. She had been working on getting the lyrics down for a new song she was writing, but it just wasn't coming out as cleanly onto the computer as it sounded in her head. She shrugged and hopped up to get a glass of lemonade. Gayle smiled to herself as she hummed the melody of the song again and bobbed her head in time with the rhythm. Even at 27, she still had a young, cheerful face. The angsty urban sophisticate expressions currently popular on the music scene just didn't work for her, and Gayle didn't really care about fashion, anyway. She was her own girl. Her fans kept telling her they liked that about her, and she was happy that way. Lean and pretty, fittingly curvy but not what most people would call beautiful, light and breezy—that was her style, and it was natural.

She tapped the display panel in the kitchen and called up her schedule for the next week. Two performances at her favorite downtown club. Three days shooting a commercial for an eco-tourism company. Some practice sessions with the band. And, wedged in-between the other things, she had marked off time for tracking down a couple of leads on the Terra First eco-terrorist group that had been plaguing the city recently.

Gayle grinned and shook her head. Eco-tourism and eco-terrorism, both in the same week. Supporting one and fighting the other. As a wind-controlling superheroine, she felt a big responsibility for protecting the environment. But destroying factories and kidnapping people to make a point, like this Terra First group did, was way out of line. Gayle was looking forward to putting a stop to their violence.

Her phone buzzed with an incoming text message. She checked who it was from. "Sheena Gardner? What in the world…?" Sheena almost never texted Gayle. This must be something special.

The text just said, *"Urgent superhero stuff, need your help, can I call you?"*

"Sheesh, of course!" Gayle tapped out the reply. She grabbed her lemonade and strode through her apartment to the balcony overlooking the river. She wondered what was up as she waited for Sheena to call.

She didn't have long to wait. The phone rang and Gayle answered, "Hello! Gayle here!"

Sheena was trying to be calm, but her voice wavered a little as she said, "Hi, Gayle! Long time no see. How are you doing?" She had asked Eric to figure out what to do about his clinic obligations so they could both disappear for a week

23

or two. He had rolled his eyes, but his expression softened as he saw the worry in her eyes and he nodded with a nervous swallow. Then, Sheena had excused herself from the men to go up to the bedroom to talk with Gayle in private.

"I'm fine, but what's going on? Do you need help? Are you in danger?" Gayle was brimming with curiosity, but she tried to stay focused and professional.

"Well... You would recognize me if you saw me, but I've just been through some... changes." She gulped a breath of air and settled her wings awkwardly against her back. "And, there's a supervillain who just shot an arrow into Eric's clinic and kind of blew it up, and she wants to take my powers, which the agents say will probably kill me, and... and I don't know what to do!" Sheena broke down, losing all her control, and started crying into the phone.

Gayle straightened up in surprise. "What? *Powers?* Whoa! Sheena, you know I'll help! What do you need me to do? What's going on?"

Sheena choked out her story through her sobs, "Something... something happened last night. I... I was on a stakeout. With the FBI and... the FBSA. Something happened and this magic stone escaped. It filled me with magic, and made me grow wings, and now I have the powers of a goddess... and I don't know how to use them right... and the woman who hired Doctor Ankh to steal the stones showed up and nearly killed us... and she wants to take 'her' powers out of me! I never in a million years thought anything like this would happen to me, but now I have to figure out what to do, and this crazy woman would just as soon kill me as look at me, and she'll track us down and kill us! And I can't let Eric hear me crying like this or he'll totally freak out!" She sobbed incoherently, all the stress and shock of the last day coming out as it hit her.

Gayle shook her head and tried to let it all sink in for a moment. "Wow, Sheena...! It'll be all right, we'll get you through this. Both of you, even! Do you need me to come there? Do you want to come here? And don't worry about the crying! That sounds scary! If you need to cry, you do it! Eric will be okay. We'll help him, too."

"Okay, okay." Sheena sniffled and wiped her face. "Let me explain what's going on." She recounted the rest of her story and pointed out what she knew about the villain called Elf Shot.

"Wow, that's pretty intense! I've never run into Elf Shot myself, but there are a lot of bad guys out there." Gayle thought for a couple of seconds. "But if she wants to take your powers, she's gonna have to find some way to do it. That's gonna take some time. For now, you've just got to get you and Eric someplace safe where it's too risky for her to come after you."

"But she's crazy! She won't let anything stop her!"

"That's what she wants you to think! It's pretty easy for her to intimidate people when she knows she's got the upper hand, but I'd like to see how she handles herself in the big leagues!"

Sheena sniffled. "Huh?"

Gayle explained, "You've got friends, Sheena. You've got heroes on your side. She can't be counting on that, yet. And we won't rest until this Elf Shot chick is behind bars!"

Hesitantly, Sheena asked, "Are you sure?"

"Yeah, I'm sure! Heck, you're smarter than me and I managed to figure it out. I've taken a whole lot of bumps and bruises and worse, but I'm still out here trying to do the right thing. You'll make it even better than I did, I'm sure!"

"All right," Sheena replied. She took a breath. "Okay, what should I do now?"

Gayle let out her own breath and relaxed. "Great! Help me understand everything that happened. Together, we can figure this out." She started asking Sheena for details and other information, her week's previous schedule momentarily forgotten.

Chapter 5 – Welcome to Venture City

Venture City was a city on the cutting edge. Sprawling along the southern shore of Massachusetts from the base of Cape Cod to Rhode Island, it had been founded in 1944 after the Nazi villain, Seaquake, devastated the city of New Bedford with a superpowered tsunami. Almost nothing of the old city had been left standing. After the villain's eventual defeat at the hands of dozens of patriotic heroes, President Roosevelt and the survivors of the disaster vowed that the city would be rebuilt as a shining example of justice, freedom, and the American spirit.

The city grew at an amazing pace, due to the genius, effort, and investment of many of North America's most powerful metahumans. The place quickly became known as a center of high tech research and development. Manufacturing, shipping, transportation, air travel, commerce, entertainment, and finance were all major industries. Post-war success brought capital, bright young minds, and profits to the city. Venture City became a mini-metropolis, rivaling Boston and New York City in prestige.

The prosperity and free-wheeling spirit of the city continued to attract many more metahumans. It was a place where being a freak wasn't necessarily a barrier to success. Genius inventors rubbed shoulders with bizarre mutants and mystic sorcerers in relative peace. Harvard Business School built an executive retreat center in Venture City. MIT opened up several research and development laboratories. The city became home to its own international stock exchange in 1989. Above all, a flock of enterprising businesspeople capitalized on the talents of anyone and everyone who wanted to make a contribution.

While most citizens of Venture City sought their success through hard work and ingenuity, the city's riches also attracted many villains. Eager and willing to prey on those weaker than them, superpowered criminals, hate groups, and secret societies grew up in the shadows of the city. There never seemed to be quite enough heroes to stamp out the villains for good. As soon as one criminal mastermind was defeated, there always seemed to be another ready to step into the gap. Venture City boasted the greatest number of superpowered heroes in North America, but the greatest number of superpowered criminals, as well.

Sheena and Eric watched the Venture City skyline grow larger through the windshield as they approached the city on I-195. It gleamed. There was no smog or ground haze and the sky was clear. Sheena shook her head and remarked, "It's so clean and shiny. Not like Chicago or New York City at all."

Eric nodded. "It certainly is. I read that most of the buildings are made with high-tech materials to resist damage from natural disasters and supervillain attacks."

"I wonder how they can afford all that?"

"It's probably less expensive than using regular materials, after you figure in insurance costs." Eric glanced at a research park as they drove by. It was almost a work of art in white synthetic stone and colored macroplast. The landscaping was immaculate. "It sure is impressive, though."

Sheena shook her head. "I don't know, Eric. It feels sort of… bigger than life, or something. It's like it's not real. I don't feel like we belong here."

He snorted. "Yeah, I hear you. This place is like science fiction."

"Or the Emerald City from Oz." Eric snorted at that, but nodded.

He drove on, following the highway across the river to the exit they wanted. At the off ramp, signs reminded drivers that they were in a GridGuide zone. Many Venture City citizens had cars equipped with automatic pilot features— the increasingly popular GridGuide system—that could pilot their vehicles safely around the city with no need for human control. Developed, manufactured, and sold by Venture City's own Scott Enterprises, GridGuide was safer, more fuel efficient, and more emissions-friendly than manually controlled vehicles. People who used it received a special tax credit and a preferred insurance rate based on the proportion of time spent in GridGuide mode.

"If we stayed here, I would want to get that." Eric nodded at the sign.

His wife shrugged. "Whatever. I like driving myself."

With a chuckle, Eric replied, "Kinda hard to manage at the moment, though, eh?"

Sheena gave him a cranky sniff in response. "Wings get in the way of the rear view mirror, yeah. I can see I'm going to have to get some modifications done. Not just the clothes, but my car, too."

Eric sighed. "Yeah, and that costs money. Temporary disability from the DNR and the FBSA 'special victims adjustment' payments will help for a while, but we're losing money while I'm not running the clinic."

"Yeah. Just another thing to worry about," she grumbled.

"Hey, don't worry about that for now. We can take care of it as we figure out what to do next." Her husband chuckled again. "Maybe you'll get your own comic book and we can live off the royalties."

Sheena made another face at him. "We're almost to Riverhaven. We can talk about silly stuff later, after we meet up with Gayle."

Gayle had wondered if she should wear one of her hero costumes to greet the Gardners, but eventually settled on normal clothes. It was going to be weird enough meeting Sheena face to face again after almost ten years. Plus, her husband was with her. Gayle loved people, but beginnings were always awkward because of her mutant powers. She flew down from her apartment to the visitor parking lot in a simple green tank top and white shorts.

Her phone rang. "Hi, Gayle, we're here," Sheena's voice said. "We're just pulling in."

"Okay, great! I'm in the visitor parking area," Gayle assured her. "There you are!" She waved as they drove up.

Sheena untangled herself from the car. She was getting used to it after two days on the road. "Hi, Gayle!"

"Wow, you look great! Those are some nice wings, too!" Gayle exclaimed. She watched for Sheena's reaction and was pleased to see her relax at her greeting.

"Gayle, this is my husband, Eric. Eric, Gayle Magnuson." Sheena made introductions.

"Pleased to meet you, Gayle," Eric offered. She didn't look like a mutant, as far as he could tell. There was just a hint of watermelon scent in the air around her, but that could have just as easily been perfume or lip balm. He smiled at her.

"You, too, Eric! How was the trip?" Gayle asked, pleased at seeing him at ease.

He shrugged. "Long hours driving. Stopped at motels after dark. We would have camped along the way, but…." He shrugged eloquently.

"Could have been too risky," Sheena explained. "Schauer and Calderón couldn't find out where that Elf Shot woman went or whether we're being watched. Safer to have walls at night."

"Not that we got much sleep," Eric grumbled with a snort. "An elbow in the ribs I can handle, but a wing flopped over my face is a different thing entirely."

"And I've been so keyed up I can't sleep. Just restless." Sheena patted Eric's shoulder. "He's been great about all this, though."

"Well, I'm glad you made it," Gayle said. She waved at the Riverhaven building beyond the low hill that separated its main grounds from the visitor lot. The apartment tower soared 35 stories into the air, looking over the parking lot, the attached building wings, and the Acushnet River park. The old Fort Phoenix state reservation lay along the shore of the Atlantic Ocean to the south of the Riverhaven complex. "The visitor parking is out here for security. If someone brings anything in, it's close enough for the monitors to keep an eye on and far enough away to reduce the risk of damage to the building. We've got resident parking in the underground ramp. Oh, yeah! And the Event Horizon nightclub is the East Wing. That's public, too."

Sheena blinked. "A nightclub attached to an apartment building?"

Gayle shrugged. "One of the ladies who designed the place wanted to try out the idea of a club where metahumans and civilians could party without worrying too much about safety. Even though the Event Horizon is open to the public, security scanning is tighter than a presidential inauguration. And—thank goodness!—almost invisible. No lines or big machines… other than the line you've got waiting to get into any popular club, anyway."

"So, do you perform there?" Eric asked.

"Yep! But it's not the only place in town for that. There are plenty of other places, too. We're playing at the Green Line tomorrow night. Assuming everything stays quiet, of course." Gayle shrugged. "Here. Let me get your luggage."

She concentrated and shaped a solid mass of air into several barely-visible human-shaped figures. "They can lift and carry your stuff, and they're actually very careful. I call them my phantom army."

Eric chuckled. "You create your own roadies?"

"Yep!" Gayle laughed. "Always on call!" After Eric and Sheena pointed out the things they wanted to bring inside, she pointed at the shimmering porters. They picked up the gear and Gayle led the way to the lobby.

At the security desk, Brian, the guard on duty, asked Gayle, "How long will your guests be staying?"

Gayle and Sheena exchanged glances. Eric shrugged. Gayle turned back to the guard. "Let's put it down for two weeks. If they decide to stay longer, um… remind me so I don't forget to let you know, okay?"

Brian smiled at the singer. "Sure, Gayle. Anything you like." She suppressed a giggle and led the way through the lobby to the elevators.

"Wow! This is your place?" Sheena asked in amazement. It was huge!

"Yes it is! I've got a whole floor," Gayle replied cheerfully. "But, there are a couple of people who have two floors. And the lower floors have more apartments to each. These upper floors are just more expensive, and stuff. With my music and public appearances, I can afford it. Actually, the rent on the luxury suites like this subsidizes the rent of the basic apartments for metas on the first ten floors who need the security but don't have the income to cover all the costs."

"Security?" asked Eric.

Gayle gestured out at the Riverhaven complex. "Yeah, the whole place is really a kind of like a 'gated superhero community' to protect the residents from villains. It's also the headquarters of a group of heroes called 'The League of Titans.'"

Sheena remembered a news article she had read about her friend. "Hey, you're a member of that group, aren't you?"

"Yes, I am. They're great people!" Gayle agreed.

She showed Sheena and Eric around the apartment, stopping at a guest bedroom suite. "It's a king-sized bed, but if Sheena's feathers are really in your face, Eric, we can get you a bigger bed. Or, separate beds…?" She laughed at her friend's frown. "No, I guess you won't need that!"

Eric chuckled self-consciously. "It's great of you to put us up like this, Gayle."

She waved away his thanks. "Oh, I'm happy to help! Besides, I don't get many visitors, and I haven't had a chance to catch up with Sheena for years. I'm almost embarrassed to say it, 'cause you guys are in trouble, but I think this is going to be fun!"

"Fun?" Sheena said as her jaw dropped.

Gayle looked abashed. "Well, yeah! I don't get to help many people who I actually know, you know? I mean, I know this is rough on you guys, but I think that we can stop Elf Shot, get you to be able to use these powers you've got, and everything will be fine."

Sheena gave Gayle a skeptical look. "Uh… why do you think so? Do you know something you can tell us about this situation?"

"Yes! I did some digging through the Titans' criminal database and called in a few favors and I found out a lot about Elf Shot and her cronies. There is a lot of weird stuff going on with them, but we've got a lot of advantages and we can keep you guys safe until we're ready to track 'em down and bring 'em in."

Eric hesitated, then asked, "You make it sound routine. Is it really going to be that easy, do you think?"

Gayle's face sobered while she thought about it for a moment. "Easy? No, not really. I mean, after all, she's a superpowered villain and she has allies, so it's not easy. But, compared to what I've faced before? And my friends who can back us up, if we need it? No, Elf Shot isn't in that class of threat at all. Mostly, we have to be keep our eyes open and make sure that we don't get sloppy or overconfident."

Sheena and Eric exchanged nervous glances. Sheena was the first to speak. "But, Gayle... I don't know how to do any of this stuff, yet! What am I going to have to do?"

Gayle smiled reassuringly. "You've got some really special gifts to figure out. I'll help you, and hook you up with more magic-types who can do it better than me. By what the FBSA people said, you've probably just gotta unlock what you've been given. So, just learn and explore, Sheena!"

Chapter 6 – First in Flight

Drops of sweat beaded Sheena's brow. "I'm doing it!" she panted. "I'm flying!"

"Woohoo!" shouted Gayle. "You got it!"

Sheena kept flapping her wings, concentrating on keeping up her forward motion. Like riding a bike, it was easier to keep her balance once she was already moving. Hovering in place or moving slowly was hard. Whatever magic kept her up seemed to work with how she used her wings. She couldn't just will herself to fly or float; she had to keep her wings moving the right way. She flew along the riverfront beach a couple of wingspans above the sand. When she came to the end of the long strip of sand, she banked and glided through a turn, then started flapping again and returned to where she started. Some of the other people enjoying the beach applauded. "All it takes is practice!" she called out happily to Gayle.

"I knew you could do it!" her friend responded. "And it's only been a couple of days you've been really working on it!"

A dozen take-offs and landings later, Sheena splashed into the river to cool off. A college-aged guy, prodded on by his friend, called out to her, "Hey, Angel! You got a boyfriend?"

Sheena held up her left hand and showed him her ring. "Married! But thanks!"

Gayle laughed. The young man did, too, and waved good-naturedly. "I bet you're gonna get a lot of that," Gayle said as Sheena waded up out of the water.

Sheena frowned. "You think so?"

"Yeah. Problem?"

Sheena thought for a moment. "I don't know. Maybe. I'm not sure how Eric will take it."

"Well, a lot has changed in the last week," Gayle reflected. "He seems to be taking it okay, but this has got to be a shock for him, too. My doctor said that it takes a while to 'find the new normal' when big changes happen."

"This is definitely a big change," Sheena sighed. "What doctor was that?"

"My psychiatrist, Doctor Swan." Gayle laughed. "Well, actually both of them said that!"

"Huh? Both?"

"Doctor Lillian Swan was my doctor in Duluth, when I had that breakdown in college. Then, when I moved out here, I kept working with her son, Doctor Joshua Swan. He was running the metahuman research center at Venture City University at the time. He was a professor there, doing research and helping people deal with the issues that come with superpowers."

"Is he a psychiatrist, too?"

"A psychologist. He's more of a scientist and he doesn't prescribe medication. But, yeah, otherwise pretty similar. Josh doesn't need to use meds because he's got some kind of 'perceptive empathy,' he calls it. He can do some pretty impressive stuff without drugs. But mostly, the thing is that the patient has to do the work, anyway. Taking shortcuts makes it all take longer to work through the issues and changes don't stick unless the patient deals with them herself."

Gayle smiled. "Josh is also a hero in his spare time and lives here in Riverhaven, too. Goes by the name of Drake Argent for hero work, using his powers for good, and all that. I've worked with him a bunch of times. Beating up bad guys. Saving the city. That sort of thing."

Something occurred to Sheena. "Has… has anyone died because of what you did? Or, because you couldn't save them in time?"

Gayle's expression froze. She looked out at the waves and nodded. "Yeah." She shuddered visibly. "I've managed not to kill anyone, but the power of the wind and storms can be pretty violent. And I've lost people when the villains got to them first." She shook her head. "And there've been a couple of times that it could've… should've… been me. And one…." She fell silent.

Sheena waited, watching her face. Gayle's eyes seemed far away, watching a painful memory.

"And one," Gayle continued, "where I saved the woman, but the villain had already started the job, and she… changed. Mutated into a horrible monster. He totally used her; made her into a breeder, to give birth to more monsters. 'A pure race to purge the Earth,' he said. And, I couldn't stop it. She busted out of the safe house we had her in and ran off to a toxic waste dump. All I could do was to go out, track her down, beat her senseless, and turn her over to the scientists to study.

"Maybe, someday, they can reverse the process. But now she's trapped inside that monster, all trace of humanity gone. And I still have nightmares. That could have been me."

After Gayle fell silent, Sheena asked, "Why could it have been you?"

"Her name was Tammy. She was the creep's girlfriend, once. And I interfered with his 'master plan.' So, later, after that case, he sent me flowers. On Valentine's Day. The card said, 'You are mine.'"

Sheena listened, horrified.

Gayle went on with forced cheerfulness. "The flowers were dusted with mutagenic pollen. I remember dropping the flowers and passing out. But I was here at home and the Riverhaven biomonitors picked it up instantly when I fainted. I woke up in the Titans' medical bay. Everyone was so worried. But, after a whole lot of tests and a week of observation, they decided I was safe. As far as they could tell, because I'm already a mutant, the pollen couldn't work anything nasty on my altered DNA.

"He's still out there, too. I've stopped a whole bunch of his plots, but I just can't get to him, personally. He keeps getting away. He wants to wipe out humanity because it's 'a blight on the pure Earth and we have to start over.' Pure, heh," she scoffed. "There's nothing pure about Ravenger or his 'Vengeful Earth.'"

"And… and this kind of thing is *normal* for you?" Sheena's voice cracked slightly.

"Oh, no! Not 'normal,' but…." Gayle shrugged. "Sheena, this is a totally different world than the one most people live in. The weird and strange gets to be… not too surprising, I guess."

Sheena shook her head emphatically. "I couldn't do that. I don't think I could ever get used to stuff like that. And, we don't even know if this is permanent, for me."

Gayle said nothing, but turned her gaze out to the waves again.

"I mean, whatever that magic thing did, maybe it will fade, or go away. Maybe it's just that I need to do something with these powers, and it will be satisfied, and… and I'll go back to being normal."

Gayle watched the waves roll up onto the shore as the river flowed by, one after another. When she glanced back at Sheena, it seemed like her friend was still waiting for reassurance that Gayle couldn't give. "Maybe," she replied. "But, whatever happens, I bet you'll never look at the world in the same way again."

"Yeah," Sheena said softly. She shivered in the warm sun. "You're right about that."

Chapter 7 – Dressing the Part

"I feel silly!" Sheena complained as she stepped out of the scanning booth. "Do I really need a costume?"

"Yes, you do," Gayle assured her. She scrolled through more of the options at the kiosk. The high-tech store they were visiting had built its business around catering to the needs of metahuman heroes and wannabes. *Image* definitely served a niche market, but its designers and tailors were masters in their craft, and in dealing with the strange and unusual. While the FBSA and superhero organizations subsidized much of their custom work, *Image* made most of its profit by licensing designs for mass market clothing manufacturers. This kept prices reasonable for registered heroes.

"Can't I just do this in my own clothes?" Sheena stepped into her tank top and pulled her shorts back on over her bikini. The scanning booth captured still and dynamic measurements of the customer's body in order to create a realistic computer model for fitting the costume designs. Sheena had just spent a good twenty minutes moving and posing according to the instructions the computer had given her.

"Sheena, the costume is not just another set of clothes. It's a uniform, so the good guys and regular people know you're not just a bystander." To Sheena's skeptical look, Gayle continued. "Look, the costume is to help you draw that line between the everyday you and who you are when you go on duty. Even if the everyday you is made of noxious-smelling smoke, like one guy I know, you want to be able to get your head out of it, sometimes. The costume lets you choose when you're going to be the hero. Mostly."

Gayle shrugged apologetically at her friend's raised eyebrow. "Sometimes it comes and plops on you, of course. But mostly, you're doing this because you're making a choice to do it. When you put on the costume, it's like going to work. Or, riding into battle. Or, whatever analogy you want to pick. It says, 'I am ready to do battle with the forces of injustice, and I'm going to do it my way, with my own style!'"

"Well, I can't fault that, I guess." Sheena scrolled through kiosk options herself as her own computer model loaded. "What should I be picking?"

"It's for fighting. Make it something that makes you feel powerful. Oh, yeah, and comfortable! Preferably durable and washable, too, but anything you get from *Image* will do that."

Sheena snorted. "Anything else?"

"Yeah. Make it match your powers and… um… theme. That way people will identify your look with what you do. It's your own style splashed like art all over you." Gayle giggled.

Sheena thought about that while she scrolled through options. The kiosk seemed to have an endless set of combinations in all sorts of styles, colors, materials, and looks. "Shanikali was the goddess of the hunt. She tracked down evil forward and backward through time, as far as I can tell. She was closely tied to the natural world. And I have to have something that works with my wings, of course."

Some options came up that looked like angelic robes or tunics. Sheena considered those, then shook her head. She wasn't an angel. She was a hunter. Her mother had named her Sheena after the main character of a television series about a girl who was raised in the wilderness of Africa and had special powers over animals. Sheena had watched the whole series on DVD many times when she was a child. The Sheena on that show was a huntress, too. She wore what amounted to a fantasy barbarian outfit of revealing, close-fitted skins.

Sheena chuckled to herself. Tempting, but no. A real huntress wasn't going to sneak through the woods with yards of bare skin exposed. An Amazon warrior style might be better. Gayle looked over her shoulder as she tried out different combinations.

"One reason a lot of heroes use the spandex is because it is light and easy to carry around," Gayle commented. "Plus, on physically fit folks it can look very good. Still, there are a lot of options."

Sheena nodded. "What about this?" She had found a leather tunic and skirt combination, with matching brass-studded armbands and knee-high boots. The tunic was designed in a way that would allow her to slip her arms into it normally, lace up the front, and then fasten the upper back and shoulder pieces to the rest with several flexible buckles. This would leave her wings ample freedom to move. "This is close to a costume I had picked out for a renaissance festival. Kind of a fantasy ranger look."

"Cool! Plenty of support, too," Gayle nodded appreciation. "You like skirts?"

"Yeah, when I can get away with it. So does Eric." She nodded. At Gayle's laugh, Sheena blushed. "On me, I mean!"

"Make sure you include comfortable bottoms to go with," Gayle cautioned, "because there will be plenty of opportunity for people to see what's underneath your skirt."

Sheena nodded agreement and explored some options. She dialed the color of the leather to a dark blue and added a cloak, shirt, and leggings to the look for cooler weather. She could leave those off for summer and just wear the basic outfit over her skin if it was hot. Belt pouches to carry things and a circlet with a vaguely Sumerian style completed the costume. It would be tough, breathable, and attractive. She liked the way it looked on her computer model.

"Good!" Gayle said. "Now, run it through the activity list."

"Oh, is that what this is?" Sheena asked, gesturing to the kiosk's prompt screen.

"Yeah. The computer will show your model in the costume doing a bunch of stuff—yoga, martial arts, running, rock climbing, flying—and will do what it can to apply physics to it. That will give you a sense for how it will work on your body. You have to think about how that would actually feel, though. The computer can't tell what would feel right to you. Then, you can make notes and tweaks and the tailors can take it from there."

"Wow. That's a pretty impressive system!"

"Yep! Quality custom costumes quite quickly!" Gayle sang to Sheena's laugh.

Sheena was pleased to learn that her costume would be ready and delivered in a couple of days. With their business at the tailor finished, the pair stopped at a local grill for a late lunch. The place Gayle picked wasn't far from the *Image* store, so she cheerfully walked down the street with Sheena in tow. The scent of strawberries swirled in the breezes surrounding them. Quite a few people stopped to stare at them.

"Ooh, it's Gayle Force!" a girl exclaimed.

"Who's that with her?" her friend asked. "Nova Angel?"

"No, Nova Angel is dark-haired, and her feathers are shiny silver. I don't know who that is. Some new hero, I guess."

Gayle smiled and waved whenever someone made eye contact, but continued to walk with purpose. Her stride suggested that she wasn't open to stopping for casual conversation or autograph signing. A few people scowled and gave them a wider berth, as if they were something unpleasant to avoid, but the pair made their way without incident to an understated storefront decorated in brushed steel trim. Painted in gold-edged red letters on the street level plate glass window was simply "Marty's Grill." Underneath the title was "Meats – Seafood – Vegetarian. Open for Breakfast. Meta-Friendly."

Gayle pulled open the big wooden door and a tumbling flood of wonderful food smells rolled over them. The main dining area stretched back from the front door with plenty of upholstered booths. Stairs led up to a second floor looking over the street. Venture City news clippings, photographs, artwork, and memorabilia lined the walls. The space felt close, but cozy and not confining. There were a few customers, but the place wasn't at all crowded. The hostess was a young woman in a casual black knit dress. She smiled at Gayle and greeted her. "Good afternoon, Gayle. Would you like something in your usual seating area?"

"No, thanks, Jeanne, not today. Could I have a table, instead, with extra wing space for my friend?"

"Certainly." The hostess nodded pleasantly at Sheena and gave her an appraising glance. She tilted her head as she considered what might be most comfortable. She checked her table plan. "I've got one in Tyler's section that should work for you. Please follow me." She picked up two menus and headed up the stairs.

Gayle gestured for Sheena to go ahead and followed her to a corner table next to the windows looking out on the restaurant's upstairs patio seating. The hostess held a chair for Sheena and helped her settle in. The back of the chair was low enough that Sheena could sit comfortably with her wings behind her. Other patrons looked at her with curiosity, but didn't stare.

As they were settling in, a tall, bookish young man wearing round-rimmed glasses and a scraggly beard on his chin approached the table. His dark brown apron was tidy and clean with "Marty's" on the front and a brass-colored name tag that read "Tyler." He made a smooth little half-bow and said, "Afternoon, Gayle."

"Hiya, Tyler!" Gayle responded. "This is my friend Sheena, from Wisconsin."

"Hello, Sheena," the waiter said cordially. He looked at her with an expression of concentration, as if he was fixing her name and face into his mind. "Welcome to Venture City, and Marty's. Please call me Tyler. If you have any questions, don't hesitate to ask. I can get you a raspberry lemonade, light on the ice, medium sweet, with a straw and a glass of ice water, extra ice, if you like." He waited for her response.

Sheena replied, "Yes, please! That would be perfect!" Then she paused and frowned slightly, narrowing her eyes at the waiter. "Heeeyyy... You picked that out specially for me, didn't you?"

Tyler shrugged a nervous apology. "Yes, ma'am. It's what I do."

Gayle cut in with a grin, "Don't give him a hard time, Sheena. Tyler's awesome."

"Uh, no problem, but ... How did he do that? I was just surprised," Sheena asked.

Gayle didn't even order, but just winked at Tyler, who nodded, collected the menus, and glided off to get their drinks.

Sheena leaned over to her friend and whispered, "Does this sort of thing happen a lot here in this city? People with weird... um, special talents everywhere you go?"

Gayle shook her head. "No, not really. I picked this place specifically 'cause it was close and it's meta-friendly. But, compared to Milwaukee? Yeah. Take this place, for instance. Marty has a real gift for food and running a restaurant. No superpowers or anything; just a talent. But he is a super-nice guy who is sympathetic to metas' situations, so he hires people, sets the menu, and runs his place so that everyone feels welcome here." She hesitated. "Well, almost everyone. He's not really set up to serve exotics with really massive or alien physiques, and he doesn't welcome hate groups or known villains. Or paparazzi, either.

"So, he makes a lot of friends and attracts a certain kind of clientele. He doesn't make a big deal about it. And there are dozens of normal, everyday places for every one place like Marty's, and maybe a dozen places like this for every one truly meta-specific business. They'll probably stand out for you because you notice those things more when you're looking for them, and because you are so obviously a meta yourself, now. Other metas who would normally politely hide their abilities will be more open with you because they can see you as one of them."

Gayle sighed and leaned back in her chair. "It's kind of sad, if you think about it a certain way."

"Huh? Why?" Sheena asked.

"Well, wouldn't it be better if everyone could just be themselves all the time?"

"Yes, but…." Sheena tried to figure out how to say what she was thinking. "But that doesn't just go for people with superpowers. That should be for everyone."

"I know! That's what I mean!"

"Yeah, that comes out a lot in your songs," Sheena pointed out.

"You've been listening!" Gayle exclaimed with a pleased expression.

"Of course! All the recordings I can find, anyway."

The singer blushed and gave her friend a pleased smile. "Even after all this time, I'm still kinda surprised when people like my stuff. Especially now that I'm on my fourth album and there have been a couple of waves of fresh stars after me since I started recording."

"It's good music, and I like it. And a whole lot of other people do, too."

"I know that in my head, but…. It was rough for a while after 'Nature Lover' and that concert in Milwaukee…."

"The one where everyone took off their clothes and turned it into a love-fest?" Sheena interrupted.

Gayle ducked her head and winced, her cheeks turning a deep pink. A dusty spice smell wafted around the table. "Yeah, that one." Tyler arrived with their drinks and Gayle nodded her thanks as she took a long sip of her own lemonade.

Sheena waited for the waiter to get out of easy earshot and grinned. "What really happened that day?"

"Well, that was just a few months after that Valentine's Day incident that I told you about."

Sheena nodded.

"It was a Memorial Day concert in the lakefront park and the event organizers had specifically invited me to headline. You know, 'cause of my mom, and the 'hometown girl turns hero and superstar' thing. It felt absolutely great, and everything was super, and we were going into the last couple of songs. I had saved 'Nature Lover' for last. The music was just flowing through me and the crowd. I started the intro to 'Nature Lover,' and you know how there's a double meaning to that one?"

Sheena nodded and smirked. Gayle's chart-topping hit was not just about appreciating nature. It was also about romance in the outdoors.

"That song was just totally rocking! I was feeling it so much that I was apparently putting out pheromones or something that started affecting the audience. And they got into the 'nature loving' mood, themselves. And started getting really friendly. And stuff." Gayle was blushing profusely again.

"My band was totally freaked out. They could see what was going on while I was completely absorbed in the music, but they didn't know what to do. The concert version runs for a good twelve and a half minutes. They just kept playing and followed my lead. We'd run through the solos in the second half of the song when I realized what was happening and managed to wrap it up early. I signaled to the guys to go right into the encore song we'd arranged. I did that one and focused on giving the audience time to come to their senses and calm down, and then I just flew out of there, right off the stage, and tried not to die from embarrassment. I mean, I had *no* clue I could do anything like that!

"For a while, I was worried that it was something Ravenger had done to me as an effect from that toxic pollen. But, as far as the experts could tell, it was just me and my own music and my air powers. Josh—Doctor Swan—thought there might have been some kind of amplification from the crowd, or some meta in the crowd that we were never able to identify, but no one picked up anything sinister."

"The headlines were incredible," Sheena said, shaking her head. "'Audience gets naked at Gayle Force concert!'"

"Yeah, and so many people who were calling for my head on a platter, too! I have had to try hard to keep it suppressed since them."

"Well, it's not as if you were using mind control on them, or making them do anything that they didn't want to do."

"Kinda…," Gayle said. "But it was in a legal gray area, actually. Pretty close to mind control, but more of a mood altering effect." Gayle sighed. "I was fighting a public relations battle and a bunch of lawsuits for almost two years afterward. And I inadvertently gave a whole lot of ammunition to the meta-haters who want us all locked up, 'fixed,' or controlled because we are 'too dangerous to be around normal people.'"

"Is there a lot of that?"

"Yeah. A whole lot. Fear and jealousy and misunderstanding and some justified worry, too. But there is a big difference between the obligation to understand and use one's powers responsibly and the call to kill or imprison anyone who has any sort of powers. And we metas don't exactly have enough votes to protect ourselves, politically.

"The same politicians who bank on fearmongering to the lowest common denominator are always bringing up new ways to regulate, tax, or take away from metas the same rights that normal people take for granted. That's what I've had to live with my whole life. I swear, it seems like it's a diabolical conspiracy, some days."

Gayle calmed herself down as Tyler arrived with their food. A chicken Caesar salad, no croutons, extra shredded parmesan, for Gayle and a spinach and roasted red pepper omelet with buttered whole wheat toast for Sheena. Sheena's mouth started watering as she smelled the meal. She shook her head and marveled at Tyler's choices. "Wow. How would he even think to put this together at two o'clock in the afternoon if he didn't know? Heck, I wouldn't have even been able to say this was just what would be perfect!"

"Isn't that just the coolest thing?" Gayle giggled.

"I have got to bring Eric to this place," Sheena sighed around a mouthful of omelet.

"Oh, Eric?" Sheena called as she and Gayle arrived back in the apartment.

"Yeah? You're back?" Eric called from the living room. He had his laptop open on his knees and printouts strewn beside him on the couch and on the coffee table in front of him.

"I ordered a costume. And had lunch at a really great place downtown."

Eric sighed and kept studying the papers intently. "What did it cost?"

"Nothing. It's FBSA subsidized, remember?" She had told him not to worry about it before she and Gayle went shopping. She slid a printed copy of the costume screenshots she had taken into the sheaf of paper in front of him.

"Huh. That is nice!" He looked at the different views. "And you make it look *good.*"

"Thanks!" Sheena leaned over and kissed his forehead. She glanced at the spread of paper across the couch and coffee table. "What are you working on?"

Eric sighed. "Research on Elf Shot. And Doctor Ankh and the stones, too. Following up on the data that Agent Schauer gave me."

"Okay. What can you tell me?"

"Those stones still haven't been reported as stolen, and the FBSA doesn't know where they came from. Ankh is a mercenary type who steals magic things to feed his own collection, and on contract or to sell to buyers. His association with Elf Shot seems to be purely business. Elf Shot herself seems to be part of some shadowy organization of villains, but I couldn't find out anything concrete about that. She doesn't seem to be known for pulling off sophisticated crimes. She's more of a brute force, intimidation, and ambush kind of villain."

Gayle looked at some of the summaries Eric was referring to and added, "She's an enforcer. That spread of crimes she's done breaks down into two buckets—some are just random violence and a few are jobs to get something she wants, but the bulk are things that benefit some sort of organization or mastermind."

"Any idea who that would be?" Eric asked her.

She shook her head. "It varies. From the checking we did before you arrived in town, we know that she does independent work for a couple of groups, like the Syndicate and the Ancients. I'm not sure, but her style seems similar to a couple of groups of mystic baddies I know. She may be a member of the Ancients, but the database was inconclusive on that. That pattern you found isn't about gaining control of criminal organizations or territories, or of any kind of high-tech corporate crap. From what you've got there and what I already know, it seems kind of…." She shrugged. "'dark fey,' I guess I would say. Which fits with her own theme, at least."

"Who benefits from what she does?" Sheena asked. "Gangs are always dealing with turf, rivals, or internal loyalty or power issues. I can't imagine superpowered criminals are any different."

"Mostly, she's carrying out dangerous muscle work for organization bosses. Stuff that might be too hard for regular toughs. Or, jobs where her in-your-face style of intimidation will get better results than if 'the regular boys' did it because she's a scary meta. Eric's right about her tactics, though. She can be sneaky and clever, but she's not much of a planner, and she's not usually what you'd call subtle."

"Do you want any of this stuff?" Eric asked, gesturing at the research he had done.

Gayle shook her head. "No, thanks. A couple of the clues you've got will give me good search terms. That'll be enough for me to feed the supercomputer."

"Oh, okay." The veterinarian looked disappointed. "Just trying to be helpful."

"Don't worry, Eric!" Gayle laughed. "That *was* helpful! You never know what kind of clue will put you on the track, so you have to start with what you've got. You picked up the ball from those agents and moved it down the field a bit."

"I just hate the waiting around," Eric grumbled. "You ladies at least have something to do."

Sheena offered, "Why don't you take some time to see what veterinary stuff you can learn while you're here? There have got to be leading researchers in Venture City to contact."

That didn't seem to make a big impression on him. "Yeah, I guess I could. It's not like I really need any super-advanced pet healing techniques out where we live, though."

Sheena rolled her eyes. "Geez, Eric. Now you're just moping!"

"Yeah, I suppose." He got up with a slight scowl. "I'm going to go work out and then I'll see what I can find."

As he walked off to change, Gayle gave her friend a sympathetic look. "He just wants to help and get all this over with, I think."

"Yeah, I know. He's used to being able to do pretty much what he wants to, and now stuff is happening *to* him... to us... instead of us choosing what to do."

"Well, it's not easy having a super-villain gunning for you. If you can't relax, the next best thing is to stay busy. We just have to find him some way to help."

"Any ideas?"

"Not yet," Gayle admitted. "I kinda thought the veterinary idea was good. Honestly, though, any research he could do with the public network access and tools he's got, a crime-fighting supercomputer could do better in a couple of minutes. And I don't think he knows anyone who can help with the face to face legwork."

"Oh." Sheena looked out the apartment windows at the broad skyline of Venture City. "Can we maybe introduce him to someone who can use his help? There's got to be a lot of opportunities out there for him, as big as this city is."

Gayle thought for a moment. "Yep. There are. I can give him a couple of names over at the University Research Center and at Scott Enterprises. Meanwhile, you need to keep working on a more important thing."

"What's that?"

"Using your powers and skills to stay alive."

"Oh."

Chapter 8 – Enough to be Dangerous

Groaning and gasping, Sheena painfully struggled back to her feet. She was bruised in a dozen places. At Gayle's insistence, she had been working at this for several days, now, but it didn't feel like she was really getting any better at fighting. Her wolf stood nearby watching her discomfort with the same canine grin she had become used to. She scowled at the beast. "Come on! You're supposed to be protecting me, wolf!" she whispered. The wolf spirit shook its ears, almost apologetically, she thought.

"Again. One rule about villains, they *will* kick you when you're down. Expect it. Consider yourself to have bruised or broken ribs, in addition to that shock to the solar plexus, eh?"

Her Canadian fighting instructor had lots of rules about villains. From her earlier days learning karate, Sheena knew that complaining never did any good, so she just gritted her teeth and nodded, then tried her attack again. Bobby Swan, or "North Shore Knight," as he was known in hero circles, advanced on her. She edged a little to her left away from his approach. Gayle watched with interest, sitting on the railing that separated the dojo practice floor from the gallery. When her wolf growled a warning and bared its teeth in her defense, North Shore dropped his left hand from his heavy wooden training sword and shot a power blast from his open palm that knocked the wolf twenty feet across the mat. The wolf spirit dissolved into smoke.

Not giving him time to regain his grip, Sheena took a step back and summoned a flurry of ravens—an unkindness, apparently, that was called—that swirled and pecked hard at North Shore. He spun in a circle and cleared some space, moving toward her as he did so. Now both hands were on his sword again.

Sheena re-summoned the wolf, and an eagle in rapid succession. She had to duck and weave as she finished because she was already within reach of North Shore's sword. The raven swarm disappeared, its magical energy used up, as the eagle and wolf attacked. North Shore sidestepped both of the attacking spirits and feinted at Sheena's face. She flinched, as he expected, allowing him to execute a reverse spin to sweep her legs out from under her. This time, though, her wolf jumped between his follow-up strike and Sheena, taking the blow meant for her.

North Shore's eyes widened a little, and he grinned. As quick as a panther, the big man shifted his stance and stepped in, inside the guard of the wounded wolf spirit, aiming an impaling blow at Sheena's belly. "Come on, lady! Give it more effort!" he shouted as he drove the point of the sword down.

Except that she wasn't there when the blade stuck. Sheena rolled back and flicked her hand at her instructor. A thin gray mist swirled around him and it was as if he was moving through molasses. The wolf bit and hung on to North Shore's leg. That gave Sheena the time to stretch out and extend her power toward the wolf, reversing and removing its wound. She was learning how to consciously use the time currents she had first seen in her initial foray into the spirit world using the psychic exercises Agent Schauer had given her back in Wisconsin after the stakeout.

Strengthened, the wolf tugged at the instructor's leg. The thick sparring gear they both wore protected his calf from the wolf's teeth, but only North Shore's experience and skill allowed him to keep his balance. Sheena scrambled to her feet and called an eagle for another swooping attack. This time, when it struck, he did lose his balance and fell over.

"Why not two?" she asked herself. She tried calling another wolf to aid the first. A word sprang into her mind, and she repeated it. Another wolf appeared, sister to the first. It sensed her danger and leaped to attack. This one was more fierce and went for North Shore's head. Even with the padded sparring helmet, this could be dangerous.

North Shore dropped his practice sword and rolled himself face down, slapping the mat with a free hand. Sheena backed up and called off the wolves. The eagle had disappeared after its attack. Her instructor paused to make sure the situation was stable before recovering his sword and getting to his feet.

"Nice!" he growled. "Where'd the second one come from?"

Sheena shrugged. "I just thought, why not two? And there was the... name, I guess... of the next wolf in my head, so I called her."

North Shore nodded and wiped the sweat from his brow. "Good tactic. That surprised me. The more you can get the critters working together, the more you can combine the effect of their attacks. That eagle attacking my head would be nasty, if I wasn't expecting it. "

Sheena groaned and winced as she hit a sore spot. "I have to stop flinching at everything that comes at me. I just keep opening myself up."

"Yeah, but not as much as when we started. You'll get it. You might not have noticed it, but I'm holding back a lot less now, since you've been able to handle it." He laid his practice sword to the side and checked his headgear for scratches from the wolf's teeth.

"Hey, Sheena?" Gayle called out. "If you can do that healing thing for the animals, can you do it for yourself, too?"

Sheena blinked and wondered. So far, she had only healed her spirit creatures. She could use the time currents to reverse whatever hurt they had suffered, but could she do it for herself? There seemed to be a wellspring of something inside her that she could draw on, swirling currents like a stream or river of time. She released it around herself, as carefully as she could. Then, in a rush, the power poured out as a swirling mist with a torrent of golden light and sparkling motes that spread out across the practice floor from where she stood. Her bruises disappeared. She suddenly felt as refreshed as if she hadn't spent the last hour practicing and taking a beating from North Shore's instruction. "Wow!"

North Shore and Gayle were also caught in the mist's effects. "Not bad, lady!" North Shore exclaimed. Then, his stomach rumbled. Loudly. All three of them felt pangs of hunger. The wolf spirits whined and disappeared.

"Okay, cut it off!" Gayle laughed. "Oh, there went my lunch! Literally!"

It was as if none of the three had eaten anything all day. Sheena had somehow managed to reverse time's effects on their bodies, but had taken them back a bit too far. The mists faded, leaving them with empty bellies.

"Well, if those are the side effects, I guess I wouldn't complain," remarked North Shore. "Better than a nasty head wound, eh?"

"Umm…," Sheena murmured. "I guess?"

"Healthy and hale, and hungry!" Gayle called out in a sing-song voice. "I'd say let's wash up, but you're both fresh as roses, now. How about some lunch. Again?"

Sheena laughed and nodded.

Her instructor shrugged. "That'd be pretty good, I guess. You two ladies going out on patrol, later?"

"I thought we would, yep," Gayle replied. "Sheena's costume got delivered this morning and her registration with the FBSA has been done for days. Got anything special for us to check out? Otherwise, I figured I'd visit a couple of folks who might have leads on Elf Shot. Start tracking her down."

North Shore stripped off his sparring gear and tucked it neatly into his bag. Underneath, his Maple Leafs t-shirt was stretched tight across broad shoulders. Sheena wondered if he used to play hockey professionally. He didn't look much older than her, but had an air of wariness and experience about him. His sandy brown hair was just long enough to be a little wavy. North Shore thought before answering, "Yeah, you might pay a visit to the Rockets' turf. There's a medical device convention going on near there and they love to mess with out-of-towners."

Sheena looked a question at Gayle. The singer smiled. "You think Sheena's ready, then?"

The burly swordmaster stood up and nodded. "She'll do. Don't get yourselves into too much trouble, eh?"

Chapter 9 – Learning the Ropes

"Hey, something is going on down there," Gayle pointed to the hotel parking lot. "Looks like we found the Rockets!"

Sheena banked to her right and looked at the swarm of motorcycles clustered around the main lobby entrance to the Kensington Suites hotel. The suburb of Westport bordered the Venture City International airport on the south, with the more run-down Sandler district to its east. The border area on the Westport side was home to a large number of hotels, convention halls, and corporate office buildings. Gayle had explained that the Rockets were a Sandler-based street gang that was big into motorcycles, illegal combat drugs, and bootleg cybernetic enhancements. They preyed on whoever they could find or intimidate on their turf, which stretched across several districts of Venture City and its suburbs. Most of the high-end gear that made them a threat was provided by the shadowy criminal organization called the Syndicate.

The roar of revving engines was easy to hear even three blocks away where Sheena circled and Gayle was hovering. Gayle's eyes flicked around the group of gangers and the hotel campus. "No civilian injuries or threats I can see, so far. Let's go take a closer look."

Sheena nodded and followed. She tapped the circlet she was wearing as part of her costume. "This thing still works, right?" she asked.

Gayle grinned and nodded, "Yep! Tap once to open the default channel—that's what we've set for the two of us—and twice to close it. It will turn itself off after six seconds of silence on the channel. All you have to do is talk and the comm unit will send it. Remember the other voice commands you can use, too, including the 'dial' command for cellular service. After you've used it for a few days, it will know your voice and whether you mean to speak to the comm channel, the phone, the voice recorder, or if you are even just talking to yourself. Once it gets all set to you, you'll hardly know it's there. But for this run, let's stay together. Just hang back a bit and let me and your critters do the fighting, if it comes to that. Hopefully, it won't."

"Gotcha, Gayle."

Gayle came to a halt behind the biggest mass of bikers and floated just above the pavement. There were close to twenty gangers parked in the loop of driveway meant for guests who were checking into the hotel, blocking the lobby doors. Another dozen were lounging on or at their bikes in the parking lot nearby. Nearly all sported some form of red and black leather vests or jackets with chromed studs and spikes. Most had a rocket design painted or embroidered on their clothes with fire spewing from the exhaust. Sheena could see that the gangers were carrying an assortment of weapons holstered or sheathed about them and their bikes. This was the kind of gathering that Sheena previously wouldn't have even thought of confronting without lots of backup and an anti-gang unit, but now she was a superpowered hero. She figured Gayle knew what she was doing. She concentrated on maintaining a hover behind Gayle, but this was still new and tiring. She whispered into the radio, "I can't hover for very long, remember."

"Oh, yeah," the green-clad heroine replied and gently set herself down on the asphalt. Gayle was wearing her most recognizable costume. Inherited from her mother, the heroine Aspen, Gayle Force wore a shimmering light green spandex outfit with matching leather boots. Her shoulders, arms, and belly were bare to the wind. She wore a golden headband with stylized metallic wings rising from either side. Over her upper chest was a circular emblem of an aspen tree in gold and forest green. Her belt and wristbands had a metallic gold finish that matched her headband. With a calf-length diaphanous cape of alternating green and spring green vertical stripes and her strawberry-blonde hair ruffling in the ever-present breeze around her, she looked every inch a hero.

The Rockets in the parking lot noticed the duo at once, but the ones hanging around the lobby doors were a bit slower on the uptake. Gayle called out sweetly, "Hiya, boys! What's happening?" Her voice carried over the roar of the engines as clearly as if they weren't there at all.

"Holy crap! It's Gayle Force!" someone shouted. The gangers now looked very attentive, watching the heroine and waiting to see what their leader would do.

A lean muscled man in a red leather duster coat lazily swung his leg over his big motorcycle and stretched his arms and shoulders. Sheena could imagine the leather creaking over the engine noise. He was more than a full two meters tall with shoulders that were almost as broad as the handlebars of the big hog that he rode. Red and white streaks were dyed into his long black ponytail. She was surprised to notice that his right eye and arm were chromed; cybernetic implants, apparently. He had some kind of sword on his back and a large-bore automatic handgun strapped to his thigh.

"Hoi, hero," the gang leader said. "Whatcha want?" His face was calm and his expression neutral, but Sheena read his stance as ready to fight.

Gayle kept her tone friendly. "Just checking on things. You don't have reservations here at this hotel, by any chance, do you? Just dropped by to mess with the tourists, maybe?"

Several gangers laughed. The leader sneered. "Nah, they won't let us in. Obstructing our rights, that is."

"Aw, come on," she grinned. "You know that's because the last time the Rockets visited, no one got any sleep and a whole bunch of stuff got broken. And a bunch of out-of-towners got robbed, somehow. You guys are just too rough on the furniture!" More gangers snickered.

"That manager guy is still being a jerk about it," grunted the gang leader.

"Pfft. What do you want with him, anyway? He works for the hotel and is just doing his job. What are you gonna do, scare all the customers?"

His glare was cold and challenging. "I'm gonna let 'em know we own this area. If they want to visit, they can be respectful. And generous."

Gayle shook her head sadly. "Why? You providing entertainment? Looking for tips? No offense, but I don't think they're buying what you're selling."

"You'd be surprised!" he laughed. "It's... what'dya call it? A 'captive market!'"

Gayle turned to a different ganger she recognized and asked, "Who is this guy? Is he new?"

"Yeah, that's Jackhammer," the Rocket replied. "Just got hooked up a few weeks ago. From Philly."

"Hey!" Jackhammer growled. "You wanna talk, talk to me!"

Gayle shrugged and said to the ganger she had asked, "Obviously not a fan of my music." To the gang leader, she replied, "Okay, Mr. Hammer, here's the deal. You guys have had your fun, but there's no profit to be made here. Time for you to take off and leave the folks here in peace."

"I'll decide when we're ready to go!" Jackhammer sneered. Sheena could see the telltale reddish glow of the Excelsior combat drug in the thug's unaltered eye. Under the effects of Excelsior, it was almost impossible for the user to back down from a conflict. Mostly, they went looking for fights to pump their adrenaline even further. More than a handful of the Rockets were on the stuff, she noticed. She hoped Gayle spotted the same signs.

"Great! When are you going to be ready to go? You've probably got more interesting things to do than to stand here and talk to me. Most of your boys know me. I think they'll be ready to head out as soon as you give the word."

"I don't think so." He paused. "Gayle Force, heh? There's a big Syndicate bounty for you. I think I'ma gonna collect it!" In a flash, Jackhammer had drawn his gun and fired three shots at Gayle.

His aim was good, but the bullets dropped to the ground in front of Gayle, stopped by an invisible barrier of nearly solid air. She shook her head as his face registered surprise. "Hold fast, Rockets!" she called out. "He's made this just between him and me!"

Most of the gangers froze in wide-eyed apprehension. Three of the Excelsior users grabbed their weapons and fired on Gayle with the same results as Jackhammer. The heroine rolled her eyes and said, "Sheena, take care of the trash. I'll handle the boss."

Sheena replied, "Got it." She called both of her wolves and sent an eagle shrieking at the assailant farthest from both her and Gayle. Jackhammer gritted his teeth and fired at Gayle again, as if sheer determination could force a bullet to hit her.

Gayle popped into the air and glided a few feet to her right to get a better angle. She held her hands out, palms facing the thug, and unleashed a blast of air with the force of a jet engine. Jackhammer went flying a dozen meters back across the parking lot.

The gangers who had joined in now each had one of Sheena's animal spirits biting or clawing at them. She concentrated and tapped the time stream, wreathing each of them in a current of slowed time. This more than countered the reflex-enhancing effects of the Excelsior, and they slowed to a sluggish crawl. Within seconds, all three were on the ground, harassed by the wolves and eagle. Sheena glanced around at the other Rockets to make sure that none of them were getting ready to join in.

Jackhammer rolled to his feet and drew a meter-long sword from the scabbard on his back. Red LEDs winked to life up the length of the blade. He stomped forward toward Gayle Force with the sword in a guard position.

"Vibroblade," Gayle warned Sheena. "Cuts through anything but a force field or another vibro weapon. But now he's in the open." She threw her arms up to the sky and a storm cloud appeared between her and the thug, rumbling with thunder. As Jackhammer approached, a lightning bolt crackled out to strike him with a loud crash of thunderous winds. Jerking spasmodically, the gang leader was flung back out into the center of the parking lot. He collapsed in a heap on the ground for a few seconds, then tried to rise.

"Not out of range, just yet, Jack!" Gayle called out. Another bolt lashed out from the storm cloud and repeated the thunderstrike the thug had just taken. He was blown into the bushes at the far edge of the parking lot. Without taking her eyes off of Jackhammer, Gayle asked, "How are you doing, Sheena?"

Sheena had reinforced the slowdown she had put on the hopped-up gangers and they were now almost unable to move at all. "Good here. No damage." She had the wolves drag the restrained gang members close together. The rest of the gang had moved out of the line of fire, to what they hoped would be safe places to watch.

Gayle whipped up an aerial servant and had it pick up the stunned Jackhammer. Another dust devil swirled about the parking lot picking up weapons that the attackers had been forced to drop. The miniature storm cloud continued to flicker and rumble periodically, but it held its lightning. Gayle had her air construct hold the gang leader immobile a couple of feet off the ground near the others. After checking with Sheena, she created more columns of air to hold the other three gangers, too. Sheena released the time currents and had the eagle circle and watch, with the wolves standing guard.

"Show's over, folks!" Gayle called out to the rest of the Rockets. The four captive gang members bobbed helplessly in their columns of air. "The police will be here soon. You might want to head out now. Thanks for your cooperation!" Several of the Rockets waved to her with smiles as they fired up their bikes and roared away from the hotel. Many had taken pictures of Jackhammer and the other three hanging in midair. From beginning to end, the fight had taken less than a minute.

The sliding doors to the hotel opened and an imposing African-American man about forty years old in a tailored navy-blue suit emerged. He struck Sheena as being in much better shape than most corporate types. He glanced around to see if all the gangers were gone and addressed Gayle. "Ma'am, I have to thank you for handling that gang with so little trouble. I've called the police and they'll be here right away."

"Thanks, mister...?"

"Killdare. Tyrone Killdare. I'm the hotel manager." He nodded respectfully to both Gayle and Sheena.

"Oh, you're new here, then?" Gayle asked.

"Yes, ma'am. The head office agreed to Brian's transfer request. After the trouble he's had earlier this year, they put me in, instead. I know the business and I don't knuckle under to hoods."

"Good for you!" Gayle giggled. "Most of those guys aren't so bad, on their own. Just when they get all whipped up and stupid is when they're a problem. Or dosed up, either way."

Killdare nodded. "I've seen the type before. Spent ten years in the army. If you keep a cool head, there's a lot you can handle." The flashing lights of the police vehicles approached. Sheena kept her eyes on the captured gangers.

"How much of that situation did you get on the security cameras, Mr. Killdare?" Gayle asked.

"Everything. With audio. They picked the second most observed spot in the hotel to go wild, other than the lobby itself."

"Excellent! That should get these guys properly sent off, then."

"I expect so, ma'am."

"Do you know why they were paying you a visit today? Anything special, or just random?"

"They wanted to deliver a threat, in addition to looking for an opportunity to shake down my staff and guests. 'The Syndicate wants you to play ball with them. And stop stalling,' was what that big fellow said. I said I would write that down and make sure that it got to the right people. Then I got the doors shut and locked before they could cause trouble inside."

"Good thinking," Sheena said.

"Yes, ma'am. Contingency planning. I was briefed on what they've done before. And, like I said, I don't knuckle under to criminals, so I put the whole staff through drills for when this sort of thing happened again. Tonight was the night."

"Well, between your preparation and the tip we got, this turned out well," Gayle acknowledged cheerfully. "Thank you, Mr. Killdare. Time to turn over the baggage and evidence to the police."

Sheena surprised Gayle by gliding efficiently through the police process. They were done and flying onward over the city in another ten minutes. Sheena explained, "Remember, Gayle, I'm in law enforcement, in real life!"

Her friend laughed. "So this isn't such a big change for you, then!"

Sheena grinned and shook her head. "You have no idea."

Gayle brought Sheena to visit Detective Lieutenant Eddie Fowler at his office in the 14th Precinct station in the Dartmouth district of Venture City. Eddie had responded to Gayle's request with a message saying that he might be able to help them find Elf Shot. Most of the police officers and staff at the station seemed happy to see Gayle and greeted Sheena with smiles, as well, although there were a few suspicious glances. No snide remarks about costumes or spandex.

49

"Strange you should mention the Syndicate," Lieutenant Fowler said. "Elf Shot has been doing work for them, lately."

Gayle exchanged glances with Sheena. "Really? What kind of work, Eddie?"

"Obstructing customs officials, mostly. Some hits on businesses that wouldn't pay protection money to the Syndicate. And, a couple of thefts from biotech laboratories, which is weird." The police lieutenant took another swallow from his coffee mug. A Venture City Neighborhood Watch program logo was printed on its side. He put the mug back on his desk blotter and turned it around a few times. A variety of scars marred his strong brown-skinned hands. Gayle had been relating the story of how they had stopped the Rockets earlier that evening when Eddie had latched on to the mention of the Syndicate's threat against the Kensington Suites manager.

"What's weird about the biotech heists?" Gayle asked.

Eddie shook his head and ran his hand across his scalp of closely trimmed hair, still hanging onto its black color, but beginning to lose the battle to the encroaching gray of age. He bore the look of a long, stressful career on the police force. "As far as I know, Elf Shot knows jack about biotech. And if the Syndicate wants something in that field, they buy and run their own labs to make it. Doing enforcement work for the Syndicate is pretty normal for her; she's usually for hire. But the biotech... it doesn't fit her pattern."

"Anything on what was stolen that would give us some clues?"

"Maybe. Some equipment used to synthesize vaccines from one place, and a truckload of materials to use in the process from the other lab, along with several crates of this year's prototype flu vaccine. The gals in the lab said that this stuff doesn't pose any threat by itself, but if Elf Shot or her employer already has other gear, this might set them up with what they need to produce a vaccine for a bioweapon."

"Protecting themselves from something they plan to unleash? Great," Sheena muttered.

"There are lots of other possibilities, too," Gayle noted. "If you wanted to infect a lot of people, why not figure out a way to tamper with the seasonal flu vaccine? Nasty."

"Fortunately, it's not that simple," the detective replied. "Unfortunately, there are plenty of people out there that could turn this stuff to some bad purpose."

"No rumors about who might have hired this one?"

"No, Gayle, nothing. That's another caution sign. It probably means that she's working for someone new, or that we haven't heard from, yet."

"That's the way it goes, Sheena," Gayle explained. "Some new villain is always moving into the power vacuum when we put down a major operation. It's like they're lined up at the edge of the city, waiting for their turn."

"So, then who's responsible for beefing up the prevention side of things?" Sheena asked. "Community policing and all that?"

Eddie nodded and leaned forward. "Yeah, you've got it, Sheena. We'll never have enough officers to cover everything, and even with the registered heroes there are still plenty of shadows to hide in. The more we can reach out to regular citizens and help them find ways to 'stay good,' the better off everyone is."

"Heroes do what they can, of course," Eddie continued, "and our patrol officers and community advocate staff spend a chunk of their time on outreach and support. Bigger businesses and major organizations work with us on security and crime prevention, too."

"This is a whole lot more complex than being a game warden in northern Wisconsin," Sheena said, shaking her head. The detective shrugged.

Gayle was thinking. Slowly, she asked, "Is there anything we can find on where Elf Shot might be holing up, sightings, or people to talk to about her?"

"One clue, and one suggestion," Eddie offered. "On her recent heists, some of the vehicles used to make the escape were found in the West Bank district near the docks and warehouses. They were recovered in the process of being prepped for sale—stripping vehicle ID numbers, repainting, and so on. The customs harassment occurred in the same area. That's where customs officers clearing cargo aboard ships in the port were ambushed and tied up while the crooks offloaded the cargo and got away into the city. I would check West Bank. She's got someplace there where she slips away."

"Cool. That should be helpful," Gayle said. "And the suggestion?"

Eddie shifted to face Sheena. "You said that Elf Shot vowed to get the powers out of you and take them for her own, right?"

Sheena nodded. "She has to figure out some way to do that before she'll be ready for me, according to the FBSA agents."

"Right. If I were you, I would figure out who or what she would go to if she wanted to get that information. Some sort of magic experts, probably. My thinking is that whoever knows how to do that is in danger from her, right now. You gotta get there first."

"Yeah...." Sheena thought about it. "Gayle? It's time to link up with those arcane scholars you were talking about."

"That makes perfect sense. Thanks for the tips, Eddie!"

"Hey, any time, Gayle. Let me know if you find anything else. I'll do likewise. Nice to meet you, Sheena, and welcome to the city." The detective rose and shook her hand.

As they were walking out of the police station, Sheena asked Gayle, "Do you do a lot of this? Tracking down clues, I mean."

"Yep. And the police, like Eddie, will call on me for help whenever they've got something that might be in my area that they need help with."

Sheena mused, "This is another kind of hunting. More of the kind that I'm used to, but the terrain is awfully different."

"What? Compared to the woods, you mean?"

"Yeah. But working with the public and doing the investigation end of things isn't too different, it seems."

Gayle smiled broadly. "Well, maybe this is your next career move! Even if you weren't expecting it."

Sheena chuckled softly. "You never know. I'd say 'stranger things have happened,' but... no, this is as strange as it gets, for me."

Chapter 10 – I Know what I Want

The leather-clad archer slipped through the rusting steel door and made her way down the crumbling concrete steps into the sewer junction. Carefully avoiding the patches of muck and fungus, she worked her way down to the landing, not deigning to even touch the rusted iron railing. As she looked out again at the corroded and decayed chamber of her employer, she paused. Her lip curled into a sneer of distaste. The filth and smell just didn't get any better with successive visits. She brushed her blood red hair back behind her pointed ears and looked about.

"Come in, Lady Elf Shot," the occupant of the chamber called in a rasping voice. He was seated in a high-backed leather executive chair behind a desk of dented and stained steel. The desk and a cluster of cabinets and tables were suspended above the sewer muck on a wide rusted iron grate that formed a sort of platform. The smell of the sewer mixed unpleasantly with the fumes of crude oil. The rail-thin creature at the desk paid no mind to the combined stench, but rose to greet his guest. He was covered with some tarry mixture of oil and sweat. A pair of dirty black feathered wings rose from between his shoulder blades. Much of his body was burned. His intact skin was a bleached copper color, as if he spent much of his time underground. His close cut black hair was as neatly groomed as he could manage, but slick with the ooze secreted by his body. The only garments covering his nakedness were an oil-soaked buckskin loincloth, a pair of stained knee-high moccasins half crusted with the muck of the sewer, and thin buckskin gloves. The gloves were smooth and tight about the fingers, opening more widely as they rose to the middle of his forearms. Leather fringes at the cuffs dripped with the oily substance the man apparently produced, preventing it from oozing down toward his fingers.

"Blighthawk." Elf Shot managed to keep a sneer from her voice as she sketched a short bow. She picked the least dirty path from the concrete landing to the iron platform where he had established his underground office. Climbing the steps to the platform, she got right to the point. "I've done what you've asked, so far. I'm waiting for my payment, and for the help you promised me."

The soiled creature in front of her smiled, but there was no warmth in it. His voice sounded like his throat had been seared by hot smoke. "Yes, you have been prompt and efficient." He gingerly picked up a small brass key with a paper tag attached to it by a piece of string. "You will find your complete payment in cash in the marked storage locker at this address."

She took the key daintily between one index finger and thumb. She glanced at the tag. "This is the same place I dropped off the vaccine equipment."

"Yes. I like to recycle, when possible." Elf Shot snorted. "I can see your skepticism. You may ask, 'Why bother, when you seem bent on drowning the world in its own manmade poisons?'"

"Yes, the thought had occurred to me," the archer admitted.

"Just because the effort is pointless doesn't mean we shouldn't exercise good habits." Blighthawk chuckled. This caused him to cough. He cleared his throat and carefully took a breath before continuing. "Just as when I occasionally use industrial chemicals to turn the corruption on the corrupt powers that be, it's a form of recycling. We get more use out of what has been produced. Like carrion. Raven feasts on the carrion left behind by the corpses of our enemies, does he not?"

"If you say so. You're poisoning the earth with its own mistakes. I get it." Elf Shot brushed on impatiently.

"Close, but not quite," the corrupter corrected. "I'm not harming the earth. Just the polluters and everyone too comfortable with the situation to do anything about it."

"Whatever. In any case, how do I get those powers out of that forest ranger and into me? You did say that you would give me what I needed for that."

"Are you sure that's really what you want? This isn't some trivial task we're talking about."

"I know what I want!" She tossed her head proudly.

"Really? Why this? Why Shanikali?"

"To make me a better hunter. To let me command the animal spirits. And more importantly, to give me the power to change the past!"

Blighthawk shook his head. "Shanikali couldn't change the past. You're mistaken about that."

She looked at him with narrowed, skeptical eyes. "Why do you say that? She controls time, so she can change the past."

He assumed a lecturer's tone and croaked, "As I understand the research, Shanikali was able to hunt in a spirit ground where the River of Time flowed. If we carefully analyze the tales, we can see from her reported deeds that she could slow down, speed up, or reverse time in limited ways. Thinking logically through the 'time as a river' metaphor which was employed here, we might also assume that anything done to the time stream in one place would be carried further down the time stream as it flowed. Yes, if you had the ability, you could go back, 'along the bank,' as it were, but whatever you do to the stream would be affected by the flow and turbulence of the 'water' until the effects of your tampering would be mostly or wholly undone at the time of your subjective 'present.' So, if you 'went back' to change the past any significant distance, the result would be negligible or unpredictable when you returned."

"I'll take my chances," the elven villain replied stubbornly.

"I should also point out that Shanikali's vessel specifically picked this young woman. The spirit carrying the power would not be a good match for your own temperament."

"It doesn't matter! Those powers were supposed to be mine!"

"Everyone has lost something, Margaret," the corrupter sighed with impatience.

"Don't call me that! I left that name far behind me!"

"Very well, then, Meg it is." He rolled his eyes and continued, "Nevertheless, Meg, everyone has lost something, had something taken from them. You've been beaten to your magic rock. I lost my family, my honor, and my health all in one day. Maybe you can steal those powers back again, with my help, but I can never be restored. Just look at me!" Blighthawk's skin oozed a slimy film of tar that spread and dripped like melting butter over his burn-scarred limbs. He stretched out oily, unkempt wings from his back, their dirty feathers pulled awry and glued by tar. With the stained loincloth around his hips, he looked like an angel of oil. "I am so sick to death of the smell of petroleum fumes, but it makes me strong!"

He flopped back into his oil-soaked seat. "The land writhes in pain, Meg. We do terrible things to it far faster than it can heal. Thanks to those burning tar sands, I am the conduit of that pain and of Raven's vengeance. You haven't lost that much, yet, but you risk all that you have serving the Dark Ones. They could show you more pain than ever I could."

"I know pain. I spent seven years in the Unseighlie Court. I'll take my chances."

"And what...? A day passed in the real world while you were there learning the most simple lessons of cruelty? I'll give you this, the death and decay of life makes Raven stronger. He feeds on the corpses of the corrupt. That's what the Dark Ones want, isn't it? The insidious corruption of beauty and life, to fall into ruin and slime? Well, I'll give it to them, at least as far as the corporate overlords and their greed-driven empire are concerned. I will let Raven pick the bones of this world, but first I have to destroy much of it."

"Exactly."

Blighthawk shook his head sadly. "You have no idea what you're doing. You simply follow the whims of the Dark Ones because there's a chance they'll let you rise in the ranks of their servants. You are not even a true elf, but just a changeling, and you mean no more to them than the tar on my moccasins."

She narrowed her eyes suspiciously. "How do you know so much about me?"

He made a careless gesture with one hand. A dozen transparent human-shaped forms, like ghosts drowned in acid, rose from the sewer water. Watery limbs and bodies appeared twisted and melted by chemicals and fumes rose from them. Encased within their outer shells appeared to be the tattered vestiges of business suits or dresses. Their hollow, unblinking eye sockets stared expressionlessly at Elf Shot. She studied them with unease. Blighthawk waved his hand and they sank back into the muck. "The poisoned spirits, my dear. I consume the corrupters and bend their shattered souls to my will. There is little they cannot see and almost nowhere they cannot go. I have my ways of finding out what I wish to know, you see. But we were talking about your dark masters. Specifically, how little they regard you. They give fickle enough favor to even their most mighty servants. How can you hope to compare your chances to those elite when you are so far from the seats of power?"

"I know that world, and in it I can be strong, free! I know the rules and I can make my own way! I can claw myself up the ranks to a place I can call my own."

Blighthawk chuckled for a moment and then burst into a croaking sort of laughter, like a raven calling. Tears ran from his eyes as he shook with the irony of it. Elf Shot's jaw clenched, but she held her tongue. The corrupter gasped, "A position and place of your own? When you last only at the whim of those lords and ladies? They are as old as the night, Meg! Your ambition is merely a few minutes' amusement to them! Ah, there is no one as blind as one who will not see!"

"I see plenty," she hissed. "And I'll take my chances."

He waved a hand and gave her an icy conciliatory smile. "Of course, of course! And far be it from me to dissuade you. Maybe I'm wrong. All we have of the past are broken memories, and all we can see of the future are hazy possibilities, no matter the skill of the mage. Yes, I will help you rip Shanikali's power from that woman you are so obsessed with. And in return, you will do what I command. When we are done, you will be free to return to claim your rightful place in the Dark Court."

"Excellent! What must I do first?"

Blighthawk tapped at one of his computer screens, careful to keep his fluids from dripping on the equipment. "You will need a vessel to hold and transfer the power. Look through that list. There are several things that might serve you for that purpose. Acquire one of them, as you please."

Elf Shot nodded with satisfaction. "At last! Now, we're making some progress!"

"The other things you must do are these: Collect your things from your current residence and move to another. You are already being hunted by the 'forest ranger' and her allies. You need to cover your tracks." To her startled look, Blighthawk continued, "I have designated several suitable alternatives for you. Then, once you have done this, send me a signal through an untraceable method, preferably one of my surface followers. I have more work for you while you consider what I have presented to you."

"Very well."

"Unless you have any questions…?" The corrupted shaman paused and fluttered his wings to sort the feathers into place as well as he could. Elf Shot shook her head. "Then, we are done, for now. I look forward to your signal and our next step toward ridding this world of that which plagues it."

Elf Shot nodded her agreement and began to make her way back up out of the sewers without a backward glance.

Chapter 11 – Cannery Row

"Do you get the feeling that we're running out of time?" Sheena grumbled to Gayle. She summoned an eagle and sent it up to the rooftop windows of the nearby warehouse. As it found a spot that was clean enough to see through, she concentrated and shifted her vision to see through the spirit's eyes. She made a quick scan of the interior, then had the bird move to a different window.

Gayle floated in the alley nearby keeping watch for trouble and keeping up a screening mist around them. In costume, they were anything but inconspicuous. That didn't mean that all villains would run and hide from them, though. Many had ego enough to try to take on a pair of female heroes caught snooping around their turf. Sheena had picked up a few new tricks over the past week of searching for clues. Perceiving through the senses of her spirit animals was one of those abilities, but she could only concentrate on one source of input at once. Gayle made sure to stay alert when Sheena was concentrating "elsewhere."

"Something will turn up," Gayle reassured her friend. "It always does."

The eagle had found another suitable perch. Sheena checked the other side of the warehouse. "Nothing. No sign of her."

"Dang. This was definitely supposed to be the place. Do you want to get inside and look for clues?"

"Yeah, let's see if she left anything. If she was even here at all, anyway."

Gayle nodded. She waited for Sheena to refocus, then moved along the alley to a side door into the building. Sheena studied the ground and the door, frowning slightly. Gayle asked, "What?"

"People go in this door, but they don't come out of it."

"Huh? How can you tell?" Gayle looked closely, trying to spot what Sheena was seeing.

"Just looking at the tracks," she replied. "The footprints all point toward the door, but there are no footprints exiting this way."

"Footprints?" Gayle asked. She giggled. "Sheena, you're serious? You can see footprints here? I'm just seeing regular city concrete."

"Really? You can't see them?" Sheena cocked her head to one side. "Sure, they're faint, but I would have thought anyone could see this if they were looking for it. They're not so much complete foot shapes like you might think, but scrapes and rubs where shoes would leave marks as people were walking and turning." She pointed with her index finger, tracing the outlines of the prints she saw one after another.

Gayle could almost follow the slight disturbances in the dust and grit. She shook her head in amusement and shrugged. "I guess your own skills are getting bumped way up by Shanikali's hunting and tracking powers, Sheena."

Sheena snorted in disbelief and was about to object, but then looked at the seemingly bare concrete and thought about it more seriously. "Well, it just seemed so obvious, but… yeah, why not? I mean, this is a plus. Still… why only in through this door?"

Gayle thought for a moment. "I've run into a couple of places where the bad guys had set up ways to shake pursuers if they were being followed. They would go into a building and leave only through secret exits. In one of those, there were traps that would have fired off if someone went the other way through the defenses. Maybe this is something like that."

"That's kind of what I was thinking," Sheena nodded. "Did that guy you got the tip from say if he ever saw Elf Shot coming out?"

Gayle wracked her memory. "No. He just said he saw her go into this warehouse, and that it was pretty much locked up until the company gets a new tenant."

Sheena glanced back at the "For Lease" sign posted on the sagging chain link fence surrounding the warehouse lot. She wasn't sure whether it was comforting or not that all of Venture City wasn't made up of the high-tech building materials she and Eric had seen in the corporate research parks and high-rises as they had driven into the city. The warehouses and machine shops in this section of West Bank near the docks were mostly made of ordinary metal and were easily 60 years old and only half-heartedly maintained. The years of hard use lay heavily on the neighborhood.

"Let's check the other doors, then," Sheena suggested.

They circled the building, allowing Sheena to get a good look at each door and loading dock. The alley door was the only one with odd signs of use. The other entrances were fully visible from the streets surrounding the lot, as well. All of those other doors were securely closed and locked. They arrived back at the alley door.

"Gotta be this one, if any at all," Sheena remarked. "Stay alert and go in?"

"Yep! Air cushions on both of us. Proceed when ready." Sheena had gotten used to the barrier of almost-solid air that Gayle could wrap each of them in for protection, but it was still a bit of an odd feeling, like a constant whisper of wind. She summoned both of her wolves and turned the doorknob. The door opened easily and the wolves slipped inside and began sniffing for any other creatures or threats. Sheena gave them a count of ten and followed.

The warehouse floor was empty except for a small beat up forklift and a faded yellow dumpster with the logo of a local trash and recycling company on its side. The dumpster and forklift sat near one of the docks. The dumpster was mostly filled with cardboard, plastic, and plastic packing strips. All of the goods or material shipped through the place by the previous tenants was gone. Loading dock doors were spaced along both sides of the bay. Dim sunlight leaked in through the windows near the ceiling and a trio of translucent skylights, but the internal lights were all off except for the red glow of the emergency exit signs. A second, smaller bay was visible beyond the first, separated by an interior wall with a large open roll-up door. An enclosed, single story office area lay across the bay from the door to the alley. Plexiglas windows and a dispatch counter for the office showed some basic office furniture remaining within. The summer heat of the enclosed space, as large as it was, was noticeably warmer than the outdoor temperature. The wolf spirits ranged about the main bay, sniffing at the floor.

Sheena looked for tracks. There were more faint marks of people passing this way toward the office. She pointed out the path. "I think they came through the door and went that way, toward the office."

Gayle glanced up at the steel support framework of the rafters. "Nothing to see inside, as far as I can tell. Any cameras or traps you can spot?"

Sheena shook her head. "No, that's the first thing I looked for. I wouldn't be surprised if they've hidden something I can't easily see, though."

Gayle looked back at the door they had come through and giggled. "Well, I can guess why no one goes out that door, at least," she said with a grin.

"Yeah?" Sheena turned to look and blushed. "Oh. The knob is missing on this side. Makes sense. Should've seen that right away." She examined it. "Looks intentional, though." She shrugged and directed the wolves onward into the warehouse.

Near the office, the wolves suddenly growled and went on guard, hackles up. They rounded the corner of the office area and a fearful voice called out, "Wait! Wait! Leave me alone! I'll go! Just keep your dogs off!" An underfed homeless man scrambled away from the dark corner where the office ran along the wall to the second bay, trying to put some distance between himself and the wolves. He climbed up on a trash can and frantically pulled himself up to the top of the office ceiling. He looked down at the wolves and the two women with obvious fright.

Gayle floated into the air and followed him. "Hi there! We're not here to cause trouble for you."

Sheena brought her wolves back to her side. They kept a watchful eye on the vagrant but stopped growling.

"I haven't seen nothin', I swear!"

Gayle frowned slightly and exchanged glances with Sheena. She turned back to the man. "It's okay. We're not after you. We're looking for someone else. Is there anything we can do for you?"

Conflicting emotions flickered across his face. Cautious hope won out. "Not unless you know a safe place I can squat 'cross town some'ere. Mebbe a job I could do."

"I certainly might be able to help with that, sir," Gayle replied earnestly. "How'd you end up here?"

"Used to work 'round here," the fellow mumbled as he climbed down from his perch. "Hit the bottle a bit too hard and m'wife left me. She took pretty much ev'rythin'. Then had an accident with a welding tank an' a couple've m'buddies got hurt bad. The union blackballed me and I lost m'job. Stayed pretty much drunk alla time, 'til they kicked me outta my 'partment and I got noplace to go. I came back down near the docks, askin' for some work, but no one would give me anythin'. Been sleepin' where I can, and I found this place unlocked a few weeks ago." He shrugged helplessly, palms open at his sides. "Don't got noplace to go, so I stay here."

Sheena looked at the man's possessions gathered in a bundle in the corner. There was a worn but serviceable sleeping bag and a battered canvas rucksack stuffed with clothes. A couple of liquor bottles lay drained by the wall. A paper grocery bag sat by the rucksack with some cans and boxes of food in it. She had definitely seen worse.

"M'name's Johnny," he offered tentatively. "Johnny Miles."

"Pleased to meet you, Johnny. I'm Gayle. This is my friend, Sheena." Sheena nodded. "Has anyone else been through here while you've been staying here?"

Johnny shook his head vigorously. "Nope. I've seen nothin'. Pretty quiet, s'long as I keep hidden."

"But there are people you're hiding from outside?" Gayle asked tentatively.

His eyes shifted back and forth for a few moments as he tried to figure out what to say. "Uh... Yeah. Don't wanna get kicked outta here, y'know. Got runnin' water an' ev'rythin' here. Just gotta stay outta the way."

Sheena went to the office door and looked in. The faint tracks she had seen were heaviest in this area. There were several interior rooms, a power box, and a restroom. The linoleum floor led to a set of doors at the end of a short hallway. She had never been here before, but there was something that still seemed familiar.

Gayle continued to talk to Johnny. She asked, "You want to get off the bottle and put your bad times behind you?" He nodded tentatively. "Are you sure? I can help you if you really want to do it, and get you someplace else, across town, like you said."

"Yeah, I do. Don' know if I c'n do it, but m'tired of livin' like this. But, no one's gonna give me a job if I don't got a place, or a phone number, and stuff."

Gayle nodded. "Yeah, I know. We can take care of that, but you've got to do your part."

He tensed up. "I don't know anythin', I told you."

Gayle smiled and waved away his protest. "No, nothing like that. I mean you've got to promise to change it all and take back control of your life."

"Oh, if you c'n help me, I'll do it!" Johnny replied. He rocked back and forth, fidgeting with excitement.

"Okay, Sheena is going to look around while I start to get you set up. Is there anything we need to watch out for or be careful of in here? I don't want her tripping over exposed wiring or anything, if you've seen anything dangerous."

"Uh, no. Storeroom door's locked."

"Hazardous materials in there?" Gayle asked.

He shook his head. "I d'know. They jus' keep it locked an' I stay outta the way."

Sheena nodded to Gayle when Johnny's back was to her and went to take a closer look. She studied each room in turn as she came to it. The wolves poked their heads in, as well, but nothing aroused their interest. It looked like the place really had not been used in many months. But there were more recent tracks to the outside doors, the restroom, and the locked storeroom door. The tracks to the restroom and exterior doors mostly matched Johnny's footprints. The faint marks toward the storeroom had a different character.

One set of these are from women's heeled boots, Sheena realized. And the nagging sense that something was familiar… she remembered what it was. It was a scent. She had only smelled that specific scent of night-blooming flowers once before, when Elf Shot had leaned in close to threaten her back home in Wisconsin. She studied the door and the knob. It was an ordinary round handle with a keyhole in the middle. No signs of any wires or scent of any explosives or chemicals around the edge of the door, just the smell of the sun-heated metal of the warehouse, warm oily concrete, and what she took to be Elf Shot's perfume.

Sheena tried the knob and found it locked, as Johnny had claimed. She was relieved to suffer no electric shock or other dangerous surprise. She realized with a start that what was locked *now* had been open *before*, and an idea occurred to her. Concentrating just on the handle and the lock, she reached out her hand and let the time currents swirl around the doorknob. Carefully, slowly, she tried to reverse the state of the lock to the time when it had most recently been open. With a gasp, she lost hold of the mechanism and the currents swirled aimlessly. *Okay, a bit more firmly, then*, she thought and tried again. This time, it worked. The pins of the lock turned back and the door was unlocked. She let out the breath she had been holding and relaxed.

Her wolves got up from where they were sitting behind her and sniffed at the edge of the door. There was nothing to alarm them, so Sheena turned the handle and opened the door. The storeroom was dark, but there was plenty of outside light from the hallway for Sheena's eyes. The simple metal shelves were mostly empty. A bucket of used paint and some cleaning supplies remained on the floor near the door. A few stray rags and pencils and a screwdriver rested on the farther set of paint-speckled shelves. At the other end of the room in front of the shelves was a seam in the floor covering. The seam looked like the linoleum had been cut to cover a square piece of the floor three feet on a side. The wolves went to sniff at it. Again, they judged it safe. Sheena ruffled a hand over each animal's ears and crouched to study the floor.

It looked like a trap door in the floor. Scratches and chips in the flooring suggested that it could be pried or levered up with something simple and thin, like a screwdriver… *or an arrow*, Sheena thought. "You're sure it's okay?" She asked the wolves. They nodded. With a shrug she looked for something to use to pry up the floor. She spotted a flat head screwdriver sitting conveniently on a middle shelf within reach. She picked up the tool and slid the head into the crack between the linoleum and the floor and was not surprised when it came up easily.

The trap door was a large metal plate over a hole in the floor. A rough concrete passage had been made into a tunnel below the warehouse floor. Wooden stairs proceeded down steeply into the darkness. "Well, this is what we're looking for," Sheena said to herself.

She left the trap door open and went back to the storeroom door. She made sure that the door was unlocked and then rejoined Gayle on the warehouse floor. Johnny had gathered his things, rolling up his sleeping bag and fastening it to his rucksack with a bungee cord. The half-full bag of groceries was at his feet. He fidgeted nervously, eyeing the alley door every few seconds.

"Find anything?" Gayle asked.

"Maybe," Sheena replied. She looked thoughtfully at the vagrant. "He doesn't want to know, though, I can tell. Probably better that way." She grinned. "No bodies, at least."

Johnny shuddered and tried to appear like he wasn't even listening.

"Josh is on his way. He'll give Johnny a ride over to the west side, get him started on drying out, and figure out how to get him a place to stay and a path back to a job."

"What? You mean Professor Swan? That Josh?" Sheena asked.

Gayle nodded confidently. "Yep! I've explained all this to Johnny, here. Josh can start him off with some hypnosis so Johnny can easily keep his commitment to stay off the alcohol long enough to really get and stay sober. He'll also get him into a work program with housing and hook him up with what he needs to get back on his feet. Johnny's trained as a welder, but like he said, the union banned him. Josh has a special program to get people re-qualified for skilled trades work. Johnny has to prove himself again, but he seems sufficiently motivated, so he can make it with the extra help. We've handled this sort of thing before."

"Huh," Sheena murmured in admiration. This was much smoother and better thought out than any homeless rehabilitation program she had heard about before. "Is this a government program?"

"It's a mix. Mostly, you just have to have someone willing to put the pieces together, and we've already done that, so we know how to get him enough help." She paused and admitted, "It's a lot harder if there are a whole bunch of people who need help at once, though. We have to call specialists for that. Heroes can only spread themselves so thin, you know."

"I 'preciate it, surely, Gayle," Johnny offered. "I'm lookin' forward to getting' outta here, though."

"Don't worry, Johnny," Sheena replied. She watched for his reaction. "No one but you has been here for about three days."

Johnny started, then turned to look around the warehouse again. Trying to sound casual, he said, "If you say so. I wouldn' know."

Sheena exchanged an amused glance with Gayle and they waited for Johnny's ride.

Half an hour later, Johnny was on his way to a better life and the two heroines were back on the job of tracking down Sheena's foe. They made their way down into the tunnel and found a sack of chemical light sticks near the bottom of the stairs. Sheena shut the trap door behind them and sent her wolves ranging ahead at the limit of the pale green light.

The tunnel wound its way through the dark beneath West Bank for hundreds of yards, twisting and turning at irregular intervals. After a time, it began to rise upward. The wolves trotted around a bend to the right and stopped. The tunnel ended at a regular steel fire door. The wolves were sniffing furiously at the base of the door as Sheena and Gayle approached. Another bag of fresh chemlights and a small wastebasket holding an assortment of expended ones sat on the floor next to the door. Taped to the center of the door was a paper sign with "**Mind your Manners!** –signed The Management" written with a thick black marker.

"Well?" Sheena asked. "Go through?"

"When you're ready," Gayle replied. She formed a trio of 'roadies' out of the air behind them and applied a fresh air cushion around herself and Sheena.

Sheena examined the door. It was latched, but not locked. She turned the knob and pushed it open. Beyond the end of the tunnel was a cramped storeroom, barely larger than a closet. Unlike the storage room in the warehouse, this one was full of clutter—cleaning supplies, three mops and a wheeled bucket, cardboard boxes of plastic cups, napkins, and other paper products, a toolbox, a stepladder, and more. The door barely opened wide enough to let them through. On the opposite wall was another door. A thumping vibration of loud dance music ran through the floor and walls; not quite loud enough to hear clearly, but more than enough to rattle the handle of the bucket.

"Huh!" Gayle remarked. "I think this is a club." She slid back a panel on one of her bracelets and checked the GPS signal. "Yeah, this is the Cannery. We're near the business section of the docks on the south side of West Bank."

"You know the place?"

"Yeah. Rough joint. Almost certainly owned by the Syndicate. Not unusual to see the Rockets here, too. The Cannery has a reputation for being a good place to score any kind of drugs, weapons, stuff like that, if you know the right people."

"Or, the wrong people."

Gayle nodded and shrugged. "Either way."

"I take it we're not going to be welcomed with open arms."

"Uh... yep."

"So, what's our strategy?"

Gayle smiled cheerfully. "Walk right out of this storeroom, find a bartender, order a drink, and let the bouncers do their jobs and kick us out, nice and peacefully!"

Sheena looked confused.

"No, really," Gayle explained. "They won't want this place trashed, which is what would happen if we got into a fight with their guards or the clientele. They'd rather just kick us out. As long as we don't make a big deal about the tunnel, they'll probably just be happy to get rid of us. Meanwhile, keep your eyes open for any sign of Elf Shot. If your sniffer is right, she came through here within the last few days."

"So, no interrogations?"

"Right. Technically, they can say that we're trespassing and the Syndicate's lawyers can make trouble for us if we don't comply with requests to leave."

Sheena shook her head. "Okay, I get it. Interesting dance you heroes do here in this city."

"Hey, we play by the rules. We're the good guys!" Gayle grinned.

"Right!" Sheena took a breath. "Okay, ready."

Gayle dismissed her 'roadies' and stepped to the storeroom door. Putting a pleasant smile on her face, she opened it and stepped through. Sheena followed, keeping her wolf spirits close to her. Out in the hallway, the music jumped ten decibels in volume. The thrash metal pulsed through the club, even though it was still the middle of the afternoon. No one else was in the hallway. With a quick glance to the left and right, Gayle turned to the left and headed for the doors to the main room. She pushed through and strode out into the club.

Emerging onto the floor of the club, the sound system rattled the whole room. The club retained the gritty industrial feel of the canning factory it had been many years ago. The DJ booth was vacant, as was the dance floor. The speakers were blaring a pre-recorded mix of generic noise. The place was lit by the afternoon sunlight streaming in through a row of windows high up on the opposite wall. A half dozen ceiling fans spun rapidly in an attempt to cool the place down. There were just a handful of people sitting in shadowed corner booths. A couple of Cannery staff members were stocking supplies behind the bar.

They noticed the heroines immediately. Gayle strolled casually over to the bar. A sullen-looking bartender with an angry purple scar across his nose and a receding hairline turned toward them. He wore a grease-stained light blue Cannery t-shirt. "Hey, we're closed!"

Gayle glanced at the people scattered about the club. They were all watching the two women with scowls. "Yeah? Is the manager in? I figured I would see if he'd like to book a band."

"Gayle Force, right? I'll tell him you called. Now get out." The bartender crossed his arms and glared at her.

"Okay, okay, but you sure he's not here? I thought he was gonna be meeting Elf Shot this afternoon. She's a big fan of mine."

"Yeah, sure she is. No, she hasn't been around in a couple of days. Go look somewhere else."

"You sure?" Gayle asked sweetly.

"Yeah, I'm sure. Now beat it before I call the bouncers."

"You gonna tell her I said hi?"

"If you want, sure, but she's not a regular. Not anymore."

"No? Why not?"

"None of your business."

"Well, I suppose not. But I am disappointed to hear that."

The bartender scoffed. "Yeah, I bet. No, you take your business with the crazy elf chick somewhere else. Leave us alone."

"Okay, I don't want to get you in trouble. We're going," Gayle replied. She turned toward the main entrance and strode purposefully toward it. She waved cheerfully toward the patrons, who were still staring at them, and called out over the music, "Good afternoon, everyone! Enjoy the day!"

She giggled playfully as she and Sheena made their exit. The Cannery bouncer and the two toughs at the door stared at them suspiciously as they left the club. Gayle casually walked the rest of the way out to the sidewalk of the street. Sheena followed with curiosity. Gayle turned to her and said in a low voice, "Let's fly. Time to put a little distance between us and this place. Then, we can talk."

"Okay. Anywhere specific?"

Gayle sighed. "Back to Riverhaven. This trail is cold."

"Oh. How come?"

"Tell you in a minute," Gayle replied and lifted into the air.

Sheena let the wolf spirits disappear and hurried after her friend. She caught up and flew alongside Gayle for a couple of minutes before the singer spoke.

"Okay, we know a few things. Elf Shot has been in the club, and they recognize her." Sheena nodded. "She is known well enough that the early shift bartender knows that something is up and she's not welcome at the club anymore. So, she did something that pissed them off, and pretty recently. And, if he had known where she went, he would have put us on her trail, too, to get us out of the club and on to a little payback for whatever she did. But, he didn't know, and he didn't know who else does, either."

Sheena played the scene back in her mind and nodded again. "Yeah, that all makes sense. Are you sure he wasn't just trying to protect her with a story?"

Gayle shook her head. "No, that all came to him too easily. He would have clammed up or tried to feed us a line if he had wanted to cover for her. That guy was in his element, pretty comfortable that he could rely on the thugs to get rid of us of anything got ugly, and was talking like Elf Shot had done something that offended his sense of 'the way things ought to be.' He was all but saying, 'you can have her, but I don't know where she went.' That's why I think this trail is a dead end."

"Well, at least we know that much. That's more than we did an hour ago."

"Yep! That is the bright side, of course. But with no leads from the magical gurus, this was our best shot at finding her before she surfaced again in some sort of fresh crime."

Sheena sighed. "I have to admit that I was hoping that one of those wizards… or whatever… would have been able to track her down magically, or something. They didn't even agree on what a ritual to strip Shanikali's power out of me would be like or what ingredients it would require!"

"Yeah, that was disappointing, but not too unexpected." It was Gayle's turn to sigh. "Magic is like that. There are as many ways to do something magically as there are magicians, plus at least one more. And it always seems like half of them are wrong, but you can't tell which half until after you've tried to follow their advice and had it fail miserably or blow up in your face."

"Aren't there any reliable magicians, then?"

"Oh, sure there are! Once one of them figures out something that works, it works almost all the time under whatever conditions he or she got it to work under. For that one magician. It may or may not be something a different magic-user can replicate, though. It's just that if you ask about something the magician hasn't personally done before, all they've got to go on is their personal theory, which may be total bupkis."

"How do you know all this?" Sheena wondered.

"I like people," Gayle replied cheerfully. "So I talk to a lot of different people and listen. Most mages are happy to explain what they know about how things work. I guess they don't get too many people really willing to listen to what sounds like total crazy-talk. But I try to be as good a listener as I would hope people would be for me. If you listen well enough, you can understand a lot. Only fair, after all, and I can learn so much that way!"

Sheena thought about that all the way back to Riverhaven.

Chapter 12 – I Worry about You

Eric was waiting on the balcony of Gayle's apartment when they returned. To Sheena, he looked relieved to see her, though he tried to hide it. When Sheena landed, he grabbed her in a big hug and spun her around in a circle. "Welcome back!" he exclaimed. "Did you find anything?"

"Whoa!" she cried, breathlessly. "What a welcome!"

Gayle patted Eric's shoulder with a flicker of a wistful look. "I'll go change and let you two catch up. It's Friday. I've got a performance tonight downstairs at the Event Horizon."

When she had gone inside and shut the sliding glass door behind her, Sheena gave Eric a big kiss. "We found things, but not as much as we wanted. Gayle got a good tip about a warehouse Elf Shot was seen going into near the docks. We took a look, but it was empty, except for a homeless guy. He definitely knew what was going on, but was terrified of telling anything about what he had seen. Based on his reactions and the half-full bag of food he was eating from, I'm guessing that he was paid to watch the place by Elf Shot. Gayle helped get him moved out to a better situation and we followed a secret tunnel underneath the warehouse. It came out in a rough nightclub closer to the docks."

"A nightclub?" Eric asked in disbelief. "Why?"

"To shake pursuers or tailers. Like us, basically. Someone goes into the warehouse and doesn't come out. Even if someone managed to follow, they'd be following the suspect right into a Syndicate-controlled establishment where the suspect would most likely have protection and friends. Except this time."

"How so?"

"When we came out into the club, we found that Elf Shot was no longer welcome there. Something happened recently and they don't want her back."

"Well, that's good, isn't it?"

Sheena nodded. "Yes. We know she has been there. Unfortunately, we have no leads on where she went after being 'uninvited' from the club. That was a couple of days ago. And we don't have any other leads. I think now we have to wait until she's spotted again. And that probably will happen when she pulls some crime."

"Oh. Darn." His brow furrowed. Sheena stretched up on her toes and kissed it. Her wings fluttered slightly to keep her balance. He chuckled and relaxed. "You know, I really worry about you."

"I know, and I love you for worrying."

"I just…." He rubbed his hand through his hair and sighed. "I just can't concentrate on anything when I know you're out there going after that woman. I keep thinking about what might happen to you."

"This is so different from conservation enforcement?" she asked.

"At least there I knew what was going on, and people weren't actually trying to kill you intentionally. I knew that you were in your element and you could handle it. This is so different! It's such a big city with gangs and superpowered villains and so much can happen that I can't even imagine. And what's happened to you is *magic*, and it makes no sense, so how can I even *begin* to figure that out? And that Elf Shot chick is also using magic, so how do we really know what we can do to protect ourselves?" He let out a frustrated breath. "And I still can't do anything to help!"

"Oh." Sheena was at a loss for words, so she just put her arms around him and held him close.

"I feel so useless," he muttered into her hair. "A veterinarian with no animals to help, stuck in a high-rise fortress where if I go out, an insane magic chick might grab me... or even kill me.... And I've got no way to fix this."

"I know you always want to fix things. You're good at that. But right now, you need to find something else to do. You're driving yourself crazy here."

"I know, I know. But how can I, when you're out there facing who knows what and making me so worried that I can't focus on anything more than watching the news? Which I shouldn't do," he chuckled, suddenly wry.

"Why? It makes you more worried?"

"Yeah. The damn news feeds just pump out more and more negative stories to grab attention, and I'm already primed for bad news. I've got to get myself out of this rut."

Sheena grinned mischievously. "I like you in rut, you know!"

Eric laughed. "You can always distract me, that's for sure!" He sighed and seemed to deflate. "And I worry about that, too. You are so damned sexy, so perfect.... What if I can't measure up anymore?"

She was taken aback. "Seriously? You?"

He extricated himself from her arms and turned away. He spread his palms apart on the balcony railing and leaned against it for support. She slid up beside him and put her arm around his shoulders. After a few moments, he said, "Yes. You've got a new improved body, a new life... kind of. It's so good for you that I don't want to hope that it will go back to the way everything was before, because I want you to be happy, but... I'm still the same. What if you get tired of dragging me along with you in your new life?"

"I would never do that! You're my husband! I love you!" she protested.

Eric nodded impatiently. "Yeah, I know. But people don't stay the same. If there's one thing I learned from my parents getting divorced, that's it. For today, we're okay. But tomorrow?" He shook his head. "I want to be with you, like I always have. I just don't know if I can keep being what you need, now."

"Oh, Eric...." She rested her head against his shoulder. They stayed like that for a few minutes, physically close, but lost in their own thoughts.

Finally, Sheena said, "Just another thing for you to worry about, huh?"

Eric nodded. "I suppose so. Maybe I shouldn't be, but...." He shrugged. "It is what it is. I mean, think about Gayle. Her mother got killed. That messed her up for a long time."

"Yeah, but she got better. And she's teaching me so much!"

"Right, but what about Gayle's dad? That's what I'm thinking about. Maybe not with Elf Shot, but some other villain down the road. After we have kids, even. Is that what I have to look forward to?"

Sheena blinked and couldn't find an answer. Finally, she said, "I hope not. I mean, I don't think so...."

"I guess part of what I'm worried about is, does being a hero mean your life isn't your own, anymore?" He straightened up. "I have to admit it, I'm kinda selfish. I want to live my life with you. Not with you having to be dedicated to the greater good, or whatever. Conservation warden, sure. World-saving superhero like Gayle? I don't know."

"I... I don't know, either. We still don't know what it is that I'm supposed to do with these powers, or why Shanikali picked me. From everything we have been able to figure out, I don't think stopping Elf Shot is the end of it. And when whatever it is gets all wrapped up?" She gestured with her hands, trying to find the words. "I don't know what comes after that, either."

Eric nodded with resignation.

She continued with a more determined tone. "But what I do know is that I choose to learn how to use as much of this power as I can, so that I can go after Elf Shot and stop her from hurting us. And I choose to use these powers to help people and nature, where I can, just as if I was back at home. And most of all, I choose to be with *you*, Eric Gardner, dragging you along with me if I have to— worried about whether you can keep up with me or not—because I love you and I always will!"

She let that sink in. Eric looked thoughtful, and an embarrassed smile spread across his face. "Thanks, Sheena. Maybe it's nothing. Maybe I just need some sense knocked back into me."

"Hmph. You're welcome."

"And I love you, too." He kissed her, and some time later they let each other go and went back inside.

Gayle glanced back at Sheena and Eric from the living room, noting the kiss Sheena gave her husband, then made her way down the hall to her bedroom. "Some day...," she murmured to herself.

She took off her winged circlet and put it on the dresser where it always went. Then her wristbands and belt in the top drawer. She checked her cape for stains and shrugged, then hung it up in its place in the walk-in closet. She lifted herself in the air and pulled off her boots, tucking them on the floor under the cape. Then she wiggled out of the green spandex costume, sniffed at it gingerly, and tossed it with a grimace into the laundry hamper. Setting herself back down on the carpeted floor, she stretched and said, "Genie, shower on, please." The shower in her master bathroom started up. She peeled off her underthings and tossed them into the hamper, too, adding a quick, "Process laundry, please."

The hamper lid closed and a soft motorized sound indicated that the mechanism was doing its job. It packaged the clothes and sent them down to the full-service robotic laundry in the basement of the tower. Gayle walked into the bathroom and stepped into the shower. Closing the shower door, she said, "Genie, relaxing shower, please." The jets changed to a pulsating spray against her tense muscles.

Gayle wondered to herself why she felt so keyed up. They hadn't even seen any action today; just footwork. *Maybe it's because losing the trail means that Elf Shot could be anywhere*, she thought. *And we don't know if she's any closer to figuring out a way to steal the power from Sheena.*

"Oh, well," she sighed, "we just have to react fast when we hear something. As usual." She tried to relax and enjoy the rest of her shower.

Thirty minutes later, she was dressed to perform. She wore a green synth-leather minidress, soft brown leather boots folded over just below the calf, a matching leather jacket with a small aspen symbol on the front left side, and a hip-hugging gold-link belt to complete the combo. She tucked a pair of gold-framed wrap-around sunglasses with green lenses into her pocket. She added a touch of eye shadow and lip gloss and a pair of simple square earrings of wavy gold to match the belt. As she left her bedroom, she grabbed her phone and slipped it into her jacket pocket.

Sheena and Eric were sitting in the living room on the couch. Eric had his arm around Sheena's waist and they were snuggling close together while they watched something on the entertainment system. Gayle gave them an approving look and continued on to her studio room. She picked up her saxophone and ran a soft polishing cloth over it once to make it gleam before putting the instrument into its case. She checked her reeds and shut the lid, snapping the latches securely closed.

"Okay, my guitar is already in the gear locker down below," she said as she returned to the living room. "You guys know where to find me, right?"

"Yeah. Is it okay if we show up?" Sheena asked.

"I would love it!" Gayle replied. "But we're not on until 8 PM, so don't rush. There's no opening act, tonight. Just DJ mix. I'll put you on the guest list."

"Thanks, Gayle. I've heard you on Sheena's playlists, of course, but never live," Eric offered.

"Oh, live is much more fun! Come see us, if you feel like it." Sheena nodded enthusiastically in agreement. Gayle waved and made her exit to the elevators.

"Do you want to go?" Sheena asked him. Eric nodded. "I think it would be fun, and I've only glanced in that Event Horizon place in the daytime when it's mostly shut down. I've just been in the restaurant side of it, not the club side."

"Okay. I'll fix us something to eat and we can get ready later," Eric said. He got up and wandered into the kitchen.

Sheena clapped and cheered with the happy crowd, her wings stretched high over her head as the last notes of Gayle's signature song, *Nature Lover*, faded away. Eric grinned like a madman and applauded just as loudly, exchanging appreciative glances with his wife. "Wow, you were right, Sheena! She is *awesome* live!"

Up on stage, Gayle laughed pleasantly and waved to her band members to take a bow. "Whew! Thank you, everybody! We're gonna take a breather for a bit, and when we come back, we've got some dance music for you all! See you in a few!"

"I'm going to go backstage and see what that looks like," Sheena told Eric. "You want to go with?"

"No, that's okay, honey. I'm going to grab a drink from the bar. Do you want anything?"

"Sure. Get me a lemonade or something. Whatever won't melt too badly before the next set and that I can drink quickly."

"Okay, why?"

She gave him a playful look. "Because I'm going to want to dance with you!" She leaned in and kissed him, then squeezed his hand and made her way around the stage to the back.

Eric admired her departing figure until she was lost in the crowd and grinned again to himself. He worked his way over to the bar as the patrons dispersed throughout the club. It looked like almost everyone in the place was an ordinary human being. Almost. He spotted a kind of alien catlike man and another person with glacial blue skin, but nothing terribly out of the ordinary, as far as he could tell. When he got to the bar, Eric ordered a strawberry lemonade for Sheena and a local lager for himself. A lean, thoughtful-looking, blond-haired man in gold-rimmed glasses picked up his own drink at the same time. He looked over at Eric with curiosity. "Doctor Gardner?"

Eric looked at him with surprise. "Yes?"

The man smiled. He was wearing a simple blue button-down shirt and grey slacks, but Eric could easily picture him in a lab coat. He had broader shoulders and a bit more of a professional swimmer's build than most academics, but not so much that he would stand out in a place like Venture City. He held out his hand and said, "Joshua Swan. I met your wife earlier and I think I've seen you in the athletic center here."

"Oh, hi, Joshua. I'm Eric." Eric shook his hand. "Yeah, I think so, now that you mention it. You're the one doing the fast laps in the pool each morning, right?"

He nodded. "That's me. Josh is fine, by the way. I understand from Gayle that you're a veterinarian?"

Eric chuckled. "I guess I'm finally meeting the neighbors, huh? Yes, I have a practice out in northern Wisconsin. Sheena's a game warden. Or, a conservation warden, technically."

"So I heard," Josh nodded. "Where in the state? I'm from Duluth, myself."

"Really? I guess it's a smaller world than I thought. We live not too far from Hayward, actually."

Josh grinned. "I've been through that area a few times, yes."

"But you live here, now, at Riverhaven?"

"Yes. My wife, Anathae, and I live on the floor above Gayle's."

Eric smiled wryly. "Which one of you is the hero?"

Josh chuckled. "Both. But I do spend most of my time running the family business empire, these days. I don't think it's much of a secret. I did spend quite a while maintaining a secret identity as a mild-mannered university professor, though."

"What happened?"

"I made enough enemies who were digging for dirt on me that it didn't make sense to keep my secret identity hidden anymore. I have dragon ancestors, and inherited some of that power. I could do more good by stepping out of the shadows and taking the fight to them, so I did."

Eric shook his head in wonder. "Seriously? Dragons, too? I'm finding out that a whole lot of things that I thought were just stories are real."

"Don't feel too bad, Eric," Josh replied. "It can be a lot to take in. Besides, there are probably a million fictional stories for every real-life case."

"And your wife?"

"Half demon, yes. Broke free of the bonds of Hell and is much happier here. Long story."

Eric was at a loss for words. Josh gave him a kindly smile and patted him on the shoulder. He offered, "You know, there are several groups that help family members adjust to their superpowered relative's new situation. Might be helpful to you."

Eric shook his head. "Thanks, but I'll pass. I think I'm still too overwhelmed by all of this."

"Well, you could skip the whole support group thing and do something more constructive, instead. A scientific colleague of mine told me that he needs to find an open-minded veterinarian or animal disease expert to consult with on his research. I thought of you when I heard from Gayle that you're a DVM. Part of the reason I mention it is also because he has been through the same thing with his own wife gaining superpowers."

"Really? What happened with him? His wife, I mean?"

"About four years ago, she was kidnapped by a group of high-tech mercenaries and given what they thought was a truth serum. She was an IT specialist for the Department of Defense. The mercenaries thought that they could get access to a special secure DoD computer system by forcing her to go in and set up secret administrator accounts, or something. The problem with the truth serum was that it was an unstable, experimental version supplied by a black market genetic lab. Instead of performing as they expected, it ended up nearly killing her. In the process, though, the drug rewired her nervous system in a totally bizarre way. She was able to escape by going through the electrical wiring and reappearing somewhere else. She has amazing abilities with electricity and any type of electronics, now."

"Wow. What happened to the mercenaries?"

"While Melanie was in the system, she sent an alarm, locked them into the building they were hiding in, and directed the military strike team right to the bad guys. She was like that proverbial 'ghost in the machine.' I guess it goes to show that it might not be smart to mistreat the IT staff." Josh chuckled. "She's fine now, and still working for the DoD. Just in a different capacity."

"And your friend? What's his specialty?"

"Greg Dawson is an immunologist. He's working on diseases that can be transmitted from animals to humans. So-called bird flu, swine flu, Ebola, HIV, that sort of thing. Viral transmission and ways to develop cross-species vaccines."

"Cross-species vaccines? Can that really be done? Or would it even be practical?" Eric was intrigued.

Josh shrugged. "That's pretty much beyond me. I'm a psychologist. As I understand it, there are just so many logistical barriers that it has been considered unrealistic. But it is theoretically possible. Greg thinks he's got a promising line of research, and he has the funding from Dynatech to pursue it."

"That could be really interesting. Honestly, I'm going nuts just hanging out around the building with nothing to do but worry. I'm just a general practitioner vet, and not a researcher. But, if you think a guy like me could be helpful, I'd be happy to talk to your friend."

"Hey, it's worth making the connection," Josh agreed, "and he has to get a qualified expert on his team soon or he misses a deadline."

Sheena returned from backstage and came up to Eric and Josh. She asked her husband, "Did you get me something?"

"Yeah, strawberry lemonade. I asked for it on the low ice side, so it should be okay melt-wise for you." He grinned at her. "You've met Josh Swan?"

She nodded and sipped her lemonade through the straw. "Yep. Nice to see you, Josh."

"Evening, Sheena," the professor replied. "Did you and Gayle have any more luck this afternoon?"

"Not as much as we'd hoped, but we know more than we did before. We've run out of clues, for now, so we'll just have to see where we can dig up some more."

Josh glanced casually at Eric, reading his reactions to the "shop talk," and changed the subject. "Gayle and the band are doing well, tonight. Are they going to be ready for the next set soon?"

"Yes, just a few more minutes. Gayle was really happy to see us here." She took another sip of lemonade with a thoughtful expression. "You know, I can understand that she would be happy to have her friends in the audience, but I wouldn't think it would be that big of a deal."

Josh shrugged one shoulder. "It's good for her."

"How so?" Eric asked.

"So many people know her, because of her music and public appearances and things, but there aren't that many people that she can really call friends. When some of them are in the audience, it's kind of special to her." He smiled wistfully. "Like an island of solid ground in the churning sea of fans."

"Huh, really?" Eric replied thoughtfully.

"Yes. More than that isn't for me to say, but it's nice to see more of her friends here." Josh nodded toward the stage. "And here they come."

Gayle and her band members came back out on stage and resumed their places. Gayle glanced around the room and smiled to people she knew, and added a mischievous grin and wave to Sheena and Eric. She stepped back to check her saxophone and guitar, then prepped a mic stand off to the side for the sax. With a wink, she nodded to her lead guitarist, Stevie, who grinned and eased into the opening notes to an old Steve Miller Band song. The keyboardist followed with the sound of a cascade of rushing winds.

Gayle strapped on her own guitar and strutted up to the front to take the microphone while they laid down the rhythm. "Okay, now, welcome back!" she called out. "We've got some dance music all revved up and ready to go. But first, I have a special one for my friend, Sheena!"

Sheena's eyes opened wide with surprise.

Gayle laughed and waved her forward. "C'mon, Sheena! Bring Eric here up front and get us started!"

Eric chuckled and said to Josh, "Excuse us. Time to get moving!" He took Sheena by the hand and led her up toward the stage.

"There we go!" Gayle said. She nodded to the band and launched into the song.

> *Time keeps on slippin', slippin', slippin', into the future.*
> *Time keeps on slippin', slippin', slippin', into the future.*
> *I want to fly like an eagle, to the sea.*
> *Fly like an eagle, let my spirit carry me.*
> *I want to fly like an eagle, 'til I'm free.*
> *Fly, through the revolution."*

A familiar burly figure glided over to Josh after Eric and Sheena went up to dance. The big swordmaster known as North Shore Knight leaned back against the bar and watched Gayle perform. He nodded to Josh and said, "'Ey, bro."

"Bobby," Josh replied with a nod.

"What do you think?"

"About what? Gayle Force? They're spot on, tonight."

Bobby snorted. "No, you know what I mean. The new girl, Sheena."

Josh considered that for a moment before answering his brother's question. "I think that she'll fit in very well as a hero. She's mastering her abilities rapidly and her head and heart are in the right place. But it's her husband I'm more concerned about."

Bobby raised an eyebrow. "Why's that?"

"His worldview has come crashing down around him." Bobby nodded with understanding. "With everything in flux, Eric doesn't know his place in the relationship and he's taking it harder than he realizes. This could turn into an exploitable weakness against Sheena."

"Figures. Psychology stuff." Bobby took a swig from his bottle of Molson. "It's never easy or simple. Is there anything we should do about that?"

"I'm already on it. Get him hooked up with the right friends and he should get through this phase just fine."

Bobby snorted again. "I hope those aren't just famous last words."

"Yeah. Me, too."

Chapter 13 – Spirit Journey

"Okay, fine. We're out of leads. Let's see if we can't figure out how to make more. Or try a different approach. Or something," Sheena said stoically the next afternoon. "I'm supposed to be a hunter. I'm not giving up just because we've lost the scent."

Gayle perked up and grinned. "That's the spirit!"

The two heroines were at the riverfront beach on the west side of the Riverhaven grounds taking a break from research. The summer sun poured down on the city with waves of joyous heat. A gentle breeze played hide and seek along the shore, but Gayle's personal zephyr tangled with it and touched it with the scent of apple blossoms before letting it go on its way. They had changed into swimsuits up in the apartment and then flew down to splash in the river to cool off. After some time relaxing in and out of the water, the friends retired to towels on the grassy edge of the beach to dry off in the sun.

"We haven't gotten anything from the magicians, right?" Sheena continued, thinking aloud.

"Right. But, we only really asked them to tell us what it would take to prevent Elf Shot from doing a ritual to take your powers, or how to find her by magic. What if we opened that up a bit to see what else they could suggest?"

"That's one thing I was thinking about, too, but there's also the question of Shanikali's powers. What is it I'm supposed to be doing? Why me? Why now? What is the threat that made the source stone pick me to give me its power?"

Gayle was lying back on her towel with her hands behind her head. She nodded slowly, considering those questions.

Sheena mused, "When I first tried the focusing exercise Schauer and Calderón gave me, I saw some things that seemed important. I've tapped into that spirit world consciously since then, but in pretty limited ways. I have this nagging feeling that there is someone or something I need to talk to there."

"A spirit journey?"

"Yes. And I think there's some sort of prophecy connected to this. I found a bit of it during my first time exploring the spirit world, but I couldn't maintain concentration long enough and I lost it partway through relating the prophecy. Something about 'Her power is to come again when the Dark Ones threaten the forest,' or something like that."

"Do you want to try that exercise again?"

"Ugh. I've tried. I can't get the same result." Sheena blew a frustrated puff of air from her lips and twitched her wings against the grass. Her feathers settled again and she brushed a loose lock of hair out of her face. "Who can give me pointers on... hmm...."

Gayle rolled onto her side on her towel to face Sheena and asked, full of curiosity, "Pointers on what?"

Sheena murmured, still thinking, "I think I've got it. Agent Calderón is a shaman. I don't know why I didn't remember that sooner! He was also helping me along the first time, I think. Maybe he can tell me how to do it again."

Gayle shrugged a slim shoulder. "Sounds worth a shot to me. Wanna take off and go contact him from the apartment, or here?"

Sheena looked around with a wary glance. "Apartment, I think. It's not likely I'm being stalked, yet, but let's not take unnecessary chances." She sat up and got to her feet, grabbing the beach towel and tying it around her waist. Gayle followed her and they both flew back up to the apartment balcony.

Eric was out at a meeting with Dr. Greg Dawson, the research immunologist that Josh Swan had mentioned Friday night. The researcher had been eager to meet Eric and had cleared space in his schedule right away. Sheena hoped that this would turn out to be something that would give Eric useful work to do. Gayle took the towels and went to toss them into a laundry hamper while Sheena found Agent Calderón's number.

He picked up almost immediately. His smooth Spanish accent answered, "It is Agent Calderón. This is Sheena Gardner?"

"Hello, Agent Calderón. Yes, this is Sheena."

"Good day! How are you doing in Venture City?"

"Making progress, thanks. I've run out leads on where to find Elf Shot, but she has been here in the city. I remembered that when I was first doing that contact exercise, I was having a vision or a spirit journey or something. I haven't been able to do that since then, and I was hoping that you'd be able to help me figure out how to do it again."

"Yes? And you think that would help you?"

"I think so. It feels like there is someone or something in that spirit world I still need to talk to, or to see, or whatever. I think that I need to get the rest of that prophecy or vision to know what I need to do with Shanikali's power."

Calderón paused as if thinking. "Okay. I will see if I can get this case we're working on wrapped up. Tom and I have been assigned to take the stones to Venture City for analysis. It sounds like we know where they came from. Someone... more or less... has claimed them."

"'More or less?' That sounds... vague."

Calderón laughed pleasantly. "I'll tell you the story when I see you. In the meantime, let me send you a few more notes to go with that original exercise you did. It really is not supposed to be a ritual that you could use to contact the spirits, but you were still brimming with untapped energy, and that energy took you to where it wanted you to go."

"And now?"

"And now you need a different way to focus outward again so that you can touch the spirit world, instead of what is just inside of you."

"Oh, I get it."

"Very good! You are a fast learner."

Sheena snorted. "I have to be. There's a psychotic killer who wants to subject me to a difficult magic ritual that is most likely fatal. I'm motivated!"

"Yes, I can see how that is true. I will send you that information as soon as we are done on the phone. Call me if you have any questions at all. Otherwise, I will look forward to seeing you again when we come to Venture City."

"Thanks, Agent Calderón."

"Please, you can call me Felix. Adios!"

Sheena chuckled as Gayle returned to the living room, "Calderón is a flirt."

Gayle laughed, "Go figure! Maybe he's a Coyote shaman. I think they are supposed to be tricksters, if they follow their totem."

"C'mon! He's as old as my dad."

"So?" Gayle winked. "You're already taken. Maybe I'll distract him for you!"

Sheena laughed and shook her head. "I think he just keeps trying to put me at ease by joking. The thing is, I don't know if that means he's worried, or he isn't."

"Hah! Once he sees how you're coming along and the people we've got to help and protect you guys, he should be pretty satisfied. All of the Titans are on the lookout for Elf Shot, now. We'll find something soon, I think."

A message from Calderón arrived on Sheena's phone. She scrolled through it. "Hmm… the pictures have a lot of detail. I'd better transfer this to a bigger screen." Gayle nodded.

Half an hour later, Sheena was ready to try the ritual. It wasn't really what she had previously thought of as a magical ritual, but Calderón's notes had showed her where she would turn a traditional magical process into her own personal thing. She explained it to Gayle as something like a three-part exercise, where she would have to do one part to get ready and into the right state of mind for the second. The second part altered the vibrations of consciousness to the right point for the actual journey, which was the third part and the real objective of the activity.

"So, like a mental mini-triathlon, then?" Gayle asked.

Sheena considered it and smiled. "I guess that's not too far off, but probably not that strenuous. Maybe more like putting on the right shoes, stretching, and then going for a run."

Gayle suggested, "Change into your costume before you do this. You might need a 'hero' state of mind, and you never know how these sorts of things will end up."

Sheena nodded and went to change.

Calderón's notes described a long, elaborate ritual that was the traditional basis for the spirit journey method Sheena would be using. Then, he broke down the ritual in detail, explaining what each of the parts did and why it was necessary. He then listed the things from the traditional form that she could cut out or replace with more modern, practical shortcuts. The traditional herbs smoked and burned in a ceremonial fire, for example, were not really necessary except as a way of calming and centering the shaman. Her own focusing technique would do just as well, and without the need for props.

Sheena settled herself into Gayle's practice studio. It was comfortable, quiet, and would not be disturbed. She summoned both of her wolf spirits and the eagle. They would act as spirit guides for her, easing the way. The eagle perched on a microphone stand and the wolves lay on the floor beside her. Gayle took a seat on the floor by the studio door, just in case she was needed. Sheena began her customized ritual.

Not long after that Sheena was glowing; a soft golden light emanating from her and spreading throughout the studio. Heartbeat by heartbeat, Gayle's apartment faded away, replaced in Sheena's view with a cedar forest. Despite the mid-afternoon sun and clear sky above her, a mist lay about the forest, shrouding the ground. She could smell the distinctive scent of the cedars and hear a stream or river nearby. The air felt dry, untouched by any moisture of the mist. As she examined her surroundings closely, she noticed a certain unreal quality. Everything was very slightly transparent, even the ground around her and the large rock she was sitting on. Her animals remained no more or less solid than she had become used to in the real world—they were as unreal as the rest of it. Looking down at herself, she found that she was just as insubstantial as the things around her.

The wolves stood up and shook themselves, then looked at her. The eagle was perched on a branch, not a mic stand. It regarded her with amber eyes, as well, as if waiting for a command. Sheena arose from her seat and turned in a full circle. The forest was not very dense. The tall cedars soared easily to 40 or 50 meters, branches spreading wide over the rocky ground beneath them. This was old growth, and might never have been logged. Sheena felt the spirit of the ancient forest around her almost as a living thing. The female wolf whined once and looked away, downhill, then back at Sheena.

"You want me to follow?" she asked. "Then lead on. Maybe we will find Shanikali."

The wolf trotted off to the north, toward the sound of the river. Sheena followed along a few paces behind. The male wolf loped ahead to run beside the other while the eagle soared into the sky and kept pace overhead. Sheena noticed that her costume was different here. It fit the same, but felt a little heavier. The tooling and cut of the leather was a little rougher. The fastenings were of thicker bronze, instead of enameled high-tech metal. Her circlet felt a little heavier, too; actual bronze, instead of a high-tech resin casing for electronics.

She did not have time to think much about this before the wolf reached her destination. A small campsite lay before her with a single tent of undyed linen stretched over a flexible frame of cedar rods. A fire was banked neatly into a circle of stones. The female wolf padded up to another larger male and nuzzled it, then sat down on her haunches. The river was an easy stone's throw away. The rushes along the bank mostly screened it from view, but the sound of water rushing over rocks was louder here. To her left along the river bank was a break in the rushes. A large smooth rock lay in the shade of the cedars at the water's edge. There was a large black leopard spread out on the rock, regarding her without concern from pale green eyes. Another leopard, a lighter gray with regular dark rosettes, watched from a cedar branch over the campsite.

Sheena heard a rustle of wings overhead. A moment later, a winged woman lithely dropped to the ground before her. Shorter by a few inches than Sheena, copper skinned, with dark hair pulled back from her face, she, too, glowed with a golden light. Unlike Sheena and everything around her, this woman appeared completely solid. Also unlike Sheena, she had a bow in her hand and a quiver of arrows slung between the dark brown feathered wings on her back. This, Sheena reasoned, would be Shanikali.

The goddess smiled warmly and made a curious sort of sweeping bow. She spoke and Sheena heard the words inside her head, with a slight echo. "Ah, Sheena, I am glad to see you here in the Forest, our traditional home of the gods!" She held out her arms—the bow and quiver seemed to have vanished between one thought and the next—and embraced the blonde-haired heroine.

"Sit. I imagine you have many questions," Shanikali said. She waved her hand and the mist cleared away from the camp. Two woven blankets lay on the ground near the fire. The goddess took a seat on one of them.

Sheena sat on the other blanket. "Yes, your... Um... what should I call you?" she asked with a blush of confusion.

Shanikali laughed. "Call me Shanikali, or Shani. I have had other names down through time—Artemis, Diana, Pakhet, Mielikki, or Skadi, for example. But you are me, and I am you, in many of the ways that matter. No need to stand on ceremony."

"You have been alive for all that time?" Sheena asked incredulously.

"Oh, no, definitely not! But my power has, borne by dozens of different women over the millennia."

Sheena frowned in confusion. "So, I've got it now? But you're still here to talk to?"

Shanikali smiled reassuringly. "You have the purest form of my power for your day, yes. There are other women out there in your time who have parts of my portfolio; the hunting side, mostly. They associate the power with one of my other incarnations. So there are spiritual daughters of Artemis, Diana, Pakhet, and so on. This power is not diminished by residing in different people, if the one who bears the power is worthy of it. And this place has no time. I am here and remain here even past my lifetime."

"Were you the first? Where did this come from in the beginning?"

"Ah, there's a question worth wisdom." The goddess paused. "I was not the first with the power of the gods, but I was the first with these specific powers and responsibilities. The power itself comes from life, and from beyond life. More than that I cannot explain in words you would understand now."

"'Any sufficiently advanced technology is indistinguishable from magic.' Arthur C. Clarke," Sheena replied.

"That works well enough for us, yes. The more important question is really, 'What must we do with this power?'"

"Right. So, why me? And why now? What am I supposed to do?"

Shanikali reached over and put her fingertips lightly on Sheena's chest. "You, because Sheena Jane Gardner, born Sheena Jane Forest in Breezy Point, Wisconsin, are the closest fit with the full portfolio of Shanikali in your own time. Now, because there is a growing threat that is Shanikali's specific responsibility to stop, as one of those protectors men used to call 'gods.' Your task is to stop the threat."

Sheena gulped. "What is so big that it would take a goddess to stop?"

"And specifically, the goddess who is a hunter through time? Who protects the spiritual domain that some call the Beastlands?"

"Uh, yes."

Shanikali leaned back. With a wry expression she replied, "That, I cannot tell you."

Sheena blinked and asked, "What do you mean? There's more to that answer, isn't there?"

"In truth, I don't know what threatens the world in your time. I can say that it will be a threat to a great number of people and animals, and that it will come from or touch this spirit world you now find yourself in. I am limited in my understanding of what happened in the world after my physical death, so long ago by your reckoning. You come from a time of wonders I cannot fully comprehend, so even though we can swim in the waters of time, I could not tell you what the threat is in a way we would both understand, even if I could go forward to see what destruction the danger would wreak."

"Wow." Sheena was taken aback. "Can I go forward to take a look, then?"

"Yes, you could. The future is easy to see, but hard to interpret. The danger of such a plan is that to come back with that knowledge, you must travel back against the current. There are two ways to ride the river—in spirit or in body. A spirit is a flitting thing and the waters of time push little against it. This is why prophecies and visions of the future are common in those who have the gift of Sight. It is a simple spirit journey forward and back to the start. But the spirit cannot fully share with the waking mind what it has seen or done, so understanding the visions can be difficult."

Sheena nodded that she followed that explanation.

"Real travel in body through time takes more energy—much more!—and one must also take into account the fluid nature of time. First, the energy. The current always carries you downstream, toward what we call 'the future.' You must have enough strength for travel in both directions. If you go upstream, back in time, you must fight the current on the way to when you want to go. When you are ready to return, you can let the current carry you at its own speed, or you can use it to make your downstream travel easier. If you go downstream, to the future, then you will have to fight the current to return."

"What if I don't return to where I started?"

"To do this traveling, you must come out of your natural place in the stream. Your body—whether spirit or physical—carries with it a memory of where you started. When you re-enter the stream, you have to compensate for any the difference between that memory of where you started and where you physically re-enter the stream. This can hurt. A lot."

"Can I rest here in this…," Sheena gestured around herself, "spirit world before returning to where I began, or to get enough energy to enter the stream somewhere else?"

Shanikali nodded. "Yes. But if you come here with your physical body, you will find that attracts the guardian beasts of this place. They will not be pacified by your powers the way that our spirit beast companions are. You must win them over with other methods."

Sheena considered that. "All right. What kind of energy are we talking about?"

"The same energy that fuels your powers, and your physical and mental stamina to work with that energy. We regain energy from rest, sleep, play, joy, and in countless other ways, but I cannot explain it with more detail. Just be careful when working with the currents of time that you do not overexert yourself. Be cautious and do the easiest thing that will achieve your goal; no more than that."

"Coming from the expert, that must be a serious warning," Sheena acknowledged. The goddess nodded with a solemn expression.

"Secondly, the fluid nature of time. If you toss a pebble into the stream at one place, it will disrupt the flow, and things will be different very near that place. But time will flow around it and resume the natural path of the current. If there is a change in events that happen in the past, it will not be very long—or very much distance downstream—before the diverted currents find their way back to the 'true' path of least resistance."

"So, time seeks the path of least resistance?"

"Yes. And that path flows over the bed of the stream. Sustained change only comes by changing the streambed."

"How do I do that?" Sheena asked.

"Everything I tell you to explain how time works is a story, or a tale, or a…." Shanikali struggled to find the word.

"A metaphor?"

"Yes, a metaphor. That is the word you use in your age. You must understand that the story I am telling you is only one story. It is true, but there are other stories that are also true. They are true for the others who can understand them. This story is true for us, for you and me."

"So, this is how time and our powers work for us. This is the way I have to understand the time stream."

"Yes, exactly. So to make a change, you must change the streambed. The simplest way is to shift sand or pebbles or plants on the streambed. These represent causes or forces or many different things in the world. You will see them clearly when you look at them and know what they represent. But remember that if you pick up a handful of pebbles, it is easy for the current to carry away some of them to a different place downstream. They will not have gone away, but they will have tumbled somewhere with the current to appear later in time. Things change in relationship to each other, but nothing is truly created or destroyed. When possible and necessary, this is the way I would do it, you understand?"

Sheena nodded.

The goddess continued. "Another way to make change is to put something into the stream that stays in place on the bottom. This changes the streambed. The ripples from this action will carry on down the stream forever. This can lead to undesirable events and complications, but it is an act of creation and less dangerous than the third way. That third way is to remove something from the time stream, discarding it in the forest or by placing it above the high water mark. In that case that specific thing will never appear in the stream at all, nor will any ripples that it could have caused ever appear. This can have unforeseen effects."

Sheena shivered. "I can imagine."

"As you will see, it is very difficult to predict how the stream will flow. The times I have done this over my history and that of my incarnations, I have been wrong almost as often as I have been right. Some mistakes I could fix. Others I could only have fixed by making even bigger changes with greater chances for bigger mistakes."

"But the threat I have to face is big, isn't it?"

"Yes. Big enough to cause events to move in ways that gave you my powers and made you my incarnation for your time so that I... you, specifically... can stop it. As you learn, you will grow to understand your limits—you are nowhere close to them now!—and what it is wise to do and avoid doing. At the start, it will be easiest and safest to rely on your hunting powers and close workings of the time stream."

"Like slowing down enemies and healing?" Sheena asked.

"Yes. You can do even more than you have done so far with the nearby time currents. Some of that I will give you to take back with you, but there are more things that I cannot even teach you because I do not know the world of your age."

"What happens when the threat is over?"

"That is up to you," the goddess replied gently. "You will continue to be the incarnation of my power for the rest of your life. What you choose to do with that power is your decision alone."

Sheena thought for a moment. "I got the power from a source stone."

Shanikali appeared confused, then smiled. "Ah, I see what you mean. Yes, I put my power into sacred vessels—jars, really—several times during my life for the times when it would be needed. After your body passes into dust, the power will go back into that vessel. There it will wait for another time and another woman to carry our shared responsibility when it is needed again."

Sheena felt strangely reassured by that. "So, it's not just me this one time only?"

"No, but it is a very select sisterhood!" Shanikali laughed. "A special order of huntresses!"

Sheena chuckled and paused, "Oh... There's someone hunting me, too. What should I do about this woman who had the stone stolen for her own use, and who wants to kill me and take the power for herself?"

Shanikali grinned. "Hunt her down and bring her to justice."

"Then she can't take the power out of me?"

"I won't say that it's impossible, but it would definitely not turn out like she expects. If she is even considering finding a way to get the power out of you against your will and into her, then she would not be able to handle the power. She would be rejected."

"Rejected?"

"Rejected. Strongly and painfully."

"Oh. I don't think telling her that would convince her to stop trying, though."

"That is why I suggest that you hunt her down and bring her to justice, whatever that might be in your age."

Sheena asked with curiosity, "What would that be in your own age?"

"I would have killed her. No torture or mess like the kings feel obligated to use to prove their power, it would just be her or me, and I would make sure that she would not be able to pose a threat to me or anyone else again."

"I see."

"The concept of justice endures. The custom of fit punishment changes." Shanikali shrugged.

Sheena said slowly, "I have never killed anyone before."

"And you do not have to. With your powers, you have many choices open to you." The goddess smiled. "And that reminds me. There are things you need."

Shanikali rose from her seat by the fire and stood. The bow was in her hand again. She held it out to Sheena. "The weapon of a huntress. You already know how to use it."

Sheena nodded. She and Eric both did bow hunting and target archery. She took the bow and examined it. It was a perfect composite bow of ancient style, a recurved weapon made of horn and flexible wood and sinew. Sheena blinked and looked more closely. It seemed like it had lengthened by a few inches when she had taken it from the goddess.

Shanikali nodded. "The object is just a representation. You can make it be whatever kind of hunting or war bow you want it to be. It is there when you need it and gone when you don't. If you drop it, you can have it in your hand again with a thought. If it is broken, you can repair it at your whim."

"What about arrows?"

"There are three types. Two are just like the bow—available whenever you want or need them. The ones I expect you will use the most often are formed purely from the time currents. These are spirit arrows. They will slow and hurt creatures with living bodies, but without doing them actual injury."

"How does that work?"

"The arrowhead jars the spirit, loosening it slightly from the body. When the spirit is far enough out of alignment with the body, the creature loses consciousness and dreams until its spirit is aligned again."

"How many arrows might that take on a strong human, for example?"

Shanikali smiled wickedly. "With your skill and mine? Only one, unless he is protected or god-touched in some way." Sheena nodded, so she continued. "The second type is a normal war arrow. These are as good as you can imagine and are also created from the time currents, but are more solid while they are needed. Use them for objects and creatures that you want to destroy, because they will be as lethal as the craftsmen of your time and your own power can make them. Even my arrows with iron heads would penetrate a thumb-length of iron. I am sure that in your age, metals are stronger and that your shots will sink more deeply."

Sheena shook her head in admiration. "I look forward to the practice range."

"Then the third type of arrow. These are not created at will from the time stream, like the other two, but must be made carefully and with the best possible craftsmanship by you alone. These are special arrows that will carry the effects of your powers through to the target, penetrating its defenses. I will give you three of these arrows. You will have to make any more by yourself."

Shanikali handed over three arrows. Each was different. One had a broad golden head and curious golden feathers. Another had a shaft of very dark material, a narrow black iron head, and black fletchings. The third was a shaft made of green wood, with soft downy feathers, and what appeared to be a carved ivory arrowhead, not of any great sharpness. Sheena took them with interest.

"These will stay in your quiver until you need them," Shanikali explained. "And your quiver works like the bow. It will be there when you need it and out of the way when you don't. The golden arrow is a special trick of mine. Instead of harming the target, it restores it to complete health. With this arrow, you can use your healing power at a distance far greater than you normally could, but I can only give you one, and you still have to hit the target."

Sheena nodded and chuckled. "Just hit it? Does it have to penetrate armor or anything?"

Shanikali shook her head. "It has to connect with the target, but just the surface. Striking the breastplate of an armored man would be sufficient, for example. And unlike your regular healing, this can restore an object. Shoot it at a wall and the wall will stop crumbling and be restored to full strength. As usual, though, if a creature is dead or if the object is destroyed, it is beyond our normal ability to repair."

"Ah, good to know. I haven't really fully explored that, yet."

"The black arrow will age whatever it hits by a thousand years. This will kill mortals and destroy most objects. It will only make gods angry. Use with caution." Sheena nodded. "The spring arrow is a special arrow of mercy. It will turn back the tide of years for a living target, restoring him or her to early childhood. He will have no memory of all of those years lost, so will have a chance to relive his life under different circumstances. I have only ever created three of these, and I am very proud of them. Both of the two I shot from my bow turned cruel tyrants into boys who grew up to be wise leaders, with the proper tutelage."

"Wow!" Sheena breathed. "I can do that?"

Shanikali nodded. "Just once. If you wish to make a tactic of it, you will have to discover how to make more arrows."

"I will remember that."

Shanikali smirked mysteriously.

"What? I won't remember that?" Sheena asked with concern.

The goddess reminded her, "This is the spirit world and you are here in spirit. When you return to your body, details will be hazy. Fortunately, you will be able to recall or discover everything we have discussed. Which reminds me...." She drew some smooth stones from a pouch at her belt and gave them to Sheena.

"What are these?"

"The names of your spirit companions. All of the ones you will use most."

Sheena looked at the stones. There were seven of them, smooth like wave-tumbled river rocks. Each had a cuneiform design etched deeply into it. She recognized the designs instantly. Two were the names of the wolf spirits she had been working with. Another was the eagle. She looked up. Another was for the alpha wolf lying by the tent. Two more were the names of the black and gray leopards. That left one more. "What is this one?" she asked.

Shanikali smiled. "Remember that I said that the guardians of this forest would be attracted if you arrived here in your physical body? Sharur is one of those guardians, but bound to and beloved by me. His name means 'smasher of thousands,' and he is a demon-wolf of iron. He will be your most clever and loyal companion and your best defender. Call him now."

All of the spirit animals around the campsite became alert, watching Sheena. With a moment of hesitation, she concentrated and called Sharur. A dark creature jumped out of the fire and landed with a thump that shook the ground. The wolf was almost as tall at the shoulder as Sheena was. He turned to regard her with eyes that glowed with the fires of a forge. His fur was like strands of iron, and smelled of heated metal. He had polished black iron claws on each paw that looked strong enough to rend steel. A jagged scar marked his forehead and upper snout, just missing the wolf's right eye. He, like Shanikali herself, was also fully real in the spirit forest Sheena was standing in. She shivered.

The wolf spoke aloud, but she heard his voice in her head, translated like Shanikali's words, "Mistress, I am Sharur, and I greet you in Shanikali's name. I have waited long for another to serve." His voice was gruff but warm. He stepped forward and sniffed at her, as if he was merely any other canine.

Sheena smiled and welcomed his curiosity. "Thank you, Sharur. You are very different from the other animals. I am new at this, so please tell me if I do anything that might offend you. If you are like Shanikali suggests, I will need your help. Be sure to advise me."

"This scar I bear was from a blow dealt by the hero Gilgamesh. Without Shanikali's touch, it would have been a mortal wound. She knew that I was doing what the gods had commanded, even as Gilgamesh was seeking the secret of immortality against their wishes. She saved me, and though I am a demon, I owe her my life and loyalty. I will do my best to serve you as well as I served her."

Sheena reached out and touched the iron wolf's fur. It was very warm, heavy, but strangely soft. "Are there any dangers I should know about if I call you into the real world?"

Shanikali answered. "He is big. If he needs to, he can extend his own wings to fly, but he cannot become smaller than you see now. He is a demon, and not a wolf. If there are places protected against demons, he will not be able to join you or pass those barriers. Also, his angered breath is like the flame of the forge. It will burn what it touches, so use caution."

"Good safety tips."

"Like the others, he cannot really be killed in the world of Man. His true place is here in the Cedar Forest. Use his service with the wisdom I know that you are capable of."

"I will."

"These are the things I can give you now," Shanikali said. "If you wish, you can remember what we have talked about here, but as if it was a dream. In this place, there is no movement of time. The river is beside us and we are outside of it. I will give you one more hint."

"Please."

Shanikali took Sheena down to the water's edge. She pointed at the water. It seemed more like flowing mist than liquid. "If you look closely, you can see what is before you. That is the streambed and the things in the time stream. If you look at the currents, you can see the direction time is taking events. You can't see both together. One or the other, position or direction. And do not be surprised if the river is different when you look at it in different ways."

"What do you mean?"

The goddess gestured at the river. "It looks only two dozen cubits across, doesn't it?" Sheena nodded. "Now think about finding the day of your wedding to your husband, Eric."

Sheena concentrated and gasped. The river was suddenly thirty meters wide and looked shallow enough to wade across.

"Now, think about trying to find the cause of a major war near your time."

After a moment, Sheena chose the most recent war in Iraq. The river widened even further and deepened to look like the Mississippi River. She shook her head. "What does this mean?"

"The nature of the river depends on what you are looking for. The more people that the event affects, the more momentum the currents of time will have behind them, and the bigger the river will be. You can still find what you are looking for at this place in time as you stand on the bank, but the cross section of the river and the pressure behind the current will be much greater. Step into the river, but only a pace."

Sheena did as instructed. The water felt tingly, effervescent, as if it was carbonated or fed by a spring. She looked back at the goddess. Shanikali explained, "You are not really there in the time stream, but you can feel the pressure just as if you were. It gets greater out in the center where the current is strongest. Now, go back to looking at that wedding day again."

The river changed. Sheena was still calf-deep in the water, but standing in the smaller river again. She looked out at the water. Her attention was drawn by something she couldn't define upstream. She searched and spotted a rock jutting just up to the surface of the time stream about thirty feet upstream. "Is that it? Where the rock is?"

"Yes," Shanikali replied. "If you walk upriver to that rock, your spirit body will be back in time four years, eight months, and seven days. Try it."

Sheena did, wading against the current. It was surprisingly difficult. She was standing beside the rock. "Now what?"

The goddess smiled. "Take a good look. Remember the good times, especially."

Sheena looked into the water and her eyes widened. She saw herself and Eric and their families and friends at her wedding. It was a still image, but just like looking at the scene from above as if she were there. "How do I see it in motion?"

"Watch with the current."

Sheena tried. It was like looking at water. She tried again. Before long she had got the hang of it. It was like looking at a series of images in a flip-book. Scanning them at the right speed made the still images seem as if they were in motion. Somewhere in that effort, she really looked at the water and realized that she was seeing faint lines, as if she was looking at a cross-section of people's lives in motion, watching them interact and separate and move. Dizzy, she closed her eyes until the effect faded.

"Yes, that is watching the time stream, and one of the reasons this can be so hard," Shanikali offered.

"Okay, if I wanted to have the bouquet go to another girl, how would I do that?"

The goddess blinked in confusion. "Bouquet?"

"Um... a tradition of my time. The bride throws a small bouquet of flowers over her shoulder. The other unmarried women try to catch it. The one who does is supposed to have good luck in being the next woman to find a husband."

"Strange custom."

Sheena shrugged. "I don't think that anyone of my time takes it seriously, but it is a bit of fun and people think that a little bit of good luck can't hurt."

Shanikali snorted in amusement. "Find the bouquet and who caught it. Then find a way to divert it. But remember that this is your spirit body. You can't actually make the change."

"That's what I thought, and why I'd rather get the idea now, instead of stumbling around when I might really need to do it later." She scanned the time stream again and found the bouquet tossing event a bit closer to the bank. She asked, "What does something being closer to the bank mean?"

"Usually, that puts the thing farther from the main current, so there is less pressure on it. It suggests that the thing you are looking at affects fewer people or events."

"Okay, that makes sense." Sheena studied the moment in time and saw that her friend Kristin had almost caught the flowers, but that Eric's cousin, Emily, had stretched a few inches more to snag the bouquet in the air. She looked at the two girls and the things that the time stream suggested that they had interacted with. If Emily had been a half second slower or had been wearing a dress with sleeves, or if Kristin had not been wearing unfamiliar heels, the outcome would have been different. Her head spun again. "So, I can see some things that would change who got the flowers. What would I do, now?"

"This is where the 'magic' happens. Trace back the thing you want to change to the place upstream where a different choice could have been made or a different thing could have happened. Then, if that is what you want, you can make that happen. This is what it means to change the streambed. Remember, substituting one thing that exists for another, especially if it's just in someone's head, like a decision, is easiest. Creating or removing something out of thin air is harder, and less likely to remain, especially if that creation or removal would violate the laws of nature in some way."

"So, if Kristin had a choice of shoes with high heels or shoes with flat heels, and she picked the high heels, and because of that wasn't in place to catch the bouquet, then I could just cause her to change her decision earlier that day to wear the flats, instead?"

"Yes, you could do that."

"Could I just move the bouquet a little bit to the left as I threw it?"

"Yes. That is still in the same category of a changed decision, but an even smaller one than the shoes."

"Could I have a wind blow it to Kristin?"

"Yes. Now you're going with a physical force, which will take more effort, but still very easy."

"Umm…," Sheena thought. "What about a five-hundred pound gorilla that only Emily sees that distracts her for a second?"

Shanikali chuckled. "Now that's getting silly. But creating the gorilla that did not exist at just the right place for Emily to see it and removing it again would take a lot of energy. An image would be easier. And you would have ripple effects from whatever Emily did at that point and afterward."

"Okay, I think I'm beginning to get this. But, this is changing things directly from within the time stream, or the river. What about going to that time, jumping in physically, doing something that makes a change, and then coming back again?"

"That is easier, but much, much riskier. It only takes the energy needed to get to the right point in time and become physical there, and then to do the return trip, as desired. But you will suffer the backlash when your real body enters that time. And you will suffer backlash again for whatever distance you have to go on your return. Because a physical body has so many possible effects on the world, it is hard to limit your impact to only the things that you want to affect. If you went to the flower throwing ceremony, and you were in the same place as the younger Sheena, how would you change the outcome?"

"No paradox from being in the same place as myself?"

Shanikali shook her head. "No."

"What if I was there then and killed myself?"

"It is not possible with this way of moving through time. The pressure of the current would make it impossible for you to achieve an outcome that would cause a paradox."

"Ah. Another important safety tip."

Shanikali cautioned her, "Remember, though, there are other true stories. Ours prevents paradox. Someone else's story may do nothing about such a paradox. I do not know what would happen, then."

"So, back to the bouquet toss. If I was there, and if I drew no special attention, and if I caused the time currents to slow Emily slightly so that Kristin got to the bouquet first, and if that drew no attention, then it would be a method?"

"Yes. But remember that your presence would be an additional factor in that time stream. There would have been another person at the wedding for that span of time, and that may cause ripples with unintended effects."

"But if the time stream wants to smooth itself out anyway, wouldn't that help disguise my impact?"

"Generally, yes." Shanikali laughed. "You are so much more thorough about this than any of my previous incarnations!"

"Chalk it up to a fondness for science fiction and fantasy," Sheena joked.

"Mmm... Science stories and tales of the gods, I take it?"

"Yes, close enough." She looked to the bank of the river. "Can I just walk out here?"

"Try it," the goddess replied.

Sheena shrugged and waded to the bank. A wave of dizziness hit her. The wolves looked like they were laughing, but Sharur padded over to prop her up. "Thanks, Sharur," she murmured.

"You just moved your spirit body four years, eight months, and seven days in less than a second," Shanikali informed her as her head cleared.

"Wow. What would that do to my physical body?"

"The same thing, but your body would feel the pain that has no effect on your spirit. You would be weakened and not so quick to recover."

"Because I didn't go back downstream to my entry point?"

"Yes."

"What if I just flapped my wings and flew?"

"If you leave the time stream, your body has to be reconciled with where it is in time. Flying out would still cause you to suffer, and you would probably fall into the river." Shanikali mused, "I've never tried that. I've flown over the river, but not out of it."

"There are good reasons not to!" Sheena replied.

"Yes. And imagine if you did not care about what effects your actions might have on the world."

"This could be horribly dangerous!" Shanikali nodded. "Are there others like us who can make changes to the time stream without being physically present in the time that they are changing? Just from standing in the river and watching and poking like gods?"

"Yes, but very, very few. Most who can affect the time stream have to go physically from one point in time to another, and have no access to the river that we see with our way. They do not have the option to study and examine and hunt for the exact thing that they want to change. They have to do what you described, go to the time and do what they could to change things by being present physically."

Shanikali fluttered her wings once and smiled to herself. She looked at Sheena and asked, "Do you know why we have wings?"

Sheena shook her head.

"Several reasons. Firstly, because it shows our higher spiritual abilities. This is just a way that this has been represented symbolically throughout history, so we are set apart from normal mortals in this way. Secondly, because we often need to fly high and travel fast, and wings allow us to do so. Finally, wings allow us to dive into the spirit world. Whether you go up or down is largely symbolic, but your wings enable you to take yourself into and out of the Cedar Forest of the Beastlands."

"Largely symbolic? What part of that is literal?"

"If you go up into the spirit world, you arrive above the ground or the river. If you fly down, you can dive into the river itself, if you choose. Or, even into the underworld, if that is your intent."

Sheena's eyes goggled. "I can go to the underworld? Am I likely to need that?"

Shanikali laughed. "No, not at all! Remember, our portfolio is the Beastlands, living creatures, hunting, and time. We are not concerned with the powers of life or death, nor the judgment of souls, or anything more metaphysical like that. Simply fly up to get here, and it will be easiest, like going to a higher place."

Sheena nodded. Her stomach growled. She was confused. "Aren't I supposed to just be here in spirit body? Why would I feel hungry here?"

Shanikali smiled. "That's just a sign that your real body is getting tired. Even though little or no time is passing, you are exerting psychic effort on this spirit journey. That can manifest as hunger pangs. I must admit that I have enjoyed this meeting."

"Me, too," Sheena said as she came back to the camp. "Will I see you again?"

"That is entirely up to you. I am here as you are here. Return when you like."

"I will." Sheena felt a wave of appreciation and gratitude for the goddess. They exchanged a hug. "Thank you, and be well."

"Go in beauty, Sheena," Shanikali replied.

Sheena awoke from her trance with a start. The wolves lifted their heads from their paws and watched her. She looked around. Still in Gayle's studio, with the two wolves and the eagle, and Gayle sitting on the floor by the door quietly listening to music.

"Hey, how long have I been gone?" she asked with a yawn.

Gayle perked up and removed her earbuds. "Not long. Maybe...," she checked the time, "just 12 minutes."

"Wow," Sheena breathed. "That felt like a *lot* longer, even if no time passed while I was in the forest."

"The forest? You got there all right, then?"

"Yes. And I learned so much! Quick, before it fades, I have to write it down!"

"One step ahead of you, sister!" Gayle said. "Pad, pencil, and your tablet by your side, whichever you prefer. And I recorded your session with audio and visual, in case it turned out to be helpful. You didn't say a lot, though. Too boring for the Internet."

Sheena nodded and grabbed the pad and pencil to record what she could. The river, the purpose Shanikali explained, the threat, the animals, the bow and arrows, everything she could remember. And just as the goddess had said, the details faded quickly, as if Sheena had awakened from a particularly vivid dream. Gayle waited patiently for her friend to finish, reigning in her curiosity.

Sheena finished, drawing a blank on some of the details. She stood up and stretched. "Gayle, you won't believe what I saw!"

Gayle smiled and guessed, "You met the goddess and had a conversation?"

"Yes! And I know what I'm supposed to do."

"Well? What is it?"

Sheena paced back and forth as she spoke with excitement. "Shanikali lived thousands of years ago, but she's not gone in the spirit world. She is always there, she said. There is some threat that is big enough that she has to intervene. Big enough to come from or threaten that spirit forest. I don't know what it is, but that's why the stone woke up and got to the right place and time to give me her powers. I am Shanikali's incarnation for this time. It wasn't random. There is a threat, and it is in Shanikali's area of responsibility, and I'm the closest match there is to her, so I got picked. And there it is!"

"But we don't know what the threat is?"

"No, she didn't know. She only has knowledge of ancient things and couldn't tell, so I'm guessing it's some sort of current-day threat to nature, maybe. Anyway, she showed me how the River of Time works and what I can do with it to change things, but it's really hard and really risky. And I got a hunting bow and arrows...." She reached out, and the ancient bow was in her hand. She nodded her head and an arrow was in her other hand.

"Whoa! That's some serious stuff!" Gayle said with wide eyes.

"And the other spirit animals, too, including one that's an ancient demon wolf, Sharur." Sheena let the bow and arrow go. They simply vanished. She concentrated and called each of her spirit animals into the studio. The alpha wolf, the leopards, and then the enormous iron wolf appeared in turn. They gathered around her with expectant eyes. Sharur glanced at Gayle and looked her over carefully.

Gayle scooted herself back against the door with alarm. "Uh, Sheena...!"

"No, no, it's okay! They're all mine!"

The trio of wolves adopted their amused canine expressions. Sharur took a step forward and bowed his head and forelegs to Gayle. A resonant voice in her head intoned as he spoke, "I am Sharur, smasher of thousands. I greet you, friend of Shee'na."

"Eep!" Gayle sputtered. She carefully got to her feet. "Uh, hi there, Sharur. Welcome to my apartment." Her phone chirped an impatient signal. She glanced down at it. "Oh, yeah. Um… one sec." She entered her thumbprint and keyed in a passcode, then looked back up at Sheena. "Security detected a dimensional incursion. I've given the all-clear and registered the extra critters."

"Really? The building detected that?"

Gayle regained some of her poise. "Yeah, Prometheus… Riverhaven's quasi-AI central control system… is really smart and on the ball. It can tell the difference between normal residential patterns and threats. Somehow, they've rigged up sensors to detect even magical stuff like conjured critters."

"Impressive!" Sheena shook her head in amazement.

"I love this place!" Gayle replied.

Sheena let the animal spirits go, and reluctantly dismissed Sharur, though she would have liked to have had a chance to learn more from him and to introduce him to the modern world. "There will be time," he replied before he vanished.

"So, what did you learn about Elf Shot, if anything?" Gayle asked.

"Um…." Sheena struggled to remember, but the details had faded. "I should hunt her down and bring her to justice. She can't get what she wants from me, but that won't stop her. That's all I know."

Gayle thought about that for a moment. "That's good enough for me. If you're an even better hunter, I'm sure we'll find the trail again really soon."

Sheena smiled and nodded, filled with renewed confidence.

Chapter 14 – This was a Good Day

The elevator doors slid closed behind him as he stepped out into the foyer of Gayle's floor. Eric waved his hand in front of the scanner and then entered the apartment as the security system acknowledged him and opened the door. He looked around, but didn't see or hear any sign of Sheena or Gayle. He shook his head with a touch of weariness and grinned ruefully. The meeting with Greg Dawson at Dynatech had gone surprisingly well. The immunologist had recognized the work Eric had done on monitoring and controlling the spread of a fatal neurological disease in the Wisconsin deer herds. It was one of the reasons Greg was so eager to bring him onto the team. This had been a good day, but it left him with a big decision to make.

"Hello? Anyone home?" He loosened his tie and wandered into the unlit living room. The late afternoon sun made long shadows on the balcony outside. The ocean beyond Clark's Point to the south was flecked with occasional lazy whitecaps in the distance. Eric reminded himself, "I suppose I can text her...."

Home from mtg. U avail?

Sheena's reply followed in less than a minute.

Practicng archery. omw

"Archery?" Eric shook his head. Well, if his wife was going to channel an ancient hunting goddess, he supposed it fit the theme. She wasn't a half-bad shot, either, even if she only practiced for a week or two before bowhunting season. Eric wistfully hoped they would be home before the season opened this year.

The sliding glass door to the balcony opened and Sheena arrived. She fluttered her wings to settle the feathers as she closed the door behind her. She was in her fantasy ranger costume, but Eric didn't see any sign of a bow. "Hi, Eric, I'm back! How was your meeting? That went way longer than just an hour or so. You were gone all day!"

He nodded in agreement and came over to meet her. "I have to admit, it was fascinating. Greg showed me around the whole lab, and I got a good look at how they are tackling that vaccine problem. It's pretty impressive what a well-funded research lab can do. And... I think they can really use me on the research team, much to my surprise." He looked her over again and smiled at how beautiful she looked. "Where's Gayle?"

"A business dinner and then rehearsal. We were trying to come up with leads for most of the day, but that didn't get us anywhere, so we went swimming."

"Oh. Sorry I missed it. You mentioned archery?"

Sheena smiled smugly. "Yeah, get a look at this." She held out her arm and she was holding a bow. Eric's eyes widened as he saw it suddenly appear in her hand. It was a composite recurve bow made of lacquered layers of different kinds of wood. The front face had a deep blue varnish that matched her costume and he could see a pattern of rubberized inlay work around the grip. With another gesture she nocked a gray-shafted arrow with natural feather fletchings and a blunt, aerodynamic head. Eric noticed that the fletchings matched Sheena's wing feathers. The whole arrow looked slightly transparent, like it wasn't really completely there. "I was out practicing, and I have to actually work to miss! I can split a dime at fifty yards!"

"Umm...," Eric murmured, not knowing what to think. He was pretty sure he couldn't even *see* a dime at fifty yards. He asked, "Bow and arrows out of thin air?"

"Yep," she replied. "A Sheena special! I had a productive day, too. Visited the spirit world. Talked with the goddess. Got a whole bunch of answers to my questions. That sort of thing." She grinned smugly again.

"Oh!" Eric's eyes widened again. He couldn't decide what to ask first. His questions eventually came forth in a flood, but he wasn't sure he was going to like the answers. "So, what did you learn? Why is all this happening to you? What do you have to do?"

Sheena dismissed the weapon and relayed her experience with the spirit journey and her conversation with Shanikali. Eric took it all in with a slight frown of concentration, trying hard to listen with an open mind. She included all of the details and sensations she could remember and came to the conclusion, "So I am the incarnation of Shanikali, and I am the closest thing to the goddess alive at this time in history, so I get the power to stop some great big threat to the world."

Eric's frown deepened, his brow furrowed with concern. That was what he had been afraid he would hear; that she was destined to bear the fate of the world on her shoulders. That she wasn't his anymore, but that she now had some sort of "higher calling." Sheena just kept looking at him calmly, which didn't help. "Okay...," he said slowly. "That sounds... big."

"It is," she acknowledged. "Because it's something big enough that Shani's whole portfolio is going to be needed. The threat is probably technical in nature, and involved with the spirit world, in some way."

"'Shani?' You're on a casual nickname basis with an ancient goddess?"

Sheena favored him with a wry smile. "She insisted."

"Okay... I guess that goes with the whole 'save the world' thing," Eric said with a snort. He noticed out of the corner of his eye that she was glowing. It was very faint, but definitely present in the dim light of the living room. "So, what now?"

"I continue to hunt for Elf Shot. But I think I am at the very least on equal footing, now."

Eric looked at her. The change was subtle, but she was different than she had ever appeared to him before. Her costume didn't look at all out of place or affected; she wore it as if it were an everyday choice of clothing. She wasn't playacting a hero any more—she *was* a hero. "I... can almost believe that. You look... different. More confident, more in charge, I guess."

"You *can* believe it, Eric. I don't think you need to be worrying about me so much. I'm still in danger... maybe even more than we thought before... but I have a much better sense of why I'm here and what I can do. And, I can take care of myself."

Seeing her standing there confidently and hearing her words uttered without bravado, Eric's heart caught in his throat. This was the woman he married, but it was someone different, as well. Now she had a bigger duty, a bigger purpose. One that he wasn't sure had a place for him in it. After a moment, he took a breath and managed to get out, "I'm... proud of you, Sheena." He felt detached as he gave her a congratulatory hug, as if he weren't really there, and this was happening to someone else and he was just watching. She didn't seem to notice.

"Don't worry. I'll take care of this, whatever it is." She looked at him with assurance.

He hesitated, then said quietly, "But we're never really going back, are we?" It wasn't so much a question as a whisper drifting free from his thoughts.

She shook her head. "Not the way it was before all this happened, no."

"Ah," he nodded absently. What else was there to say? He looked away and then took a deep breath, then let it out slowly. Softly, as if it was a goodbye uttered to the woman he used to know, he said, "I love you."

Sheena looked at him with a touch of puzzlement. "I love you, too."

Eric shook his head and brought his attention back to the present. With difficulty, he forced a smile. "Well, I should get changed out of my 'work clothes.' It's been an, uh... interesting day. Do you want to do anything special tonight? Dinner out?"

The puzzlement changed to amused suspicion. "Out?"

"Well, yeah. Figuring all this out, talking to the goddess, my almost certain job offer... it seems like an appropriate occasion for a little celebration." He smiled ruefully, determined not to spoil her accomplishment with his petty misgivings.

"You didn't tell me it was *that* good a meeting!" she exclaimed with surprise.

"Yes, it was *that* good of a meeting." He sighed. "Normally, research fellowships really don't pay that well, but I am in the right place at the right time, and they have a lot of funding. This is a pretty promising situation."

"Are you going to take it?"

"I was going to ask you if I should. It means I have to be tied down here in Venture City more, and maybe selling the practice back home...." He shrugged and turned to look out the windows at the panorama of the coastline and the sea beyond it. "I was hoping maybe we wouldn't have to."

"That's a big step, Eric."

"So is deciding you have to be the one to save the world!" he snapped. He rubbed his eyes and sighed. "I'm sorry, I didn't mean that. They warned me about this. I'm... this... is going to take more getting used to."

95

Sheena put an arm around his shoulder. "Eric, it is what it is," she said softly. "If it could have been another way, it would have. But, I'm the one this falls to."

"I know, I know." He put his arm around her. "I was just afraid this was going to happen. We had a pretty sweet setup, and I liked it like it was. I knew where I stood. Now... now I feel like I don't know anything."

"Well, don't give up on me, yet. Keep an open mind and roll with it."

"Yeah, that's all well and good for you to say."

She snorted. "Put your money where your mouth is, Doctor Gardner! It's your own fault for coming up with that 'open mind' saying, you know." She chuckled. "Besides, you might find that you like new things opening up for you, like that project at Dynatech."

"Well, yeah... It *is* a great opportunity..." He sighed again. "And if this pans out, we don't have to worry about the money angle for a while...."

"Yes! Now, *there's* a positive!" Sheena said with enthusiasm. "Come on, years from now you're going to look back on today as a very good day. And, yes, let's get out of this building and go somewhere fun."

Eric cocked his head and asked, "Not worried about the psycho chick popping up out of nowhere?"

Sheena smirked and shook her head. "Nope. She would feel compelled to monologue for at least a few sentences, and by that time, she'd be facing my own little army of pets. And my arrows. Not too worried."

"As long as we don't get overconfident," he cautioned.

"Right."

"Okay." He chuckled. "I did offer, didn't I?"

"Yes, and I won't let you forget it. Let's get some recommendations and go exploring. Venture City awaits!"

Chapter 15 – Hunting for Clues

"Okay, I'm game. Why are we in Dartmouth?" Gayle asked as they landed on the rooftop of an office building.

"I'm supposed to be the tracking expert, right? Well, I did some work early this morning with Josh and the Titans' supercomputer while you were on that teleconference with your business manager. I wanted to put together the clues we have and see if I could maybe find a trail. This is more 'waiting at the watering hole' than real tracking, but I think I've got a lead we can follow."

"Really? Neat! What do you have?"

Sheena summoned her eagle and sent it up high to watch for trouble. She hopped up onto a ventilation duct and sat down, arranging her skirt so her bare legs weren't pressed against the hot metal. She had to speak louder to be heard over the thrum of the air conditioning fans. "We check out the medical companies that make stuff that Elf Shot's employer might need, in case she pulls any more thefts. The ones we want are here in the Dartmouth district."

Gayle nodded appreciatively. "That works. Any idea how we can recognize her if she's wandering around in disguise?"

"If she keeps wearing the same perfume, that's pretty distinctive. Other than that…?" She shrugged.

"What about… oops. Hold a moment."

Both Gayle and Sheena looked at their wristband displays. An emergency call for help was going out over the VCPD Hero Request channel. According to the guidelines established by the FBSA, any "on duty" hero could receive such a call for help from law enforcement. Calls were usually limited to situations that ordinary police officers might find too dangerous to handle without SWAT or superpowered backup. Data flowed across the heroines' wrist displays—alert ID, the nature of the emergency, address, and other details, including a threat rating. In this case, the threat rating was a series of red question marks. The authorities knew that at least one superpowered individual was involved, but had not yet been able to identify the villain.

"A jewel heist? Seriously?" Gayle exclaimed in disbelief.

"What's wrong with that? I mean, other than the obvious—robbery, jewels, stealing, you know."

"It's so cliché!" Gayle complained. "Still, we're closest. Let's get on it!"

Sheena and Gayle just happened to be less than three blocks from the store that was being robbed, Vicente's Fine Jewelry. As they got airborne, they could see flashes of light accompanied by an explosion of glass and rubble onto the street. Sheena sent her eagle ahead to look for trouble and prepared to wing off after it. She waited for Gayle to apply the air cushions that would protect them from most damage.

"Okay, we're bubbled," Gayle affirmed. They flew off toward the commotion. "And there he is."

Flying over a rooftop, they paused to look at the scene. The jewelry store was part of a single-story suburban commercial building that housed several other high-end shops. It stood on its own, surrounded by a small parking lot with access to the street. The roof extended out from the storefronts about three meters all the way around the building to provide shade and cover from rain or snow. An organic foods superstore lay on the other side of the parking lot to the north, with its own parking lot loosely connected by a grassy median that held a long drainage pond. A simple fountain was spraying half-heartedly into the air at the center of the drainage pond. In the middle of the summer afternoon, the parking lots were both only about one quarter filled. Frightened shoppers were running from the shops, ducking behind cars and trying to get away from the danger. Vicente's Fine Jewelry occupied the entire southwest quarter of the building. It had a white marble façade, much of which had been blasted to pieces as a humanoid figure in shiny blue and silver power armor stepped out through the massive hole in the front of the store.

The armored powersuit appeared to be heavily built and reinforced for the protection of its wearer. Major surfaces were polished silver, with the rest painted or constructed of some electric blue material. The helmet had a reflective, blue-tinted face plate that completely covered the front of the wearer's head. It gleamed in the sunlight brightly enough to make Sheena and Gayle squint. The powersuited bandit waded through the wreckage of the storefront, casually blasting parked cars as he moved. He had beam emitters in the palms of his armored gauntlets that made a snapping noise like a bug zapper as they fired brilliant white energy beams. To Gayle's experienced eye, it looked like a professionally manufactured suit, and not a garage-built hobbyist's project. Therefore, it would be more dangerous.

"Target, identify and threatcon," Gayle commanded her headband electronics. She centered her gaze on the armored villain so that the imaging system could pick out the correct target. The device chirped that it had captured the visual and was searching the database to identify the threat.

"He doesn't have the loot," Sheena noted. "Look for a partner."

"Right." They were still more than seventy-five meters away from the villain, hovering over a three-story parking garage across the broad four-lane avenue from the store. Gayle wrapped herself in an obscuring mist and swooped closer to the other side of the street. She created a trio of shimmering air servants and sent them after the armored threat.

Sheena flew off to the right and around to the opposite side of the building from the jewelry store. She landed in the shade of an ornamental tree at the side of the avenue and summoned her army of spirit animals. She gave the wolves the order to hunt for someone taking a lot of shiny things from the jewelry store. To the leopards, she said, "Find anyone sneaking who could be a threat." To Sharur, she said, "The big guy making all the noise probably has a partner stealing jewels. Help me find the thieves and capture them all."

"At once," the demon wolf growled.

The animals ran off while Sheena checked with her eagle flying overhead. So far, the bird had seen only the powersuited blaster in front and a lot of people running from the scene. None moved like they were escaping with stolen prey, according to the bird. Meanwhile, the phantom army Gayle had conjured was busy distracting the armored foe while she summoned a miniature tornado to lift and spin the villain. Gayle hoped this would be enough to disorient and immobilize him, but she was preparing more tricks in case the suit was as good as it looked.

The armored blaster snapped off shot after shot at the shimmering forms of the air servants, but the beams did nothing to them. Gayle's tornado spun its way into the villain, lifting the suit into the air and throwing it around violently. After only a few quick rotations, the suit regained its equilibrium and stopped whirling. It hovered in the middle of the tornado. Cutting the jets but keeping the gyros spinning, the armored robber settled with a thump onto the parking lot. The air servants were still blasting and battering the villain with high pressure winds of their own, but it appeared that the armor could withstand these attacks for quite some time.

"Target identified as Snapflash," her headband notified her. "Threat rating 25. More available."

"More," Gayle commanded. A rating of 25 on the 50 point scale was extremely dangerous to normal police units or low-powered heroes, but almost trivial for Gayle. It would just take a little time and care to capture the villain without too much extra collateral damage.

"Armored heavy power suit. Operator identity unknown. Affiliation independent. Suit designed by Syndicate technologist, Gearbox." The device went on to list major capabilities of the suit and specific crimes Snapchat had committed. Gayle nodded, having heard what she had expected to hear.

By now, the armored villain's targeting computer had spotted Gayle, as well. Finding an actual opponent to fight, Snapflash shifted his aim to her and fired. The bright hot white power beam caught her right in the chest. Her shielding held, but she was knocked back a good ten meters by the converted energy of the beam. Still hovering three floors off the ground, Gayle made a circular gesture and swept up trash, grit, and ruined bits of the marble façade in a whirling zephyr around the suited thug. "How about a little sensor blindness?" she muttered.

"Bring it, lady!" Snapflash called out in a filtered mechanical voice. He braced himself and aimed his palm at Gayle, trying to hold it steady in the windstorm surrounding him.

The zephyr battered the surface of the suit with its debris. It sucked in even more loose objects and road grit from the parking lot to add to the swarm. Still, it was able to only partially obscure the villain's senses and scour the outside of the suit. Fortunately, this was enough to cause his next volley of rapid-fire energy blasts to miss the hovering singer. The blasts gouged big chunks out of the reinforced concrete wall of the parking garage across the street. Gayle took the opportunity to strengthen her shields and fill in Sheena on the threat.

"Standard powersuit, so far," Gayle reported to Sheena. "Identified as Snapflash, a TL 25 villain. Not too tough for either of us, but way dangerous for ordinary folks. Heavily armored, blasters on palms and feet, flying thrusters, gyros. I'll keep watching for surprises. Find anything, yet?"

"No… Yes," Sheena reported as one of her wolf spirits was suddenly sliced almost in half by a nearly invisible attacker. The unknown assailant had just stepped out an emergency exit door on the north end of the building farthest from the jewelry store. The destroyed wolf spirit vanished as the other two rounded on the threat. Sheena squinted at the attacker, trying to more clearly see what it was. Her leopards stalked along the wall of the building, staying in the shadow of the overhang. "Someone in a really good stealth suit, I think. With blades. Took one of my wolves out with one shot."

"You got him?"

"I think so. I have to move to get a decent shot, but the pets are on him now."

"Okay. I'm gonna have to build up layers on this guy. The suit's too strong to hold with just one funnel."

"Got it." Sheena flew to the north edge of the parking lot near the drainage pond and ducked behind a minivan. She kept her eyes on where the wolves were trying to engage the thief. Strangely, her leopards had not pounced, yet, even though the wolves snarled and bit at their target. Sheena spotted a flicker of movement—an unnatural shimmer in the air—near the northwest corner of the building. Neither of the wolves had taken any damage. "Are they fighting a decoy?" she wondered. She spread slowing currents of time in a large puddle around the corner and side of the building. The sneaking thief was much easier to spot in the slow field. The shimmer slowed as the mists surrounded it, revealing a slim human-shaped form by the wall of the building.

Sheena leaned back at a sudden movement from the thief and a buzzing dart slid past her through the air, fired at one-quarter speed by the stealthed villain. Then, the foe had more immediate threats to deal with than her. The leopards both identified their target and pounced, the black one right after the gray cat in sequence. As they entered the field of time currents, their leap slowed to a crawl, as well. The slow-motion attack of the big cats was amazing to watch, but Sheena mentally kicked herself for getting distracted, as well as forgetting that her pets would also be affected by the wide area currents. She changed the flow of her time slowing field to a more precise effect, seeking to capture the sneaky foe with a concentrated current. By the time she had done so, the villain— moving at the same speed as the cats—had opened a long gash in the gray leopard's throat and chest. The cat's claws scrabbled off the body armor underneath the stealth suit and it landed with a painful cry on the sidewalk before dissipating in a cloud of mist.

The black leopard had better luck and took the villain down to the ground. It struggled for a hold with its teeth on the thief's neck or shoulder. The pool of slowed time was surging in to concentrate just on the villain. The thief rolled to the side, dropping his sword. The villain's weapon, a straight 60 centimeter blade of darkened metal attached to a non-slip two-handed hilt, fell to the ground with a soft "thunk." Far from disarmed, the thief extended claw-like blades from his left forearm sheath. The blades slashed across the jaguar's shoulder, breaking its hold for a moment.

As quick as a thought, Sheena grabbed her bow and drew a spirit arrow, then let it fly. The thief's body jerked and slackened. That was enough for the leopard to pin him to the sidewalk. Sheena wrapped the time current more tightly around the villain until he was completely restrained, enveloping him with all of the misty currents that had previously spread over the ground around the building. It was still very difficult to see details, but much easier to target now that the stealth suit could no longer adapt to its wearer's movement. The black leopard obtained a solid grip on the thief's neck; only the time hold kept it from crushing the villain's throat.

Sharur appeared by her side protectively. He reported, "This one and the armored warrior are the only foes. There are people bound inside, but none are injured."

"Can we disarm him safely?" Sheena asked. She was trembling with adrenalin, even though the threat was passing.

"Yes. I will do so now," the demon wolf replied. He moved quickly across the parking lot to the thief. Much to her surprise, with teeth and claws far more nimble than they appeared, the great wolf pulled pieces of gear off the thief and flicked them out of reach.

"Stealther down and immobilized," Sheena reported. "Sharur found no additional perps. No injuries, but people tied up or something in the store."

"Gotcha. I've finally got this guy held, too. The VCPD SWAT team will be able to drain off his energy and neutralize him. Can you hold that one until they get here?"

Sheena was concentrating on keeping the currents wrapped tightly around the immobilized thief. It was not difficult, but it took a bit of her attention. "Yes. Bagheera's jaws will get tired, though."

"Bagheera?"

"The black leopard. That's not his real name. Just a nickname. He's got his jaws around the guy's throat. I'd better call him off."

"Uh, yeah. You think?"

Sheena snorted. "The time currents will hold him, as long as I don't get too distracted. I hit him with a spirit arrow, but he's pretty strong and it only numbed him a bit, instead of sending him off to dreamland."

"Why didn't you use another one of those dream arrows on him, then?" Gayle asked.

"Uh... I didn't think of it?" Sheena replied. "I can do a lot of things, now. I just have to figure out what to use when, I guess."

"More practice," Gayle agreed.

Sheena walked up to the restrained thief. She looked him over to be sure he would not be able to move and then gathered up the gear into a pile. She found a slim backpack bulging with stolen jewelry among his belongings. She called the wolves over and re-summoned the one slain earlier and set them to guard the pile. Making sure that the bonds had not loosened, she healed Bagheera's shoulder wound and re-summoned Misty, the gray spotted leopard, as well. She gave them the task of keeping people and vehicles clear of the area until the police arrived. Sharur she kept close by, just in case.

"What about you?" Sheena asked over their private comm channel. "Do you have to concentrate to keep up your grip on the tanky guy?"

"Nope," Gayle chirped. "I've been doing this long enough that I learned how to put a little 'twist' into the wind and that keeps it flowing until I release it or get so far away that I can't affect it anymore."

"How far is that?"

"Oh, about two hundred yards."

Sheena whistled appreciatively. "I can probably hit stationary targets with my arrows pretty well at that distance, but I'm not sure I can work these time currents at more than maybe fifty or sixty, right now. And I do have to pay attention to what I'm doing."

"More practice," Gayle repeated. "That's all it is."

By this time the police SWAT unit and patrol cars were arriving. With the proper equipment to capture and restrain metahuman criminals, the SWAT team took over quickly and efficiently. Lieutenant Fowler also arrived on the scene to talk with the two heroines. Sheena dismissed her pets back to the Beastlands, having been relieved of guard duty over the prisoner.

"Thanks, you two," the detective said. "That was a whole lot easier and cleaner than it could've been. Especially with that Snapflash guy being able to fly. We might not have caught them at all."

"Happy to help, as always, Eddie!" Gayle responded. "We just happened to be in the area when the alert came through."

"Still looking for Elf Shot?" he asked.

Sheena nodded. "My guess is that she's going to be sent to get more biotech supplies for whatever her boss is working on, and that's probably going to put her here in Dartmouth with the research labs."

Eddie nodded. "Unless they've got everything they need, yeah. I haven't heard anything new on her, sorry. If I do, I'll let you know right away."

"Thanks, Eddie. What about these guys?" Gayle asked. "What's up with them? Just a smash and grab for loot, or do you think they're after something specific?"

"Won't be able to tell until we talk to all the witnesses and the suspects, of course, but it looks like a simple smash and grab. These guys have done it before about five months ago. We didn't catch them, then. Snapflash and his buddy, Quickblade, are independents, but not too greedy or dumb, as mercs go."

"Quickblade?" Gayle asked. "Wasn't he part of that gang trying to steal the Dynatech super-soldier formula?"

"Yeah, he was, but he was never caught and gave up on that ring before they got busted by the League of Titans."

Gayle snorted. "Well, we got him now."

Eddie congratulated them once more and went to supervise the investigative cleanup. A reporter and camerawoman had arrived from one of the local news stations. The reporter waved at Gayle from outside the police line, trying to attract her attention.

"Hey, Gayle Force! What happened here?" the reporter called out.

"Hi there! How are you guys?" She walked over to the news team with a pleasant smile on her face, nodding to the woman with the camera. Sheena followed with mild curiosity.

"Dan Rogers, Channel Nine News," the reporter said, shaking her hand. He grinned as a sweet-smelling breeze ruffled his hair. "Good to see—and smell—you again!"

"Oh, yeah!" Gayle laughed. "You covered that traffic pileup when those mutated chimps got loose and went berserk last year! Some nice shots and background on that story, if I remember correctly."

"It was fun, thanks. Can we get your story on what happened here, Gayle?"

"Sure! My friend and I were in the area working on a case when the call came in for help with a jewelry store robbery." She turned to Sheena. "Dan, this is Shee'na. She's new to Venture City but has a background in law enforcement."

"Really?" the reporter asked, brimming with curiosity.

"Yes," Sheena replied. "I've worked with the FBSA a bit, but most of my experience is at the state and county level in Wisconsin." She figured that would be a safe enough answer.

"How does that help you, as a hero?"

"It makes working with the police a whole lot easier, and it also helps to know how to protect people's rights, whether they are normal folks or potential suspects. Maybe working with clues and evidence, too."

"If you don't mind sharing, what's your story? What do you do, as a hero?"

Sheena glanced over at Gayle, who nodded enthusiastically. "It's kind of a long story, but I guess I'd boil it down this way. I was on an FBSA operation when I inherited the powers of an ancient Sumerian goddess. Her influence is apparently needed in the world to stop a dangerous threat. I'm not sure just what that is, specifically, but I'm working on finding out."

"Wow! That sounds pretty important!" Dan responded. His camerawoman was capturing the interview. "What sort of things do you do?"

"I'm a huntress. Using Shanikali's powers, I track down criminals and capture them with the help of my spirit animal companions. They come out of the mists of time to do what I need them to do."

"Can we see a demonstration?" the reporter asked eagerly.

At a nod from Gayle, Sheena called the wolves, the leopards, and then the eagle, who flew in to land on her shoulder. She felt it would be best to keep Sharur in reserve. The others were enough to provide a good demonstration.

The reporter looked very pleased. He asked some other questions of Sheena and Gayle, including more about their role in stopping the robbery. As they were wrapping up, he asked, "How should we refer to you, Sheena? Do you want us to list your name as Sheena, or Shanikali, or what?"

"For official purposes, Shee'na is spelled with an apostrophe after the second E. That's what I'm registered under in the FBSA database. Wouldn't want to get me confused with someone else," she smiled. She checked the spelling with the camera person taking notes and thanked both of them for the opportunity to share her story. With a smug grin, Gayle waved to the reporter once more and the additional bystanders who had gathered, and then urged Sheena into the air to follow her.

"Sooo...? What's that about?" Sheena asked as they flew.

"Just happy to get you your first media appearance," Gayle sang cheerfully.

"And?"

"And, it went perfectly!"

"So, that was good, yeah. Why the big deal?"

"Public opinion is a huge advantage to a hero. As long as you are humble and focused on protecting the public, good PR can open doors and get you leads and clues that you might never have found, otherwise. If you have a reputation for being tough and fair, even to the defeated bad guys, you earn respect. You never know when you're going to need to draw on that pool of respect and goodwill that you've saved up."

Sheena thought for a moment. She grinned and asked, "Like, after that Memorial Day concert in Milwaukee?"

Gayle blushed. "Yeah. Like that." A dusky rose scent wafted around her and faded into the wind behind them.

Sheena laughed, "I'll keep that in mind!" They flew on to continue their search for Elf Shot.

Their last stop before quitting for the day was Dynatech Research Labs. This was one of the shining white and blue macroplast buildings that Sheena and Eric had seen on the way into Venture City almost two weeks earlier. Most of the eight hectare campus was occupied by carefully preserved natural grasses and trees. The Dynatech facility was made up of a central office tower and a half-dozen two-story labs connected to the office building by enclosed glass walkways. The buildings were made of a specially formed material that was as resilient and flexible as plastic, but as strong as titanium alloy. The design and construction of the facility would easily withstand virtually any type of natural disaster, up to an 8.5 Richter-scale earthquake. Each lab could be sealed off physically and with force fields, if needed. After his visit to the campus, Eric had assured Sheena that the safety measures and emergency systems to manage biological contaminants were state of the art. Today was his first day on the job.

Sheena and Gayle took a good look at the place from the air before landing near the visitor parking lot. A sandstone sidewalk led to the Dynatech entrance lobby. Sheena asked, "We don't need to have an appointment, do we?"

Gayle shook her head and replied, "Nope, but we may or may not get to someone who can help us. I suppose I could check the Titans' computer to see what we know, but we can probably do just as well walking up and asking."

Sheena shrugged. "These guys haven't had anything stolen, yet, as far as I know. But, they do work that puts them on the possible target list. I'm kind of grasping at straws here, but forewarned is forearmed."

Gayle nodded and accompanied her to the entrance.

There were two people behind the big blue desk—more like a control station—inside the Dynatech lobby. Both were wearing blue Dynatech shirts and black pants. One was a fiftyish redheaded woman who exuded quiet competence as she watched the heroines arrive. The other was a younger fellow with Asian features and an outgoing, easy smile. He stood as they approached the desk.

"Good afternoon, I'm David! Welcome to Dynatech! How may we help you, today?"

Gayle smiled engagingly. "Hi there, David! I'm Gayle Force, and this is Shee'na. We would like to speak with your security director, if possible. We are tracking down a criminal who has been stealing from biotech firms, and we would like to do what we can to help Dynatech protect its people and property."

"Well, that sounds serious," he responded with an earnest expression. "One moment, please." He turned to the woman at the desk, who nodded and started working with her keyboard and screens.

"Would you mind giving me your FBSA verification codes, please?" the woman asked after a moment.

"That's the…?" Sheena started to ask Gayle.

"Yep. We call it up on whatever we've got for a display, and show it to the person asking for ID. She will check the generated code against what she sees on her app. It's like those keyfob devices. Each eight-character code is only good for a minute." Gayle held out her bracelet with the FBSA verification code showing. The woman nodded and then looked at Sheena's.

"That checks out, thank you," the woman behind the desk said.

"It can be done even more easily with close-range chip readers, and your device can do that, too, but if Joe Citizen on the street wants to check your hero license and identity, this is a pretty simple way to handle it. The FBSA keeps it secure and constantly changing on their end," Gayle finished her explanation.

David offered to provide literature about Dynatech and answer questions while his partner contacted someone with her headset. Even with her enhanced hearing, Sheena wasn't able to make out any of the conversation. She guessed that there must be some kind of special privacy or security devices protecting the desk. Gayle chatted happily with David while Sheena waited and looked around. The large, open atrium extended up for three floors and back from the desk to a bank of elevators. A series of glass-walled meeting rooms of various sizes ringed the lobby, along with a discreet set of restroom doors tucked along one corner of the atrium. The whole area appeared to be sealed off from the rest of the building. This made sense to Sheena from a security perspective.

"Ladies, Ms. Coffee would like to meet with you," the redheaded woman said, finally. "She is finishing up a conversation and will be available in just a few minutes. Would you mind waiting for her?"

"No problem!" Gayle responded.

Sheena and Gayle waited around a bit more while David returned to his post behind the desk. A trickle of people left the building, either shaking hands with the Dynatech employees they had come to meet and departing, or walking out with the purposeful air of employees who had put in a full day on the job. Most cast curious looks at the pair of costumed women as they went by; only a few were less than friendly. The heroines did not have long to wait. Less than three minutes later, the redheaded woman announced the security director. "Gayle Force, Shee'na, Ms. Coffee, Dynatech's Directory of Corporate Security, is available now."

As she looked at the approaching executive, Sheena was quietly impressed. Ms. Coffee managed to make a fully functional security uniform blend in seamlessly with the expected corporate business dress code. The mahogany-skinned security director was an athletic woman of Gayle's height who appeared to be about thirty years old. She was dressed in a blue silk blouse over a tasteful dark gray scoop-neck top of ballistic cloth. Her black skirt was carefully tailored to fit closely over thin black fibermesh leggings that Sheena knew would be as rugged as thick leather. She wore stylish black calf-length boots that managed to imply a high heel without actually having one. She wore bracelets very similar to Gayle's, and Sheena was sure that they contained the same sort of high-tech electronics. Ms. Coffee's face was an interesting mix of features, with broad round cheekbones, a petite nose, and pale green eyes, like a cat's. Her hair was a silky-smooth wave of black, parted mostly to her left in a shoulder-length ripple. Sheena didn't see any obvious weapons, but something about the woman suggested to her that the security director wouldn't be unarmed and helpless even if she were somehow blindfolded and bound hand and foot.

"Good afternoon, Gayle Force, Shee'na," Ms. Coffee said calmly. "I hope I didn't keep you waiting long. Let's grab a conference room and you can fill me in."

She led the heroines to one of the glass-walled private rooms on the north side of the atrium. Sheena and Gayle followed her into the room. Ms. Coffee gestured to the chairs and took a seat at the end of the table nearest them. "What's this about, then?"

"We are hunting a villain named Elf Shot," Sheena explained. "She is responsible for some recent thefts of biotech equipment and supplies from other companies in the Dartmouth area. We would like to do what we can to prevent loss to Dynatech."

"And to track her down, of course," Ms. Coffee added. Sheena nodded. The security director glanced at her hand and smiled. "Ah! And to protect your husband and yourself, as well."

Sheena and Gayle exchanged confused looks. Sheena looked back at the Dynatech security director with a puzzled expression. Ms. Coffee laughed casually and grinned. "You and Eric have rather distinctive—and matching—wedding rings."

"Oh. Thanks." Sheena blushed.

"It's my job to be observant, as you might guess. Anyway, I'm aware of the situation with regard to the thefts. I have taken extra steps to boost security. Elf Shot will find it difficult to predict our routines well enough to pull off anything important for a while."

"Oh, good," Sheena said. "Uh, did you get the list of the stolen goods?"

"Yes. I was invited to investigate by the VCPD detective handling the case. I think the police missed a couple of things from the list, actually. They got the important items, but details count. I'm not sure the victims really realized what else was missing until I pointed it out."

"Really? What else was there?"

"Storage media. 25 and 100 microliter aliquots. Cryogenic vials. Cryopreservant agents." At Sheena and Gayle's blank looks, she summarized, "A small variety of technical items needed for the safe transport and storage of virus samples and related things they would be working on. They had a list detailed enough to suggest that an expert is behind this, even if the thefts were carried out by hired muscle."

"Ah. So, thinking about possibilities, what would they be able to do with all of the things they stole, and what might they do if they combined that with things that they might already have?"

"For this particular combination, it appears likely that someone is trying to create a vaccine or a cure for a virus or viruses that they already have in their possession. This is the main thing. It means they already have existing samples of the target virus to work with. There is a lot of complex preparation and supporting equipment and safety procedures that would be needed to do this work. It is extremely unlikely that a rogue villain working alone would be able to pull it off. It requires a controlled lab environment, so that might be a place to look."

Gayle asked, "Who might have a lab like that, and would be willing to give access to a criminal to use it?"

"Most likely one of the Syndicate's higher-end drug labs. No reputable business or university lab would be able to hide something like this unless a bunch of people at high levels did some hiding and cover-ups. I have been looking for that, myself, and right now there are no indications of trouble."

"Right now?" Sheena asked.

The Dynatech security director nodded with a cynical quirk of her lips. "It has happened before, and unfortunately all too often. That is part of why I keep an eye on that sort of thing. Not all of my industry colleagues are trustworthy all of the time, especially when corporate pressure or outside blackmail is involved."

Sheena replied, "Ah, I see. I wonder if that might be what Elf Shot did to anger the Syndicate."

"Misappropriate one of their labs?" Gayle guessed.

"Yeah." Gayle nodded thoughtfully and Sheena turned back to Ms. Coffee. "So… if they commandeered the lab, moved in the equipment, set up and used it to make a vaccine, how long would the vaccine stay good, and how long would it be before the vaccine became effective in the people they injected?"

"If it is a vaccine, it could remain effective for a very long time if kept at the right temperature and conditions. Usually, it takes about two weeks after administration of a vaccine for the patient to produce enough antibodies to be considered safe from the pathogen. But it is equally possible from the data that they are attempting an anti-viral cure."

Gayle mused, "Hmm… either way, the clock may be ticking!"

"Do you think Elf Shot or her employer will need any more equipment or supplies, under this scenario?" Sheena asked.

Coffee shook her head. "No, not if this explains everything. But if they are trying to protect certain people against a virus, and they plan to use the virus in an attack, they may still need to find a way to mass-produce and then spread the virus to the targets, whoever they are."

"We *really* need to find that employer, then."

Gayle nodded.

Sheena asked, "Ms. Coffee, based on what you know, are there any other scenarios that seem possible for this situation?"

The security director chuckled. "Dozens. But, this is the strongest likelihood. You'd still need to know what they were planning to spread and how. Any missing or stolen samples of biological agents might provide clues to both the pathogen and the nature or identity of the person or group behind this plan." Her expression grew serious and more thoughtful. "This is a lot of work, so it suggests something on a fairly major scale."

Gayle felt a buzz against her forearm and glanced down at her wristband. "It's a message from Lieutenant Fowler."

Sheena nodded. Gayle shared the message, "*Elf Shot linked to a kidnapping last week by security video footage. No witnesses, and the main security cameras were fooled by a hacker, but the gals in the crime lab recovered data from an on-camera buffer with help from a local hero. The victim, Walter Herschel, was the COO of an oil pipeline services company. He was going on planned vacation, so he wasn't missed at work for a while. No ransom demands, no claim of responsibility by any group, just gone. There were two other masked assistants with Elf Shot. They drove off in the exec's own car. Stay alert and see if you can find anything. We'll stay in touch.*"

Gayle asked Ms. Coffee, "Any thoughts?"

The security director nodded. "There is a new eco-terrorist group active recently… Feathers of the Raven, they call themselves."

"Feathers of the Raven?" Sheena broke in with a thoughtful frown. "Interesting…."

The Dynatech exec nodded. "Raven is a powerful being or spirit in many cultures. There may be some sort of link there to investigate. They certainly made use of that imagery in explaining how their enemies would become carrion for the ravens."

She continued her explanation. "They started off by issuing threats to anyone connected with the exploitive extraction of the earth's resources—oil companies, logging and paper, chemical industries, financial industry and investment banking, military and government officials responsible for promoting or protecting the exploiters, industry lobbyists… a pretty broad brush of the powers-that-be. Sounds like a populist, power-to-the-people, sustainable development sort of group gone over the edge. Demanded that they change the way they do business in several ways or face increasingly severe consequences.

This guy....," she indicated the kidnapped executive, "showed up as a vocal critic of the group's threats in the media. That seems to have made him a target."

"Where does Dynatech stand on all of this stuff?" Gayle asked.

Coffee stood and paced as she tried to answer that question. "It's complex. Dynatech wants to create medicines that will help humanity. Mostly, we do a good job at that and stay within both the law and the spirit of the law. We do the research and testing, and license the formulas to manufacturers, who provide most of the funding for the research in the first place. Grants from foundations and various governments provide the rest of the money. Those sources of revenue, and a guidance board, set the research priorities. We work on the biggest problems and the best opportunities for profitable treatments for the pharma companies. We have received a lot of criticism for working on 'first world, white people diseases' from people who don't understand how this all works.

She stopped and tapped her fingertips against the surface of the conference table. "What the man on the street doesn't really understand is that real research takes a huge amount of time and money. Even then there are vested interests, government interference, and a whole lot of scientific ignorance that make it harder to find solutions and win approvals. But in the end, the laws of nature set the limits and the scientific method discovers what we can and can't do within those limits. There is no magic pill for anything—it always involves trade-offs. Medicines come with side effects and different people can react differently to the same drug. The cost of doing all this safely comes with the process, and even then it is imperfect. Science doesn't do miracles, though it might seem that way, sometimes. It is impossible to provide effective medicine for every disease and condition without side effects—sometimes fatal—for free to everyone, regardless of what popular opinion might suggest.

She started pacing again. "And, with all the scientific tools and knowledge we have at our disposal, there is tremendous attraction for the unprincipled. There are some people with limited ethics and big egos who would try to use the science for their own aggrandizement. I have personally shut down five 'private, off-the-books' projects at Dynatech in the eight years I've been working here full-time. I have helped the FDA, CDC, and FBSA stop thirteen more situations in the industry and six 'wild' in so-called 'secret labs' of rogue researchers. I have defended the company and its employees against twenty-seven acts of terrorism and assorted federal crimes. I have also provided investigative support to nine additional ethics inquiries. That's what Dynatech pays me to do.

"So, back to your question, where we stand is that Dynatech wants to make a profit using science to do what's right, helping the world in the process. Terrorists and self-righteous crusaders might label us an evil corporation because they don't understand how this all works, but we have people dedicated to the search for cures and preventions for all kinds of diseases and debilitating conditions. And, some more exploratory research into safely enhancing human potential, too. And at least we're privately held, so we don't have additional direct pressure from the Street or its analyst community. With all of that said, we would be happy to prevent the bad guys from hurting people and destroying our property or anyone else's."

Gayle grinned and admitted, "That was way more than I was asking for, but thanks! I can definitely understand the pressure you must be under."

Ms. Coffee blushed slightly. "My apologies."

The green-clad hero waved away her discomfort. "No worries. We're here to help."

Gayle looked back at Sheena. "So, it sounds like we have some possibilities."

"Right." Sheena nodded. "Check for Syndicate labs or other facilities under inappropriate use. Check out this Feathers of Raven organization. See if we can find the kidnapped exec...."

"If this is all linked," pointed out Ms. Coffee, "then the absence of a ransom demand may mean that he is intended as a test subject, with his corpse to be displayed as a warning."

Sheena raised her eyebrows with a worried look as Gayle nodded. "That would be the terrorist way, all right," Gayle agreed.

"If I can be of any assistance," Ms. Coffee offered, "by all means let me know. And, if you need another meta working with you, backup, anything... give me a call."

Gayle grinned as Sheena blinked. The singer asked, "Are you registered?"

The security director nodded. "Just call me Coffee. I don't usually do 'hero work,' as such, but I can when the need comes up. This job and the extra investigations usually offer enough excitement." She smiled less formally, her corporate demeanor slipping for a moment. "And I am definitely a fan of your work, Gayle."

"What? The hero stuff, or the music?" Gayle asked with a pleased grin.

"Both."

Sheena laughed and shook her head. "Another Gayle Force fan!"

Gayle grinned even wider. "Hey, no problem! I like people! Especially nice, capable ones!" To the security director, she said, "Any time, Coffee. If you can find out anything more with what we've shared, or if you just want to chat or get together, here's my number." She beamed her contact information to her device. Sheena did likewise.

Coffee gave Sheena a curious look. "Does your husband know you stopped by?"

She shook her head. "I wasn't sure until earlier this morning where we'd be going today. Dynatech was likely, but I didn't want to intrude on his first day here with a personal visit."

The security director relaxed. "Oh, okay. He and Doctor Dawson are headed out together. Probably going to get dinner."

Sheena cocked her head. "How do you know that? I didn't even see you look at a device or anything!"

Coffee tapped her temple by the corner of her right eye. "Retinal display. One of the handy little augmentations Dynatech has provided, along with the rest of the experimental bioware."

"Bioware?"

"Like cybernetic implants and enhancements, but biologically grown, tissue matched, and worked into my body more organically. This is actually how I paid for college, as a research subject, and I've been happy to work for the company ever since."

Gayle made a low whistle of appreciation. "Nice! If it all works pain-free, of course."

Coffee nodded. "I have been one of the fortunate ones. Everything we've done has fit perfectly, been integrated perfectly, and been almost completely natural for me to use. My phenotype is an adaptable one—only six percent of the population has this combination—and they really liked my psych profile, so we've had a good match."

"We should compare notes, when you get a chance," Gayle suggested. "Sheena's got a law enforcement background and the powers of an ancient Sumerian goddess. And, well… you know what I can do!"

The Dynatech security director smiled warmly. "Get through the rest of your evening and suggest a time at your convenience. It would be fun. Let me walk you out."

Coffee walked with Sheena and Gayle back out through the lobby and shook their hands. "Let's keep in touch. If anything appears that might be helpful, I'll be in contact."

"Thank you!" replied Sheena as Gayle nodded. "Have a great evening!"

As they left the building and walked down the path, Gayle remarked, "That seemed like a pretty cool visit. Clues, progress with Elf Shot, and maybe a new friend!"

Sheena nodded. "Yeah. Does this happen often to you?"

Gayle grinned and shook her head. "No, not really all that often at all. I might pick up a new heroing contact, but things just kind of fell in line today."

"Maybe it's a bit of good luck after all the dead ends."

"Well, whatever the case, I'll take it!"

"Me, too!" Sheena glanced around. More people were leaving from the employee parking lot on the other side of the building. "Back home?"

"Well… we stopped a robbery, visited Dynatech, found clues, et cetera… I'm hungry."

"Then I vote for takeout!" With a burst of energy and a flurry of her wings, Sheena launched herself into the air with Gayle right behind.

Chapter 16 – Blood for Oil, Blood for Power

Walt Herschel moaned again weakly. He felt like he was burning up, and the sweat just kept beading up and rolling down his forehead as he turned his head from side to side on the table. The rest of his body was tied down securely with plastic restraints. It had been chilly at the beginning, dressed only in the red surgical scrubs they had put him in. Now, he alternated between chills and waves of fever. The oil company executive had no idea how long he had been in this concrete cell. Long enough to come down with the flu, though. How long did that take to incubate; two, maybe three or four days? It must have been in the stuff they puffed in his face when they had brought him here.

Surely someone would miss him by now. The terrorists had said that they were keeping his wife safe but isolated at home. He hoped Marta was all right. She was strong, he knew, but she would be worried about him. He wondered for the hundredth time what these people were going to do to him. All he had seen since the strange pointy-eared woman had tranquilized him and shoved him into the back of his car were people in biohazard gear. After he came down with these symptoms, that began to make sense, even though they would tell him nothing specific. Was he supposed to be some kind of walking biological bomb to be used against innocent people? Would someone figure out that he was gone in time to rescue him? Had the terrorists made any demands? He just didn't know, and with the fever raging it was hard to concentrate on anything for more than a couple of minutes at a time.

His innards cramped up again and he groaned in dreadful anticipation. He didn't have anything left in his stomach to bring up at this point, but the diarrhea was terrible. They kept the IV drip going to keep him from losing too much fluid, but this whole thing was just pure misery. He just didn't have the energy to fight or even protest anymore, not that it had done any good when he had. With the cramps, he kept tasting blood, and he wondered what was happening to him yet again.

He barely registered the door opening and the attendants coming in to do whatever they were going to do to him. Walt's insides convulsed and spots were swimming across his vision. He heard one of the attendants say from behind the hood, not to him, but to the other one, "Remember the oil." He wondered what that was supposed to mean as they turned him on his side with another bout of heaves. More spots in his vision and blood in his mouth and nose. He cried out, wondering when this torture would end.

"He's into stage three," the scientist informed his boss. "Severe hemorrhagic manifestation."

"Ah, then it is working," Blighthawk replied calmly. His voice rasped, "Blood for oil."

"Yes, sir," the scientist agreed, nodding. "My kids will be avenged."

The corrupter nodded with satisfaction. He stood apparently unprotected from the hazards beyond the door. The field clean room they had set up in an abandoned factory basement would contain the contamination of their unwitting test subject, but no hazmat suit would either fit or last long on Blighthawk's strange physique. He was immune, anyway, and was more concerned about not getting his own fluids all over the makeshift lab. "This is the point where I would put my hand on your shoulder and console you, but that would waste your hazard suit."

"I'll consider the word for the deed, sir. Thank you."

"You're welcome, James. This is a hard thing we do, but it is necessary, and it will be delivered only to the completely unrepentant. They will take us seriously, from now on. They will change their ways, or they will all end up like this."

"It's actually a stroke of genius, sir, making the virus mutate through three separate stages. I still don't really get how you managed to make that work, but it's inspired!"

"Magic, James. It isn't possible, but for Raven's power. A controlled, polymorphic virus? Magic."

The scientist went over the virus' characteristics again with admiration. "First stage, a normal rhinovirus like the common cold with mild symptoms and spreading quickly. Second stage, an influenza variant, but only morphs into that stage if the patient supports the corrupt order, in general. Avoids ecological patriots. Third stage, a hemorrhagic fever that only appears if the patient actively supports the corrupting power structure. Leaves everyone else alone in stage one or two. Brilliant!"

"Thank you. And with the virus progression dependent on the individual himself deciding his own fate? It *is* elegant, isn't it?" Blighthawk smiled wryly.

"And I'm still working on the cure for the second and third stages, sir, as you requested. Are you sure that we should wait for that to be done, sir? Every passing hour makes it more likely that we will be discovered by the powers-that-be. And the Syndicate probably wants their lab back, too."

"Yes, I want the cure. For one thing, I want to be able to offer it if someone important and influential does have a change of heart. But more importantly, I don't want to subject the innocent to any mistakes. Nothing in this life is certain. I want to be as prepared as possible."

"All right, sir. Also, the advanced bioreactor we acquired has been working well. We have close to one hundred and fifty canisters ready now."

"Good. We are more than halfway there. High density traffic hubs, like airports, train stations, and cruise ships, will give us the reach our limited numbers cannot provide. With thousands of people acting as carriers, spreading it across the globe, the outbreak will be complete. Now that we know the virus works, we are waiting only for the cure. I think we can start distributing the virus canisters and sending our volunteers off to their targets. But we must time the release carefully. If it doesn't spread globally at the correct rate, some very clever doctors and healers will find a way to defeat it too soon, and all this work will be wasted."

"The sooner the better, sir."

Blighthawk sighed and mopped at a stray drip of oily fluid that had spattered the scientist's console. "Yes, but we'll make sure we're fully prepared, first. Raven only needs to feed on the corpses of the guilty. We can take our time getting the anti-viral cure right for the sake of the innocent. This plan will come together soon enough, you can be sure of it."

The garage door rolled up. Elf Shot stood at the loading dock with a sour expression on her face. The night was dark and silent, and the fun had been over too quickly. She touched the transmit button on her headset. "Bring in the truck. The area is secure."

"Are all the guards down?" asked her driver over the radio.

Her lip curled with cruel satisfaction. She glanced over at the twitching security guards and warehouse workers. Each lay on the floor where she had shot them, fluttering blobs of darkness surrounding each of them like a parasite, slowly draining their souls. It was actually too easy for one of her abilities, but at least her newest arrows were providing some entertainment. "Yes. They'll soon be wishing I had killed them, as the Dark Ones torment their waking dreams."

A hooded man garbed entirely in black with a mask over his face and a calf-length black cloak across his back verified the readings on the barcode scanner as he bent and checked the last tag. From beneath his hood, he said, "These are the crates, Your Ladyship. Everything you wanted."

"Excellent," she purred. She switched the channel on her headset. "Vincent, report!"

From a different part of the city, the ready answer came back, "It's here. I'm just waiting for you, Your Ladyship. My location is secure and everything is quiet. Whenever you're ready, jump to my beacon."

"Very well. Expect me momentarily." She cut the transmission. The unremarkable delivery truck had backed up to the dock and her team was loading the crates. Security was down, the escape route was clear, her obligation to the oilbird was fulfilled. She could pursue her own goals.

Elf Shot jumped down from the dock and strode a few paces out into the night. The warehouse parking lot was silent and still. Nothing threatened. "Follow the plan," she commanded. The black-clad thieves nodded and kept working.

The villainous archer made a complex gesture with her free hand and a black circle appeared upright beside her like a door in the air. She stepped through it and was gone.

"Everything is in readiness, your Ladyship," the thief whispered.

Elf Shot looked around the corner. The vault stood open. Two museum employees were blindfolded, gagged, and tied to chairs in the entryway to the secure storage area. They were either drugged or unconscious, judging by their lack of movement. The thief, Vincent, was merely a blur in the shadows behind her.

"Cameras?" she asked imperiously.

"Fooled by illusion."

"Sensors?"

"Showing only what they are allowed to detect."

"The Arama Hallada?"

"The top box in the stack, ready for you to claim it, Your Ladyship."

She sniffed with pleased surprise. "This is too easy, Vincent!"

He shrugged. "If you say so, your Ladyship. I have merely taken care of all the details that are unworthy of your notice. The act of claiming your prize is for you alone. I assure you that the planning and execution of this little acquisition was no trifling matter, if it will help you feel the worth of what you are about to take into your hands. The dagger coming to this city and specifically to this museum on loan was a stroke of luck. The rest, as you can see, is simply a matter of careful attention to detail. You provide the opportunity, I clear away the distractions, and you get what you wish. As always." He bowed respectfully to her.

She inclined her head as if to dismiss the difficulty. "So be it. Time to take my prize."

Elf Shot walked casually into the vault. The thief followed. She strode up to a reinforced aluminum shipping case atop a stack of other crates. It was unsealed, but latched. With a nod, she opened the case. Inside in a specially fitted foam cutout was a carefully-wrapped knife. She lifted out the inner package. Wrapped in red silk, it was old, ornate, and beautifully curved, with a blade like pure silver. The hilt had an eagle's head in gold with ruby eyes, and a guard shaped like wings. It felt good in her hands.

"The Arama Hallada. From the ancient executioner down through the years to my own possession," the villain breathed. "And with it, the receptacle I need to regain the stolen powers."

"As you say, your Ladyship."

She held the knife up to the soft light of the vault and admired it. With a wicked grin, she said, "Her blood will flow, and I will fix this error that has wasted so much of my time. And then my enemies shall know what it truly means to be hunted. As they fall, my place will be assured in the court of the Dark Ones!"

"Perhaps you mean to lead the Wild Hunt, my Lady?" Vincent breathed in surprise.

She nodded smugly. "You have guessed it correctly, Vincent." The thief bowed deeply with even greater respect. "The oilbird misses the significance of all this, but you got it immediately."

"Such power, my Lady! I only hope that I will continue to be of meaningful service to you."

"Perhaps, Vincent. Only time will tell." With prize in hand, she summoned her exit and disappeared again into the night.

Chapter 17 – The Scenes of the Crimes

"I thought you ladies would like to see this," Lieutenant Fowler said quietly.

Sheena stifled a yawn and nodded. "Thanks, Detective." She looked over at the EMTs working on the victims. They looked worried and frustrated and far more alert than she felt at two in the morning. "What's the matter with them?"

"Got hit with some kinda arrow, but very little in the way of wounds. Instead, it put 'em asleep and it's giving 'em nightmares. Bad ones." He sighed. "They've called for a specialist. I don't know when he can get here, though."

Gayle looked at Sheena. "You want to try? Maybe you could reverse the effect off of them."

She nodded. "I'll give it a shot."

Sheena walked over to the nearest stretcher. The guy was one of the warehouse workers—a middle-aged Italian-American with thinning hair and bushy eyebrows. He was twitching and mumbling erratically in his sleep. His forehead was creased with anxious lines. A faint aura of darkness flickered across his body. The medical responders had removed the arrow and bandaged the puncture wound to his chest muscle below the collarbone. There wasn't much blood on the man's shirt, which Sheena found odd. "Can I see the arrow?" she asked.

"Here." The EMT held up a clear plastic evidence bag containing the arrow. The arrow was black. Not painted black, but made of something black. The feathers and shaft were all a dull black. There was no head to the arrow. Sheena looked closely at the end of the shaft where the head should be.

"No arrowhead in the wound, right?" she asked. The tech shook his head. The bag was closed, but not sealed, yet. Sheena opened it and took a cautious sniff. "Oh!"

"What?" the EMT asked anxiously. "What's wrong?"

"Nothing... exactly. I recognize this, that's all. This is definitely Elf Shot's arrow."

"What can we do? We can get them on the stretchers, but they aren't coming around. They seem completely unresponsive, and they won't wake up. And there's that dark... uh, glow on them."

"I can try to take him back to before he was hurt," Sheena offered. "I'm not sure if this will work, but it's worth a shot, and I'm sure it won't hurt him further."

The EMT looked confused. Gayle finished her quick look around and came over to watch. Sheena explained, "I can heal by making the body or the wounded parts 'remember' when they weren't hurt. That fixes the problem. With most things, at least."

"Hey, that sounds good to me. Give it a shot," the tech agreed.

Sheena concentrated for a count of fifteen, centering herself and relaxing to "feel" the time currents. Then, smoothly and deliberately, she waved her hand in a small spiral over the man's wound. Golden mist flowed from her into the wounded warehouse worker. He tossed and turned rapidly, as if he was trying to escape or break free of something. She frowned and moved her hand a few inches above his body, feeling where the magic or poison of the villain's arrow had buried itself.

"Heart and head, both," she said softly. Gayle nodded as she looked on. "I think I can do it, though." Sheena made the spiral motion with her left hand over the man's chest and then held her hand steady while she repeated it with her right hand over his forehead. A swirl of golden mist poured out like vaporous clouds and wrapped around his entire body. He stopped twitching on the stretcher and lay more comfortably. The dark aura was much easier to see when contrasted with the golden light. The malevolent darkness flickered and lost its hold on the man, becoming dimmer rapidly and then disappearing. He opened his eyes with a start.

"Where am I?" he gasped.

"At work. In the warehouse," Sheena answered. "You're safe."

The man let out a deep breath and sighed. Then, he sat up and quickly began looking at his arms and legs. "The bites! No... no bite marks. God, what a horrible dream! But... you're sure I'm okay? These rat things were chasing me all over a graveyard and every time I thought I found a place to rest and get away, they'd jump out at me again."

Sheena nodded, "Yes, you're okay, sir. You're back in the real world. How's the shoulder?"

He rolled his shoulder twice. "Fine. Is that where I got hit? I remember that red-haired elf lady shooting arrows. And one hit me, and then... and that's all I remember before the nightmare. The arrow did that to me?"

"Yes, sir. That's what it looks like. You'll be okay, I think. I need to go help the others, too."

"Oh! Okay, sure. Please, yeah... help my buddies." He relaxed back onto the stretcher while the EMT checked his vitals again and made notes.

"Not bad, Sheena!" Gayle offered. "Nice job!"

"Thanks, but I have to get the rest of them up, too."

"How's the drain on your energy? Is this tapping you out, or anything?"

She shook her head. "No, it just takes some concentration. It's not really... hard, I guess, but it is a lot trickier than the regular healing currents. I have to make sure I'm touching the right thing with this, if that makes sense."

"Heck, I'm just glad you can do it at all. This isn't a simple effect she's caused with those arrows."

"Yeah, me, too." Sheena got to work on the other victims. Lieutenant Fowler called Gayle over.

"Hey, Gayle, you won't believe this...."

"What?"

"We've got a robbery from the Venture City Museum of Fine Art, too. It looks like this was a simultaneous hit. But, get this... it also looks like Elf Shot."

"Huh? How come?"

"You know how we got the camera data from that garage kidnapping? Off the memory buffer?"

"Yeah, I remember you telling me how the gals in the lab pulled that one off. It sounded like a special thing, though. Did they do it again?"

"Yes they did. Or, she did, anyway. Essie's her name. She's the analyst on duty. As soon as the museum alarm went off, she tapped the security feeds and did the memory capture. The cameras and sensors at the museum were fooled the same way the garage cameras were, and Essie just pulled the real data out of the hardware, somehow. Clear video of Elf Shot walking into the collections vault. Not much of an image of the guy who did all the work, though. He must be a real pro. Anyway, they only took one thing—an ancient Turkish dagger that just came into the museum on loan. The staff hadn't even prepped it for display in the exhibit, yet."

"A dagger?" Gayle didn't like what she was hearing.

"Yeah. Something called the 'Arama Hallada,' if that means anything to you."

Gayle shook her head absently and chewed her lower lip. "No, no clue. But I think it's going to be very important." She glanced over at where Sheena was finishing up on another victim.

Eddie followed her gaze. "You think that's what Elf Shot needs to do her power stealing thing?"

Gayle sighed. "I'll find out, but my gut says it is. I'd better tell her." She ambled slowly over to the stretchers. No sense disturbing Sheena's concentration before she finished bringing the people out of effects of the nightmare arrows. Still, the slight delay wasn't going to make the news any easier to deliver.

"Okay, so if what you're telling me is true, she now has a weapon that might be what she needs for a ritual to kill me and take my powers," Sheena said calmly. She considered that for a moment. "What else do we know? For certain, not guessing."

"The recovered camera data from the museum shows Elf Shot," Lieutenant Fowler added.

"You're sure that this evidence is reliable?"

The detective nodded. "Yes. Our analyst's work has been on target and corroborated by physical evidence on other cases; she's solid. We may find more evidence at the museum."

"Good. Can I get a look at the scene before a bunch of people get to it?" Sheena asked. "With so much activity going on with the emergency response, this place was pretty useless by the time I got here. No tracks left to find. Maybe the museum will give me something to work with."

"Yeah, and they will have more info on what that thing is, too," he added. "I'll let them know to hold up on disturbing the scene for you as an outside expert." He stepped aside to make a call.

"We need to know more about that dagger, but this really doesn't change anything," Sheena told Gayle. She turned over the possibilities in her head. "We've been assuming that she would figure out what it would take, and this is just a part of it. It may be the final piece or just one ingredient. Either way, I'm still in danger. Not more danger or less than before."

"Dang, you're taking this calmly!" Gayle marveled.

Sheena shrugged. There was an edge to her voice when she replied, "What else can I do? It's not like I don't already know that she's trying to kill me. But, she has to catch me alive, first. That gives me the edge. This is going to come down to her and me, and I'm determined to win. If I'm going to catch her, I need a trail to follow. This might get us closer to predicting where we can find her. That's the goal—hunting her down and bringing her to justice—and I'm going to stick to it."

"I suppose you're right."

Sheena pressed her lips tightly together and scowled in frustration. "I need clues, a scent to track… something. Let's head to the museum. And, can we call one of our real experts? A mage you can trust? One of the Titans, maybe?"

"Yeah, I'll call Leo. Sir Vincent Leo, that is. We haven't talked to him before, because he's been out hunting down some of the Ancients' supernatural creatures, but he's back in town and he's the best friendly mage we've got for this sort of thing. I got a message from him just before you and Eric turned in for bed."

"Not Arcanus, or Grey Bull? And, who are these Ancients? You've mentioned them a couple of times."

Gayle shook her head. "We need someone who is more than just a theorist or researcher, and who is actually a caster. Leo is an elf, besides, and that can't hurt, considering who we're talking about."

"Another elf." Sheena raised a skeptical eyebrow.

"Really, truly."

"All right, fine. Why not? And the Ancients?"

"A group of mystic troublemakers who once ruled an ancient empire through arcane magic. Now, they are some sort of secret cabal. The original wizards or mages—or whatever you call them—never actually died out. Instead, they have been possessing new bodies down through the centuries. They keep trying to get enough power or whatever it is that they need to reclaim their ancient thrones. That seems to involve things like kidnappings, thefts of magic artifacts, summoning monsters from who knows where to kill their enemies… typical dark magical conspiracy stuff."

"So, what's stopping them? Why haven't they won already?"

"Leo told me once that the big reason that they haven't succeeded already is because there are so many mystic factions fighting each other from the shadows. So, it's the Ancients against the Coven of the Nine Sisters, against the Circle of Thorns, against the Atlanteans, against the faerie, with factions sometimes inside of each of those groups, and so on. Some of the factions are on speaking terms with others, and some aren't. I think that the Ancients have some sort of ally-type connection with the dark faerie court, or fey lands, or whatever."

"'Or whatever?' You don't do much with those guys, I take it."

Gayle shook her head. "Never really got sucked into all that stuff."

"Okay. But this Leo guy has?"

"Right. And if Elf Shot is connected to either the Ancients or the fey in some way, he is the most likely to be able to help us. He's the best source of information about what she can do with that dagger. If he doesn't know right off, he'll know where to go to find out."

"And he won't just be guessing, like some of those other mages."

"Right. He's about as scientific as you can get as a spellslinger." Gayle paused and pouted slightly. "And we weren't really giving those others much to go on, you know. This is a solid lead."

Sheena snorted. "We're making that assumption. It is still possible that she stole that dagger for an employer."

Gayle blinked in surprise. "Oh. Yeah. I guess that's possible."

Sheena shrugged. "Personally, I think you're right and she was after it for herself, but we don't know for sure. Anyway, we're wasting time." She walked over to check with Lieutenant Fowler on the name and address of the museum, and gave it to her armband device for navigation. Gayle followed. Within moments, they were in the air and headed toward their next stop with the city lights passing by beneath them in the night.

"Do you smell that?" Sheena asked.

Gayle sniffed. "Um... you mean me? The wilted lettuce smell? Sorry. I'm tired."

"No, not that. Or the dusty museum smell, either. Elf Shot's perfume."

Gayle sniffed again with a look of concentration. "Uh... maybe? I can't tell."

Sheena turned her head from side to side, sniffing and scanning the floor. Lieutenant Fowler's instructions had been good. The police investigators had waited for her. The scene was mostly undisturbed. She spotted signs on the carpeted floor that matched what she was looking for. "Yes, definitely traces of her perfume. And here...." She knelt and pointed. "The same women's boot marks I picked up at the warehouse. Pretty faint on carpet like this, but just enough of an impression to register."

She rose and walked carefully to one side of the tracks and toward the vault. She paused before the vault door and looked back at the police sergeant. "Two museum people? Tied to... no, duct-taped to chairs?"

The sergeant's eyebrows nearly leaped off his forehead. "Yeah! But, we moved the chairs out when we cut 'em free! How'd you know?"

"Scuff marks, a shred of the tape strand, smell of duct tape where I wouldn't expect it here, and a hint of some chemical. Probably chloroform or an equivalent, I'd guess." She pointed at the spots where she could catch the barest hint of the clues she mentioned.

"Huh. You want to check the chairs or door for fingerprints or anything?"

Sheena shook her head. "Elf Shot just showed up and walked into the vault, judging by the easy line of her tracks. No fighting or anything strenuous. But, you just gave me an idea. Please stand back. I'm going to summon a very large wolf." The sergeant quickly stepped back to the opposite wall. Gayle also gave her friend some more room.

Sheena summoned Sharur. The demon wolf almost filled the hallway. The smell of heated iron wafted about, spread further by the gentle breeze blowing around Gayle. "I am here," the wolf intoned.

"We are hunting Elf Shot. Here is her scent, and her tracks." Sheena pointed out both trails of evidence to Sharur. "What else can we learn here?"

The wolf turned and sniffed at the floor, then took several steps around the corner. The police officers moved back as he did so. Sharur stopped and sniffed the air with a puzzled look. "Her tracks go no further, and there is the scent of sick forest."

"Sick forest?" Sheena asked. "Of the cedars, or something else?"

He shook his massive head. "Of something else. Willows, elms, bushes, dampness, some oaks, mushrooms, toadstools, decay, rot. Scum on stagnant water. But nothing on the ground; only in the air."

"Did she maybe come through that sick forest to get here without touching it?"

"Yes. There is also the scent of magic. A sick sort of magic that matches the forest."

Sheena nodded. "Okay, I've seen her do that trick once before, I think. She opened up some kind of doorway and stepped through it when she left after setting our clinic on fire."

"That fits with her file, too. She can use a sort of magic doorway or portal to get around," Gayle added.

"Anyone else, Sharur? Can you tell if anyone was with her?"

The wolf sniffed again. "Yes. A male human. The scent is quite faint, and mostly masked by a metallic smell. And these people, here. I assume you do not mean them. And two men, drugged. And older scents from many hours ago that I assume are not of interest."

"Yes, good. Remember the scents of Elf Shot and the male human."

"Of course. Your female prey left the same way she arrived, but from that metal place." The wolf pointed his nose toward the vault.

"What about the male?"

Sharur swiveled his head back toward the stairs at the end of the hall. "He left the way you came in."

"Excellent. Could you track him?"

"Yes."

"All right. Let me take a good look at the vault, first." Sheena went back to the vault and the now-empty metal case while Sharur remained where he was. She sniffed the air again and studied the outside of the case before opening it with a pocket multi-tool. She read the labels on and inside the case, which the villain had left behind. Another close sniff of the case and she nodded to herself.

"Well?" Gayle asked. "Any conclusions?"

"Yes. But hardly earth-shattering. She took the knife. She already knew what she was after, the other man prepared the scene and left the knife for her to remove from the case, for some reason. She took it and left. Presumably, so did the other guy. The knife did not spend much time in this case, I would guess. Not much of a scent and very little lasting impression on the padding, so it would not have rested inside for long. And I can smell the 'sick forest,' too, as Sharur put it."

"Okay. That's good, I guess. Now what?"

Sheena emerged from the vault. "Now we let the sergeant and the rest of the team get on with their work." She turned to the police and museum manager. "Thanks, guys. You're sure nothing else is missing, misplaced, changed, or added?"

The sergeant looked at the museum manager, who blinked in surprise. "No, no, nothing else is missing. But, I hadn't thought to check for anything added or moved. I'll make sure to do that. There's nothing obvious, but I came right in here when I arrived."

"Let's get started on a quick inventory, then," the police sergeant told the manager. "Nelson, go with him. The rest of us will get rolling on the evidence collection. Uh, Shee'na, can we get your statement before you go?"

"Sure. If I was more awake, I would have remembered to record the whole thing." She rubbed her eyes. "Sharur, if you can, follow the trail and let me know where it leads. Don't let him know he's being followed."

"As you command, Mistress." He faded away into mist and stalked down the hall, an insubstantial outline as big as an ox. When he reached the stairway door, he simply walked right through it.

The rest of the people in the museum basement, including Gayle, stared in amazement. Gayle turned back to Sheena. "That was... different!" she said with a delighted grin.

"Shanikali said he would be my most trusted and clever companion, or something like that. I've had no reason to doubt her," Sheena replied. A big yawn managed to escape her lips. "Let me get that statement out of the way before I start forgetting things from fatigue."

"Uh, yeah. Right," the sergeant mumbled.

"I can't believe I'm actually getting up and going to work at an office," Eric complained.

"Mmph," Sheena muttered incoherently into her pillow. She twitched her left wing over her head to shade out the morning sun slanting in through the window.

"Oh, sorry!" her husband apologized quickly. He hastened over to adjust the blinds, throwing her back into shadow. Eric leaned over and kissed the top of her head. "I'll see you later. Have a good day. Love you!"

Sheena's mind drifted between sleep and wakefulness for a while after Eric left. Somewhere in that lazy wandering, the smell of the cedars on a cool summer breeze drew her back into a peaceful dreamland. She nestled down into the blankets with a hint of a smile on her face. In the cedar forest of the gods, the branches swayed high above her. The earth beneath her smelled clean and cool, just the way it should. She picked up a handful of dirt from the ground and left it run through her fingers. The sun crept higher in the sky. It felt good to walk among the trees, up and down the rocky hills. The scent of the forest shifted to something heavier and more metallic. She looked around. Sharur sat on his haunches behind her, tongue hanging out, waiting. She stretched and bowed to him, arms and wings counterbalanced in a graceful, synchronized motion.

"Good morning, Sharur," she said to the demon wolf.

"It is morning, Mistress. I have news for you."

"Thank you." She waited.

"News of your world," he added after a lengthy pause.

"Yes? I am listening."

He grinned at her, tongue lolling with canine amusement. "You must wake up, or it will do you no good."

Sheena's eyebrows rose in realization that she was still asleep. "Oh." She shook her head and chuckled at herself, then closed her dream eyes and felt with her senses for the boundary of the waking world. She opened her eyes to her bedroom in Gayle's apartment at Riverhaven. Sharur was not there, but there was scant space for him, even in a bedroom as large as the one she and Eric occupied in the luxury high-rise. She extricated herself from the bedclothes and rose from the bed, slipping into a short blue kimono-style robe she had modified.

She tied the belt about her waist and reached around to pull the back piece up past her wings to her shoulders, fastening the buttons to keep it in place. Then, she poked her head out of the bedroom and walked down the hallway to the living room. She heard a shower running from the direction of Gayle's master bedroom. Sharur was lying in the middle of the floor between the living room and the studio beyond, waiting. "Good morning, again, Mistress."

"Good morning again, Sharur. What news?"

"Tracking in this city is far more difficult than in the places of old. Many more smells and distractions. Foul substances with a great stink to cover the natural scents of the quarry. Greater distances to travel. Wagons that move faster than swift horses to carry the quarry away. I will enjoy sharpening my skills here."

"Well, that's a positive, at least."

"I followed the trail of the man, though he tried to hide it. He is skilled." Sheena nodded.

"His trail led to a statue of a hero in a park. There, he disappeared."

"Like Elf Shot did?"

"Yes. His scent was on the hand of the statue, but no further. I smelled a different sort of doorway scent from that of the sickly forest, but the same kind of magic."

"Interesting." Sheena turned over the possibilities in her mind. Sharur waited. "No scent of Elf Shot there, or along the way?"

"None."

She considered further. Hesitantly, she asked, "Can Shanikali stalk prey without being seen or scented?"

"Yes." Her heart thrilled to the answer. She had hoped he would say that.

"Can you show me how?"

"I can try."

"Please, do so."

The next fifteen minutes found Sheena trying to emulate the technique that was so simple for the demon that he could not express it in words. For Sharur, he simply *was* stalking and he virtually disappeared. To Sheena, he changed from "there" to "mostly not-there," but she was not sure how to do the same thing herself. The more she watched him, the better she felt she understood what he was doing, but she still couldn't grasp the feeling or technique or whatever it was that she needed to do. All Sharur could offer as a hint was, "when you start hiding, get your body out of the way."

Gayle emerged from her bedroom dressed in jeans and a green brocade vest laced loosely over an unbleached cotton peasant blouse. Her hair was drying in the sweet lemon-scented breeze and her bare feet were tucked into simple leather sandals. "Morning, guys!" she called cheerfully as she walked past them into the kitchen.

Sheena tried sneaking up on her friend from the living room, moving as quietly as she could. Gayle looked up at her with a curious expression, a box of breakfast cereal in one hand and a jug of milk from the refrigerator in the other. "Umm...? What's up?"

Sheena let out an exasperated noise. "I'm trying to be stealthy. Sharur is trying to teach me, but I am definitely not getting the hang of it."

"Oh. Well, it will come, I'm sure." She made a quick gesture and an aerial servant brought a bowl, spoon, and juice glass to the table where Gayle seated herself.

"If I could figure out how to do this, I could sneak around much more safely, I think." Sheena sat down at the table herself. "I get it, but I just can't... *do* it!" Sheena grumbled.

"Maybe it's like working with the wings," Gayle offered. "The more you try to concentrate on it, the more muddled it gets."

"Yeah, probably. I'll keep working at it. Knowing that it's possible is half the battle."

Gayle ate her breakfast. She said, "I'm guessing you'll want to change before we meet with Leo?"

"Leo? Oh, yeah. That would be good." Sheena looked down at herself in just the robe. Gayle wasn't in costume, so she asked, "Normal clothes?"

"Yep. No need for heroics, just yet."

Sheena nodded and went off to the bedroom to change.

When she returned, Gayle and the demon wolf were talking about how he would fight creatures of air. Sheena listened with curiosity as Sharur explained his tactics.

"If it is a creature or spirit of wind, my teeth will be enough. My nature is fire and metal, and my strength is enough to fight the wind without tricks. If it is a thing of magic, such as you create, I must go after the one controlling it. My teeth will do nothing to the spell that binds it into shape."

"That's what I usually find," Gayle replied. "People and things that I fight can't fight the wind directly. Even magical creatures can't usually hurt the phantom army of air servants or the tornadoes or storm clouds."

"No, faced with an attack like that, I will attack the sorcerer."

"Yep, that seems best. Mmm... What happens when lightning hits you?"

"It may cause me some pain, but most passes through me into the earth beneath my feet."

"You're well-grounded? Nice." Gayle asked Sheena, "All set? I can see if Leo is ready now."

"Yes. Ready when you are."

Sharur made one comment before vanishing. "Mistress, I recommend that you keep practicing. I know that you can do it, but I am sorry that I cannot explain better how to do this thing."

"That's okay, Sharur. I'll figure it out." After he disappeared, she remarked to Gayle that, "It probably involves turning at right angles to reality, or something."

Gayle looked up from her phone. "Speaking of right angles to reality, Leo is available. Are you ready to talk with a real elven mage?"

Sheena grinned. "No time like the present!" Gayle snickered.

Lean. Exceptionally lean, tall, and elegant. That was Sheena's first impression of Sir Vincent Leo, Knight of the Wyvern and elven combat mage. Even in relatively simple clothes—black jeans over deep gray cowboy boots, white shirt with sleeves rolled to mid-forearm, black silk vest with a gold lion tastefully embroidered on the breast—he conveyed a sort of nobility and style that impressed her. His skin was fair, but not too pale, his features strong, but not too rugged. His physique was well-muscled, but again in a lean, rather than brutish, way. He wore his fine golden hair a comfortable medium length that nicely set off his close-trimmed beard. His eyes were of a keen, piercing green of a color more vibrant than normally found in humans, but his expression was relaxed, confident, like a GQ model. And, of course, the long pointed ears were the most obvious evidence that Leo was not of the human race. But beyond the physical appearance, there was that certain... something... in the way he carried himself that just wasn't quite what normal people could manage.

"Good morning, Ms. Gardner, Daughter of Shanikali," Leo said with a bow. His voice had a touch of Texan drawl to it that surprised her. The greeting had a sort of courtly quality in the way he included her incarnation of the goddess as a title. "Gayle has told me of you."

"Good morning, Sir Leo," she replied.

Both of them stood there assessing each other in a polite way while Gayle bustled into the conference room. Sir Leo offered Sheena a seat, tucking it in behind her before taking a chair across the table from her. Gayle had already taken a place at the center of the table and was connecting her electronics to the Titans' computer system. Finishing her task, she activated the room's projection equipment and brought up an image of the stolen dagger. The singer turned her attention to her companions.

"All right, introductions, first. Sheena Gardner, this is Sir Vincent Leo. He is a Knight of the Wyvern, a combat mage, and a member of the League of Titans. He has a great deal of expertise in the politics of the magical and supernatural. He is also an authority on arcane magical theory and its practical applications." She turned to Sir Leo. "Did I leave out anything important?"

"No, that will do well enough, I think."

"And Sir Leo, this is Sheena Gardner, chosen incarnation of the goddess Shanikali, huntress and mistress of the currents of time, guardian of the Beastlands. She is a conservation warden of the state of Wisconsin, a recent guest of Riverhaven, and wife of Eric Gardner, veterinarian. She is also a personal friend of mine. She acquired her powers very recently through contact with an artifact storing the powers of Shanikali, which was contested by the huntress villain known as Elf Shot. Both Sheena and Elf Shot are hunting each other; Sheena to bring the other to justice, while Elf Shot seeks to take Shanikali's powers for herself and dispose of their current host. Any questions?"

The elf grinned mysteriously. "No, you make yourself clear." Sheena shot a questioning glance at her friend.

Gayle ignored the look and smiled cheerfully. "Cool! Now, let's figure out what Elf Shot might be after with the Arama Hallada that she stole last night, and what we might do to protect Sheena and catch the villain."

"The Arama Hallada, mmm? I have not seen that, but I have heard it mentioned once or twice," Leo said smoothly. He tapped at the table and activated a set of desktop controls. "Let's bring up some data on it."

Gayle passed control of the display to him and sat back in her chair to watch him work. Sheena looked on as Leo set up and ran multiple searches on the dagger and related histories, legends, and rumors. The application he was using assembled the data into categories and built a sort of map of the relationships between items. As he worked, more and more icons were added to the map, with the Arama Hallada at the center of many connections. Two other "hubs" on the display appeared, as well. One was related to the subject of magical executions. The other was cryptically labelled "Soul Theft."

"Interesting," the elven mage murmured as his pace slowed. He leaned back with his arms folded and his long legs crossed in front of him at the ankles.

"What is it?" Sheena asked.

He nodded at the display. "The Arama Hallada is a jambiya-style dagger originally forged in or about the year 640 of your Christian era calendar. A secret society of Arab witch hunters created it as the means to strip an infidel Magi's powers during his execution. It was thought that without this extra surety, the most powerful and sly of the Zoroastrian mage priests—those 'Magi'

127

I mentioned—would otherwise be able to use their powers to defeat execution and return to life. Of course, this was mostly superstition. However, among the dozen or so such daggers created, there was one, this one, that was empowered by an actual practitioner of the arcane arts. His name is not known, but several sources point to his skill in enchanting the Arama Hallada with the power to steal the soul of the one slain with the knife. Not only would this prevent the victim from returning, it would also grant his magical powers to the one who dealt the killing blow."

Sheena shivered despite herself. "Does... does a ritual have to go with that?"

The mage shook his head. "That is unknown. Of course, there was a ritual to accompany the execution of the infidel mage, but whether this or a supplemental ritual was required to invoke the power transfer, I cannot say from the research, so far."

"What would you guess?" asked Gayle.

He considered for a long while. "The ritual is probably not required. The soul theft seems like a side-effect, or a means by which the primary purpose of the blade was achieved. On the positive side, at least for present circumstances, only the death blow will rob the victim of her powers. There is no need to fear a scratch or minor wound suddenly leaving the victim without her abilities."

Sheena snorted. "I don't think that will matter much, if they've already lost their life to it!"

Leo smiled slightly and nodded. "An entirely accurate and pragmatic assessment of the situation."

"So, the soul stealing thing isn't for the purpose of driving black magic or anything, right?" Gayle asked.

"Correct," Leo nodded. "That would have been anathema to the early Muslim witch hunters who were, after all, fighting against what they felt was Persian pagan fire-worship."

Sheena asked thoughtfully, "What would this thing do in the hands of an evil, dark fey? Or, one aligned with them?"

Sir Leo chuckled. "Exactly what it was enchanted to do, and no more or less." To her questioning look, he explained, "It is no bane weapon and has no special power inimical to the faerie of any side. At that place and time, the pagan demons were of far more concern to the magically aware Muslims than the mythical fey of northern lands... such as my folk." He quirked a half-smile.

Gayle looked at Sheena. The winged heroine had a look of concentration as she tried to follow a chain of thought. "I have to track her down. It sounds like she doesn't need a specific place or setup to do this power stealing. What can I do to find her and stop her on my own terms, instead of hers?"

"Ah, good question," the elf agreed. He looked at the network map on the display and thought for a moment. "I could enchant something to track the dagger itself, magically. A sort of... compass, as it were."

Sheena nodded. "Good. I think I'm at my best hunting her, and not sitting around waiting for her to strike."

Leo nodded. "Yes, you seem like one who would choose her own future and move toward it." He studied her searchingly for a moment. "Waiting for things to happen to you is in your past, now."

Sheena frowned slightly, then tilted her head hesitantly, trying to interpret what he meant. "All right...."

Gayle asked, "What about Elf Shot's employer? Can we figure out who she is working for?"

"Perhaps. Tell me more," Leo offered.

Gayle and Sheena explained what they knew about the kind of work Elf Shot had been doing, the recent changes to her pattern, and everything they had learned over the past two weeks. The elf listened calmly, stroking his beard. When they were done with their initial relating of the story, he asked about details and additional things that he thought might fill out the picture.

"Well," he said slowly, "I do know that she is not currently working on anything for the Ancients. And, the theft of scientific equipment is certainly not their style."

"That's what I thought," Gayle agreed. "Someone new, maybe?"

"Does the term 'Feathers of the Raven' suggest anything?" Sheena asked.

Leo thought about it and shook his head slowly. "Not from the groups of magical villains we usually encounter. Something about that suggests a crossover, though. Raven is a good lead to investigate, I believe."

"Can you ask around?" Gayle asked him. The mage nodded. "Thanks, Leo. I appreciate it."

"I remain, as always, your devoted servant," he said as he stood and bowed to the singer.

"If only that were true!" she giggled.

Leo winked at her. "Friendship is magic, they say."

"Arrgh! That's terrible! Shoo!" She pretended to chase him out of the conference room as he exited, laughing.

"What was that about?" Sheena wondered aloud to her friend.

"A play on pop culture. He loves puns. Never mind that; we should check in with Eddie on our Syndicate lab lead."

"Oh, yeah... Maybe someone over there will have information for us on whether anyone has lost control of a lab recently. If Elf Shot's boss is going to use the equipment, then whoever it is will need the facilities, like Coffee said."

"Right. And speaking of coffee, I could use a latte," Gayle mused. "Let's visit the Event Horizon restaurant section and see what we can wrangle. They should still be on the breakfast menu, if you want anything."

Sheena nodded and followed.

Chapter 18 – A Night on the Town

"Thanks for showing me around, Eric. This place is amazing!"

"Hey, no problem, Greg. Yeah, Riverhaven is pretty neat." Eric looked around the atrium again and wondered at the chain of events that led to him and Sheena living there. He had gotten permission to show Greg Dawson the residential common areas and Gayle's apartment. With Greg's wife, Melanie, having superhuman abilities, Greg had a natural curiosity about the facilities of one of Venture City's premier metahuman living communities. Gayle had cheerfully agreed to make security arrangements, and Greg just had to go through a brief DNA scan when he arrived with Eric after work.

"Overall, though, Mel keeps a pretty low profile. She's not a registered hero, or anything. We don't need this kind of security." Greg chuckled and shook his head. "But the amenities and living spaces are gorgeous!"

"Doesn't the Department of Defense help out with your situation any?" Eric asked with some curiosity.

He wasn't really surprised when Greg replied, "No comment. But, certainly not like Riverhaven, even if they could." Greg Dawson grinned to take the edge off his response. He had an easy smile. In fact, Eric had found him really easy to get to know. Despite being almost fifteen years his senior, Greg Dawson didn't talk down to him, or to anyone on the team, for that matter. He would challenge facts and conclusions about the research, pushing each of the team members to make sure that they accounted for as many possibilities as possible, but he would always do it in a very collegial way. Eric especially appreciated that Greg and the other medical staff on the team didn't talk down to him because his specialty was in animal medicine, instead of humans. Greg made it a great team to work with.

"Fair enough," Eric snorted. He glanced about at the building interior again. "I like how the security is pretty much tucked into the background. Normally, I can just drive into the residents' parking garage. The system scans the vehicle and passengers on the way and does its verification. It's only if there is someone who isn't already on the cleared list that I have to use the visitor lot, like today."

"I heard that Dynatech is considering that for our campus, too," Greg mentioned. "It would make it a bit more convenient. But, that takes money, and there's always something to spend it on. Better equipment, salary increases, security upgrades, new projects... the list goes on."

"Huh. They seem to do a good job, though. I've been constantly impressed this week."

Greg nodded. "I have to admit, I'm pretty happy there. I think the execs have their heads screwed on pretty straight."

"I can sure appreciate that," Eric agreed. "Running your own independent veterinary practice is one thing, but managing all of that is in a completely different world."

"Yes, and I'm glad I can pretty much focus on the research and project leadership. I'll help steer things to meet what they tell me the corporate goals are, but I'd rather leave the management to the experts."

Eric nodded. He asked, "Are you sure you're okay getting back to your car at Dynatech after dinner? Do you want a ride back over there?"

"No, thanks. I'll just open a call to the car and Mel will zap us through the wireless signal carrier wave, or however that works. Then, I'll just drive home from there."

Eric chuckled, "All right. That's pretty neat. Sheena should be ready in just a couple more minutes."

"Are you guys planning on getting an apartment of your own here?" Greg asked.

Eric thought about it. "Well, I guess we really are staying here, at least for now. I should probably look into it with the building manager."

"If someone is actively going after Sheena, then both of you need a safe place," Greg pointed out. "I hate to say it, but villains just love to target unprotected family members."

Eric nodded grimly. "Yeah, I have thought of that, way more than once."

"That's why Mel got me a charm that protects me from magic, just in case. My phone has a panic button that goes directly to her, too. And she can get to me almost instantly from that with her own abilities. Kinda nice, that way."

Eric scratched his head and wondered, "Mmm, that sounds pretty slick. That makes me think—again—what I should do if Elf Shot showed up?"

Greg shrugged. "Forewarned is forearmed. Having a couple of contingency plans is a good idea."

"Yeah, I just wish there was something I could do to help. I still feel like I'm letting her down, or being a vulnerability, instead of a help."

"Eh, you can't worry about that too much. Think about it this way: she's got a different job than you do. You can't do her job for her, so this is just part of that whole package." He pursed his lips in a cynical expression. "It took me most of a year, myself, to get that into my head after her hostage experience. I mean, I knew it right away, but it took that long to really *get* it."

"Mmm." Eric turned that over in his head for a moment. "Good point."

"You'll figure it out. It's kind of like she's in the military, or the police. There's always this worry that goes with the job, but I can make her job easier by not loading her down with my own anxiety. Might end up being the same for you, but at least Sheena was in law enforcement before all this happened."

Eric chuckled. "Yeah, but the danger scale went way, way up. There's not a whole lot of daily imminent personal risk as a game warden."

"I suppose not," Greg grinned, "but we doctors always think we're right, anyway, so that can't help the process, either!"

They both laughed and waited for Sheena to come down.

"All set for the night?" Gayle asked from the living room.

"Just about. Making sure the shoes match. I don't have much that's dressy, in general. Most of that won't fit anymore with the wings, and I brought even less of it with me here to Venture City. I mean, not that we're really going anywhere dressy, but it would be nice to have everything match." Sheena looked at herself in the mirror and shrugged. The blue sundress looked fine, but she would have liked pockets. "Why does women's fashion always skip the practical stuff, like pockets?"

Gayle laughed. "I have no idea. Tradition? They want to avoid anything breaking the clean lines of their designs? Take your pick."

"I think I need to get some wristbands like yours that I can wear with more normal clothes."

"Remind me tomorrow. We'll get you hooked up." Gayle looked into the guest bedroom where Sheena was finishing up. "Anything new come in while I was out at that commercial shoot today?"

Sheena shook her head. "Eddie and crew are still working the lab angle. He thinks they will have something from a Syndicate contact in another day or two. It's no secret that Elf Shot betrayed them and took out one of the North Docks bosses' headquarters, but getting the location of the labs that guy had running is tricky. They have to get someone who will give up the location without any word getting back to the big bosses or the source ends up dead. No new word on Elf Shot's whereabouts, either, but it's only been a bit less than three days since those last jobs."

"And Leo?"

"He's working on a thing to track the Arama Hallada. It won't take very long, because that is a pretty unique item. He's verified that Elf Shot is not working for the Ancients right now, and that whoever she is working for isn't associated with them, either." She brushed out her hair quickly one more time and tucked it into an elastic ponytail band. "He also discovered that the Feathers of the Raven is not a fey-affiliated group, but that the Unseighlie Court approves of whatever it is that they are doing."

"Okay... is that bad?" Gayle asked hesitantly.

"For now, no, because the Unseighlie Court has not committed any strength to them. But, Leo did say that could change, if the Feathers succeed in their plan. Something about increasing the influence of the Dark Ones, which I did not really understand."

"He didn't explain?"

Sheena frowned slightly and picked up her phone. "No. He basically brushed it off as fey politics that will only matter later."

"So, we have no idea what Elf Shot is up to now."

"Right."

"And you are going out to dinner with Eric and Greg and Melanie Dawson."

"Yeah."

Gayle shook her head. "Far be it from me to caution you against having fun, but just be careful. She's had enough time to figure out how the knife works, if she knew what she was after to begin with. The longer she has that dagger, the greater the chances are that she's started actively hunting you."

"Yeah, I know. I figure that with Melanie and me both, we should be pretty safe."

"Well, stay safe and have fun, then! I'll be at practice until late, probably. I'll have the chance to ask someone about whether anyone in the eco-terrorist underground knows about the Feathers."

Sheena stopped and stared at her in confusion. "At your band practice?"

"Yep! A couple of my guys know some people who know some people, if you know what I mean. I can at least catch up on rumors, and that might get us a lead."

"Okay, all right." Sheena thought about it for a moment and shrugged. "I'll go join the guys in the atrium and we'll head out. Have a good session!"

She slipped her phone into a little sport purse that mostly matched her dress and left the apartment. The floor numbers flashed by as she rode the elevator down to the lobby. She spotted Eric and his boss immediately and made her way out through the security fields to the main atrium. The men were sitting in a trio of comfortable chairs in a small waiting area. Approaching Eric, she leaned over and gave him a kiss on the cheek. "Hello, I'm sorry I kept you waiting."

"You are worth the wait," Eric assured her with a grin. He stood up and introduced her to Greg. "Sheena, this is Greg Dawson, from Dynatech. Greg, Sheena."

"Pleased to meet you, Sheena!" Greg replied with a friendly smile.

"Likewise, Greg." She asked Eric, "We're taking our car, right?"

"Yeah. We'll meet Melanie at Marty's and she'll get him back to his car at Dynatech after dinner. Come on. Let's head out."

The three of them made small talk as they walked out to the Gardners' SUV in the visitor parking lot. Greg was curious about Sheena's duties for the Department of Natural Resources. Eric had already explained enough for him to realize that a conservation warden's job was far bigger than just enforcing hunting and fishing regulations. Sheena was happy to elaborate. When they reached the SUV, Eric helped Sheena into the front passenger seat.

"You're sure you're okay in back?" she asked Greg.

"Oh, I'm fine. There's plenty of room. Plus, you've got to be more comfortable where you don't have to squish your wings against the seat, I'd think."

"Yes, that's true. I just don't want to put you to any trouble. You're the guest!"

"No problem. Don't worry about me." He slid in and buckled himself in behind Sheena.

Eric pulled out of the Riverhaven parking lot and turned north toward the city center. He asked Sheena, "Marty's, right? I can park off Sawyer Street?"

Sheena tried to remember where the garage entry was. "I think so. Gayle and I were flying, so I wasn't thinking about driving in, so much. Want me to check the GPS?"

"No, that's okay. Once we get to the area, I'll find my way."

Sheena nodded and noticed a movement out the windshield, on the right side of the street and ahead most of a block. A wave of panic ripped through her. "Oh, crap! It's Elf Shot!"

The villainous archer stepped out on the street side of a light post and loosed an arrow at the Gardners' vehicle. Sheena's mind froze. Try to slow the arrow, or speed the SUV, or summon a pet, or...? Too late to make a decision, the arrow hit somewhere in the lower front of the vehicle with a peculiar metallic crumpling sound. Then it exploded.

The truck bucked like it had hit a wall. Fire and heat and metal slammed into the three of them from below. The whole SUV flipped over backward and came crashing down on its roof. The airbags popped and deflated, cushioning some of the impact, but doing nothing about the explosion. As Sheena's head cleared from the initial shock she felt heavy and her left side hurt all over. Her ears were ringing badly and her vision was still swimming. "Ow, damn." She glanced to her left at Eric, who was wincing, but certainly alive. She called out, "Greg? You okay?"

There was no response.

"Damn!" Sheena tried to look over her shoulder but a spasm locked her neck halfway through. "The heck with this," she muttered and called on the time currents for a pool of healing on all three of them. The golden motes of light poured forth and she felt her injuries vanish. Eric gasped suddenly.

"You okay, Eric?" She asked. "Greg?"

Still no response from the back seat.

This time, she was able to see Greg dangling upside down, like they all were, in his seatbelt, but he was unconscious. His left arm had several big gashes that she could see, and the same with his left leg. His chest was covered with blood, as well. "Damn it!" Sheena spat. "That didn't heal him at all! What's the problem?!?"

"We've got to get out of the car," Eric urged her. "Psycho chick is out there!"

"Crap, yeah. You get Greg, and I'll cover you." With difficulty, she popped the release on her seatbelt and fell to the roof of the car. Cramped, almost upside down, but orienting herself, she took a breath and summoned Sharur outside the vehicle. "Protect us, Sharur!" she called out.

"I hear and obey, Mistress," came the familiar rumbling voice. Sheena also heard a squawk of surprise from the elven huntress not far from the turtled SUV. The demon wolf cautioned her, "Your chariot is aflame."

A ferocious growl and then a hunting howl erupted from Sharur as he leaped toward Elf Shot. Sheena tried to open the door, but it was too badly crumpled to move. She fumbled the vehicle escape tool from the glove box, mentally thanking the sheriff for insisting that even the DNR officers in his county carry emergency tools. "Breaking the glass! Mind your eyes!" she warned. She tried to shield the rest of the front compartment with her wings as she wound up and smashed the point of the tool into the corner of her side window. The window shattered. She slithered out on her stomach and jumped to her feet.

The vehicle was facing backward in the direction they had come from. The traffic had stopped and begun to pull to the side and around the SUV. Halfway down the block, Sharur faced the pointy-eared archer, advancing and snapping at the villain a step at a time. Elf Shot was wreathed in the billowing armor of darkness Sheena had seen the first time they had met. Several black arrows were sticking out of the demon wolf's shoulder and chest, but he seemed to be suffering no ill effects. As Sheena turned to try the passenger door, Elf Shot summoned a black doorway and jumped through it. Sharur's teeth almost caught the archer's leg, but she escaped through the portal.

Sheena caught a flicker from the other side of the street on the roof of a three-story apartment building. Elf Shot had stepped through to a new location midway between Sharur and the burning SUV. "Sharur! Up there!" she pointed. She crouched and yanked at the door handle, but the frame to that door was deformed, too. "How're you doing, Eric?"

"Uh… I don't know," came the reply from inside the flipped vehicle. Sheena could see that some parts of the engine compartment were still on fire.

Sheena pointed at the driver of a car stopped behind the accident scene and made eye contact. "You! Call 911 and report this, now!" The man nodded and fumbled out his phone. Sheena nodded at him and the others. "Stay back! Stay safe!" she called out. As she turned, a black arrow grazed the SUV, barely missing her wing. "Damn!" she exclaimed and summoned her bow.

Sheena drew an arrow, popped up over the side of the SUV, and ducked back again just as quickly to avoid another of Elf Shot's black arrows. Having located her opponent, she stepped to the side and fired. It was at least seventy-five yards, but only the rippling black waves of the elven archer's magical protection stopped the tungsten-tipped war arrow from penetrating her leather tunic. Without waiting to see the full effect of her first shot, Sheena drew and loosed another arrow, then crouched behind the SUV again. Her arrow scraped Elf Shot's left shoulder guard, but did not draw blood.

Meanwhile, Sharur had leaped toward the villain, an impossible distance for even a creature as strong as he was. As he reached the apex of his leap, wings sprouted from his back and he flapped furiously toward his target. Elf Shot swiveled and fired another explosive arrow at the wolf as he closed the distance. The blossom of fire and heat rocked the neighborhood with a hammer blow of sound. Knocked out of his flight path, Sharur crashed into the edge of the roof and scrabbled for purchase. Elf Shot had already drawn another arrow, this one of glowing blue ice, and fired it at the demon wolf's forehead. The freeze arrow wasn't enough to fully hold the wolf, but it did slow him enough to make him slip off the edge of the roof. He crashed through the bushes and tumbled to the ground.

In the wrecked SUV, Eric yelled, "I've got him! I'm coming out the back!"

"Come to my side when you do. She's on the roof across the street, driver's side." Sheena eased up again and loosed another arrow. This one flew true and pierced the dark armor of the elven archer as she turned, scoring a long gash at the ribs along her right side. Elf Shot's hand went to her side and came away bloody. She turned an even angrier eye on Sheena and laughed. She must have been counting on Sheena's acute hearing, because she raised her voice only slightly to say, "Almost, little ranger, but not good enough! I'm glad you've got the guts to fight back! A little pain makes the hunt more interesting!"

"Crap. Pay attention, Sheena," Sheena muttered to herself. "You're supposed to be capturing her, not killing her!" Her next arrow was one of the misty spirit arrows. It caught Elf Shot squarely in the chest before she could duck or dodge. It tumbled the villain back against the rooftop air conditioning unit. Sheena saw Sharur struggling to his feet beneath the eaves of the building.

She readied another spirit arrow as Sharur shook himself and took to the air. The elven archer rolled to the other side of the A/C unit, using it for cover. She fired another arrow at Sheena. Sheena ducked behind the SUV. The arrow embedded itself in the light pole behind her. It snapped with an electric discharge and the bulbs at the top of the pole exploded. Sheena slid to her right and popped back up to loose her own arrow. Though a touch woozy from the effect of the first spirit arrow, Elf Shot managed to slip to the side, dodging Sheena's shot.

That gave Sharur enough time to flap himself up to the villain. He gained a purchase on the roof and snapped at Elf Shot. She cried out in surprise and pain as the iron teeth tore through her dark armor and punctured the leg of her leather outfit. She twisted to the side and looked around desperately for a safer place, then created another portal and jumped through it.

"Sheena, I've got him out. Heal him!" Eric shouted.

Sheena scuttled over and crouched down beside the wounded researcher. Holding her hands out, she poured golden energy into him. Still, nothing happened. "What is wrong with this?" she cried out. "Why won't it heal him?"

"Oh, no," Eric said with a sudden realization. "He's got a charm on him that protects him from magic!"

A flicker of light behind the wrecked SUV, from the opposite side of the street that the elven archer was just on, and Sheena saw Elf Shot emerge from another portal.

"Well, see if you can get it off… Never mind, just get him stable. Help should be on the way. I've got to deal with this." Her bow was in her hand again.

"Okay, got it," her husband replied and he went to work. "You just take care of psycho… Ahh!" A black nightmare arrow pierced his arm. His eyes glazed and he slumped to the ground as Sheena summoned and fired another spirit arrow at the villain.

Elf Shot was closer, this time, only thirty yards away. She fired again as Sheena's own arrow was in flight. The spirit arrow caught the elven villain in the side of her head. Rings of light flashed through the elven archer's vision and she staggered back against the side of a parked car. Sheena registered the black arrow speeding toward her and desperately threw up a current of slowed time at it. The arrow dropped to a mere snail's pace just an arm's length from her as she stepped to the side.

"Got… to get out… of here," Elf Shot muttered. She summoned another portal and tottered toward it. Sharur arrived, bowling over the archer. Sheena saw that he was not in great shape himself, but the wolf managed to get to his feet before the elf did. He was between her and the portal. Both archers drew and nocked arrows.

Sheena let hers fly, another spirit arrow for the villain. Elf Shot loosed an ice arrow at the wolf and stumbled toward the doorway. Sheena's shot did something to make the dark ripples of magical armor fade away. Sharur shook his head to clear it from the effect of the ice, and took in a great breath. He blew it out again with a blast of forge-heated flame just as Elf Shot fell through the doorway into somewhere else. As before, the portal closed behind her.

Sheena quickly summoned her wolves and the leopards. "Stay nearby and protect me," she commanded the wolves. "Search the area for Elf Shot, in case she is still nearby," she told the cats. She turned to Greg and Eric. In the fading early evening light, Greg Dawson looked terrible. Eric was twitching and moaning as she had seen the other victims of the nightmare arrows do. Greg was her first priority. She hurriedly began first aid and hoped that an ambulance was on its way.

The sirens of approaching emergency vehicles reassured her. She had just finished putting a pressure bandage on Greg's worst leg wound when the police and ambulance arrived. The EMTs quickly assessed and worked on Greg. "What the hell is wrong with *him*?" one of the first responders asked in a near-whisper, nodding at Eric.

"Magic arrow," Sheena responded in a shaky voice. "You take care of that guy. I can handle the arrow." She wiped as much of the blood off her hands as she could and knelt by Eric's side. Full of worry, she plucked the arrow out of his arm and tried to concentrate on what she was doing. As she did several nights earlier, she held one hand over his heart and the other over his head. She poured out the golden mists, but nothing seemed to happen.

"Mmm! Come on, come on!" she whispered urgently. She took another breath and tried again. The light poured into him, but Eric just continued to twitch and cry out in his nightmare. Sheena cried out with worry and frustration, "What am I doing wrong?!?"

Sharur dragged himself over toward her. He breathed out, "You are not fighting the darkness."

"Oh! Yes!" She realized that she was focusing on healing the internal wounds, but was doing nothing to the black aura that rippled across his body. Sheena centered herself as best she could and reminded herself of what the healing had felt like before. She attempted it again, this time working to banish the darkness, first.

The black aura withered in the golden light. Eric cried out, "I can't! I can't do it! I…." He stopped and looked around, nearly in shock. Sheena burst into tears and hugged him with relief, kneeling on the street beside the wrecked SUV.

"Oh my god! What was that?" Eric sobbed.

"Elf shot. Real magic nightmare arrows," she sniffled.

137

"Oh, that was… What's happened?!? Where's Greg?"

"The EMTs have him. They're loading up and headed to the hospital." As she said it, the ambulance turned on its siren and pulled away from the scene.

"You two should probably go, too," the police officer said.

Sheena nodded and stood up. She noticed Sharur lying quietly in a pool of blood nearby. "Oh, Sharur! I'm so sorry!" She threw out her arm and enveloped him, Eric, and herself in a pool of healing energy. The demon wolf shook his head and rose to his feet with a canine grin.

"No fear, Mistress. I am as good as new. Remember, my life is to serve you. I am as eternal as your spirit animals. If I die here, you can summon me again, as you please." He nodded to her. "Just try not to make a habit of it."

Sheena hugged the wolf as Eric shook his head in disbelief. She tried to explain to her husband what had happened as they collected what they could from the ruined SUV. Sharur and the spirit animals found no further trace of Elf Shot. They got Eric a ride to the hospital with one of the police officers. Sheena dismissed her pets and followed from above.

A short time later, the Gardners arrived at the hospital.

The triage nurse looked them over, glanced at his advance case notes from the police responder, and said, "You don't look like you came from an exploding SUV. Except for the clothes."

Sheena shook her head. "No, I fixed us up at the scene. We're really here to help with the other passenger in our car, Greg Dawson."

"Uh huh," the nurse said, scrolling through the status board. "Can you verify identity, please?" At Eric's exasperated look he added, "Just for the record."

Eric and Sheena showed him their ID. "Okay, he's in the OR and they're working on him. Is his emergency contact a… Melanie Dawson?" He checked the record and Eric nodded. "Okay, she's being contacted now. If you could wait, the doctor might have some questions for you to help with treatment. Thanks."

"Oh, this is all my fault!" Sheena cried anxiously as they stepped to the side. "If I hadn't been in that car, she wouldn't have hurt you and Greg!"

Eric snorted, "Donkey dung. She would have fired on the SUV just to get you close. And he's got some sort of charm or amulet or something that makes magic not work on him. How could you have known?"

"An amulet? Can we get it off? I could still help him!"

"Worth a shot." Eric turned back to the desk and tried to get the attention of the triage nurse as other patients and staff bustled through the area.

At the other end of the admitting desk, another ER staff member took a quick step back from the desk with an alarmed look on her face. A woman with short brown hair in a navy blue business suit slowly appeared next to the desk. To Sheena and Eric, it seemed as if she were being poured into existence from out of the phone, becoming solid from her feet up to the top of her head. This took only a few seconds, but it was a startling thing to witness. With an intense, worried expression in her dark brown eyes, she asked the nursing assistant, "Where is he?"

The ER staffer called over her shoulder, "Uh… um… Bernardo?"

"Okay, yeah. Ms. Melanie Dawson?" the triage nurse asked the woman in the suit.

"Yes, that's me."

"Could I verify your identity, please, for the record?" Melanie pulled up her DoD security badge on its retractable holder from her suit coat. The nurse nodded. "Operating Room 102, right down the hall here. Your husband is in surgery, at the moment. Janice, you can take her there."

The woman who had been on the phone nodded and escorted Melanie down the hall. Sheena followed, with Eric in tow. The nurse looked as if he was going to say something, but glanced at Sheena's wings, shook his head, and turned back to his work.

"Here it is," the nursing assistant announced. She glanced at the status board. "They're working on him now. He has suffered wounds to multiple areas on his body and is currently in critical condition." She gestured to a padded bench nearby out of the path of traffic. "You can wait here, if you want. We will send you a text at changes in condition, if you like."

Melanie nodded, stiff lipped and trying to control the leaking of tears from her eyes. "Yes, please."

The nursing assistant went back down the hall to the admitting desk. Sheena hesitantly reached toward Melanie, but stopped herself. Instead, she said quietly, "Ms. Dawson?"

Melanie turned, seeming to see the Gardners for the first time. "Yes? Oh, you must be Sheena. And Eric? I…." Words failed her.

"I am so sorry!" Sheena exclaimed. "But I think I can help Greg if we can get the charm or amulet off him!"

"Wait, what charm? What are you talking about?"

Eric explained, "Greg told me that he had a charm or something that protects him from magic. Sheena healed me and herself, but it didn't work on Greg. We think it's because of that charm. If we can get it off, Sheena can heal him."

Melanie sank onto the bench with an expression of shock and dismay. "It's… it's not a charm like a bracelet; it's cast on him. I can't get it off." Tears began to flow freely down her cheeks. "I never thought it would…."

"Wait here." Sheena hurried back down the hall. She caught the triage nurse between patients, working at the admitting desk. She glanced at his nametag. "Hey, um… Bernardo. Can you tell how critical a patient is? I think I can help Greg Dawson in 102, but it would take a while for a specialist to get here and if it's not needed, I shouldn't bother him. Or the surgeon. Suggestions?"

"Ah, let me check," the nurse replied. He tapped and scrolled through a series of readouts and data on the patient. He pursed his lips, trying to judge the situation. "No guarantees, but I've seen lots of trauma patients much worse off come out of Doctor Chang's OR doing well. You can never tell what exactly will happen, but my guess is that he's doing okay for now."

"Then, I don't need to get the specialist?"

"That's up to Doctor Chang, but everything looks like it should for this kind of work, so far. Why, are you a healer, or something?"

"Yeah, but he has a magic spell on him that prevents my powers from working on him. The specialist would be able to get that spell off so I could heal him."

"Uh... okay." He shook his head and in a low voice muttered, "Only in Venture City."

"Thanks," Sheena said and went back to Melanie and Eric.

Melanie looked up at her with a question in her eyes.

"According to the triage nurse and the data he can track, Greg is doing okay for his condition, for now," Sheena explained. "I thought that I would check and see if I should try to get someone here to get the protection spell off so I could heal Greg. The nurse doesn't think it's that urgent."

"Go ahead. Do it anyway," Melanie choked out. "That was a dumb decision on my part. I thought it would help him, not hurt him when he really needed it."

"Hey, how could you possibly know something like this would happen?" Eric reassured her.

"And I am *so* sorry about all this! I never would have put Greg in any danger if I had known she was... um...." Sheena waved her hands in the air trying to find words.

"Wait, what really happened?" Melanie asked. "Eric told me some, but was that the woman who wants to kill you that Greg told me about?"

Sheena nodded and related the story. While she talked, she pulled her phone out of her blood-stained sport purse. The face had a big crack in it, but it otherwise appeared to be functioning.

"Oh, geez. Greg sometimes has more good intentions than common sense," Melanie muttered. "I didn't realize that this Elf Shot woman was so close to her goal. I would have told him to keep his guard up and stay at a safe distance until you caught her. No offense."

"None taken. Let me make a call." Sheena stepped away and looked at her phone, then realized she didn't have Sir Leo's number. She hesitated, and then tapped a call to Gayle with an "emergency" flag on it. Then, she plucked idly at her shredded sundress while she waited for Gayle to pick up.

"Gayle here. Go ahead, Sheena!" came her friend's concerned voice from the phone.

"Elf Shot ambushed us a few blocks from Riverhaven. Eric and I are fine, but Greg Dawson is in critical condition. Elf Shot took a beating and escaped, but Greg has some kind of spell on him that means my healing can't affect him. Can we get Leo over here to the Miller Memorial ER to strip off that protection and let me heal him?"

"Uh... I'm on it. It may not be Leo, but I'll get someone from the League of Titans. Anything else?"

"No. Thanks, Gayle."

Sheena turned back to Melanie and Eric. "Gayle will send someone from the League of Titans to help."

"Okay, good. Thank you, Sheena. This isn't your fault," Melanie replied. She turned her gaze back to the OR window forlornly.

Outside the hospital an hour later, Eric paced and fumed, "That bitch must pay! Bringing innocent people into this thing...."

"She is a *villain*, Eric," Sheena sighed with exasperation. "What part of that do you not get?"

"Whatever. I hope you get her, and soon. She needs to be hauled off the streets and put away."

"I'm trying."

"Yeah, well...." Eric paused, tight-lipped. "Tell me what I can do to help. Anything I can do. Track her down? Trace whoever is paying her for the other stuff she's doing? Just let me know how I can help."

Sheena sighed, "I don't know, but I am definitely going to ask. There has to be something."

Eric let out a frustrated breath and hailed a taxi.

Chapter 19 – Way Out of his League

"You're sure you want to come along, Eric?" Sheena asked, really hoping she could leave him at home. "It's okay if you stay here, you know."

"No, I'm going. I need to hear this, and I have some questions of my own for those guys. Besides, I've got a lot to do today." The set of his jaw told her that she wasn't going to be able to talk him out of it. He stuffed his laptop and tablet into his computer bag and straightened his tie. "All set. You want me to call a taxi and meet you there?"

Sheena sighed. This would make getting to the FBSA building more complicated, to say nothing of whatever conversations would come from the meeting with the agents. But at least the chances were very slim that Elf Shot would already be back on the streets and watching for Eric. "Yeah, go ahead. Gayle and I will fly there."

Eric nodded. "See you in a bit." He went out to the elevator foyer and pressed the call button.

"He's in a determined mood," Gayle observed wryly after Eric had departed.

"Yeah, that's his 'I'm going to fix this mess myself' look. It usually doesn't work out well."

"Mmm, I can imagine," the singer sympathized.

"Costumes, I think," Sheena said after thinking it over for a bit. Gayle hadn't asked, but Sheena had the feeling that this meeting with Agents Schauer and Calderón was going to turn out to be more than just a casual chat.

"All right." Gayle asked with a touch of concern, "Are you doing okay, circumstances-wise?"

Sheena started to offer the easy "I'm fine" reply, but took a breath and forced herself to share what she was really feeling. "Not really okay, actually, no. I'm worried. I'm worried about what she's going to do next. And, I'm worried about Greg, even though Drake fixed him up. And I'm worried about Eric thinking he has to somehow step in and protect me when he's totally out of his league... And, you know what else? I'm worried that I find that kind of insulting, that he thinks he can and should protect me! Like I'm some delicate flower!"

Gayle's eyebrows went up a notch. "Ah! He's gonna play the alpha male protecting his mate?"

"Yeah! Come on, he is not only out of his league, he is so *far* out of his league that it would be laughable... if it wasn't something that would get him killed!"

"And that's also what you're worried about?"

"Damn straight! Who got us out of the ambush last night? Me. Who went down at the first thing she threw at him? Eric. And you know what? I could have done it myself with the spirit animals, even if I didn't have Sharur helping. And healed up all of us if that stupid spell on Greg hadn't mucked it up. I don't need his protection. And, what if that had been some other kind of arrow that hit him?

I can't fix death, Gayle!" She felt a knot in her chest. She had been so close to losing him and didn't even realize it until afterward.

"And that's...."

"Just another thing I have to worry about on top of tracking this bitch down and stopping her without shooting her full of real arrows, which I started to do, too."

"Oh." Gayle came up and put her arms around her friend as she started to cry. Sheena's tears of worry and frustration poured out on Gayle's shoulder.

"Heh," Sheena said through her sniffles. "A literal shoulder to cry on. I'm sorry."

"Pssht. That's what friends are for, right?"

After short while, Sheena let her go and wiped her cheeks with the back of her hand. Gayle patted her friend on the shoulder and ventured a hesitant, "He's worth it, though. Right?"

"What? Eric? Of course!"

Gayle nodded. "Good. I thought so. I mean, that's what I *don't* have in my life."

Sheena's eyebrows knit together in confusion. "But, why?"

Gayle sighed with a puff of air from her cheeks. The breeze around her took on the scent of fallen leaves. "Not for lack of looking. It's just never seemed to work out, for lots of reasons."

"Oh, I'm sorry. And here we are just parading it around you all the time...."

"There, you did it again, saying you're sorry," Gayle chided her with a grin. "You aren't responsible for everything that happens, so quit apologizing."

"I'm... all right, I'll try."

"I keep my eyes open for possibilities," Gayle said. "Someday, I tell myself, I'll find the right guy. But, I'm not waiting around for him, either. I'm not a princess waiting for a prince to 'complete me.' I've got a life to live, and friends to live it with. So, I'm only a little lonely, in that one corner. I can live with that."

"I suppose that works," Sheena said hesitantly.

"It does."

"So, suit up?"

"Let's. And then we can go find out what your agent friends have found out about the source stones and Elf Shot's mysterious employer."

The district headquarters and special offices of the Federal Bureau of Superpowered Affairs looked like an ordinary modern office building, with none of the high-tech flair that characterized many of Venture City's structures. Most of it was made up of a large six story building with what looked like a black and gray glass exterior covering most of two city blocks. The parking garage was entirely underground and the roof boasted a bustling heliport. It was located on the northern edge of the city center district near the eastern border of the Sandler district. The north side of the FBSA headquarters had a great view of Cedar Swamp Park.

Eric arrived shortly before the 9 AM meeting with the FBSA agents. After checking in with building security, he was shown to a small conference room on the second floor. Agent Schauer arrived to greet him as he was trying to decide where to sit.

"Good morning, Doctor Gardner," the agent's low-key voice said from the doorway. Schauer was dressed, as always, in his generic black suit and white shirt. He looked exactly the same as the last time Eric had seen him. He gestured to a chair for Eric and observed, "You appear physically healthy, after last night's incident."

"Yes. I'm fine, thanks. I have a lot of questions, though." He took the indicated seat along the side of the table.

"I imagine you might. Officer Gardner and Gayle Force will join us shortly, I understand. If you wish to ask questions now, I will do my best to provide answers." Schauer sat down at the end of the table nearest the door and then adjusted his chair so that he could see the whole room.

"The biggest one is this: How can I help Sheena find and stop Elf Shot, given that I don't have any special training or background?"

Agent Calderón came in and waved to Eric. He answered for Schauer, "Tough question. You want the tough answers?"

Schauer smiled politely as Eric nodded.

Calderón sat down across from Eric and leaned forward. With a serious expression the veterinarian had not seen him display before, Calderón said, "First off, you stay safe and out of the way. You go about your business and follow her instructions about how to keep off the field of battle. She's the expert and the main target here, like a queen on the chessboard. Unfortunately, you are an exposed pawn, no matter how much you'd like to be a white knight."

Eric was completely taken aback. Before he could respond, the agent continued. "You wanted the tough answers. That is the toughest reality you've got to face, right now. You are a way to get to Sheena. A potential bargaining chip. A way to hurt her with almost no risk to Elf Shot or her people. A soft target. An easy...." He suddenly broke off and leaned back with a casual smile, glancing at the door. "To be continued."

Sheena and Gayle walked into the room in their hero costumes. Eric and the agents stood up and Schauer welcomed them. "Good morning, ladies." He offered Sheena the chair he had been sitting in and moved around to the other end of the table, pulling out a chair for Gayle between Eric and himself.

"Hi, guys. Have you met Gayle Force before?" Sheena asked.

"I have had the pleasure of working with her, yes," Schauer replied. He shook Gayle's hand professionally. "Good to see you again."

"While I have only heard many, many good things about her," Calderón finished with a grin. "Welcome, lady of the winds!"

Gayle chuckled. "You would be that shaman who helped Sheena. Thanks for that. It really seemed to get her to where she needed to be." She winked at him. "And it's not like I haven't been in this building before."

"I'm sure you have the advantage of me, there. I started working with Agent Schauer just this time last year, in Phoenix. This is the first time I have done more than visit Venture City."

They sat down and Agent Schauer glanced at Gayle and Sheena. He asked, "Would you like us to tell you what we've learned, first, or to share with us what you've discovered?"

"I'll fill you in, first. Then, you can see if that opens up new perspectives on your information," Sheena replied. She proceeded to explain everything she and Gayle had done or found out since she and Eric had arrived in Venture City. Calderón asked some questions, but Schauer just took it all in. Eric sat quietly and listened, as well. Hearing it all related in such a matter-of-fact way, Eric felt even more out of place. Sheena and Gayle were involved with magic, mythology, ancient history, spirit journeys, bio-terrorists, superpowered thieves, and other strangeness that made his head spin. The determination he had entered the room with was rapidly leaking away.

"So...," Sheena concluded, "with the aftermath of her ambush last night, that brings us up to today."

Schauer steepled his fingers and nodded. "Very interesting."

"This Feathers of the Raven group may have a tie-in to Elf Shot's activities," offered Calderón. "More on that in a minute. The source stones, first?"

Schauer nodded. Calderón used the conference room's display to show images of the stones. "These source stones and other similar items have been in the possession of a specific collector for a very long time. Periodically, he lets certain items get out into the world. They do what they are supposed to do, and then they find their way to new homes or back into his collection. In this case, the collector loaned the pre-Sumerian source stones to a researcher, knowing that they would likely be stolen from that researcher."

"What?!?" Sheena exclaimed. "The collector set up the theft of his own stuff?"

"Not exactly," Calderón explained. "He allowed the theft to happen, but without specific knowledge of who would steal the stones, where they would go, or how or if they would be recovered."

"Why?" asked Eric.

Calderón gave them a wry half-smile. "To bring power into the world." He let that sink in for a moment. "He is fully aware of what these things do. He also knows quite a bit about the conditions under which they will grant their stored powers to individual mortals—probably more than anyone else alive, in fact. He also has such a long view that he may see this all like a library, making temporary loans of his collection as a sort of public service."

"Well, who is he?" Gayle asked, brimming with curiosity. "Or is that a secret?"

Calderón shook his head. "We do not know the collector's name, just that of his chosen spokesperson. We may simply call him The Collector. But we have been told that he is very, very old—centuries—and the records we can find seem to verify that."

"And so..." Sheena reasoned.

"Yes. He let the source stone of Shanikali out into the world specifically so that it would find you," Calderón acknowledged.

"Then, he must know what the threat is!"

"Not necessarily. He sends items of his collection into the world through different methods, and by signs that show those things are needed. I asked his representative if he knew the purpose of the stone, and he said that The Collector saw the signs that these should be back in circulation, and had arrangements made accordingly."

"Wow. That is totally cosmic!" Gayle breathed.

"Yes," replied Schauer. "And can you guess who loaned the Arama Hallada to the Venture City Museum of Fine Art?"

"The Collector?" Sheena asked with wide eyes.

"Exactly."

"But... why?"

"We do not know," answered Calderón. "Perhaps he is or sees himself as an agent of prophecy, or a servant of the powers...."

"Or, a colossal mischief maker," interjected Schauer. Calderón chuckled. "As you can tell, Agent Calderón and I do not necessarily agree on the interpretation of this information. But certain things happened that coincided with the emergence of the Feathers of the Raven group, the loans of the source stones and the dagger being among them."

"How do you know there is a link?" Sheena asked.

Calderón grinned. "We asked. The Collector's agent confirmed it when we asked why these items were put into circulation at this time. He said that the various conditions for all of the different items were all met on the same day. In his experience, that meant that there was a threat that needed more power out in the world to counter. The common factor was the public announcement of the demands of the Feathers of the Raven."

Schauer added, "To be accurate, there were over two thousand common factor possibilities. However, The Collector's agent stopped us when this group's activity was displayed and said that must be it. To the extent it is reasonable, we are taking the advice of that... 'expert.'"

"Well, it is awfully circumstantial," Sheena agreed. "But, if he has the experience to be confident, we can treat it as expert witness testimony. The things that have happened after the release seem to be connecting events together."

Calderón grinned again. "Yes. The network analysis agrees with you." He tapped at the display controls and brought up an image of icons and connections similar in style to the one Sir Leo had used at Riverhaven three days earlier. There were several places on the map where relationships converged. "It doesn't predict the future, but it can show the strength of possible relationships between things that have already happened."

"What does this tell us?" Eric asked. Interested again.

Calderón circled the network hub points. "Sheena and Elf Shot are central. So is Elf Shot's as-yet-unknown employer, who is closely tied by association to the Feathers of the Raven group. Gayle is a supporting connection who, in this analysis, brings a great deal of support to Sheena. Another high-connection element is the biotech thefts. We have been able to link six other thefts or irregularities to the ones you already mentioned."

He continued. "A couple of interesting things here. There is a lot of suggestive evidence that Elf Shot's mysterious employer is the leader of the Feathers of the Raven, and that he is some kind of magically-powered metahuman. The Feathers have some expertise with virus-based biotech. We know where they got some of it, in this guy, here." He circled another node on the network map. "James Kadorsky."

"Who is he?" Gayle asked.

"A former employee of the Centers for Disease Control and US Department of Homeland Security whose family, and dozens of others, died because of an oil refinery accident in his community. The companies involved denied all wrongdoing and responsibility. Clean-up of the site and further operations at the refinery produced... less than desirable results, including more toxic accidents and harm to the environment and community. A class action settlement didn't even cover the property and health insurance deductibles of the victims and survivors. The town was abandoned, but the refinery and supporting buildings were not. They keep running today, using non-union contractors and replacement workers from other towns. Kadorsky asked his friends in government to investigate, but they were stonewalled. Kadorsky himself disappeared without a trace a week after the class action settlement was announced."

"Wow," Gayle said. "No wonder the Feathers gain support. Do you think Kadorsky is in with them?"

"Yes. Informants have confirmed it. He is close to the leader, and helping with some plan to bring justice to polluters and their supporters across industries and in government."

"Can we find him? Or this leader?"

"All signs point to the Feathers, Kadorsky, and their leader being based in Venture City at this time. We've also identified the location of the lab Elf Shot took from the Syndicate, with the help of the Venture City Police Department. The Feathers are definitely occupying the lab, and have managed to defend it from Syndicate metahuman counterattack. Sources suggest that the Syndicate is going to destroy the whole block and cut their losses, soon."

"The whole block...? What does that mean?" Sheena asked.

Schauer used the display pull up a map of part of Venture City. "This city block would be destroyed, and everything in it, if the Syndicate plans are not stopped. Fortunately, the Pillars of Virtue supergroup has volunteered to help with this."

"Oh," Gayle said. She seemed a little disappointed. "So, you don't need our help with that?"

Schauer shook his head. "No. The Pillars have made the Syndicate a major focus of their crime-fighting efforts in Venture City. They are not only the natural choice to handle this threat, they leave you free for another mission."

"Oh! And that is?" Gayle perked up.

"Discovering the identity of the Feathers of the Raven leader," Schauer said simply.

"Okay… Any suggestions on how to do that?"

"Yes. This is from a tip we got late last night. The leader is meeting with another group's boss tonight. An informant has given us information about the meet. You might recognize the other fellow." He put a picture up on the display. It showed a bulky, vaguely man-shaped creature with tentacles dangling from an overhanging jaw, brilliant violet compound eyes high on its broad, hairless head, and thick, pebbled skin like a cross between a rhinoceros and a snake. It had no nose or external ears and wore no clothing. It was a dark brown on its back, a muddy gray on its front, and mottled with earthy brown spots across its head and shoulders. Its arms and legs were thick and powerful, equipped with hard claws for burrowing. What looked like a second set of more delicate manipulating hands were tucked into cavities under the creature's forearms. A criss-crossing of something that looked like dark green veins but might have been roots, or just large patches of fungal growth ran across its body.

Gayle jumped out of her seat. "*Ravenger?!?* They're working with Ravenger and the Vengeful Earth?!?"

Schauer remained as imperturbable as ever. "Apparently, the Feathers and the Vengeful Earth are going to explore that possibility. Are you interested?"

"You dang well know I'm interested!" Gayle was scowling and madder than Sheena had ever seen her. The air smelled like thunder. Her permanent breeze had grown into swirling gusts around the room.

"Excellent. With a little luck, you may be able to take down the heads of two villainous groups at once and protect the lives of millions." At Sheena's quizzical look, he added. "That's no exaggeration. We may not know exactly what the Feathers are up to, but the Vengeful Earth work on a scale that threatens entire regions or metropolitan areas. Unlike human villain groups, all of the minions of the Vengeful Earth are either quasi-sentient vegetable and mineral creatures or humans converted into powerful, grotesque monstrosities. They are not all that dissimilar from Ravenger himself, but fanatically loyal and with no memory of their human lives. We barely even know how Ravenger communicates with his horde, but they are extremely dangerous."

Eric was horrified. "You're going to fight that?"

"First opportunity I get," growled Gayle. She dropped back into her seat and crossed her arms. The wind faded back to normal levels, but a peppery dark chocolate scent wafted about in the breeze. "Okay, drama time's over. Your presentation was great, Agent. What's next?"

"I can give you two all the details we've obtained on the groups involved, Elf Shot, the Ravenger meeting, Kadorsky, the Feathers of the Raven, and its leader. I'll help you plan and arrange for backup." He looked up at Calderón. "Did you want to finish your conversation with Doctor Gardner?"

Calderón nodded. "That would be a good idea. I'm sure Eric has other questions. You stay here. I'll use the Cedarview room." Calderón stood up and gestured for Eric to follow him, leaving Schauer and the heroines to work out their plans.

Eric followed Agent Calderón along the hallway to another conference room about the same size as the first. Calderón closed the door as he came in after Eric and he sat down next to the young veterinarian. Eric let out a nervous breath.

Calderón gave him a wry half-smile and asked, "So, now that you see what they're up against, do you still think you can help?"

Eric slowly shook his head as he considered it all. "No, not that way. But isn't there some other way I can be useful that won't put me in danger or distract Sheena from what she has to do? Or, should I just go back to Wisconsin and carry on with my life there?"

"What? Giving up so easily?" Calderón smirked. He made Eric want to smack him.

"Not giving up, but trying to get realistic, yeah. Come on, either there is something I can do, or there isn't. If there isn't anything that someone else... or some computer... can't do just as well or better, then let me know."

"Why all the pressure?" Calderón asked.

Eric struggled to explain. "Sheena's my wife. I love her. If there is something I can do to help her or protect her, I've got to do it, and not just sit by. I can't just be a bystander! Don't you get it?"

The agent dropped the prodding sarcastic attitude and gave Eric a considering look. He let out a long breath and admitted, "Yes, I get it. And, I'll do what I can to help you. There are a couple of things you can do. One of them is pretty simple, but not easy to do. The other is not safe and may end up creating more trouble in the long run. But, I will at least give you the choice."

"All right. What are my options?"

"First, the simple thing, but not easy. You let your wife tell you what signs to watch for, what to do in emergencies, and how to stay as safe as possible so that she can do her job. You protect yourself and listen to her, support her, take care of her when she gets beaten up... not necessarily physically, because she can fix that, but when the villains get the upper hand. You be the normal, stable one she can lean on for sanity when all the rest of her world is crazy. But that's not easy. I think you already understand that."

"Er, yes. I haven't been doing really well at that, have I?" he admitted reluctantly.

Calderón shrugged and grinned. "That's not for me to say; I don't sleep with you. Ask your wife!"

Eric snorted. "Okay, I should probably do that anyway. What's the other thing?"

Calderón chuckled wryly to himself. "You become a hero, too."

"Huh?"

"Oh, no, it's not easy or assured or anything! But, if it could be done, at least it would make your wife worry a little bit less, and you would be able to help her more directly."

"But... how in the world would I do that?"

The agent winked in a conspiratorial fashion. "You do remember The Collector, and the objects he has sent out into the world?"

"Yes, but… oh."

"You see? It may be… *may* be… that there is something that needs you to do it, like the something that needs Sheena."

"Isn't that a bit of a long shot?" Eric said skeptically.

"Yes! A very long shot!" agreed Calderón. "But, we never know unless you try, eh?"

Eric sat in thought, possibilities tumbling through his head. "What's the down side of trying?"

"The biggest down side?" Eric nodded. Calderón answered honestly, "You might succeed. And your life changes even more than it already has. Just think about that for a moment."

He did think about it. Having to go through the trials that Sheena had already been through, the changes, and putting her through it, too. Could he do that to her? On the other hand, could he not take the chance, if it meant he might be able to protect her and help her? Was just being a normal guy enough for her? He knew she would say it was, but would she grow apart from him and regret her decision later? Would she lose patience with him falling behind as just a normal man?

"What do you think I should do?" he asked Calderón.

The agent looked satisfied. "Say hello to the stones, expect nothing, and go pursue that first path of supporting your hero wife."

"'Say hello?'"

"Look, touch, see if anything happens. Just in case. If something is meant to be, accept it graciously. But, don't try to power it up. Don't go searching for other ways to make yourself a hero." He shook his head sadly. "The odds are more in favor of a hideous and painful death or permanent disfigurement, instead of success."

"Ah." He continued to think, and Calderón seemed content to let him do so.

Eventually he had thought long enough. "If there is a chance I can be what she needs me to be, I'll do it."

"Very well, then follow me."

Calderón got up and took Eric with him to an office further down the hallway. It had the look of a temporary or guest office. There were two desks and not nearly enough clutter or personal items to show that people "lived" there. One of the desks was in complete order, despite the routing envelopes and paperwork. Eric guessed that was Schauer's. The other was more natural, with some things piled loosely and a bit more of a human touch to it.

The agent bent down and pulled a cardboard shipping box from underneath his desk. "Here we go. Ancient source stones. Very important!" he joked.

Eric chuckled in disbelief, "You keep priceless magic artifacts in a cardboard box under your desk?"

Calderón paused and looked at him. "What? You have a better place? It's just a temporary office."

He lifted the box up and put it down on the desk. He opened the top and Eric could see three silk bags packed into the box with wads of bubble-wrap surrounding them. Calderón reached in and pulled them all out. One by one, he took the smooth, fist-sized polished rocks out of the bags and put them on the desk. He gestured at the stones. "Go ahead. Say hello."

With an amused snort, Eric hesitantly reached out toward one. He touched it with a finger. Nothing happened. He picked it up and looked at it closely, trying to feel if anything was happening. Still, nothing did. He put it down again and looked at the other two. He repeated the process with a second one, and still felt nothing unusual. As he was looking at the third, he asked, "Which of these is Shanikali's?"

"That one you're looking at now."

"Huh." He picked it up and looked at it more closely. "I'm trying to imagine this thing floating in the air and doing all those things Sheena told me about. Wow." He shook his head. "Nothing."

As he put it back down, something like a flicker of electricity rippled over one of the other stones. He pointed at it. "Is that one the storm god's stone?"

"Yes, Horgan. Why?"

"Well, lightning just flickered across it."

Calderón suddenly appeared very interested. "You saw that? What did you see?"

"Just an arc of purple-white, like from a plasma globe or a lightning bolt, rippled from around the top of the stone toward the bottom once."

"Interesting! It appears that you are not completely dead to such things, Eric."

"Uh, and that means... what?"

Calderón looked about to speak, then stopped himself. He frowned and rubbed his chin. "Actually, I'm not sure what it means."

"What were you going to say, though?"

Calderón chuckled. "I was going to say it means that you might be able to activate it. But then I realized that I was projecting my own tradition onto it, and that is not wise to do, and I should know better."

"Should I try activating it? I'm willing to give it a shot."

The agent swayed back and forth as if caught between two possibilities. Finally, he came to a decision. "All right. I found enough data on this one to suggest a way. You have to wait for a thunderstorm. Then, go out into the thunderstorm and hold up the stone. And you say a specific phrase. If it's not working after five minutes, it won't work and I'm wrong." He tapped and swiped through the contents of his tablet for a moment. "Here we go... Let me print this off and I'll translate it phonetically."

The printer hummed and printed off the cuneiform phrase. He sat down and worked out the syllables in English characters for Eric, writing them on the sheet. He bagged the stone and handed it to Eric again. "One way or another, deliver the stone back to me. I've signed for it."

"Go out into a thunderstorm and hold up the stone. Uh huh." Eric cocked his head to one side and asked, "That's not particularly safe, is it?"

"What? And trying to unlock an artifact full of magic powers is?"

Eric laughed. "Point!"

"But, in all seriousness, Eric. Yes, this is dangerous, and you are better off supporting Sheena than chasing after power, for whatever purpose," Calderón said with a fatherly tone.

"All right, I will give this some serious thought before the next thunderstorm." He tucked the stone and the translation into his computer bag.

"Good man. Here, I'll get you back down to the security desk. Where are you going from here?"

Eric snorted. "Off to work at Dynatech. But first, the SUV was more than totaled. So… Car rental agency."

They both laughed.

Chapter 20 – A Dangerous Alliance

"You don't mind pain, do you?" Blighthawk asked the elven archer. "This will burn a bit, but you will be on your feet again in no time."

Elf Shot clenched her teeth on her leather glove and nodded her assent. "Ged id ofer wif, alreddy!" she growled around the glove. She was lying uncomfortably in a worn out vinyl-upholstered recliner in the walled-off basement of a Mackey's grocery store. Blighthawk had been displeased to learn of her failure to capture the winged huntress. Not only was his most capable lieutenant nearly incapacitated, he opined that this would likely provoke Shee'na and Gayle Force to greater action, and he had previously made it clear that they were already getting closer than he liked.

The corrupter paused and struck a thoughtful pose. "Hmm... I seem to remember you saying something about knowing pain. Well, I guess you'll have a chance to get re-acquainted."

He concentrated on her leg wounds, first. A wave of his hand, a clenched fist, a few magic words to Raven, and fire engulfed her leg, searing into muscle and skin, burning away the injury. Elf Shot stiffened and groaned in agony. The flames vanished, leaving her flesh whole and undamaged. She gasped for breath. "I've had worse," she croaked.

"Good, good. Ribs next." He repeated the process. She jerked and arched against the recliner. Her groans were louder and tears of hot pain ran down her cheeks. The flames vanished again and she panted deeply, trying to suck in more air to relax and relieve the pain. "You flinched," Blighthawk remonstrated cheerfully.

"Bastard."

"Sticks and stones, Meg." He was entirely too cheerful about the healing for her taste, but at least it was effective. She lay back as easily as she could and tried to catch her breath. "You are done. Fixing your outfit, I'm afraid, is up to you. I can only work miracles on living flesh."

"Fine," she grunted.

"So curious an irony that the knife you have stolen was intended to prevent the flame-worshipping Zoroastrian priests from using essentially the same magic I just employed on you."

"Yeah. Did it do them much good?"

"No. In the end, the Persian Empire fell to the Arabs and the few remaining true magi went underground. And Raven picked the bones of the fallen, as he always does."

"Well, this dagger will let me take back those powers. But I have to take her alive and do the ritual, you said. Any more hints?"

"None needed. The Arama Hallada will steal her powers with its killing stroke and give them to you. The ritual ensures that you can control those powers when they flow into you from the knife."

"Excellent."

"On another topic, I have a meeting tonight. And, I have a meeting tonight. I am considering which one I want you to attend."

"What?" Elf shot squinted at him in confusion.

"We need more time for James to finish his work on the cure, and the Syndicate is getting desperate to show everyone that they won't let our theft of their drug lab go unpunished. Lobo is working on our plans to deliver the virus. He'll be back in the city soon. That leaves us short-handed. As much as I hate stopping work, I have already started the crew moving to a new lab. We'll let the Syndicate destroy the one we've been using."

"What new lab? I thought we couldn't get a backup."

"Ingenuity, my dear archer! I happen to know of an individual who still has several under his control, and I have negotiated for the use of one of them. Plus, said individual has a burning antagonism for a certain nature-loving hero we both know."

"What, the ranger?"

The shaman rolled his eyes elaborately. "Gayle Force, your ranger's friend."

"Okay, so...."

"We are going to form a temporary alliance of convenience. We give him what he wants, and a little boost to his capabilities, courtesy of Raven, and he provides the lab facilities we need and keeps the heroes off us for a few more days. Or, on the slim chance he actually pulls off the plan successfully, permanently."

"And you have two meetings."

"Yes. One is a face-to-face with our ally, at which I work out the rest of the details and give him something he can use to wreak absolute havoc on Venture City. The other is a decoy meeting that I have arranged to be leaked to the police. That is where they will discover the corpse of the individual you grabbed for us some weeks ago; our test subject, Mister Walter Herschel. I am tempted to send you to that meeting for another shot at your forest ranger. However, the opposition will be stiff, they will be very well-prepared, and I cannot afford to lose you at this stage of the plan."

"Are you sure, Blighthawk? Too risky? Even when they are expecting someone else?"

"Well, they don't know who I am, yet, but they will be expecting you there. And because they know you, they will be prepared for you. We need a better venue if you are going to succeed the next time."

Elf Shot snorted and wearily got to her feet. "At least I have a much better idea of what she's capable of, now."

"Indeed. I don't think that you'll underestimate her again. Maybe." He snickered to himself.

"That huge wolf is tough. She's got a lot of tricks in her quiver, now." She grimaced. "And you see why I want Shanikali's power."

"Well... yes," the oily mastermind reluctantly admitted. He flicked some of his excess fluids into the corner. "I think we have some options with regard to both of those ladies. Again, continue to help me get what I want, and I help you get the power you want."

"Agreed."

"Now rest up those pain-jangled nerves and get yourself back into top form. I am going to need you tonight."

"James, how goes the transfer?" Blighthawk rasped later as he hastened down the last few steps of the iron spiral staircase and strode into the underground transfer station. Some of the Feathers were moving boxes and equipment on wheeled carts through the area.

"Carefully, sir, but we're moving quickly." James Kadorsky respected Blighthawk for a variety of reasons. He was a genius, unquestionably. He was a former military pilot who had defended the country and the world against the K'rk'ti aliens, nearly giving his life to do so. He had borne unquestionable suffering with dignity, despite the changes that suffering had wrought upon his physical form. He held fast to his philosophy and loyalty to a powerful patron that probably cared nothing for him. He continued to care for innocent people while he fought a war against widespread corruption. And, most importantly, he had a vision of how the world could be so much better that inspired the technologist. In bringing that vision to pass James Kadorsky would avenge his family.

"How close are we to isolating the Stage 2 antigen?"

"Close, sir. Another two days at most. This influenza variant isn't very common, given that we're using a predominantly avian variety, but we're into the last... oh, say ten percent... of the sequencing."

The villain nodded. "But using the uncommon variant means that the immunity will be low in the general population. It will spread more effectively."

"Yes, sir. Just a couple more days and then we can start producing the cure. And a vaccine, if you wanted one."

"Good. We are now racing against time. The spirits are ready to spread the disease to Venture City, Boston, Providence, New York, and Washington, D.C. The volunteers are ready to receive their canisters and head out on their worldwide journeys. We just have to finish and disperse before the government and corporate minions can stop us." Kadorsky thought he looked worried.

"We'll do it, sir. The new lab is great. State of the art. More, even! Who did we get this from?"

Blighthawk looked away from the technologist and scowled unhappily. He considered carefully before answering, "The Vengeful Earth."

Kadorsky's eyes opened in disbelief. "Wha... *Ravenger*?"

The corrupter nodded reluctantly. "The man... creature... is a total, dangerous loon. I have no doubt whatsoever that he will turn on us once he perceives our usefulness is over. Where we are trying to change the world, he wants to completely destroy anything to do with civilization or humanity. Yes, I know what I'm getting us into."

"Then, why...?"

"Because we need time! Ravenger will distract the heroes and give us facilities long enough for us to finish our work. We maneuver him into an open battle, he fights the heroes, the heroes fight him and his horde, the powers that be get a wake-up call about the wrath of nature, and we get a few more days. And if his twisted monstrosities gain too much of an upper hand...." He smiled coldly. "Well, then, Raven plucks away his support and Ravenger and his minions come crashing down again, the trick completed."

Everything Kadorsky had ever heard about the Vengeful Earth told him that this was a bad idea. The Vengeful Earth did not make deals; they smashed things. They did not take allies; they assimilated and mutated anyone they captured. They were an implacable, inhuman fungal rot trying to spread across the entire face of the earth. "This sounds risky, sir."

Blighthawk sighed. This started him coughing. When he recovered his breath, he replied, "It is. But it is what Raven suggested. I think he is impatient and hungry, and it is even riskier to deny him. Especially when we are already so close!"

"Do you want me to make emergency evacuation plans?" Kadorsky offered tentatively.

"Yes, please. By all means. And if we have anti-fungal and anti-bacterial agents available in quantity, make them handy. We may need to use them as a weapon against Ravenger's creatures if he turns on us early."

"Yes, sir. I'll arrange for it."

"One more thing."

"Yes, sir?"

"The body of our test subject, Mister Herschel, and our message to the powers that be."

"Double-bagged, sealed, labeled, and the message enclosed on a thumb drive. The files have been forensically scrubbed to remove traces, and have been instead peppered with a variety of alternate organizations' fingerprints. We had help from Terra First on that, which you said was all right. The content of the files lays out the steps toward change; dismantling the corrupt power structures and imbalances. They explain that what happened to Herschel will happen across the world to those who greedily abuse wealth and power. And, it describes how they have grown greedier than Raven, but his power is far greater than theirs."

"Excellent. And his widow?"

"The police made sure that she was properly treated after they found her. She was not able to give them any useful information. We've also sent the members who did that part of the job into the underground."

"How are they doing?"

Kadorsky shrugged. "Okay, I guess. Pretty happy to have succeeded without a hitch."

"I will drop by and give them my thanks. It would only be natural for them to be questioning the cause after extended contact with their captive. It may seem a small and cruel thing they've accomplished, but I will help them recognize the value of what they have done for the future of mankind."

"Yes, sir."

"And thank you, James. This plan is coming together largely thanks to your hard work. Keep everyone safe and leave Ravenger to me and Elf Shot. Your family will be avenged, soon."

Kadorsky nodded. He turned back to his work with a sense of uneasiness as Blighthawk walked off deeper into the tunnels.

You are skinny and broken. You could be strong.

Ravenger stood before him in one of the sewage settling ponds of the Destruction Brook Effluvium Treatment Plant. The creature was massive. The corrupter imagined him sucking in nutrients from the muck. Blighthawk himself preferred to remain on the bank where he slowly dripped much more modest quantities of effluvia. Elf Shot remained at a distance, where she would be most effective if things turned sour.

"Thank you for the offer, Ravenger. I have work left to do for Raven before I give up this form, however," Blighthawk replied to the creature before him. He knew that Ravenger had once been a brilliant genetic research scientist. He still retained his intelligence, even in the monstrous body he had chosen to inhabit, and the corrupter wondered why he chose to communicate in simple sentences like a brute. The words came in a hollow mental voice, like a grunt from the bottom of a well. The tentacles depending from Ravenger's upper jaw quivered slightly as he spoke.

You would be a strong ally. We could make the earth pure faster.

"I think that working together as we are now, we will be able to accomplish much. And later, perhaps, will be another opportunity. I don't know how much of my magic I would retain if I transformed to join you." Actually, Blighthawk strongly suspected that none of his magical ability or connection to Raven would remain. The metahumans absorbed and mutated by the Vengeful Earth spores never again displayed any of their original powers. Blighthawk greatly preferred to keep his shamanic bargain with Raven intact. It gave him much greater flexibility and certainly more free will than becoming a minion of Ravenger possibly could.

The creature shifted in what Blighthawk presumed was a shrug. *I give you the lab. What do you give me?*

"A seed," the corrupter croaked simply. He plucked a light green walnut-sized item from a pocket at the wrist of his left glove. "An ancient tree blight seed, in fact. Plant this and the blight will grow to mighty size from the ground. Then, it will make the forest come alive to do your command. As long as the blight stands, it will continue to produce lesser blights. These, also, will follow your command and will bring even more trees alive to your cause."

How long?

"The tree blight is a withered cedar. It could stand for a hundred years, under suitable conditions. I think you will have to protect it from your enemies, but it will stand long enough."

Will it give more seeds?

"No. It is brought from the spirit world where Raven corrupted one of the celestial trees to produce that seed."

That concept seemed to give the nature-loving Ravenger a moment of pause. The compound eyes and lack of virtually any human features made his expression unreadable. Finally, he said, *That seems excessive.*

Ah, a multi-syllable word! Blighthawk repressed his amusement and responded, "What? That an eternal and godlike spirit would deign to destroy one tree in an infinite forest in order to make a thing of horror for you to use in your campaign to cleanse this earth? It does seem unlikely, but nevertheless, that is what we have."

The corrupter watched patiently, noting the slow pulsation of the dark green vein-like growths on the creature's skin. Eventually, Ravenger responded, *You have your plans. What do you suggest?*

"You might perhaps start with Cedar Swamp Park. There are plenty of trees there, and it is near to residences, factories, the airport, and the city center is not far away... take your pick. The important thing is this: The longer you can keep the blight alive, the more minions it can create and the stronger your army. And there is one more element to consider."

What is that?

"It would be nice if you could take good care of Gayle Force as you avenge the earth. She and her friend have been getting too close to my business. I know you two have had dealings in the past."

Ravenger did not really nod, because he no longer had a neck with which to do so, but he made an acknowledgement. He took the seed from Blighthawk in a hand the size of a backhoe scoop. The seed disappeared into his skin.

This is good. I will use your blight seed. I will distract your enemies. We will purify more earth. She will be mine. Agreed.

Ravenger lumbered out of the settling pond and onto the opposite bank. He turned back to Blighthawk and added. *Seven days.* Then, he seemed to collapse slowly, as if melting into a pile of decaying fungal matter. The pile itself grew smaller, sinking into the ground. The corrupter wondered if Ravenger traveled through the ground that way. He watched and listened until the night sounds of the nearby pond and woods started again, free of the unnatural presence of the Vengeful Earth leader. A raven croaked in the trees, which he took as a good sign.

"Come, Lady Elf Shot," he called. "We have what we need."

She jumped down out of a tree and sauntered over to rejoin her employer. "All finished?"

"Yes. We have seven days. That should be more than sufficient. Let's get back to the factory, and I'll tell you what I have in mind to trap your forest ranger."

"About time." Elf Shot opened a portal, and pulled the corrupter through with her.

The moon cast long shadows across the graveyard. Long creepy shadows. Gayle would have preferred more illumination, but the main lights at the Richter Cemetery in Acushnet were turned off when the place closed at 10 PM. It was now approaching midnight. The weathered headstones stood as mute reminders of lives long past, the famous and forgotten, alike. Gayle crept through the trees with Sheena close by her side, both shrouded in a deep obscuring mist that swirled lazily in the night air. An owl hooted nearby; enough to send a chill up her spine but not enough to startle her from her deliberate trek toward the central mausoleum.

Just before closing, two men in a pickup truck had dropped off a package at the mausoleum that stood at the center of the cemetery. They departed after unloading the coffin-sized box from the truck. Nothing had stirred since then, according to the FBSA monitor cameras. Agent Schauer had informed Gayle and Sheena of this before they headed in to try to observe and interrupt the meeting of the villainous masterminds.

Gayle stopped behind a large granite monument near the gravel road that ringed the central part of the graveyard. She sniffed the air, then turned to Sheena. She whispered, "Smell anything unnatural? Any fungus or strange disturbed earth?"

Sheena took in a slow deep breath, rolling the air between her nose and mouth. She shook her head and replied in a similar low whisper, "Nothing out of the ordinary for a graveyard... except that box."

"What about it?" Gayle studied it as best she could through the darkness and intervening rosebushes near the mausoleum.

"Smells like hospital. Disinfectant wipes, plastics, and...." She paused with a frown. "Petroleum?"

"Huh?" Gayle turned and looked at Sheena, instead.

"An oily, refinery kind of smell. Faint, and mostly cleaned up by the disinfectant, but distinctive. Probably on the outside of the box."

"Hmm...." Gayle turned back to look around the cemetery again. It remained still. "Any sign of either party, yet?"

"No, not yet." She made sure that she couldn't be observed from the road or the mausoleum and summoned the leopards, Bagheera and Misty. She cautioned both cats to remain unseen and had them stalk in opposite directions to look for anything out of place.

"Then we wait." Gayle refreshed their air cushions and the mist, making sure to blend it in with the natural obscurement available in the night air. They settled down to watch for the villains as comfortably as they could while remaining hidden. Sheena kept her senses alert for any departures from the natural sights, sounds, and smells of a graveyard in the middle of the night. The long shadows shrank bit by bit as the moon rose higher and higher in the night sky.

A rapid electronic beeping rang out through the quiet, jerking Sheena out of her reverie. It was coming from the mausoleum. It was midnight and a digital watch alarm was sounding off. She scanned the cemetery again, but nothing was moving. Gayle watched the mausoleum closely. The alarm continued into the night. Still, nothing happened and eventually the alarm stopped.

"Nothing," whispered Sheena.

Gayle huffed, "Hmph. I think we've been played or they called it off or moved it. Ravenger can't help but be punctual."

"Really?" To Sheena, that sounded odd for a creature bent on rejecting and destroying humanity.

"Yeah. He's obsessive about detail, even if the detail seems irrelevant or petty. Even mutating himself into a half-fungus, half-superhuman monster didn't do anything for his mental issues."

"Uh… there's still the box."

"Yeah. Assume it's a weapon of mass destruction, and let's take a look." Gayle got up and summoned her phantom army. She floated forward and the aerial servants followed.

Sheena blinked and tried to find words to explain why that just sounded wrong—something about Pandora and another box crossed her mind—then gave up and called Sharur, instead. "Let me know if there are any other humans, demons, ghosts, or anything else that could be threatening. I need to investigate that box up there."

"I hear and obey, Mistress." The demon wolf regarded the box without moving. "There is a corpse inside."

"What?" she asked in surprise.

"A dead human. Tightly packaged. Diseased."

"How can you tell…? Never mind." She called louder, "Gayle! There's a body in the box. Diseased. This may be our kidnap victim. Don't touch the box."

"Ooh! Okay."

Sheena used her headband electronics to call Schauer and report what they had found. The agent suggested that they do a sweep of the cemetery to secure it and make sure that it was unoccupied. He would get the bomb squad ready to move in. Sheena first checked with the leopards, but they had found nothing in their patrolling. With Gayle and Sharur helping, they quickly cleared the rest of the cemetery. The only footprints of interest were those of the men who had unloaded the box, but the FBSA had already picked up and questioned them hours ago. They knew nothing except that they had been hired to pick up and drop off the box earlier that day, and to ask no questions. There were no traces of Ravenger, his minions, or the Feathers of the Raven, except for the box.

The FBSA experts arrived and methodically determined that the box was not booby-trapped. They got it open in the same methodical fashion. As expected, biohazard stickers were plastered over the body bag inside. A separate bag contained the victim's personal effects: clothing, jewelry, watch, phone, and wallet. The watch alarm was set for midnight. The FBSA added another containment field around the corpse and moved it off to a secure facility. In the process, Sharur and Sheena both detected the oily scent much more strongly from the package.

Gayle was talking with Agent Schauer when Sheena walked up. "Even if the informant was reliable, he could still have been deliberately fed misinformation to get us here."

Schauer agreed, "Yes. That seems most likely. We will start the analysis of the body as quickly as possible. There appears to be a flash drive between the outer and inner bags. It will probably yield as many answers as questions."

"Well," Sheena asked, "does this mean that there was a real meeting somewhere else, or what?"

"Most likely, yes. This is a pretty classic distraction," Gayle sighed. "Whoever this leader of the Feathers is, he's still a step ahead of us."

"All right. Then the lab people work on analyzing clues and we watch for the next thing. Is the Syndicate strike still going off as planned?"

Gayle looked at Schauer, who replied, "Yes. That is underway as we speak."

"Good. I can add a couple of bits to the evidence pile, too. There is a specific scent of petroleum or oil present on the box. If we can get comparison samples, I'm sure I can pick out what it matches."

"That will be helpful, Shee'na. I will make arrangements and inform you as soon as we can assemble olfactory samples," Agent Schauer agreed. Sheena noticed that he had switched to using her official hero name as soon as they began planning this operation, instead of continuing to call her Officer Gardner.

"Can we track the box back to its origin with that scent?" Gayle asked.

Sheena shook her head regretfully, "No, unfortunately it's not strong enough to track through a city full of other masking smells, even if we started at the place the deliverymen picked it up. But we will definitely recognize it again."

"All right. Enough of the spooky graveyard, then. Let's go home, get some rest, and leave the labwork to the experts." Gayle bobbed into the air, waited for Sheena to dismiss her extra pets, and they headed back to Riverhaven.

Chapter 21 – The Classics always Work

"How did those clumsy monsters build something like this?" Elf Shot asked with a sneer. The lab she was poking about was, as Kadorsky had said, even better than the state of the art. Bioreactors, reagent tanks, cryo-containment chambers, it had everything a genetic or biological researcher could ask for.

"Mind control," Blighthawk replied easily.

"How?" She looked up from the cabinet she was searching.

"Spores. As brutish as the Vengeful Earth minions are, Ravenger has designed some very sophisticated abilities into them. The fungi-based ones include a type of mind control spore that works on humans and other creatures with similar mammalian biology. Somehow, he knows what he's doing, and the minions follow orders to the last decimal place. No-one knows how he communicates with or commands them, and he can do so over hundreds of minions and thousands of miles of distance." The corrupter shook his head in awe.

"So, the VE make people build and install all of this stuff for them?" The archer was more than a little skeptical.

"As far as I can tell, yes." Blighthawk arranged a drop cloth under a desk and chair and carefully moved things out of the way that he did not want to drip on. "And then they go on about their daily lives with no hint that they've designed, planned, built, moved, paid for, and installed all of this. Amazing… and frightening."

Elf Shot nodded with a frown. "I've never even heard of the faerie doing that sort of elaborate trick."

"No, they are typically content to copy what has been done before, and to charm mortals into doing their earth-bound work for them, with payment in service or faerie gold, depending upon their loyalties and whims." He took a seat and dabbed at a couple of stray drops of oil. "At least, as far as my knowledge extends."

"Yes. But just because it is a copy of something the humans have created, don't think that it isn't terrible and dangerous. The Dark Ones have their own hidden operations here that rival the Syndicate in profit and exceed them in cruelty. There is a thriving market of trade in the vices that choke humans' innermost hearts."

Blighthawk raised an eyebrow. He had never heard the archer speak this way before and it piqued his curiosity.

"One thing that I have never understood," he ventured, "is why they bother with the human world at all."

She sniffed cynically with a hard-edged smile. "Entertainment. Diversions. New sources of beauty, cruelty, and innovation. And to have a neutral battleground for their wars with each other. It would not do to spoil their own lands with such things."

"But ours are fair game; as disposable as the people caught in their games." He sighed. "That much I knew."

Elf Shot shrugged.

"Do you owe fealty to any particular lord or lady, Meg?" he asked. "Merely out of curiosity, of course."

She shook her head. "Not really. The lady I was bound to was killed. She stuck her head out where it didn't belong and got it whacked off by the light-siders. The new lord hasn't gotten around to extending me an 'invitation' to his service. By the time that happens, I want to be in a place of my own power where he can't touch me."

"Ah, I see." He steepled his fingers in thought, keeping his hands elevated so that the fluids he produced would dribble down, leaving his gloves clean. "Well, then let's be on with that."

Other Feathers bustled around the lab, bringing in or hooking up equipment and getting ready to carry on their work. Blighthawk glanced over the preparations with satisfaction. "You will need a place to hold a captive for several days. Up to a week, in fact. Unfortunately, that should not be here. Part of the plan is to draw in your ranger, and there is likely to be a lot of collateral damage when she arrives."

"Good."

"I know that you hate the sewers. Is there anywhere else you would prefer to hold a captive and then defeat your foe and complete the ritual to take back those powers?"

"Could I go back to the warehouse in the Docks?"

"You could, but I believe that the Syndicate is still using it as an entry to the club. You might draw unwanted attention."

She thought for a minute. "How about that maintenance garage and park building on West Island?"

The corrupter considered it. "Can you stay unobserved for up to a week there?"

"Sure. With a glamor or two, no one will know I'm even there. How long do I have to prepare?"

"A day or so. Once Ravenger has begun his attack in earnest, we are going to strike at Shee'na's weakness."

Elf Shot smiled in a most unpleasant way. "Her husband."

"Exactly. And rather than threaten to kill him—which is too cliché—you are instead going to threaten to hurt him, torture him, and sell him into slavery to the Dark Ones. From what I have been able to glean, that may be worse for her and harder to resist."

"I like this plan already!" she chortled.

"We will prepare the battleground to our satisfaction, first. Then, once you take him, be sure to play it out for time as long as you can. We can use the time to get more of our people into position to spread the virus."

"All right," Elf Shot grumbled, "but that delays my victory."

"I know, and appreciate that, but it makes our bigger victory that much more certain. I am not really confident that Ravenger will be able to keep the heroes busy for more than a day, or maybe two. That's all the time we need, but we still have other things to do before we can release the virus. Besides, this gives you more of an opportunity to play with your prey."

She sniffed. "Very well."

"All right, tell me more about your fight and what you have learned about her abilities, and we will make our plans. I have every intention of helping you personally, and then we will kill two birds with one stone."

Chapter 22 – Feathers of the Raven

Thursday was overcast, sticky, and warm, but Sheena still enjoyed flying over the river to the FBSA headquarters building. She didn't need a weather forecast to tell her that a thunderstorm front was moving in. All of those things that had she had shared with Gayle the previous morning were still gnawing at her in the back of her mind, but they weren't enough to prevent her from trying a couple of barrel rolls for fun. Well, all but one were still there, anyway. Eric had been much more his old self after she returned from the meeting with the FBSA agents. He made them dinner and then sat down and asked what she needed him to do to make her hero job easier. They talked and came up with a number of ideas that they could agree on. A nice backrub was part of it.

This morning, she had worked on her combat skills again with North Shore, focusing on drills to get her decision speed up. She didn't want to be caught like a deer in the headlights again trying to figure out what to do the next time Elf Shot showed up. He could only spend an hour with her before getting dressed for his own job, but it was enough to start getting several reactions burned into muscle memory. He also surprised her by escaping her time effects, which she did not know was possible before. She realized that she would have to be just as accurate and focused with her slowing or immobilizing time current tricks as she would with her arrows when fighting a skilled opponent. It was a good lesson.

There was still no sign of Ravenger or the Feathers of the Raven leader, yet, but Schauer had called her and Gayle in just after lunch to share more information on the developing case. Gayle would be joining her at the FBSA, coming from a meeting downtown with her business manager. That seemed both perfectly natural and very odd to Sheena. Gayle had a manager and staff who arranged for publicity, promotion, scheduling, and even legal support for her multi-faceted career as a musician, hero, and celebrity. Looking at it from the outside and thinking about the business, it just seemed to make Gayle's whole life even bigger than it already was. While Sheena felt a flicker of guilty pleasure at being close to all of that, she really didn't feel it was for her. She wondered again for the umpteenth time how Gayle managed to stay so... normal... in the midst of that pressure and attention.

Arriving at the FBSA building, she carefully watched for helicopters and landed at a safe corner of the roof. She passed through the security checks and went down to the operations center the agents were using to manage the investigation and response. Gayle was already there with Schauer and Calderón. The singer waved her over.

"Hiya, Sheena! How was your morning?"

"Good, thanks. I got in a really helpful workout with North Shore."

"Learn any new tricks?" Gayle asked with a curious tilt of her head.

"Yeah. I'll have to fill you in later. Stuff you probably already know, but great for me."

"All right, remind me if I forget... Oh! That reminds me!" Gayle grinned. "Before Elf Shot popped up and shot your truck out from under you, you were talking about getting wristbands like mine with the hero-grade electronics that you could wear around with normal clothes. Those came in from *Image*, but you have to authorize the device replacement with your wireless carrier. They're back at home, next to the microwave."

"Next to the microwave?"

Gayle blushed. "I was gonna surprise you by getting them unpacked and ready, but I didn't realize that I was running late and I took too long answering a fan email."

Sheena chuckled and shook her head. "Okay, fine. Later."

Schauer was talking with some other members of the team, but Calderón just leaned against the wall grinning at the ladies' conversation. "Buenos tardes, Sheena. How is Eric doing?"

"Umm... Good?" She gave him a curious look. "Anything special I should know about?"

He straightened up and adjusted his black suit coat. "I was hoping that our conversation yesterday helped him decide what to do."

"Oh, that. Well, he was much more relaxed and very helpful last night, yes."

The shaman smirked knowingly. Gayle laughed, and Sheena exclaimed, "That's not what I meant!" She laughed and mock-punched his arm. "Control yourself, or I'll sic Sharur on you!"

"All right, all right!" he chuckled. He noticed Schauer's nod from the front of the room. There were almost two dozen people gathered for the briefing. "We might as well laugh while we can. The news isn't pretty. Are you two ready for the update?"

"Let's get to it!" Gayle replied. They seated themselves and waited for Agent Schauer to begin.

"Ladies and gentlemen, we have gained a lot of information over the past twenty-four hours. Section leads will provide the detail as we go, but here is the summary. Forty-eight days ago, a newly formed group calling themselves the 'Feathers of the Raven' announced itself by issuing a series of demands and a manifesto through regular and social media. At the time, no specific threats were made. As per standard procedure, the FBI began monitoring of information regarding the group.

"Thirty-six days ago, the first of twelve thefts of biological research equipment, material, or information was made by agents later traced to the Feathers of the Raven organization. Such thefts have all been carefully planned and executed with no prior warning to the targets. Metahuman freelancers have conducted or led all known thefts. The most recent was four and half days ago. These thefts have not only given them the capability to build a biological weapon of mass destruction, it has also given them the ability to deliver it... potentially globally... and to vaccinate against it, if our logic is correct.

"The primary motive for this organized criminal activity seems to be a combination of ideological disgust and vengeance. Specifically, their ideological disgust is directed at what the group considers to be the unchecked greed and exploitation of the earth by for-profit corporations and the collective failure of the governments of the world to safeguard ecological and economic sustainability and protection of individual rights. Vengeance is directed specifically at the leaders and decision makers of organizations that inflict suffering, as they see it, on the earth and injustice on its people. Putting it simply, if you have knowingly made a decision that favors corporations, profits, or political convenience over people in any meaningful way, and it caused significant harm to the earth or third-party individuals, then the Feathers of the Raven sees you as guilty of a crime punishable by death.

"Walter Herschel, the Chief Operations Officer of Hardy Oil Services, was kidnapped twelve days ago from the underground garage of his office building. He was not reported missing until six days ago because he and his wife were scheduled to fly to San Francisco on vacation and they were not expected back for a week. The Venture City police identified the threat level 35 villain Elf Shot as the leader of the kidnapping. Law enforcement officers have not been able to locate Mr. Herschel until early this morning, when his corpse was discovered in a well-sealed casualty bag delivered to Richter Cemetery late last night.

"Mr. Herschel's body contains evidence that not only are the Feathers of the Raven capable of weaponizing a deadly virus, they have already done so and tested it on one of their ideological enemies. They have delivered Mr. Herschel's corpse as a proof of their capabilities, but they have made no additional demands. Instead, they explain that they expect 'the successors to the current positions of global leadership to display wiser judgment and stewardship of the people and ecological systems under their care.' They give a succinct, but complete, set of suggestions and governance proposals in their revised manifesto accompanying the body. They make no suggestion that they will be dissuaded from their plans, and semantic analysis suggests that this plan is already in motion on a global scale.

"There remains some uncertainty about the distribution vector of the virus. There are some signs that the virus that killed Mr. Herschel was not the virus that infected him. This may mean that the terrorists have discovered a method for making the virus mutate, or for attaching a more deadly virus to one that is less dangerous but easier to spread. The labs continue to work on this, and we are now marshalling the best technology and expertise available to reinforce and expand this effort.

"We still know very little about the leader of this group. Two members of the Feathers of the Raven were captured by the Pillars of Virtue supergroup last night as the Feathers withdrew from a drug lab that they had taken over from the Syndicate. They have so far insisted on legal representation and remained silent under legal forms of questioning. We do know from traces and clues found in the lab that the group expected it to be destroyed by the Syndicate, instead of captured intact by the Pillars. A forensics team is working at that site now to collect evidence.

"We have some information that suggests that the Feathers of the Raven have formed a temporary alliance with the Vengeful Earth eco-terrorist group. The purpose of this is unknown, since they already have their own plan in motion. It could be to provide a diversion or delay that would allow them to stay hidden or to finish mass producing and moving the virus. We are putting our agents and allies specializing in the Vengeful Earth's activities on highest alert. We should expect some form of threatening activity from them within the next 24 to 48 hours.

"The Feathers of the Raven have employed the villain named Elf Shot in a number of crimes, and we should consider her a lieutenant of the group's leader. She is probably not connected to the group by ideology, but by mutual benefit. The group's leader seems to be providing Elf Shot with resources she can use to pursue her particular vendetta against the hero, Shee'na. Specifically, Elf Shot seeks to capture Shee'na in order to perform a ritual that will kill her and take her metahuman powers, which she believes were supposed to be granted to her, and not to Shee'na.

"Priority for this investigative team is to locate and identify the leader of the Feathers of the Raven and his capabilities. Additional priorities are to analyze the viral threat and find a counter or cure. Ideally, we can find a way to prevent the release and spread of the virus. Secondary priorities are to prepare for and counter threats from the Vengeful Earth and from Elf Shot. Subject to general questions, I will turn this briefing over to the team leads."

There were no big questions for Agent Schauer and the group split into its specialist teams. Sheena asked Calderón, "What do you want us to do?"

The shaman looked thoughtful. "Something big is coming from the spirit world. I can feel it brewing, but I cannot see it clearly, yet. I think that Raven is the key, but the Raven I know is not like the one they describe in the group's messages." He shook his head. "We need to figure out where that Raven is coming from. With this, I do not think you can help me, Sheena. I suggest that you both keep looking for clues. And, you should prepare for a Vengeful Earth attack."

"Have you talked to Raven before?" Sheena asked.

Calderón frowned for a moment. "Yes, I have. But I have seen no traces of him for a long time. I wonder...."

The heroines waited, then Gayle asked, "What?"

The shaman shook his head. "I wonder what happened to Raven. Excuse me, please. I think this is something I need to find out." He quickly made his way over to Schauer and drew him aside. Calderón seemed to be explaining something to his partner quickly and with barely restrained animation. Schauer simply nodded at the end and Calderón hastened out of the room.

"Well, that certainly got him moving!" Gayle muttered. "Do you think he's going to go find Raven in the spirit world, or something?"

Sheena nodded. "That seems like a good bet. I hope he can manage it okay. I have a feeling that this is the big threat Shanikali called on me to stop. If the Raven of these terrorists is coming from the Beastlands of Shanikali, then this isn't simply a biological terror plot. There's something bigger wrapped up in it."

"I think you may be right," Gayle replied quietly. "And if it's big enough to need a goddess to fix it, is Calderón going to be all right?"

Sheena didn't answer, but set off after the shaman. Gayle followed close behind.

She followed Calderón mostly by scent. The government shaman was hurrying quickly through the building. She caught up to him at the non-descript door to a room on the first floor of the FBSA headquarters. The door was numbered simply 128, but it didn't smell like an office. To Sheena, it smelled like... something else entirely; what it was she could not be sure.

"Hey, Felix, wait up!" she called.

Calderón stopped at the door and looked back at her. "Sheena, thank you, but I do not think you can help me with this."

"Have you considered that this might be why Shanikali is involved?" she shot back at him.

He froze, one hand on the doorknob. Several thoughts and expressions crossed his face in the space of seconds. His hand dropped to his side.

"What if you find Raven, and he is the Raven of the terrorists? And angry? Could you even get back to tell us?"

Calderón grinned. "I am not without my own tricks, Sheena."

"Of course. Show me."

He hesitated. "All right. Come with me." He opened the door.

Beyond the door was not so much a room as an enclosed bit of the outdoors. One wall was almost completely transparent. The transparency somehow extended over the outside half of the ceiling to show the sky, though Sheena knew they were inside the FBSA building. The other walls were paneled with natural wood. The floor was dirt and natural grasses. A tidy fire pit sat in the center of the area. Sheena noticed several piles of different kinds of wood against the interior wall. Strangest of all was what looked like a fish pond near the opposite corner of the room. It all smelled natural and felt connected to the outdoors. The grasses waved softly in Gayle's breeze.

"Wow! Interesting place," Gayle breathed. "For magic work?"

"Yes," Calderón acknowledged. "The room is protected, but this is the real, undisturbed earth. The pool taps a spring brought to the surface by natural forces; aided by magic." He was removing his black agency shoes and socks.

Sheena said, "One question. How do I make sure that I go where you go? I can get back to the Cedar Forest easily, but I don't know where you are going."

The shaman smiled broadly and sat on the ground next to the fire pit. "Track me!"

"Huh?"

"Come, Sheena! If you have the power of the goddess enough to help me, then tracking me through the spirit world should be child's play for you!"

"I'll watch here, like I did before," Gayle said softly to her friend. Sheena nodded.

"Catch me if you can, goddess!" Calderón said with a playful grin. He turned his gaze on the fire pit, but did not prepare a fire. He placed the backs of his hands on his knees and relaxed. After a breath or two, he started muttering words under his breath. Sheena did not recognize the language, but could tell it wasn't Spanish. Shortly, his lips moved but his voice stilled. Then, even his lips ceased moving.

"Hmph. If I'm as good as I should be, he can have whatever head start he wants. I'll still catch him," Sheena said to Gayle.

"Good hunting," the singer offered.

Sheena nodded and then concentrated for a moment. Then, in one smooth movement, she spread her wings and launched herself straight up out of her body and into the spirit world. The cedar forest appeared around her, unfolding almost like a child's pop-up folding storybook. The air was crisp and clear, in contrast to the muggy afternoon air back in Venture City. Calderón was nowhere in sight.

In the corner of her mind still attached to her physical body, Sheena relaxed and sat herself down back in Room 128. She was dimly aware of Gayle settling in to wait and of the soft rise and fall of her own chest. She could hear Calderón's breathing, too. She grinned to herself. Using the same kind of technique she had used to study the time currents before, she slipped her perspective midway between the cedar forest and the physical world. In that halfway border, she studied Calderón and saw the trail he had left stretching as clearly as a set of muddy footprints off into the spirit world.

"Sharur, come to me."

The demon wolf appeared. "Mistress. We are hunting?"

"Tracking, certainly. Hunting, maybe. What do you know about Raven?" She brought her perspective back fully into the spirit world. Now that she knew what to look for, the tracks remained easy to follow. She hefted her bow and started walking after the shaman.

"A black bird of great power. Feeds on carrion and whatever else he can find. Always hungry and greedy for food. Enjoys shiny things and playing tricks on mortals. Sometimes acts with enormous wisdom, and sometimes is as foolish as a newborn cub. He has been a protector and a spirit guiding the dead to the afterlife." He walked along with her, sniffing the air. "Do you stalk your friend, or merely follow him?"

"Umm...," Sheena considered. Practice wouldn't hurt. "Stalk so that when he finds Raven we two might come up unseen."

"Very well." He faded into a barely detectable outline. Sheena did the same thing, getting herself "out of the way," and feeling very pleased with herself. The wolf nodded. Sheena picked up the pace.

"Have you seen Raven recently?"

The wolf shook his head. "That question has no answer here."

"Ah, I see. Do you know where I can find Raven?"

"Yes. If Raven is willing to be found, you can go to his home. You will know the way."

"And if he does not want to be found?"

"Then it will be a contest of your will, skill, and power against his, but he will still be found in his home. It may just be hidden, or you may face challenges along the way."

Sheena considered that for a bit. She spotted Calderón up ahead as he walked along the rocky shore of a river. This was not the River of Time, she noticed. The water here was rushing along its shallow rock-tumbled bed just as almost-there as the rest of her surroundings, without the misty, ephemeral quality of the time stream. In the spirit world, the shaman was wearing plan white cotton trousers and a sort of loose wrap-around tunic of the same material tied at the sides. He wore a colorful beaded belt over it and carried a smooth redwood walking stick. Here the sun was bright overhead. Calderón looked back the way he had come and shaded his eyes, but did not seem to see Sheena or Sharur. He shrugged and shook his head. Sheena grinned to herself.

Calderón waded into the river and watched the water carefully. He adjusted his position and took a few more steps, then waited. Some minutes passed, during which Sheena and the wolf moved into a shady spot further up the shore. Calderón leaned over and whispered to something in the water, then reached down and gently pulled a fish from the river.

"Fish tickling?" Sheena whispered to Sharur.

"He is a kind hunter," the wolf replied. "He apologized to the fish, explaining that he needed a gift of food for Raven. The fish allowed itself to be caught for this."

"Hmm...."

Calderón looked back along the path he had taken once more, obviously wondering where Sheena was. He looked onward. She decided to take pity on him. Striding out of the shadows, she said, "Well, Felix? Are you going to stand there all day with your fish, or will you go on?"

Calderón jumped and nearly dropped the fish. "Aha! Oh, you startled me! You have been watching me?"

"Yes. I have been practicing my stalking. I am still trying to master that in the real world. Doing fine here, though!"

"Apparently!"

"You have a gift. We move on?"

"Yes. I am ready."

"Sharur and I will follow." She stepped back and made herself fade away. Calderón nodded and waded across the river. He followed a path in the grass of the prairie that wound its way up a small embankment. He did not go very far before reaching the top, and then he stopped. Sheena and Sharur came up alongside him.

Before them was a scene of destruction. A wide plain seemingly two miles across stretched ahead of them. To the left, the low mountains that bordered the plain rose in barren, rocky heaps. To the right, the river bent around the other edge of the plain, but it was stinking and polluted, with streaks of oil and bright colored chemicals running through the sluggish water. Sheena turned back to look at the pristine river they had just crossed, and saw that it was now dirty and polluted, with jagged rust-streaked rocks and sharp bits of metal and trash dumped everywhere along the banks. The plain itself was littered with smoldering piles of trash and bones. She could see a few leafless trees rising here and there from the land. Pools of bubbling muck dotted the landscape, giving off both an acrid and a petroleum-laden scent. And bodies. Human and animal corpses, mostly picked free of the juiciest bits of meat, but otherwise left to rot in the heat beneath the low-hanging overcast. Sheena turned back to look again. The sunny afternoon sky she had been walking under before was gone. Now the dark, ominous overcast stretched to the horizon. There was nothing to show what had slain the creatures whose corpses littered the plain. No weapons or signs of battle, just death and poison everywhere.

At the very center of the plain was the ruin of an enormous tree. Barren of foliage like the rest, this one towered high over the landscape. Sheena could see the silhouette of a bird perched in the tree. She glanced over at Calderón. "Not what you were expecting to find?" He shook his head silently. "Didn't think so."

The shaman trudged forward with his fish and Sheena stalked along behind him. Calderón avoided the corpses and sludge pools, making his way toward the great tree. This part of the journey had the strange, dreamlike quality of seeming like it went on interminably, at the same time that it seemed like just an instant before they arrived near the trunk of the tree.

"Ho, Raven!" Calderón called. "I bring you a gift!"

The bird in the tree looked down at him. It was dull black and shaped mostly like an ordinary raven, but other than that it had little in common with what Sheena expected. It was at least seven feet from its feet to the sticky, scabrous feathers poking up at odd angles from its head. The feathers all over its body and wings seemed damaged in some places, matted and coated with oily goo in others. Its eyes oozed a bright green fluid. Patches of its body kept bursting into flame and then going out nearly as quickly. The strange substances that seeped from the bird's feathers dripped to cover its perch and the ground beneath the tree.

"What do you want, son of Man?" the bird croaked.

Calderón lay the fish down as close to the tree as he dared and then backed away respectfully. The fluids smoked slightly where they touched the yellowed grass. "I would like to know something."

Raven fluttered down and examined the fish with one eye. He drew his head back and stabbed the fish with his beak, crushing its head. "Not ripe, yet." He picked up the fish in his beak and tossed it into a nearby pool of oil. He flew with what seemed a great struggle up to one of the low branches. He croaked again, "What do you want to know?"

"What happened to you since the last time we met? Your home was not covered with all of this trash, then." The shaman waved his hand at the dismal surroundings.

"I helped a man. He was a warrior, riding wings of metal, sent by his elders to defend their gold in the north. The elders were greedier than me! The people the elders should have protected were left to the invaders. Many of the people were killed, including the warrior's family. The warrior was wounded and his wings were seared by the fire arrows of the invaders. He fell into a hole in the ground, where he would have died in pitch and poison. His ancestors made a bargain with me, long ago, so I saved him and shared my power with him. But to do that, I had to get him out of the stinking hole and I got pitch on my feathers. The pitch makes me sick and angry. It is not right for those elders to be greedier than me, for I am Raven! Now, we will turn the trick on the elders and then I will have millions of corpses to pick clean, at my leisure."

"But, this is not right!" Calderón protested. "You don't need all this... trash and poison to do your tricks!"

"It is justice."

"Justice, to destroy the land and water like this? To hurt the people with poisons?"

"It is justice! Until none of the elders of the sons of Man are greedier for their treasures than Raven is for his!" croaked the spirit emphatically. The bird's eyes gleamed brightly for a moment. "You serve those elders, son of Man! I think you will need to ripen, too, before I feast on your soft bits."

Raven lunged forward to impale Calderón on his beak. The shaman stumbled backward and managed to avoid the blow. He held up his walking stick to ward off another peck. Raven swooped down and splintered the stick with a single swift blow. Calderón gasped with dismay. The great bird landed without grace and hopped forward as the shaman backed further away.

Sheena commanded Sharur, "Protect Calderón!"

The iron wolf leaped between Raven and the shaman and growled at the bird. Raven flapped up into the air croaking in alarm. He fluttered about in a circle before returning angrily to his perch higher up in the tree. He fluffed his feathers and croaked, "Bah, I'll feed on you soon enough! Diseased corpses still have plenty of meat, too. I can wait. I always get what is mine. And you, Shanikali...."

Sheena stepped forward and asked, "What?"

"Do not interfere, goddess! This is within my purview." With a wave of his wing, Raven cast them out of his domain. Tumbling through the air head over heels, Sheena and Sharur were cast back to where they had started in the cedar forest. She caught a hazy glimpse of Calderón snapping back into his own body and falling over on his side back in the physical world. She regained her balance and stretched. *Nothing broken, but that was weird!* Sharur growled once with indignation on her behalf.

"Thank you, Sharur. I had best get back." The wolf nodded and Sheena closed her eyes and slipped back into her physical body. It felt like going down a twisty playground slide. She scrambled to her feet and rushed over to the shaman. "Felix! Are you okay?"

"Unh..., sí. I am okay."

"Well. I think we know more about what's going on, now! There *is* a spirit world influence on the Feathers. And it started with this person that Raven saved."

Calderón still seemed shaken. "Raven has been corrupted, somehow."

"Huh? What do you mean? What did you guys find out?" asked Gayle. Sheena explained what they had seen and heard. "Wow... that's pretty serious. What can we do about it?"

Sheena turned to Calderón, who shook his head slowly in puzzlement. "I do not know. I have run into corrupted shamans and toxic spirits, before, but... the totem itself?"

"Well," Sheena sighed, "it looks like it's time for more research, then. And in the meantime, we'd better get ready for all of the other stuff Schauer went over in the briefing."

Gayle nodded and Calderón added, "I will go fill Tom in on what we've discovered. I think this tells us a lot more about the Feathers' leader, but it may not be enough to be practical, yet."

"There are some important details in what Raven told us. I don't know if this will get us any closer, but it sure is getting us in deeper and deeper," Sheena agreed.

Chapter 23 – The Angry Earth

"Sheena! The trees are moving! Get up!"

"Mmph?" Gayle's voice roused Sheena from sleep. Light was peeping in through the blinds. The clock read 5:47 AM. Eric was in the bathroom getting ready for work. Sheena called out in a groggy voice, "What about the trees?"

"Get up! The Vengeful Earth are on the move! They're bringing the forest in Cedar Swamp Park to life and it's headed into town!"

That got her attention. She scrambled out of bed. "Be there in a minute!"

Sheena dressed quickly in her hero costume and made sure everything was in place. Eric emerged from the bathroom. "Whoa, what's up?" he asked.

"It sounds like Ravenger is animating a forest and the trees are headed into the city. I have to go stop it."

Eric blinked. "Uh… Should I stay here or go to work? Whatever you need me to do."

She considered that for a brief moment. "No, go ahead. At least while the Vengeful Earth are on the outskirts of town, Elf Shot shouldn't be looking for me anywhere else. That should leave you clear."

"Okay. Thanks for filling me in on the situation with the Feathers and their virus stuff. Good luck, stay safe, and I love you." He kissed her cheek. "Call if you need anything."

"Will do, thanks, Eric." She hurried out to the balcony to join Gayle.

"Trees only? No VE shroominators, or anything?" Gayle asked over the League of Titans channel as she was flying with Sheena toward Cedar Swamp Park.

"No, nothing. No shrooms, crystals, weed whackers, or anything," responded the distant voice of Icelock, one of the Titans' leaders. "Just trees. But angry trees. They're bashing anything that gets in the way of their morning walk. Ice blasts aren't doing a whole lot other than slowing them down."

"Do the trees show any sensory organs or weak points? Any anthropomorphizing?" asked Syngularity, another one of the Titans, a figure skater with gravity control powers.

"No. Just trees. Except that they are walking on big clumps of roots like feet," Icelock replied.

"Are we sure this is the VE doing this, then?" asked Sheena.

Gayle nodded emphatically. "Yep. I'm sure. Even if the 'nature-gone-wild' theme wasn't a giveaway, Ravenger posted to my SpaceBook page, 'Go take a walk in the park, Gayle Force, before the park comes taking a walk to you!' Arrgh, I hate that guy!"

Sheena laughed at the ridiculousness of it all, and then flapped harder to keep up with her friend. She had been patched into the Titans' network on a temporary basis. She asked the heroes, "Okay, so how do we defeat trees?"

Jet Flash, the League's powersuited captain responded, "Draw them off of roads and areas where they might clog traffic and cause a lot of property damage, and then chop, burn, or otherwise take them out at the base of the trunk. Even if that doesn't de-animate them, it will slow them down. In the meantime, I'll call the tree service."

"Good," Gayle said. "Heavy hitters on the trees. Who do you want looking for the instigators? Something has to be causing this and we need to find it and take it out."

"Already got a couple of my drone suits on it, Gayle, but you and Sheena as the nature-sensing types would probably be the best choice. See what you can find, but be careful."

"That's good," Sheena remarked privately to Gayle. "I don't really think my critters or arrows or time powers are made for cutting down trees. Especially a lot of them."

"Right. Everybody has something they can do to help. Sometimes, it might just be healing and scouting. It all depends on what we end up fighting."

They cleared the West Bank district and could already see the tops of ambulatory trees bobbing and waving back and forth as they shambled into the city. It was unreal to see the wet, fresh-turned earth in the center of the park reserve where the trees had started uprooting themselves. Their departure had left a large cleared area in the middle of the park. From the air, Sheena and Gayle could see two other similar holes in the forest further west and north. It looked like the clearings were getting larger as more trees shambled toward different parts of the city.

"Okay," Gayle reported, "one group is headed west toward the airport. Another is moving north toward the center of Braley and the university campus there. The southeast group is wandering south toward Scott Industries Industrial Park and across Highway 140 into the commercial district."

"Oh, I hope they don't scratch the paint on my wind turbine factory," Jet Flash's voice muttered over the league channel. "I just had the place landscaped! We even painted fresh lines on the employee parking lot!"

"There's a thunderstorm brewing already, so I can really crank up the tornado power," Gayle said over the main channel. "I'm gonna check the park to make sure that there's a safe place to drop all the lumber."

"Good. Let us know what you find," Jet Flash replied.

Gayle swooped over the walking forest, heading back the way it had come. None of the trees seemed to notice her or Sheena. Even when Gayle dipped down within reach of their upper branches, they ignored her and kept on walking. Sheena looked at the trees as they moved, but couldn't easily see anything unusual about them. They just plodded along at a slow walking pace with a shambling sort of gait. The smell of freshly turned earth, roots, and bog mold accompanied the trees, but Sheena didn't find anything specifically unusual to home in on as a source of whatever was animating and controlling them. She flew on with Gayle further into the central section of the park.

There, shrubs, grass, and young trees still stood, but the earth was churned up all over the area from the uprooting of hundreds of mature trees. Sheena watched as still more trees on the edge of the area lurched to one side or the other and pulled their own roots up to start walking with the others. A few paved trails through the park were torn up as the roots underneath them were removed. A boardwalk near the water was completely splintered. In most places, swamp water was already seeping into the holes left by the uprooted trees.

"Any tracks?" Gayle asked.

"None worth following, yet. Let's try to find the center," Sheena replied.

They glided another hundred meters further north. A tabby-striped form on a large boulder waved at them. Gayle seemed to recognize her and waved back. Sheena looked at the lithe little woman perched atop the boulder. She was a head shorter than Sheena, covered with fur, and sported catlike features—eyes, ears, tail, and whiskers. A full-size Japanese-style katana sword was strapped to her back. Other than the sword, she wore only brief running shorts and a sports bra over her fur.

"Hiyas, Windy!" the catgirl called from below.

"Hiya, Leaf!" Gayle returned the greeting. "See anything useful?"

"Nopes. Just the trees goin' walkies. Gonnas keep lookin,' They're messin' up the park!"

"Yeah, that's for sure! No sign of the Vengeful Earth?" The catgirl shook her head. Gayle shrugged and said, "We're going to try to find the center, where they started pulling themselves up. Keep in touch!"

As they continued further, Sheena asked, "Who was that?"

"Leafchaser. She's a Titan, but she doesn't live at Riverhaven. She just visits. Leaf was an actual stray housecat caught on the edge of a magic spell cast by the Ancients, and she got turned into a human... kinda. The wizard who lived in the park and left food for her took her and her kittens in, but he couldn't reverse the spell. She decided to stick around as a protector. She knows the park better than anyone."

"And the sword?"

"She says it extends her claws. Goes with her theme, too, I guess." Gayle giggled.

"Hey, there's something," Sheena pointed. The ground was low and marshy, but they had found the central place where the tracks of the trees through the area were all moving away. Sheena swooped low and hovered. "Wow, there's almost no stable ground here. It's either turned up or bog."

"Yeah, be careful. The VE can easily come up out of the ground."

Sheena regained some height and studied the earth. "Are we freshly bubbled? I'm going to land and look more closely."

"Yep, you're covered. Go ahead." Gayle summoned a trio of aerial servants as Sheena landed. She sent them squishing around the churned up dirt and mud to see if anything would jump out and attack them. Nothing did.

Sheena summoned her own pets, too, to be on the safe side. She gave them all orders to stand guard, then she called Sharur. He appeared as usual, and sank to the tops of his paws in the soft earth.

"Good morning, Mistress. What would you have me do?"

"The Vengeful Earth have made all the trees get up and walk away. We think they are going to attack different parts of the city. This is one of the places at the center of the spell, or whatever it was, that made them come to life. We are looking for the cause. Take a sniff and a look and see what you can tell me."

Sharur raised his nose to the wind. Suddenly, he splayed his legs wider and growled, "The ground underneath moves! Beware!" The wolf and the leopard spirits were also agitated, detecting tremors through the ground right after Sharur did. Sheena launched herself into the air and flapped urgently to gain altitude.

With a wet slurping sort of noise, three creatures the size of bulldozers burrowed their way up out of the swampy earth. They looked very much like giant wrinkled potatoes with the digging claws of moles attached to short, stubby root-like legs. Each also had two long woody roots roughly ten centimeters thick and at least six meters long attached to joints above where its shoulders would be, if it had shoulders. They had no obvious heads, eyes, or sensory organs. They ignored Sheena, Sharur, and her pets. Instead, all three lashed out with their roots at Gayle. The roots stretched and lengthened easily to catch her near what would have been treetop height, had there been any trees left. Each root wrapped instantly around whatever it could catch—arms, legs, or torso—then pulled itself tight, and began to squeeze through her air cushioning and drag her closer to the ground.

Sheena noticed another ring of the creatures burrowing up further away in a circle around the site. "Go for the entangling roots! Get Gayle free!" she called to her pets. Gayle's phantom army was already jumping into action, as well, converging on the monster nearest to her.

Gayle gritted her teeth and wrapped her arms and legs around the roots that had a grip on each. Then, she started with her left arm and began sending blasts of air down the root into the top of the creature, using the root as an aiming guide. The creatures were already pulling her lower.

Sharur slipped to his side, and then scrambled to his feet and leaped to the top of the closest creature. With his iron teeth, he bit down fiercely into a root and then shook his head from side to side. The root began to tear apart. The spirit animals did the same thing, but with considerably less success. Their teeth, while impressive, were not meant for hacking through green, woody plant material.

Sheena toggled the League of Titans' channel as she quickly targeted each of the three creatures in succession with a current of slowed time. "We have contact with some kind of root roper creatures at the center of the central point. Three of them are pulling Gayle down. I can see at least six more further out converging on our position. Please send assistance."

"Roger, Sheena. Leafchaser and Liberty Girl are closest," Jet Flash responded. "Let me know if you need more help. The trees are falling over on things, then getting back up. Pretty crude, but with so many of them, it's surprisingly effective. We're working on stopping them before they do more damage."

"On my ways," added Leafchaser.

"Be there in a flash," another voice, presumably Liberty Girl, responded.

"Mistress," Sharur reported, "there is some sort of poison on these roots." He kept chomping and managed to sever the one he was working on. It loosened its hold.

"Sheena, I'm going numb!" Gayle called. She shook off the root that the demon wolf had bitten through and tried to climb again, but the other five kept reeling her in.

Sheena reached out and poured a healing current of golden motes into Gayle; one designed to wash out poison, as well as to repair injury. The singer's look of panic vanished instantly.

"Thanks! That's better!" With an arm free, Gayle churned her hand in a circle and whipped up a storm cloud near the creature that her phantom army was battling. The "root ropers" were continuing to ignore anything other than Gayle. While the repeated battering of the aerial servants was turning the potato-like flesh of the creature into mush, it was not letting go of its target.

Sharur had switched his bite to the second root on the creature he was facing. He dug in and started tearing at the root. Because they were not having much effect on the entangling roots, Sheena commanded her other pets to attack the body of the middle creature, hoping to tear it apart. She took her bow in hand and produced a broad-headed war arrow, and took aim at a spot just above the joint of one of the roots holding Gayle's other arm. She released the arrow with all of the power behind it that she could muster. It pierced all the way through the root and sank out of sight into the ground next to the creature. The root continued to pull, but the arrow had cut through enough of its fibers to weaken it.

The storm cloud began spitting out lightning bolts, too. They were not precisely targeted, but lashed the root ropers with electricity and enough force to rock them slightly on their feet. Sheena tightened and reinforced the slowed time currents on each of the creatures, then drew another war arrow and repeated her shot. She aimed for a slightly higher spot on the same root. All it was doing was tugging in one direction, so this was not a difficult shot. Again, it weakened the root, but it would still take more arrows to cut through the thick plant material.

By this time, Gayle was getting closer to the ground, despite the slowing effects that Sheena had managed to apply. She turned her attention to the same creature that her phantom army was attacking, and started bashing it with narrow, rapid-fire blasts of air. At this closer range, she quickly blasted away chunks of the potato-like creature around the root joint and pulled the root free of her waist. Sharur severed the second root joint and Gayle pulled that root free, as well.

"That works!" Gayle shouted over the crash of her thunder cloud.

"Great!" Sheena replied. "Then, do it faster!" She wrapped Gayle in a current of quickened time and reapplied another anti-poison healing dose to counter the speeded up metabolism she would be experiencing as a result. Gayle's rapid-fire blasts became an air hammer machine gun, carving more chunks out of the monsters.

The second ring of root ropers was getting closer, Sheena noticed.

"Here's to help," came the cry from the katana-wielding catgirl, Leafchaser. With a single flashing stroke, she severed the remaining root around Gayle's left leg. "Gots to have the right tool for the job!"

"I'll take care of these," a woman in red, white, and blue spandex called out. Standing well over two meters tall, she was wearing red high-heeled boots with a white star on their sides. Her long, muscular legs were uncovered up to where her uniform began with a blue boy-short unitard with short sleeves and a high collar. Her powerful arms were bare down to a pair of white finger-gloves. Her face was concealed by a red mask that covered from her cheekbones to her hairline, leaving a short crop of brunette hair visible. On her chest was a red and white stylized Liberty Bell. She landed in front of one of the oncoming creatures and hoisted it into the air above her head. Before it could lash out and grab her with its roots, she had thrown it bodily into the next one along the circle.

"Thanks, Lib!" Gayle sang out, a half octave higher than her usual voice. Liberty Girl waved and moved on to the next Vengeful Earth monster.

"Heads up, everyone!" Sheena shouted. "Big bubbling from the swamp behind you, Gayle!"

"A massive creature. Much larger than these," Sharur reported to Sheena.

Gayle finished freeing herself from the initial set of root ropers and turned to look for the new threat. She reapplied her shield of air that had been worn off by the ropers. Sheena decided later that this was what saved her from what happened in the next few seconds.

First, three enormous eyestalks rose up from the swamp. Each eye was the size of a basketball on a rubbery tentacle-like stalk a dozen meters long. Then, the eyestalks were followed by a frog-like body the size of a whale shark. The chief feature of the body was a wide, gaping mouth big enough to swallow a small truck. Its tongue was a long sticky lash similar to a frog's, but there was a sort of duct attached to the bottom of its base. The monster seemed to have legs, but Sheena could not really be sure. They were hidden beneath the surface of the swamp. The eyestalks terminated in a bony cluster at the top of the thing's spine, or where a spine should be.

Like the root ropers, it ignored the other heroes and the pets, and focused solely on Gayle. It opened its mouth, lifted its tongue, and blew a jet of some kind of particles all over her. As far as Sheena could tell, the air cushion prevented any from actually touching her. The tongue lowered slightly, and it shot out and slammed into the singer like a wet, meaty freight train. It was obviously meant to stick to her and then withdraw into its cavernous maw, but it only succeeded in disorienting her and knocking her back through the air a few dozen meters.

"Oh, I knows what to do with giant frogs!" Leafchaser said gleefully. She jumped into the creature's mouth and started raining blow after blow on the thing's tongue. Then, her ears and tail began to quiver and she shook her head back and forth. "Oh, ick! Nots good! Poison spit!"

Sheena immediately sent out a stream of healing energy and antidote to the wobbling catgirl. Sharur snorted his amusement and bounded over to the thing's side, sinking up to his shoulders in the swamp. He took in a deep breath, and let it out again as a white-hot blast of fire against the creature's flank. The mud beneath his iron paws couldn't support his weight, and Sharur sank beneath the surface, bubbles of steam rising from the water. Leafchaser renewed her assault on the massive tongue, and then leaped out of the mouth and back onto muddy ground as it gave way.

Sharur scrambled out of deep water and into the shallows, apparently none the worse for the dunking. Liberty Girl finished battering all six of the second-string root ropers into mush as Sheena turned her healing back on Gayle, adding the antidote effect for good measure. The behemoth frog-creature sank halfway back into the swamp and then seemed to deflate. The eyes glazed over and the eyestalks flopped over limply.

"Strange," Sharur remarked. "It is dead."

"Maybe it just knows when it gets beaten," opined Leafchaser.

Sheena's wings were tired from all of the hovering. She landed and looked at the frog creature closely. It was not just playing dead. Sharur was right; it *was* dead. So were all of the root ropers, though she was certain they had not done enough damage to kill all of them. She dismissed her extra pets, keeping just Sharur. The other currents of time she had used had run their course, as well.

"Ravenger knows he lost this round and he's cut their strings." Gayle floated wearily to the ground. "Ugh. Thanks, Sheena. That thing packed a wallop, and I think the stuff it shot at me were more spores. I was feeling really light-headed there, for a bit, and not just because of that hit."

"Well, isn't that normal for an airhead?" joked Liberty Girl with a wink.

"Wind control, Alexa! It's wind control!" laughed Gayle. It seemed like an old joke between them.

Sharur made his way out of the swamp water and onto semi-solid ground. He shook himself dry, spraying muddy water everywhere. Sheena raised a wing to shield herself from the spray. The clouds overhead chose that moment to rumble with thunder and start releasing the rain they had stored up during the past few humid summer days. She knelt to look at the ground beyond where the battle had churned it into mud.

"Any more monsters? Gots more sword for 'em," Leafchaser remarked.

Gayle looked around. "No, I don't think so. But, there might be more VE ambushes like this at the other two central points. He apparently put a lot of effort into creating these things to capture me. Bastard." She shuddered and looked over at her friend. "Sheena? Find anything?"

Sheena nodded slowly. "I think so. Sharur, have a sniff at this." The iron wolf padded over and nosed a set of scrapes in the earth.

"This is different from the monsters, and different from the trees. It is a different kind of tree. It is a sickened tree like I smelled from the archer woman's doorway."

"Yes, I thought so, too," Sheena said. She turned back to Gayle. "I have something to follow. Are we in good enough shape to do that, now?"

Gayle took a deep breath and let it out. The other two nodded. "Okay, I'm pretty battered around, but I'll get my wind back soon."

Liberty Girl made a report back to the league communication channel and checked on how the rest of the Titans were doing. Several teams of heroes were spread out managing to contain the march of the trees not far from the borders of the park reserve. In addition to the animated trees' mindless lack of tactics, they had discovered another major weakness: They could not climb over steep obstacles. The Titans had taken to using felled trees to create makeshift log barricades that the other trees could not cross. This channeled the marching forests into easily-managed chokepoints. The most puzzling thing was how the trees just kept on coming. Most of the park reserve had now been emptied of its mature trees.

"We had better get on with the tracking," Sheena said. "The rain is going to get heavier, and the scent will be washed out. Maybe this will lead us to an answer for the thing that's causing all this."

"Okay, let's go, then," Gayle replied.

Sheena followed the trail of the different tree across the broken ground toward the edge of the reserve. It was difficult going on the ground, because the Acushnet Cedar Swamp Park Reserve was originally a very dense growth of trees and foliage. With so many trees uprooted, the ground was very uneven. Eventually, they came upon the back side of one of the big groups of walking trees. The trees still looked normal, but Sheena gave them a much more thorough look, trying to identify one that was different from the others.

"Got it," she said. She pointed. "There it is. It's sickened or blighted, and it looks like it has more of a face and arms the way it's carrying itself."

"Yes, Mistress. I can smell the sickness of the tree. It is not a natural thing."

Sheena pointed out the blighted tree to the others. "Hang back a bit, but be ready to smash it, please. I want a closer look."

She relaxed and centered herself for a moment, then began stalking the tree blight. She "moved her body out of the way," as Sharur had described it and faded away. Only a faint outline remained. Sharur did the same and followed her as she stalked toward the trees.

The blighted tree was a scrawny form of the same kind of white cedars that made up most of the forest. It smelled of rot and disease, and gashes in its trunk and major limbs seeped an orange sort of goo. Most of its leaves were yellowed and drooping. As Sheena watched, it stopped and settled itself on its roots. About ten seconds later, another cluster of trees nearby began to uproot themselves and the blighted tree began moving again.

"I think we've found our quarry," Sheena murmured to the wolf. She drew her bow and a spirit arrow, and loosed it at the center of the trunk. The tree blight shuddered as if hit by something far bigger than an arrow and it turned toward her. The bark on its trunk was contorted into an angry sort of face. It made no particular sound, but waved its limbs about wildly. The rest of the trees stopped in place. Then, they turned and began stomping toward Sheena.

Sheena fired another arrow and backed up a step. Again, the tree shuddered as if struck by something as large as it was, but Sheena could not tell if the arrow was actually doing any damage. She still had plenty of range, so she drew and shot two more arrows. The tree blight stopped waving its limbs. Its "face" drooped with a decidedly human expression of weariness. The rest of the animated trees continued moving toward her with a creepy creaking of wood and shambling of roots through the loose earth.

"Now?" asked Liberty Girl.

Sheena shook her head. "Hang on for a minute. Let's see what these arrows can do to it." She loosed another, backed a step, and then another. The tree blight's branches and roots went limp and it slowly fell over. The rest of the trees stopped moving. Then they, too, started toppling haphazardly to the ground. Packed as tightly as they were, most simply fell over on their neighbors in a tangle of branches, limbs, and roots.

"Okay...," Gayle said. "That works, but not very fast."

"Yeah. I think you guys would be much faster just smashing it into firewood. Let's get a little height and see how many trees this blight was controlling." Sheena took to the air and Gayle followed. Liberty Girl made her way over to the blight and started breaking it apart.

"You know," Sheena said, "when I've been out hunting or practicing with my bow back home, I never thought I would be shooting a tree for real. Target practice, maybe, but shooting magic arrows at a magic tree until it falls over? Huh."

"You probably never thought you'd be shooting arrows at people, either. Even if they're bad guys," Gayle added.

Sheena made a wry smile and nodded. "That, too."

A large swath of trees was now down and immobile, but there was still a much larger patch that was continuing its march out of the park. "There must be more blights controlling big groups of trees," Sheena observed. "This could take a while."

"If each blight has a limited range, then there have to be a lot of them. They have to come from somewhere, wherever Ravenger is creating them," Gayle replied. She looked out at the army of trees that was still moving and sighed. "I think we need to take down the current crop of animators, first, and then track down whatever is spawning the blights."

"Are you sure?"

"Not completely, but that seems safest. That's the way Ravenger usually works, and our highest priority is to protect the civilians."

"Okay, but stopping it at the source seems like a more direct strategy."

"Yeah, but only if we can be sure that's an overall less damaging plan than containing and pushing back the threat. We don't know enough about whatever it is, yet."

"I suppose you're right. Having met that corrupted Raven spirit, this has the same kind of feel. I worry about spending time on distractions while the Feathers churn out more of that killer virus that they're working on."

"Mmm, yeah. Good point. Let me call this in." Gayle got on the Titans channel and explained what they had discovered. She passed on the details about how to spot and deal with the tree blights, and the effect that had of stopping the animated trees they controlled. Informed of what to look for, the Titans swung into high gear, finding and destroying the blights. With no immediate threat to handle, Leafchaser and Liberty Girl bounded off to help other Titans tackle the blights.

As Sheena predicted, the rain got progressively heavier with flashes and flickers of lightning. The rain had no effect on the walking trees, but the thunderstorm slowed down the Titans' efforts somewhat. They worked their way around the borders of the park reserve, finding and destroying the tree blights. Sheena watched for more clues while Gayle used the natural power of the storm to create tornadoes that picked up the fallen trees and deposited them back into cleared areas of the park.

"Couldn't you do something about the rain?" Sheena shouted during a break from standing watch over a pile of downed trees. She was soaked through, as they all were.

"Could. Shouldn't," answered Gayle. "Messing with the weather is something I leave for emergencies, because it's not my main strength and there is so much more behind it than just wind. I tend to mess it up if I'm not really concentrating on it, and I don't want to cause a bunch of tornadoes to run over a school or housing area, or something by accident."

"Oh, okay. I'll just stay wet. It's a fine day to be in the DNR!" Sheena joked. Gayle laughed and continued her work.

It was just past 11 AM when Sheena received an urgent call from Coffee at Dynatech.

Chapter 24 – The Storm King

Eric buried his worry as best he could and headed off to work. Several sections of highway were closed surrounding the Cedar Swamp Park Reserve due to the sudden march of trees across the roads. Fortunately, he didn't have to travel that way. He just came in through the city center on the elevated US-6 highway and turned south on 140 toward Dartmouth. The rental car didn't have GridGuide, so he had to drive through the heavy traffic manually. Without the automated traffic control, this meant his speed ended up being about fifteen miles per hour less than the GridGuide lanes were managing.

This left him extra time to think. The weather service was predicting thunderstorms for today. He had Horgan's source stone in his bag. Should he try the activation ritual, or leave well enough alone? He was tempted to try it just for the novelty and thrill that just *maybe* something would happen. But, the whole point was to be less of a liability and more of a help to Sheena, if by chance the stone did something for him. Eric sighed. That whole line of thought was depressing. The more she got hooked into the hero stuff, the less of an asset he was and the bigger the liability side of the equation looked.

What good is a man who can't protect his wife when she is being threatened? he asked himself. But he sure hadn't been able to do much when Elf Shot attacked the other night. He didn't even see the arrow that laid him out on the street with vivid nightmares churning through his head. He didn't tell Sheena about what he saw in his nightmares, and he wasn't going to. They were too humiliating. But they had been haunting him since then.

But she doesn't need you to die trying to protect her, he told himself. *She needs you to succeed or to get the hell out of the way so she can do it herself. And so she can save your own sorry ass in the process, too.* Ugh. Like that hadn't occurred to him dozens of times in the last couple of days. He was out of his league. Eric Gardner, mild-mannered veterinarian. Good with pets, livestock, and kids. Mostly caring and supportive, but sometimes too pig-headed for his own good. *Calderón's right. I'm just a liability to her. I should just lay low and stay out of the way so she can do her job.*

But maybe he could be more. Just a chance, maybe, but not zero. Calderón had thought that it was a possibility worth exploring. He reminded himself, *Yeah, but more because he was intrigued than because he actually thought it was a good idea. Remember, Eric, he said you should just suck it up and support Sheena.*

"Arrgh!" he groaned. "And she's out there right now, probably risking her life fighting something… whatever… that would kill lots of people if she didn't! And I'm stuck in traffic."

He still hadn't made any real decision by the time he got to the Dynatech parking lot.

"Quite a storm that's blowing in, isn't it?" Cherie said conversationally as Eric shook the rain off his jacket. Eric had quickly noticed that she had a habit of randomly stating the obvious whenever silence had reigned for more than five minutes.

"Yeah, it sure looks like it." He hung up his jacket on the coat hook in his cubicle. "Anything special coming up in the lab results?"

"Nope. But we got approval for our 3X dual sequencer-manipulator. Greg already signed off on the purchase and we're going ahead with it." Cherie was the project team's technology specialist. She had started off in the field about twenty years ago with an associate's degree in medical lab technology. Along the way, she had continued her education with a bachelor's in microbiology. Eric had learned that she had such a talent for technology that Greg had snapped her up eagerly at the start of the project, even though she wasn't technically a researcher. Cherie had been largely responsible for keeping the team on its timeline ever since.

"Nice! When will we get that?"

"Only two weeks, installed!"

"That's pretty impressive," Eric agreed. "Took me almost three months to get a simple ultrasound machine delivered and set up in my clinic. And that's a pretty standard model; way behind what they use in human clinics."

"Maybe you had to wait for the secret cow medical approval board?" Cherie grinned with a silly expression.

"You never know. Sometimes, it feels like it." He chuckled softly, and then it built into laughter.

"What? I know you weren't laughing at *my* joke, there. Spill it!"

Eric explained, "Somehow, you reminded me of something my wife's friend, Gayle Magnuson, said the other day."

"What? You mean Gayle as in 'Gayle Force'? That Gayle Magnuson?" Cherie looked impressed.

"Yeah, her. She was talking to a bunch of protesters last week. She was trying to calm them down and get them to see both sides of the issue, and she said, 'Don't be too hard on GMOs. After all, I *am* one!'"

Cherie's eyes widened. Then she tried to hold it in, but she burst out laughing, too. "Oh, that's too funny!"

Eric smiled wryly. "Yeah, I like her."

"Well, I hope they're okay. I saw on the news that weird thing going on with the walking trees up in the Cedar Swamp. But, I can't imagine that would be too tough for a bunch of superheroes, right?"

Eric shrugged and shook his head. "Yeah, I'd think so. But, really, what do I know?"

"What do you mean?"

"Well, I don't even really know everything Sheena can do, to say nothing about Gayle or the rest of those folks. They can describe it to me, or I can read about it, but that's different from really knowing and being able to say, 'Yes, this is something easy,' or 'Wow, that's really impressive!' I mean, I hope that everything they face turns out to be easy, but I don't really know. And, there are enough things that I know are super dangerous that I'm not even sure I want to know about. So... I just worry and try to let it go."

Cherie thought that over. She shook her head in awe. "Well, if I can be of any help to you... you're in worse trouble than I thought!"

Eric chuckled at her attempt at humor. "So be it!"

He glanced through the team schedule and flagged the things assigned to him. "Working the H3 avian-transmitted variants? Hey, Cherie, how come we didn't get those into last year's seasonal flu vaccine?"

"Not enough of a threat, according to epidemiology. Aside from the cost implications, you can't just load it up with every strain we've got...."

"Yeah, I know. It doesn't work that way." He looked over the past project work record. "But it's all ready when needed. You finished that work last year, and this is...." He frowned at the report.

"What?" She looked over at his change in tone.

"So easy to weaponize." He paused. "Uh oh...."

Cherie's eye widened. "What are you not telling me?"

"Um... bioterrorist risk. I'll be back shortly. I have to make a phone call." He grabbed his computer bag and headed for the nearest private conference room. It was in use, so he kept going until he found one that was unoccupied. He ducked into the room and closed the door, then dug his new phone out of the bag. His hand brushed the source stone as he did so and he paused. Did it feel warm against the back of his hand? *No, that's silly. Keep your head straight, Eric,* he chided himself.

He pulled up Calderón's number and called it. The raindrops pelted the outside window as he waited. A lightning bolt flickered thinly across the sky.

"Hola, Eric. It is Calderón."

"Hi, Agent Calderón. I have just put a couple of things together, and I need to pass on something to the people working on that virus."

"What? Oh, really! Okay, go ahead and give me the rundown."

"I was reading an article in a veterinary medical journal last year—it was a year ago last spring—and the article was reporting on some research into avian H3 flu strains. The researchers had done some great work on showing how the virus could cross species barriers from birds into humans. They mentioned how some of the strains were uncommon, which meant that neither the bird nor the human population had much immunity to them. And, they provided some technical details that I realized at the time could be really dangerous if capable terrorists got their hands on the data. They made it almost a cookbook for creating a weaponized virus. Again, they didn't mean to, but what if that got into the hands of people with the equipment and an axe to grind? I was almost at the point of sending an email to the journal and the companies that produce vaccines, pointing out that the researchers had accidentally given a recipe for a nasty biological weapon. I was going to suggest that those strains should be included in the North American flu season vaccination to start building immunity, in case this stuff got out."

"But, you did not send that email?"

"No, I didn't. And I'm kicking myself now, because it sounded like one of those influenza strains may be part of what you've got included in that supervirus they're studying in the lab."

Calderón was silent on the other end of the line. "Okay. I will pass that on. They will probably want to talk to you directly about that if that is what they find."

"And one more thing. Dynatech already has both a vaccine and an antiviral medicine formula available for those strains, in case it's needed. It's not common enough for us to have gone into production or clinical trials, but it's on the books."

"Okay. That's good to know, I think."

"Umm… That might be a company trade secret, though. Please keep that as whatever counts as Homeland Security classified. I'm almost certainly not authorized to share that information with anyone."

Calderón chuckled. "I get it. Anything else?"

"Not that I can think of."

"Okay, I will go pass this on right now. Thanks, Eric."

"You're welcome. I hope it isn't even needed, but just in case…."

"Sí, just in case. Gracias."

Eric ended the call and stood looking out the window at the storm for a few minutes. It would make sense to tell Greg, too. He would know who inside Dynatech to alert. He tucked his phone back into the bag. As he did so, he noticed another flicker of electricity from the stone. *I wonder if it's reacting to the storm,* he thought. *But, it's not flying around searching for a host, so… I guess I'll leave it for now.*

He headed back down the hallway to his desk. Greg was just coming back from a meeting. Eric waved him over. "Hey, Greg! I've got an… I don't know, security issue? I need to fill you in and see if there's anything that we need to do about it."

"Okay. Does it involve anything that Sheena's working on?"

"Yes, but it's actually bigger than that."

"Really? Wow…." He thought about it and added, "Let me get Coffee in on this."

Greg took Eric into his office and called the security director. After a brief explanation and putting the phone in conference mode so Eric could explain, Coffee thanked them for bringing the issue to her attention. She promised to coordinate with the FBSA investigation and to determine whether Dynatech would need to activate its outbreak response agreements with the manufacturers.

"Okay, I'll get that rolling. And, Greg, how are you doing after that attack Monday night?"

Greg chuckled ruefully. "Thank heavens for metahuman healing powers, that's for sure! But, really, I was unconscious for almost everything. Not much trauma by the time I woke up except for a scolding by my wife. How about you, Eric?"

Eric shifted uncomfortably in his seat. "I don't really know, yet. I'm okay, I guess. Still having nightmare effects from that arrow that she shot me with."

Coffee said, "I want to make sure that we get you two what you need to deal with this, so contact me or drop by any time. Both of you."

"Will do, Coffee," Greg replied.

"Eric, the violent experience itself can pose recurring mental trauma. If that crops up, or if the effects of that arrow continue longer than this weekend, let me know. I know a couple of specialists who can help you work through that."

"Understood."

"And thanks for connecting with us so quickly on this, Coffee. If the virus risk that Eric noticed materializes, Sheena and her friends are going to need all the help they can get."

Greg ended the call and sat back in his chair. "Well? That seems to be about as well-handled as it can be, for now."

"Hmm? Oh, yeah," Eric responded. He was still thinking about what Greg had said before that. "I'll go get working on those H3 comparisons again."

"Sounds good. Let me know how those turn out."

Eric nodded and went back to his desk. He looked down at his bag and then out the window at the storm. It showed no sign of lessening soon. *She's going to need all the help she can get.* He shook his head and sat down to do his work.

After a while of looking at tables and protein chain images, he started seeing the Lichtenberg pattern of branching lightning every time he shifted his view back to the screen. He blinked hard and tried to clear his head. The thunderstorm was still rolling by. *If there's a chance, you should try. She's going to need all the help she can get.*

He made a decision. Eric stood up and reached over for his computer bag, taking the stone out from the bottom pocket. He checked the phrase one more time to be sure he remembered it. He left his jacket on the hook where it was. He was going to get soaked out in that storm with or without it. With a determined stride, he headed out to the exit.

Sure enough, the wind was driving a steady shower of rain sideways toward the ground. Eric made his way to the other side of the parking lot squinting to keep most of the water out of his eyes. He was already soaked. Lightning flashed overhead and thunder boomed almost instantly, making him duck reflexively. *Well, that's gotta be close enough to count! If this doesn't work, it's not 'cause the storm wasn't near enough.*

He held the stone in his left hand and raised it slightly above his head. Feeling embarrassed and wet, he repeated the phrase Calderón had prepared for him. Nothing. But, he kept it up. The whole thing was a long shot, anyway, but if there was a chance, then he owed it to....

Lightning stuck.

Twice.

Shocked would be a good word to describe the feeling he experienced. Astounded, too, but definitely shocked. He felt electrified and mostly it *hurt*! Eric's perception floated over his body as it crumpled to the sodden grass near the Dynatech parking lot. *Well. Ouch. Now what?* he wondered.

"Sorry, lad. You're a scholar, not a warrior, and I can't do with a scholar." The voice boomed. A bigger-than-life Sumerian god with light blue skin stood... no, floated... before him. Barrel-chested, vaguely Arabic features, leather kilt edged with brass, and somehow looking windblown and not a bit wet. "Yes, lad. I'm Horgan. Sorry about the mix-up there, but you did call for the power, you know."

Eric looked down at his unconscious and quite possibly dead body. *She's going to **kill** me,* he thought.

"Oh, no, not at all! I'm sure Shani will understand! She's very forgiving, you know... At least, as long as you haven't insulted her." The storm god shook his head sadly. "Made that mistake once. Completely unintentional, I swear."

"What did you do?" Eric asked out of idle curiosity.

"I, ahh... told her to get back to the hearth and... um... let the men talk." He looked very sheepish.

"Yeah, that would do it. What'd she do to you?"

"Kept me from eating at my own feasting table for a month!" Horgan looked affronted. "Every time I tried to sit down at the table, I blinked, and dinner was over. Done! Everybody... and all the food! ... was gone!"

"Huh. Clever trick."

"Yes, and she kept it up until I... me, Horgan! ... apologized."

"Go figure."

"Hah! No sums needed. It was a full month of 28 days! Anu finally told me what I had done, and told me what Shani wanted. So, like an honorable man, I told her that I was sorry, and she let me eat at the feast table again."

"That sounds like a solution to the problem," Eric offered hesitantly.

"It was. But, it just goes to show, Shanikali can be a tad touchy about some things. Best not to upset her too much. Women, huh?" He guffawed.

"Uh, yes. So... You need a warrior to inherit your powers?"

"Yes, 'fraid so. You're not bad, lad, but not what I need." The storm god seemed genuinely apologetic.

"Am I dead?" Eric continued to watch his body lying before him, getting increasingly wet.

"Bah! No such thing! It might tingle a bit... or a lot... when you wake up, though."

That was a relief, but somehow it was a very mild one. "Okay, is there anything I can do to find a proper warrior for you?"

Horgan blinked in surprise. "I don't really know. Maybe you can. If someone can see my lightning mark on the stone, he would be a candidate."

Someone was running up to Eric's body. Three people, actually. Eric noted with detachment that he didn't appear to be breathing. He realized that he couldn't hear them. Or the rain and thunder, either. Interesting. He supposed they would be bringing up an AED device next.

"When will I wake up, and what should I do then?" he asked.

"Oh, they'll get you all started up in no time! Honestly, lad, you're a scholar. Do...." He waved his arms about in the air aimlessly. "...whatever it is that scholars do! And, if I were you, I would do whatever Shani wants you to do."

"Should I try to become a warrior?" Eric really didn't think that was likely, but figured he had to ask. If that's what was required, then he'd find a way to do it.

"Oh, by the wheel of the sky, no, lad!" Horgan laughed. "You've got a better chance of getting Lilitu away from a tasty mortal soul! You're a clever one, a thoughtful one. Even I can see that. Stick with it! Besides...," he leaned in and added with a conspiratorial grin,"Shani seems to like that type. Stick with her, lad!"

Now there was a real relief. "All right, I'll do that. Sorry that I couldn't be what you need. I'll see if I can't help you get the power where it needs to go." Yes, sure enough, they were bringing up the automatic external defibrillator in its yellow box. That seemed sensible to Eric, in a detached sort of way.

"Thank you, lad. You're an honorable fellow, you are." Horgan looked over at the gathering of people getting wet on the grass. "Seems our talk is about over. Travel well, lad!"

It was horribly disorienting when Eric's perception snapped back into his body. And the tingling was excruciating.

"What were you thinking?!?" Sheena shouted at him. She looked as bedraggled as he felt, dripping with water and even the leather of her costume soaked through. She still looked beautiful to him, though.

"If there was a chance I could help, I owed it to you to try." Even his lips were numb. Eric was sitting up in the hospital bed at Atlas Southwestern. Everything still felt numb and tingly.

"That is a... a... a stupid reason!" He didn't think so, but she drove on. "I have been out fighting trees... Trees, Eric!... all morning in the rain. And bigger weirdness that came up out of the swamp like God knows what, and Ravenger almost got Gayle, and then this! Whatever it is that is creating these things is still out there, and those terrorists are still out there, and Elf Shot is still out there, and I'm here instead of being out there where I should be just because you had to see if you could get powers of your own! This isn't a competition, Eric!"

That stung. Because that's just what it felt like. Eric just kept his mouth shut and said nothing.

"You do... not... need... to protect me!" She glowered at him with tears of frustration in her eyes. "You can't! Period! Full stop! End of story! You do not have the capability, so stop trying."

"But...."

"And even if you could, I'm not sure I would accept it anymore!" She drilled him with her eyes, then sharply turned away.

He drew in a breath, but held his tongue.

"How about a little goddamned self-discipline, instead?" she muttered with her back to him, rubbing her eyes. "Just... keep your head down. Do your work at Dynatech. And stay out of the way."

"I was trying. It was just this one leftover thing."

Sheena turned toward the door and looked over her shoulder at him. "That's *not* what I need from you." She shook her head and quickly left.

Eric let out the breath he had been holding in.

There were sounds of another one-sided argument somewhere down the hall, but he couldn't make out any details. Not long after it ceased, he heard a soft knock at the door. Calderón came in.

"Hi, Agent. You get your stone back?"

Calderón nodded with an abashed half-smile. "And a piece of her mind, too."

"Well, you warned me." Eric sighed and sank down against the elevated back of the bed.

"I'm sorry, Eric. I thought there might be a chance." Calderón sat down in the chair across from the bed.

"Oh, there was! But, not for me. I'm not Horgan's type." He chuckled. At Calderón's curious expression, he explained what had happened.

The shaman looked both impressed and unsure about how to take that. "I did not expect that, certainly. That gives us more to work with, I guess...."

"And properly shuts down my search for powers." He sighed again. "Let's face it. I messed this up. Like the guy said, I'm a scholar, not a warrior. I should stick to what I do well."

"No, you are right. This is not your path. I saw that, but I was curious, so I let you try it. I apologize, my friend."

"No, it was still up to me. Even being willing to try, now is not a good time. I should have known that."

"But, what would you think if something happened to Sheena that you could have stopped, if only you had activated the stone today?" Calderón grinned. "We can go on like this forever, though."

"Yeah, I suppose so."

Calderón changed the subject. "How long do you have to stay in here?"

"Probably just overnight. Maybe physical therapy tomorrow. They'll want to test me to see if everything is still working after getting hit twice by lightning. My whole body is numb all over. EKG is normal, though."

"That's good, right?"

"For having my heart stopped for a few minutes? Yeah. And no burns at all to speak of? Really good." He chuckled and waved at the ceiling. "Thanks, Horgan!"

"So. What do you do now?" Calderón asked with a look of curiosity.

"Now, I be the good boy and do what mama wants."

"Ah." The agent didn't sound convinced.

"For a while, anyway."

"Ah, yes. That sounds more believable."

"And... I decide what it is that I really want to do."

"Ah? How so?"

"Sheena said... well, yelled, really... that this isn't a competition. But, it is. Not that I want it to be, or because we're actually counting points or anything, but I have to be honest with myself. I am okay with our relationship when I know the score, and Sheena has tipped it so far that I don't think I can catch up. And I do have to catch up. But, she really is in a different league, and I am far, far out of that league.

"Elf Shot hit me with that arrow, and I didn't see it coming, and I couldn't have done anything about it, anyway. And I have nightmares, still, from it that I will never, ever tell her about...." He clamped his lips shut and swallowed nervously.

He looked down at his feet under the hospital blanket. "I am not a house husband, or even just the guy supporting us financially. I am not okay with this. I thought I was an equality-minded, women's lib kind of guy, but deep down, I'm the man. I feel like I should be in charge. I feel like I should be the protector. And... and... that's just not happening any more, and it won't. So... I have to figure out what it is that I really want to do."

Calderón bowed his head and looked at his hands for a minute. When he looked up again, he stood up and said, "I understand. If there is anything I can do, Eric, just call me."

"Will do."

Calderón nodded and left, drawing the door shut behind him, leaving Eric alone with his thoughts.

Chapter 25 – Ship It!

James Kadorsky looked at the green indicators on the console and felt a thrill of excitement, followed immediately by a shiver of dread. It was done. To the best of his knowledge, no one had ever created a cure for a polymorphic virus before. Not even Ravenger. Of course, Ravenger's efforts were entirely bent on destruction, not even considering the possibility of saving lives. And with the anti-viral cure complete, Blighthawk would order everyone to go to their assigned positions to start spreading the disease. And a week later, people would start dying. And he would be responsible.

"Two hundred and twenty-three dollars per person," he reminded himself. "That's all they were worth to them."

"What, James?" Blighthawk croaked as he stepped through the doorway into the lab.

"That was the settlement. Two hundred and twenty-three dollars per person affected by the accident. Per life extinguished. Per homeless family member. With no admission of wrong-doing."

"Ah. I see. Not even enough to scratch the surface of a guilty conscience, but too much for the ones who were convinced they were in the right all along." The corrupter entered and sat down on the dropcloth covered seat. "How are we doing?"

"We have a cure for the virus."

"What? That's excellent! Well done!" His eyebrows went up enthusiastically and a big smile spread across his face. Then he noticed Kadorsky's expression. "But, you don't sound excited."

"I will be responsible for the deaths of those people."

Blighthawk inclined his head and gave an ambivalent nod. "Partially, yes. Truthfully, I think I have to carry that mostly on my own conscience. You, however, do get karmic credit for the cure. That is your own achievement."

"That's why I was reminding myself of what they did. And it was intentional. For business. They must have bought the lawyers and thrown us scraps. Even if it had been millions, it would not have brought back Emma and my kids."

"Yes. And remember, this virus strikes down only the ones who make such deals and decisions. For everyone else, either a bad case of the flu or just the sniffles." He paused and shrugged. "Well, subject to the usual complications of influenza. That is the risk that bothers me."

Kadorsky nodded sadly. "Well, we'd best be on with it. I'll get this ramped into a new membrane accelerant matrix and loaded into the bioreactors. We'll make as much of the cure as we can before we run out of material or Ravenger kicks us out."

"There's the spirit! And I have instructions to give to our volunteers. Lobo has got everything set for us on the logistics side. We have the product, and tonight we ship it out!" He stood up and looked toward the production room of the lab.

"Sir, you said you were going to have spirits spread the virus, too. How will that work? Aren't spirits… I don't know, insubstantial?"

Blighthawk turned to explain. He took a careful breath, trying to avoid triggering a coughing fit. "Yes, they are, but they can carry material closely aligned with their nature. Earth spirits can carry dirt, rocks, or even gold and jewels from the ground. Water spirits can carry water or other liquids. Corrupted spirits, such as the ones I command, can carry filth, diseases, and poisons."

Kadorsky got the idea and shuddered. "That's scary, sir."

The villain chuckled wryly. "You have no idea."

He stepped over to a clear spot on the floor, then wiped off some of the oil dripping down his body. He flicked the fluids to the floor. "A demonstration, James. Please, do not approach it."

Kadorsky shook his head quickly.

With a dramatic two-handed gesture, Blighthawk brought his hands close together, fingers grasping like claws, and then raised his hands up into the air and out to his sides like wings. His real wings spread at the same time. The technologist saw a momentary image cover the toxic shaman, like a hologram of a raven superimposed over his features. A bilious green figure shaped rudely like a human being rose from the drippings Blighthawk had smeared on the floor. It appeared almost like a watery, melted corpse. A tattered business suit floated within its outer fluid shell. The eye sockets were empty and staring. It stared at the shaman with slack jaw and slumped shoulders.

"You see?" Blighthawk asked loudly. Other Feathers had stopped work to stare at the spirit in horror, as well. "This is the spirit of a poisoner killed by his own poisons. It is not pleasant. It is a thing of horror. But it is just. When I summon these spirits, it forces me to think of their victims; the ones they killed with their poisons and treacheries and corruption in life. This reminds me that there is work left to be done, until there is no cause for such a spirit to walk the earth ever again."

Many heads were nodding. The corrupter said more quietly to Kadorsky. "The spirit can absorb the virus and spread it perfectly as vapor. This is how the most important targets will be affected—JFK, Grand Central Station, Logan International, Roosevelt International here in Venture City, the US Capitol, and so on. But, for now, I need it to go spying for me." He whispered to the spirit in a language the technologist did not recognize. It vanished from sight.

"Where did you send it, sir?"

Blighthawk smiled sadly to himself. "Not far. I need to find out where a certain veterinarian is to be found, that's all. I need him to pay a house call."

Chapter 26 – Not Just a Side-Chick

"No, I want you to take a break from this."

The last tree crashed to the ground as if to emphasize Gayle's point. Sun Man had just finished off the last tree blight on the western side of the reserve with a fiery beam of sunlight that dazzled Sheena's eyes. The trees it controlled toppled in bunches and rows. The approach to Roosevelt International Airport was safe, for now. The elder Titan waved to the heroines and flew off to the league meeting point.

"But there is something out there creating new tree blights!" Sheena protested.

"Yep! And we'll find it and then we'll deal with it, but it's getting dark and you need a break." Gayle leveled a no-nonsense look at her friend. Sheena's eyes slid away from her gaze. "Just about everyone else has rotated out for at least a couple of hours already."

"I already had a break," Sheena said bitterly. "And I feel like a sidekick. You're doing all the work."

"No, you didn't. That wasn't a break. And you flew all the way back here in the worst of the storm and kept going. You can tell me what happened when you're ready, but you look more tired and miserable than I've seen you before. If we fight anything serious now, you are going to make mistakes and that will get your butt kicked, whether you feel like a sidekick or not. And you're not, anyway."

Sheena wanted to argue with that, but it really wasn't worth the effort.

"Come on. It's time for a warm drink." Gayle shot up into the air and waited for her. With a final grumbled complaint, Sheena followed. The rain had softened to a light patter. Gayle took them across the highway and down the street to a soup and bakery place where the rest of the Titans were gathering. She glanced at Sheena's exhausted, downcast face and tightened the set of her lip.

On landing, she sent a quick whisper to Irish Fury, the big red-headed hero coordinating the clean-up. Carried by the wind to his ears only, she asked, "Hiya, Irish. Would you grab a kind of private-ish table for me and Sheena and see that no one bugs her? I have to figure out what's eating her." The broad-shouldered bruiser raised a bushy eyebrow and then looked over and made eye contact with the singer and nodded.

Sun Man, resplendent in his classic orange and gold hero costume—tights, belt, gloves, boots, and headband tied jauntily above his brow—was standing near the door sipping tea and chatting with fellow Titans and anyone else brave enough to get into the conversation. From the tips of his pointed Mercurian ears to the toes of his boots, he looked like a classic comic book hero. Sun Man was also providing a quick air dry for the wet and the cold making their way into the restaurant. He bowed graciously to Gayle and Sheena as they came in. "Good evening, ladies. Again." In less than five seconds, they were dry.

Gayle giggled and thanked him, and then pulled Sheena off to a small table along the far wall that Irish Fury indicated with a nod of his head. As they were sitting down, he came over. He had just a touch of accent when he asked, "Hey, ladies. Can I grab you coffee or something?"

"Spiced orange tea, for me. Sheena?"

"Nothing," she mumbled.

"She'll have a large hot chocolate," Gayle told Irish Fury. He looked at the singer skeptically. "And if she doesn't drink it, I will."

He went off to put in the order at the counter.

Gayle leaned in and asked in an earnest whisper, "So, what happened? And don't tell me, 'He'll be fine,' again. People don't look like their dog got run over if everything really is fine."

"Gayle, I really don't want to talk about this, yet." She was surprised at the weariness in her own voice.

"Did Elf Shot get to him? Does that have anything to do with this?"

"No, she didn't. It's… It's that Eric is still on that alpha male crap."

Gayle sat up in her seat. "Huh?"

Sheena cradled her head in her hands and rubbed at the tension beneath her eyebrows with her thumbs. "Yes, he was hit by lightning. Twice. And do you want to know why?" Her voice picked up a ragged edge to it. "Because he was trying to use one of the other source stones. The one from the storm god."

"Oh, wow!"

"Yeah. It didn't work, but it did get him smacked with lightning."

"But, why? Is he still stuck on protecting you?"

"Yes!" She clenched her fists and then carefully put them down on the table and forced herself to relax, restraining the urge she felt to hit something. "I thought I had gotten through to him, but apparently not!"

"But, you said he'll be okay…."

"Yeah, yeah. He'll be fine. And then what?" She cocked her head to the side and glared at Gayle, waiting for her to answer.

"And… he… stops? Tries again? Learns his lesson? I don't know?"

"Right. I don't know. I have no freaking clue what he's going to do next!" She leaned back into her chair and crossed her arms over her chest with a sour expression. "And that's the problem."

Irish Fury brought over their drinks and set them down on the table in front of the two women. He glanced at their faces with a neutral expression, nodded once, then turned and walked off.

Sheena regarded the tall paper cup on front of her. With a quick shrug, she took it and popped the plastic lid off. The cocoa and whipped cream smelled good. She took a nice, long sniff. Very good. A sip. Not just milk chocolate, but dark chocolate, too. It left a slight bitter taste.

With a deep breath, Gayle asked, "So… what now?"

"Destroy whatever is making tree blights. Defeat Ravenger, if he even shows up now that his ambush attempts are done. Go back to finding the Feathers' leader and Elf Shot. Pretty obvious."

"No, I mean about Eric."

"Oh, I'm sure they'll let him out of the hospital tomorrow, probably." She took another sip of the cocoa and licked the whipped cream off her lip.

"And then?"

Sheena snorted. "What do you want me to say? I try to keep him safe while I track down Elf Shot, which he will probably make substantially harder with his attempts to help. It's like taking a puppy for a walk. Dang things wrap the leash around your legs and tangle themselves and you up in the process."

Gayle chuckled. "I suppose so."

Sheena let out a weary groan. She leaned over and propped her head on her hand with her elbow on the table. "Oh, gods… You were right. I am *so* tired. I do need a break."

"Well, there is one advantage to the current situation in the park reserve," Gayle offered.

"What's that?"

"There really aren't any more mature trees left to animate."

"Thank heaven for small favors."

"The night crew can contain this. I suggest some rest, and then we do more tracking first thing in the morning."

Sheena roused herself to a morning that gave every sign of being dreary, misty, and wet. The overcast still hung low in the sky, the kind that kept raining sporadically in little patches here and there. She didn't feel much better than the day looked. Sheena had kept waking up during the night to wonder what was missing only to remember where Eric was. Even though she was still mad at him, she hoped he was doing okay, alone in the hospital.

The situation wasn't totally bleak, though. The Riverhaven robot laundry had cleaned and polished her costume to be as good as new. At least she didn't have to pull twenty pounds of cold, wet leather on over her shower-warmed skin. While she was getting ready, she called Sharur and sent him back out to the ruined park reserve to scout.

Gayle downed another strip of bacon and then finished her fourth slice of wheat toast with butter and jam. She mopped up the last of the egg yolk on her plate and licked her fingers. "Hungry this morning. Pulled a lot of power through, yesterday. You want any?"

"I ate something when I woke up at four. Ready to go now."

The singer looked at her with narrowed eyes. "You look tired. Not much sleep?"

"Not as much as I would've liked. I kept waking up."

"Mmm." Gayle nodded. "Want to visit Eric before we do this?"

Sheena snorted and shook her head. "No. He's a big boy, or thinks he is. He can take care of himself. Let's get tracking."

Gayle shrugged. "Okay. Find the thing spawning the blights. Strategy?"

"The strategy is simple. Find a blight, follow its tracks back."

"I like it! Let's do it."

Their flight over the park made for a fresh reminder of how badly Ravenger had damaged the place. Downed trees were piled in heaps around the periphery of three sides of the reserve. It looked like a tornado a mile wide had slammed into the forest. The swamp that made up the main basin of the reserve looked much more open and wet with the rain and lack of tree cover. There were only five members of the League of Titans still on duty. They could get back and forth easily between the three points in the park where the blights had marshalled the trees for attack the day before. These now formed the only good choke points where more trees could get through, if any were coming.

The land rose from the swamp level up toward the hills in the northwest corner of the park reserve. This was the area not yet denuded of trees. Sheena found a patch of reasonably solid ground and landed. Sharur appeared by her side.

"Greetings, Mistress. I have found a tree blight."

"Excellent."

"It is standing among many other trees."

"It hasn't animated the trees, yet?"

"No. There are tracks where the blight has walked from somewhere else to where it is now. I think we will be able to easily follow the tracks."

Sheena scanned the forest ahead with a careful eye. "This is too easy."

"Well, if Ravenger is working with trees, there is only so much he can do to hide them," Gayle replied. "Not like with his burrowing minions."

"I suppose. Still, let's be careful." She took a moment to summon her eagle and send it aloft. She studied the area through the eagle's eyes. None of the trees were moving and there were no signs of unusual activity other than the tracks of the tree blights that had gone before. In fact, the tracks of several blights were easily visible from the air, despite the summer's lush growth. It was actually easy to see where they had come from. They had started in one particularly densely wooded area about one hundred meters from the northernmost tip of the reserve. There was a well-worn path of trampled foliage and disturbed earth leading south from that "origin thicket" downhill toward the swampy area. The easily visible path disappeared in the region of uprooted trees, where it was obscured by all of the tracks of the hundreds of animated tree roots.

She looked back up the trail to the origin thicket with her eagle's eyes. There it was. A massive cedar tree half again as large as any nearby, with most of its branches bare and the others bearing sickly yellowed leaves. Fungus covered it in patches and creepy-looking moss was draped about like a garnish. Even its limbs were gnarled and twisted like some artist's idea of a scary Halloween tree. With the eagle's sharp vision, Sheena could spot several other blighted trees nearby, but they had not yet moved from where they had grown. Still, that offered the big creepy elder blight some potential defenders.

"No sign of Ravenger or VE monsters, from the air," she reported to Gayle. She pointed to the northwest. "I found a really big blighted, scary, unnatural tree off that way about 250 meters from here. There are about eight blights near it that haven't moved and a lot of trees for them to animate."

"Any sign of movement from that elder blight thing?" Gayle asked.

"Just from its branches, swaying a bit under their own power, but it hasn't uprooted itself."

"Let's assume that this whole area is going to be brought to life at once to attack us. We should call in the Titans on duty." Sheena had no complaint with that. Gayle placed the call and soon the other heroes were on their way.

Liberty Girl arrived in two giant bounds from the east side of the park. "Good morning, Gayle! Hi, Sheena! Thanks for the call. I was afraid I wouldn't have anything to do this morning but split and pile lumber."

Gayle laughed. "Morning, Lib! No, I think we'll be in for a fight here."

"But that will probably involve splitting and piling lumber," Sheena cautioned her with a wry half-smile.

Three more Titans arrived by air and a fourth bounded along through the brush. He was the first to arrive, a hulking seven-foot tall werewolf in rugged fibermesh cargo shorts and a pair of pocketed bandoliers crossing at the center of his massive chest. He ran up with his tongue lolling out of the side of his mouth. He winked at Sheena and called out, "Morning, Gayle! Someone said you needed a big bad wolf to handle the house of sticks?"

Gayle grinned. "Yep! But I'm pretty sure these sticks are gonna fight back! So, be prepared to fetch!"

"Sticks, twigs, logs, squeaky toys... hey, it's all the same to me!" the wolfen hero joked. As the others landed, he introduced himself. "Hello there, Miss. Pleased to meet you. I'm Steve Volk, also known by these jokers as Steffanwolf."

Sheena waved self-consciously to everyone. "Hi. I'm Sheena Gardner, going by Shee'na. Thanks for the assist."

One of the others she recognized as Sir Leo, dressed in a sleek green suit of high-tech armor. He bowed gracefully and smiled at her. The second was a thin male figure in a white head-to-toe unitard with a golden eye design on the chest. His eyes were a bright yellow glare behind the mask. The young man in the suit said, "Hi, Sheena. I'm PsiKid. Mental powers. Goes with the name. I'm not sure how much help I'll be against trees, but you never know."

"We're probably going to be stirring up trouble with the Vengeful Earth, too, PsiKid. If you can keep our minds clear, that would be a major help in itself," Gayle explained, clearly relieved that he was on the team. "I think you know how often I've been held down by those VE things, and not in a good way."

"Ah, okay. Mental resistance for everyone, then. Happy to help!"

"Good mornin', Sugah. Ah'm Serendipity Blue," said the last addition to the group in a sweet Southern drawl. She had smooth chocolate brown skin, bright blue hair down to her shoulders, and one of the warmest smiles Sheena had ever experienced. She was wearing a reinforced spandex and fibermesh outfit of white with blue side panels and a red cross on her chest. "Ah'm the healah on duty, and happy t' help out. Jest call me Blue."

"Okay, folks, here's what we've got," Gayle explained. She told the team about what she knew about the overall plot by the Feathers of the Raven, and the apparent alliance with Ravenger. She detailed the previous day's Vengeful Earth ambush meant to capture her. Sheena also filled them in on what she had discovered nearby this morning, and guessed at what they might find when they moved in. She also told them about her encounter with the corrupted spirit of Raven and cautioned them that these blights had the same toxic flavor of magic that she had experienced in Raven's home in the spirit world.

"Ooh, that sounds nasty!" growled Steffanwolf appreciatively.

"It appears that magic might be needed to set this right, then," observed Sir Leo.

Gayle nodded. "That could be. And frankly, I'm expecting Ravenger to make another attempt at capturing me when we go for the elder blight and are distracted by the tree blights and the animated trees."

"Whoa, there, honey," Blue said. "Elder... blight?"

"The big one that created the other blights. The big scary Halloween tree that Sheena found up there."

"Oh, ah see."

Gayle suggested a plan, Sir Leo offered a few tweaks, and everyone was satisfied with how that was likely to work. Sheena, Gayle, and Sir Leo would focus on the elder blight while Liberty Girl and Steffanwolf drew the attention and ire of the tree blights and any trees they animated. PsiKid and Serendipity Blue would support with protection and healing and offer their own brand of firepower as they could. If Vengeful Earth appeared, Gayle would take the job of defeating as many as she could and holding the rest at bay, with PsiKid's help. If possible, Liberty Girl and Steffanwolf would drop trees or blights in a defensive ring around the team.

"Remember," Gayle cautioned everyone, "we don't know what that elder blight can do, yet, and Ravenger is always coming up with new VE mutants. Stay careful. And if Ravenger shows...." Her expression hardened. "I have something new for him."

They moved out, Sheena and Sharur sneaking ahead along the track left by the previous blights as stealthily as possible. This time, Gayle had not only protected herself and Sheena with air cushions, she bubbled the rest of the team, too, including Sharur. He apparently found this uncomfortable, shaking out his metal fur several times, but made no complaint to Sheena. She patted his shoulder sympathetically and stalked onward up the trail.

The shrubs and trees were so tightly packed in the thicket that there was no real space to maneuver. Only the ground within a few meters of the elder blight was open, and it was suspiciously free of all vegetation. The wide ring of moist black dirt underneath the elder blight was freshly turned, with a scattering of mostly-buried bones in the dirt. Sheena wondered for a moment if this is what had happened to the wildlife in the reserve. She realized that she had not seen many animals that should have been displaced by the uprooted trees. Normally, they would have been frightened away by something strange like that. She made a mental note to warn the Titans about that ring of earth.

The tree that formed the elder blight was as twisted and unnatural as she had seen from the air. It looked even more like a caricature of a scary, haunted tree than she had thought possible. It seemed copied straight from a low-budget horror movie poster, artificial plastic-looking bark, groaning facial expression, dangling vines, and all. Sheena could also pick out most of the lesser blights from where she stood. She whispered to Sharur to keep watch while she went back to fill in the others.

"All right," Gayle said after getting Sheena's report. "Things stand pretty much as we thought. Everyone ready?"

Everyone nodded. Liberty Girl gestured to Steffanwolf. "I'll take the left, you take the right."

"Got it," the werewolf growled softly.

Sheena kicked off the assault by summoning her wolf spirits and sending them running at the elder blight. While she proceeded on to bring out the leopards, as well, the roots of the elder blight snaked up out of the dirt to defend the tree. They lashed out and grasped at the wolves. Within seconds, all three of the wolf spirits were grappled. The roots pulled tightly, strangling the animals and dislocating limbs. Each spirit dissolved into mist. "Sorry, guys, but at least you showed us how the monster works," Sheena said softly.

"That may not be all it does," Sharur growled.

"Of course not. But, it's a start." She raised her bow and fired a spirit arrow and a war arrow in quick succession to test their effects. The Titans were already spreading out to do their work. Sheena watched closely as the spirit arrow hit the elder blight between the ersatz eyes of its trunk. As with the lesser blights, the tree shuddered as if it had been hit something massive, but with its greater size and bulk, Sheena did not think that the arrow did much damage. Still, it was good to know that the spirit arrows would have some effect, if needed. The war arrow hit the same spot and buried itself up to the fletchings with the soft "thock" of a solid object hitting rotten wood. The elder blight scowled and looked about for its assailant.

Sir Leo casually finished casting a spell and a silvery-green bolt of light stabbed out to hit the tree just above the base of its trunk. The bolt left a deep scorch mark, but did not seem to have much other effect. Leo narrowed his eyes as he assessed the impact of his spell. "Hmm… That would have blown one of the lesser blights apart. This is definitely a much tougher creature."

"Let's see how it handles lightning," suggested Gayle. She had summoned one of her storm clouds and the lightning bolt zapped the tree. It, too, left little more than an isolated scorch mark. She snorted, "Personally, I don't think it's really wood."

"There are only simple psychic presences here," PsiKid informed his companions. "Like ghosts or spirits inhabiting these blighted trees. The partial consciousness of the elder blight is no stronger than that of the others, though it is physically more powerful. And… I'm getting something else, shielded, nearby. I will keep seeking it."

Liberty Girl and Steffanwolf had already waded through the dense thicket to the first of their blights, and were in the process of destroying them. Liberty Girl's went down first. Steffanwolf shredded the trunk of the blight with his claws and then punched the tree several times until it fell over. Meanwhile, the entire thicket came to life.

"Here we go!" Gayle called out. She summoned a troop of six aerial servants to be her phantom army. She instructed them, "Keep the walking and falling trees off of us."

Sheena threw a slowing current around the elder blight. "Want to risk it, Sharur, or wait for another opening?"

"Try a stealthy leopard."

Sheena sent Bagheera in and re-summoned the wolves to her side. None the worse for wear, they waited for a command. Sir Leo tried a different kind of spell and hurled a firebolt at the tree. It smoldered briefly and went out, leaving little more than another scorch mark on the elder blight's trunk. He followed with an ice blast. That, too, did little the heroes could detect. In the meantime, Liberty Girl and Steffanwolf were busy with trees. So far, neither of the powerhouses had taken enough damage from the attacking trees to warrant Serendipity Blue's healing. She held herself alertly in reserve.

The elder blight's "eyes" glowed like burning coals and it waved its arm-like branches as if it were casting a spell. A sickly yellow glow surrounded eight of the animated trees and they stopped where they were. As Sheena watched, those trees grew thicker, shrank slightly, and discolorations ran along their bark and leaves. They turned into tree blights. The elder blight's eyes faded again as the freshly-created tree blights began to attack. Half picked up the task of coordinating the attacks of the otherwise-normal animated trees. The remaining four started flinging clumps of leaves at Liberty Girl and Steffanwolf.

"Ouch! These are sharp!" Liberty Girl announced after a few seconds of this. Each made barely more than a pinprick, but the blights were churning out a lot of them in a nearly continuous stream. Serendipity Blue prepared her healing powers, but both of the humanoid tanks seemed to be doing fine. Gayle refreshed the air cushions on them for additional protection.

The black leopard, Bagheera, had crept up to the side of the elder blight like a shadow in the night. The massive tree was still wreathed in Sheena's slow current, but it responded quickly when the leopard's claws started digging into its trunk. A tree limb swung down and crushed the leopard like a bug against its trunk. Sheena flinched and shuddered in sympathy.

"Focus on the point between its eyes," instructed Sir Leo. "Let's see if we can whittle it down a bit. For the moment, we have time. Let's use it to concentrate our fire." He threw an energy bolt to mark the spot and began preparing another. He ducked as a tree came crashing down where he was standing, only to be stopped by one of Gayle's aerial servants. The elf nonchalantly continued his spellcasting.

Gayle threw concentrated air blasts at the target spot on the elder blight. This direct physical impact seemed to do more than the energy bolts. Her storm cloud continued to hit the blight with lightning, too, but its effect remained negligible.

Over the crash of thunder, she said, "I could wrench this whole bunch of trees out of the ground with a real tornado, if we needed to."

"Keep that in reserve," Sheena called. "You never know."

"Man, these things are pinching me in!" Steffanwolf complained. He ducked and weaved as branches pummeled him and the blights peppered him with sharpened leaves. He wasn't taking much actual damage—none of the attacks involved silver, and he had the traditional weres' resistance to most other forms of injury—but it was a lot to deal with. He had managed to tear down two blights and a bunch of trees, so far. True to the plan, he and Liberty Girl were keeping everything but the elder blight busy. Liberty Girl was ahead in the arboreal body count, with four blights and enough fallen lumber to build several log cabins. She had stacked it roughly to the left side of the central group, preventing the blights and animated trees from getting close to them.

Sheena had an idea. "Liberty Girl! Steffanwolf! When you can, toss them down into the elder blight's circle! Let's see if we can make a deck that's safe to stand on."

The werewolf chuckled and edged around to get a better angle for that work. Sheena asked Sir Leo, "Do you have a fire ball or something that would burn off foliage and small branches? There's going to be a lot of brush in the way if they can pull that trick off."

"Of course, lady. I will watch for the right opportunity."

"It's coming closer," PsiKid warned.

On that word, Ravenger himself burst up through the soft earth. He towered to his full height and stretched out his arms, releasing a cloud of russet spores in a wide area around himself. Gayle held her breath and nodded to PsiKid and quickly swept the spores away with a sirocco of wind. She had experienced this attack before. She yelled, "Good morning, Ravenger... you creepy jerk!"

Gayle Force. You are mine. Your fight is pointless.

"Yeah, I've heard that before. It's not any more true now than it was the last eight times you've said it." She crooked her arm and put a fresh storm cloud right behind the villain. It rumbled into existence and zapped the creature with a bolt of lightning. Ravenger twitched slightly, but did not seem seriously hurt.

The violet compound eyes of the monstrous villain swirled with color. A flash of light leaped from his eyes toward Gayle, but it faded before it reached her.

~Mental resistance, up and running,~ PsiKid sent in a relaxed telepathic voice to everyone.

You cannot stop me. The creature moved forward with a speed that belied its bulk and aimed a two-fisted flurry of his mighty claws at Gayle. *You can only delay the joining.*

The elder blight chose that moment to let out an unholy screech. Sheena and several of the others clapped their hands to their ears. Her pets, including Sharur, to her surprise, vanished. So did Gayle's phantom army and both of her storm clouds. The sound was excruciating. In the moment of distraction, Ravenger's clawed fists pummeled the singer and drove her back toward the elder blight.

Her air cushion shield held, but it could only lessen the impact, not protect her completely.

PsiKid remained calmly focused on countering Ravenger's mental attacks. Liberty Girl picked up one of the nearby trees and threw it at the elder blight. This cut off the wail, but Steffanwolf's sensitive ears had been particularly hurt by the sonic attack and he was being buried beneath a pile of falling trees.

The other blights and the trees they controlled pressed their advantage, closing in on Serendipity Blue, PsiKid, and Sir Leo from the right as best they could. The elder blight began to wave its limbs and glow as it had done before when summoning a wave of tree blights. Sheena quickly raised her bow and fired a spirit arrow at the elder blight. This interrupted whatever it was that the tree was doing. She wasn't sure what it was, but it probably meant more trouble for the heroes.

"I suggest physical attacks on the elder blight, not energy," Sir Leo offered quickly. He switched his own spells to produce a stream of razor-edged flechettes instead of energy or fire or magical force. The projectiles slowly began to chew a hole in the trunk.

Sheena thought something was strange about the way the mage's shots were sinking into the tree, but she wasn't sure what it was. She raised her bow and fired a spirit arrow, and then a war arrow, as before. The tree quivered from the spirit arrow and the war arrow sunk deep into the rotten wood.

Ravenger swung both fists in an overhead blow at Gayle. He was fast. Gayle dodged to her right but took a glancing blow that scraped down her left arm and hip, drawing blood. Her face screwed up in pain. She side-stepped again and bobbed into the air to get over the loosely stacked trees in her way. Ravenger released another load of spores, and then turned and picked up one of the trees and threw it at PsiKid. Sheena wasn't sure between PsiKid gently waving his hand or Gayle's blast of wind which one deflected the leafy missile, but it missed its target and continued far past the thicket before landing. Serendipity Blue focused her healing on Gayle and the green radiant glow rippled up and down the singer's body, instantly healing the wounds she had taken and preventing the spores from taking effect. Gayle brought out her phantom army again inside the elder blight's root circle, but on top of the logs that Liberty Girl had managed to put down. The aerial attackers began to pummel Ravenger and hammer him with air blasts. This seemed to Sheena to be more of a distraction than an actual source of damage, but she supposed that every little bit helped. She continued to alternate arrows against the elder blight.

The elder blight's roots tried to creep up to attack the phantom army, but they had little success worming their way around the trees that pressed them down. Sheena was satisfied with that.

Liberty Girl called out, "Hey, 'Wolf, how are you doing over there?"

From under the stack of trees, Steffanwolf replied, "Stuck."

"Okay, hang on," the liberty belle said. She jumped past Ravenger, smacking him with a backhanded fist as she did so. The massive villain barely moved, and kept his attention on Gayle. Liberty Girl grabbed a tree like an unwieldy baseball bat and smacked it into the cluster of trees over Steffanwolf. Most of them started falling over, so she gave them another push to help them on their way. This was enough for the wolfman to heave a couple of trunks off of himself and scramble to his feet. Blue bathed them both with healing energy and they separated to push back the trees and the blights again.

Sheena, Leo, and Blue kept their distance from Ravenger and the trees as best they could, and Sheena and the elf mage also kept firing at the elder blight. It seemed more that they were scraping it than that they were doing any real damage. Sheena silently cursed when she noticed that the bark was quickly growing scars over the damage they had done.

You are not powerful enough to stop the tree. You are not powerful enough to stop the Vengeful Earth. Give up. Your bodies will join the Vengeful Earth. Ravenger levelled another mental blast at Gayle, and then turned and stomped toward PsiKid, who had blocked the attack. The villain kicked a shower of dirt at his face as he closed on the psychic powerhouse. The teenager waved his hand again and the debris was simply turned aside.

Gayle suddenly pushed her hands out toward the villain. She scooped up the air around him and spun it into a whirling ball with Ravenger inside. Her slender eyebrows were knit in concentration and her jaw clenched with effort as the aerial hamster ball rapidly picked up speed and strength. It lifted the villain off the ground and contained him.

"Whoa!" Serendipity Blue said. "What d'yall want me to do, Honey?"

PsiKid was concentrating on Ravenger, his eyes glowing with a bright light. His was a look of total focus. With a gentle and relaxed voice, he answered for Gayle directly into the heroes' minds. ~Stand back, and be ready to heal. Take out the blights, first. Then, we'll deal with Ravenger. Gayle and I will keep him contained until then. His psyche is extremely powerful; well beyond threat level 50. And it's not entirely present here in this body. Weird.~

The elder blight began its summoning motions again, so Sheena repeated the trick with the spirit arrow. As before, she was able to interrupt the tree's activity. She noticed that there were far more than just eight targeted trees, this time. "We can't let the big one get off that blight creating spell! It's getting more powerful each time it tries!"

"Yeah, and we have enough to handle with the ones we've got," Steffanwolf added. He finished breaking up another blight, but the animated trees kept on pressing forward. "I don't think taking out the lesser blights is doing anything to stop the trees they are controlling."

"Gotcha," Liberty Girl said. She kept fighting, too. "Sheena, any progress on the big one?"

Sheena shook her head. "Slim. We'll have to think of something else. Leo?"

"I threw in a couple of alternate spells over the last couple of cycles, but they are not having any real effect. I must admit that I am more prepared for fighting things truly living, fully dead, or built by man. I am usually protecting the forest, and not attacking it myself."

Beads of sweat began to form on Gayle's forehead as she kept the ball of air compressed and spinning. The phantom army dissipated, her full effort needed to contain the master villain. "Any time, folks...."

Sheena shook her head and muttered, "Time... Oh, yes, that's it! Am I the goddess of time or not?" She reached deep into the spirit world and pulled a thick, fast-running current out of the time stream. Concentrating on just what she needed to do, she looped it around the elder blight and got it flowing securely in one direction. Then, she flipped one half of it over to counter its own flow. The current, visible to her alone, became a still pool that trapped the massive tree creature like a fly in amber.

"That should buy us more time!" Sheena laughed. "Now, take out the blights. The big one is stuck."

"Excellent," Sir Leo responded. He picked out the lesser blights farthest from the heroes and burned them down with his energy bolts, one after another. Liberty Girl and Steffanwolf did their part, too, moving from blight to blight and pulverizing the trunks of the sickly trees until they splintered. As the blights went down, so did the trees they controlled, just like the previous day. In less than a minute, the whole thicket was clear of moving trees. The roar of the spinning capsule of air dominated the clearing.

"I've got you now, Ravenger, and you are going to face justice!" Gayle called out through the sound of the wind.

Do you think so?

"Yes, I do."

The villain's mental voice was suddenly much smoother and easy to understand, as if it was more human and divorced from the monstrous body the wind controller had trapped. *Foolish girl. My consciousness is distributed among any and all of my creations. I can be anywhere, and I cannot be stopped. I am patient, Gayle. You *will* be mine. It really is only a matter of time.*

"Oh, no... Get him! Now!" Gayle shouted. She tightened the wind capsule as much as she could, and even the clouds dipped lower toward them in the sky as she sucked in air. She continued to push the sphere as hard and fast as she could.

The glow from PsiKid's eyes faded and he relaxed. He said by mindspeech, ~Gayle, he is gone.~

"No! I still have him!"

~You have a ruined mass of fungus. Ravenger has left it.~

"Noooooo!" Her frustrated shout was almost as loud as the elder blight's wail.

"I'm sorry, Lady Gayle, but while you have won the battle, the monster has escaped to continue the war!" Sir Leo called out. "No life remains in that sphere!"

"Damn it all, anyway!" The frustrated singer began relaxing her grip on the storm. The ball of air began to slow. "I had him."

"Well, that's it for Ravenger today, at least. As much as I hate to say it, there's always next time, Gayle," Liberty Girl said. "What did you do to the elder blight, Sheena?"

"I trapped it in time. I'm going to have to let it out, but I remembered something important. All it will take is one shot." She felt a little smug at the surprised looks of the other heroes.

Gayle was carefully winding down the trap she had been spinning for so long. She looked exhausted. "Good. I'm not sure how much more I'm up for. If I just let this go, it will flatten what's left of the park and spin tornadoes out of control for a couple of miles."

"Wow! Overkill much?" Steffanwolf asked.

PsiKid shook his head. "Not overkill at all, actually. Ravenger is incredibly strong. Between the two of us, we could keep him contained, but I'm not really sure what it would take to truly capture and hold him."

"Oh. Sorry." The wolfman looked abashed.

Sheena called Sharur again. The enormous iron wolf appeared at her side.

"I am here to serve, Mistress. What would you have me do?" he asked.

"Sharur, I have trapped the elder blight in time."

The demon wolf managed to grin. "You have discovered the full legacy of Shanikali!"

"Yes, thank you. Can you tell if its wood is rotten all the way through?"

The wolf studied the motionless tree and sniffed carefully. "I believe so, Mistress, although I cannot fully scent it, trapped as it is. Is that important?"

"Oh, yes, it is! Tell me, oh aged one! You have seen much. How long does it take for wood to rot?"

"A small span of years, but longer if the tree is preserved or the temperature is low."

"Surely, less than one thousand years."

"Yes, much less."

"Even for a magical tree such as this one?" Sheena was grinning now, and playing to her audience a bit.

Sharur studied the tree again. He responded, "Yes, Mistress. This tree was created rotten. I do not think it would last long naturally."

Gayle had finally spun the capsule down to where she could safely let it go. She did so and it collapsed with a thunderclap. She fell to her knees panting. Serendipity Blue helped her to a seat on a downed tree trunk.

"Are you all right, Gayle?" Sheena asked her friend.

"Oh, sure, I'll be fine! Just have to get my wind back, is all."

Steffanwolf extended a claw and experimentally scratched at the trunk of the tree. "Huh. It's frictionless, or something."

"If it's frozen in time, that would be only logical," Sir Leo agreed. He looked back to Sheena.

She nodded and asked, "All right, then. Is everyone ready for me to take the elder blight off of 'pause?'" Heads nodded and the rest of the Titans took up ready positions. "Like I said, this should take just one shot. But, if I'm wrong, battering that rotten wood ought to finish it off."

Sheena reached into her quiver and drew out the black arrow and fitted it to her bowstring. She lifted her hand and flipped the pool over, "spilling" the time stream and letting it flow away at its normal pace. The enchanted tree started moving again, intent on continuing its battle with the heroes. Sheena drew back the string and let the arrow fly into the heart of the elder blight. With a shimmer of light like sunlight reflected from the surface of a river, one thousand years passed the tree. Its rotted hulk fell into a large pile of dust on the ground.

No one said anything for a long moment. Smiles grew on the Titans' faces. Gayle looked at Sheena and laughed, "Okay, it's official. If you were wondering before, I think you've proven what you can do today. You are way more than just a sidekick! Do you have anything to say to the group?"

"Uh, thanks for the help, everyone. Something this big takes a team effort, and I'm glad we were all here to pull it off. This was some impressive work!"

"All right, then!" Gayle hopped up from the tree trunk and saluted Sheena. "By the dubious mutant powers invested in me by my mother, and especially given your feathery wings and all, I hereby promote you from side-chick to full-fledged hero, with all duties, rights, and privileges and so forth!"

The applause and cheers of the heroes rang out over what was left of the park reserve. Sheena laughed and realized that she felt at home. There was still a lot to do, and some very serious threats to stop, but for the first time, saving the world didn't seem so far out of reach.

Chapter 27 – Classic Villainy 101

"Eric Gardner?" The nurse stepped into the hospital room.

"Yes. That's me." Eric looked up from his laptop where he was finishing up the H3 analyses. Coffee had brought his things by the previous afternoon after Eric had put in a call back to Dynatech. He figured that he should at least keep working on the project assignments for the team.

"You can sign out and go home. Go ahead and get dressed, and then open the door. I'll be waiting outside for you."

"Oh. No physical therapy?"

"No, that will be rescheduled."

Eric shrugged and swung his legs out of bed. The numbness and tingling had disappeared by nightfall. As far as he could tell, the only lasting effects of the incident with Horgan's source stone were his bruised ego and the damage to his relationship with Sheena. He sighed. "Okay. I'll get dressed."

The nurse nodded and stepped out. At least they had dried his clothes overnight. He shut down his computer and tucked everything back into his computer bag, then opened the door.

"All done?" the nurse asked.

"Yeah, thanks. What do you need me to sign?"

She waved her hand back and forth oddly and it seemed almost like she was drawing something in the air. Eric squinted as he tried to follow it with his eyes. He looked up at her face. She looked familiar. "Oh, come on…! Not you!"

The nurse sneered, "Yeah, me. Let's go for a little walk, Gardner!" Elf Shot dropped her disguise and grabbed for his arm.

"No, I don't think so!" Eric quickly leaned over and hit the call button on the hospital bed and then snapped his hand down on the archer's wrist, breaking her grip. He shouted as loud as he could to the hospital staff, "Help! Assault! Call the police!"

Elf Shot rolled her eyes. "Blood of the queen, Gardner! What a wuss! Stand still!" She drew a pair of knives from her belt.

Eric pulled the sheets from the bed and spun away from her. He flicked the sheets at her hands and face, grabbed her right wrist, and turned it over. He stepped to the side and slipped the knife from her grip.

The elven woman slashed at his grip on her wrist with the other knife, opening a three-inch gash on his left forearm, as she tried to recover her balance. "You aren't making this easy, are you?"

"What's going on here?" cried the floor nurse as she pushed the door open, a physician's assistant right behind her. She gasped and jumped back on seeing the knife-wielding, leather-clad villain.

"Bah, enough of this!" The archer cast the spell that opened a shimmering doorway in the air. She made another grab for Eric with her free hand. Eric took the opening and threw a karate kick into her ribs. Air whoofed out of the villain, but she grabbed his leg before he could pull it all the way back. With a gasp and a sneer, she backed through the portal and dragged the veterinarian with her. They both vanished and the temporary doorway to somewhere else disappeared, as well.

After a few seconds of shock, the hospital staff ran to call the police.

"So, this time you underestimated the ranger's husband?" Blighthawk shook his head in mock sadness.

Elf Shot glared at her employer. "Just fix him. And make it hurt."

Eric looked at the corrupter with wide eyes. He barely noticed the blood staining his clothes. "That's really not necessary...."

"Actually, the fixing part is. We don't need you to bleed yourself to unconsciousness," Blighthawk replied. A trio of the toxic spirits surrounded the young veterinarian in a garage normally dedicated to Park Service equipment. Eric and Elf Shot had landed in a heap on the other side of the portal and he had taken two more cuts before the toxic spirits moved in and scared him into submission. Elf Shot had taken a few more bruises in the process, but the outcome was never in doubt. The corrupter pointed to a nearby chair. "Sit."

Eric winced and sat. The elven archer drew a black arrow from her quiver and twirled it in her fingers. "Remember these?" she asked smugly. He nodded apprehensively. "Just give me a reason, vet boy!"

Blighthawk cast his fiery healing spells, and quickly sealed and removed Eric's wounds, leaving him wide-eyed and gasping for breath against the pain. The corrupter backed off and asked Elf Shot, "Did you make sure to leave all of his electronics there?"

"He rushed me a bit, but yeah."

"All right." As much to Eric as his lieutenant, Blighthawk explained, "This area is warded so that magical detection methods will fail. You've removed the standard technological tracking methods, so all that our guest has to do is sit tight and wait for eventual rescue."

He turned his attention fully to Eric. "You see these three spirits, of course. These are manifested specifically for your benefit. Their touch is acid and poison. Their breath is deadly. There are many more of these things roaming the area. All of them have orders to restrain you—painfully—if you try to move from this building. My advice to you is to wait patiently and to follow any instructions you are given."

Eric nodded.

"Excellent. My apologies, because this is not your fight, and you seem like a decent fellow. Still, a bargain is a bargain, and I mean to give the lady here what she wants." He bowed to Elf Shot, who sniffed cynically.

"Are you finished?" she asked with a scowl.

"Yes. I will go about our work. You know what to do." He went to the door and opened it. Eric could see a gravel parking lot with trees beyond. The corrupter spread his oily black wings. "Time for me to fly."

"Go already."

Blighthawk nodded and left. The elven changeling waited to be sure he was gone, then sneered at Eric and looked him over disdainfully.

She drew a curved dagger with a golden eagle hilt and turned it this way and that so he could appreciate it. "See this? When I cut your wife's throat, I will get my powers back. Until then, that will just give you something to think about." To the spirits, she said, "Bind him to the chair and guard him."

The spirits extruded sticky strands of goo that tied Eric to the chair. The strong chemical fumes given off by the spirits made his eyes water and burned his sinuses. "Good," she said. "Now, I am going to deliver a message. Back soon."

She created a doorway and stepped through it, leaving Eric alone with the toxic jailors and his own thoughts.

"Sheena, it doesn't matter how they knew where he was. What matters is what we do next," Gayle tried to calm her friend. They were standing in a briefing room at the 14th Precinct in Dartmouth.

Sheena couldn't help it. All of the emotions were swirling around inside her like a storm. She couldn't stop crying, even though she knew it wasn't helpful. "I'm sorry, Gayle. I can't think straight. Just, tell me what to do."

Gayle hugged her again. She reflected that maybe it wasn't so fun helping people she knew closely. Lieutenant Fowler waited patiently. Gayle let Sheena go and took a deep breath. "Okay, metahuman hostage taking situation. No contact, and no demands, yet. Elf Shot wants you, and doesn't care about Eric one way or another, except to indulge her petty little cruel streak. The Feathers' leader... no clue what he thinks of this, but he doesn't seem the wanton violence type. This elaborate multi-tiered virus plot is too complex. They've got your attention and you have something Elf Shot wants." She paced while she talked.

"Okay, check," Sheena agreed. She sniffled and wiped her eyes.

"We've put in a call to Schauer and Calderón. Right?" Gayle glanced at Eddie, who nodded. "So, the FBSA is aware of the situation. The Feathers gain by keeping us off their trail, so it's probably not personal for them, just a stalling tactic while they execute their plan. It's Elf Shot who needs to get in the killing blow on you with that knife. That pushes her into a very specific set of conditions that we can take advantage of."

"Yeah. She's got to get me helpless where she can stab me in the heart, or slit my throat, or whatever. I'd like to avoid that part."

"You know," offered the detective, "the Feathers' leader benefits from drawing it out as long as possible, but Elf Shot is probably pushing to get this done as fast as possible. She is not a patient lady. That may also be a wedge we can use."

"So... finding Eric is the next thing," Gayle continued. "And, maybe getting an update from Schauer's team on the virus plot."

"I am *tired* of waiting for other people to piece together clues! Let's go out and find her!" Sheena shouted. Her fists clenched and the feathers of her wings bristled.

Gayle responded with a calm voice. "Have you discovered some way to track her through her portal jumps?"

Sheena gritted her teeth. "No."

"Do you have some way to find her—or Eric—that we haven't tried, yet?"

She wracked her brain, and reluctantly shook her head. "Just the thing Leo is building."

"Right. And he's working on that as fast as he can."

Sheena let out a dejected breath and her anger collapsed. She whimpered, "Don't let him die!" as her tears started again.

"Then stay with me! If we put them on the defensive, they'll let something slip and we have a much better chance of finding Eric before something more happens to him!"

"Okay." She brushed away the tears again, but they kept falling.

"Eddie? Is there anyone we can lean on who might know something about the Feathers?"

"If you can find the thief that cracked the museum vault, he'd be my first recommendation," the detective suggested. Gayle shook her head reluctantly. "Or, Elf Shot's accomplices for the biotech thefts."

"Any lines on them?"

"Maybe. If we can have someone approach the Broker and ask for the same crew that Elf Shot used, but for a new job."

"Oh! There's a sneaky tactic! I know just who to ask for help with that." She turned to Sheena. "The Broker is a neutral underworld guy. He makes it possible for people to get anything they need or want with no questions asked and a lot of 'insurance' against cheating and treachery. He's like the honest broker for the bad guys, and also for police and heroes who need information... if they play by his rules. He's got enough leverage and power that it's really impractical for the police to shut him down. Elf Shot probably got the muscle for her heists through the Broker, or through someone he can point us to."

Eddie gave Gayle a skeptical look and asked, "So, yeah? Who you gonna ask for help on that?"

"My friends at Curiosity Kilz."

The detective's eyebrows went up. "Are you serious? Those are assassins and killers, Gayle!"

The singer waved away his protests with an air of assurance. "That's just what they want people to believe.... Well, yes, they do those things, too. But, they also do spying for the good guys, locate missing persons, and rescue people right out from under the noses of the really bad guys."

Eddie sighed. "The 'really bad guys?' You're gonna do what you want to, of course, but I can't condone this! You can't trust villains like that."

"No, Eddie, I agree. You can't. But I can. Some of them, anyway."

"Wait, what? Work with the bad guys?" Sheena was confused.

"Not really bad guys. Or, not all of them. They're more like gray than black or white. And some of them owe me favors."

"Seriously?!?" Eddie just threw his hands in the air and made an exasperated noise.

"Yeah, seriously." Gayle looked back and forth between the two of them. "We need a lead followed, and those people with the Broker aren't going to cooperate with heroes, right? And, it would be suspicious for the VCPD's undercover officers to suddenly ask about this. So, we need someone else we can trust. That's who I'm going to call." She paused and then cocked her head and looked at Sheena. "Or, we can just wait around for something to happen."

Sheena hesitated for only a second. "Do it." Eddie shrugged and nodded reluctantly.

"All right. I'm on it. Give me a few minutes." Gayle excused herself to make a call.

"The Arama Hallada compass is gathering energy from the moon. It will be finished by dawn on Sunday morning. I'm sorry. I can't make it go any faster than nature allows." Sir Leo seemed at once sincerely apologetic and also as if he was explaining to a small child why she couldn't have the moon. They were using one of the situation rooms in the Titans' underground base beneath the Riverhaven complex.

"If it is any consolation, I have done an astral scan of the city, and Eric is not to be found therein. I believe that he is hidden by magic. That led me to search Underhill. He is not in the fair folk's realm, and none of my allies have scented him in the Dark Ones' lands, as yet. Elf Shot does not have enough standing in the Unseighlie Court to call in a favor big enough to keep him Underhill, which lends more weight to the theory that he is still in Venture City, but hidden."

Sheena nodded sadly and accepted the news. "All right, Leo. Thank you. I know you are doing what you can. It's just...."

He touched her arm gently. "It's hard. I know. I will do everything I can."

"Thank you," she replied. The elf turned and left.

She noticed an incoming call from Calderón and answered it. "Yes, go ahead, Felix."

The shaman's voice and accent was soothing. He said, "Hola, Sheena. I am calling with your six o'clock update. No contact from Elf Shot. No location on her or Eric, yet. But, the lab has figured out the supervirus. Let me know if you want the technical details. We have also determined the identity of the man who Raven rescued. This man is probably the leader of the Feathers of the Raven. I don't know if that gives us much on his current appearance, identity, or location, though. And, there is one more opportunity for a tracker, if you are interested...."

"Yes! Whatever it is, I'll do it."

"The police have secured the Syndicate lab that the Feathers were using. When the Feathers left, they moved a lot of material and people out. One section of the sewers they used was trapped, but EOD has cleared that. It has been a few days, but if there is anything left to track, you are the one to do it, I think."

"Great. Where do you need me?"

"How about Howard and Belleville?"

"Okay, um...." Sheena calculated the distance on her wrist display. "About five minutes."

"I will meet you there."

Sheena, Sharur, and Calderón stood in a surprisingly large sewer tunnel staring at the pile of rubble that blocked further progress. The ceiling had been collapsed with explosives. The FBSA agent played his light across the rubble again.

"At least it's not beneath the river," Sheena muttered.

"That would smell better, I am sure. This will take some effort to get through. It looks like the rest of the tunnel ceiling is unstable, now."

"Can we go to the surface and get around the blockage that way?"

Calderón shrugged. "Let's try. At least we know that the Feathers did move this way, and that petroleum smell was here, too."

"Pitch."

"Whatever. I think it is the same thing."

"I think it's the leader. The toxic shaman that Raven rescued."

"And who corrupted Raven."

"I wonder if that was intentional," Sheena said as she walked back the way they had come. "What does getting shot down by the aliens have to do with anything that would corrupt a powerful spirit?"

"I don't know. What I do know is this. The story Raven told us matches with Captain Bryan John, Royal Canadian Air Force. born near Vancouver. Last flight over the Fort McMurray oil sands production region to protect the facilities during the K'rk'ti attack ten years ago. His ejection seat was found in a sort of large waste oil sump pond in the area. The pilot was missing and presumed captured by the K'rk'ti, but apparently not."

"So, what in that background would turn him into a terrorist, or did that come later?"

"His family was killed in the invasion when the K'rk'ti smashed big chunks of Vancouver. John's squadron was supposed to protect the city, but was diverted northward. There is an email record of his protest against the diversion. The response from command was 'we can rebuild Vancouver, but we can't just let them have our country's mineral wealth.' That may have something to do with it."

"Mmm... Similar story to Kadorsky, in a way. They may have reason to be angry, but this goes way too far."

Calderón grimaced. "Terrorists make their own reasons. They start with an injustice— real or imagined—and fantasize about 'getting even.' They surround themselves with people who are like them and keep telling themselves and each other that the other guy 'deserves it.' They do that so long that they push themselves bit by bit out of sanity and into crazy, rationalizing every step of the way."

"Yeah?"

"I see it every week, in this job."

"Really? Why?"

Calderón stopped at the stairs to the basement access and looked at her. "Because all of these villains that I chase down—or help heroes chase down—every one of them thinks he's justified in doing what he does. They think that because something bad happened to them, they are justified in doing things to others. From taking what they want to killing because it amuses them. But they are not. They are just lying to themselves."

Sheena nodded.

"That's why I joined the FBSA, to protect people from that. And why I like heroes, because they made the other choice, to use what the spirits have given them to help, and not just to get what they can for themselves." He climbed the rest of the stairs and opened the door.

Sheena followed. Sharur walked through the doorframe, as he had done before. Calderón told the officers guarding the crime scene what they were going to do. He and Sheena headed upstairs to the street level. After consulting some satellite images and city public works maps, they settled on a possible access point.

As they walked, Sheena was thinking. She asked, "Do heroes... people like me, anyway... get to retire from this business? Or do we end up giving to others until we give our lives to protect someone?"

Agent Calderón stopped and looked at her with a frown. "Why would you ask...? No, never mind. I think I know." He sighed and looked like he was trying to put together an answer. Sheena glanced around for trouble while she waited for him. Eventually, he said, "Metahumans retire all the time. It's just not very exciting for the news, which is why you don't hear about it. Some go on to become mentors to younger heroes. Some simply get out of the hero business to do something less dangerous, especially as they get older or as their abilities fade."

"Heh. As if," Sheena snorted.

"Maybe not for you, but a lot of metas have abilities that depend on a healthy body. Super strength isn't all it's cracked up to be when you pop your age-weakened joints every time you lift a truck!" He chuckled. "Or, whatever."

He continued. "The point is, it's up to you. Having powers? That just happens to you. What you do with them? That is a choice."

"Like the villains." She added, "They chose to be that way."

"Sí. Personally, I am glad that you chose to be a hero."

"You're welcome. Now, let's find that hideout and get my husband back!"

Sharur nodded and vanished. He set off into the night to follow the scent from the garage to wherever the rest of the Feathers went.

"Finding that truck may be the best we can realistically expect," Sheena groused, "but I'm still going to cross my fingers and hope for a breakthrough."

"If we find where the truck went, we might find where they are holding Eric. That might be the breakthrough you are hoping for," Calderón assured her. He glanced up and down the street as he waited.

She shook her head doubtfully. "I doubt that a guy as smart as this 'Blighthawk' would keep a captive in the same place as his virus factory. I mean, if the whole point of this on his side is to delay us and keep us away from his operation, he won't want us to stumble onto that in our search for Eric. And Elf Shot just wants to get me, so she'll want a place that gives her an advantage."

"At least we found out more about him. A name and appearance will help. The move out of this hideout was very recent. These two were just cleaning up anything the rest of the Feathers had missed."

"Still a step behind." She scowled. "I want to catch up. I've got to catch up!"

A VCPD cruiser and van pulled up. Calderón waved to the police officers. "Two. Just inside the doorway. Do not mind the animals. They are guarding the suspects for you."

The police responders gave Sheena admiring looks and went into the parking garage to fetch the captured members of the Feathers. Calderón made sure that the officers got the arrest report and statements from the two of them. The police could do a more detailed search of the hidden rooms beneath the garage for evidence. Sheena had already noted the important things in her report.

"Is there anything else we can do now?" Sheena asked as she fidgeted.

"No. I have sent the new evidence and information back to Tom. Now we wait."

Blighthawk wiped the oil off his face with a carefully folded paper towel and resumed eating his takeout. He was on his fifth container of pasta and second order of garlic cheese bread and was only beginning to feel full. There was a price to pay for using the power of Raven, and being hungry all the time was part of it. "They got caught, then."

"Yes. Shee'na is getting too close. Gayle Force wasn't with her, this time, but some secret agent-looking guy in a black suit was. He smells like magic. They didn't spot me, of course." The young man sitting across the table from him had an intense, almost feral face with pale blue eyes and chiseled features. His dark brown hair was pushed back from his tanned face and fell most of the way to the collar of his red t-shirt, past slightly elongated, pointed ears. The t-shirt had a black wolf's head on the front outlined in gold. Below a web belt supporting a half-dozen pouches and clips, he wore a pair of black and dark gray camouflage pants tucked into black leather SWAT boots. The pouches at his belt and the pockets of his trousers bulged with compact tools. A custom matte black automatic pistol was tucked into a worn holster at his right hip. He had the kind of lean, dark, and dangerous vibe that a lot of young movie stars and gangers tried to emulate, but with him the wolfish feel came naturally. The hand of his cybernetic right arm clenched and released with a soft, metallic click. He sniffed the air. The pasta was making him hungry. "That wolf that is with her isn't natural. It's made of metal, somehow, but living." He seemed to be trying to explain it.

"I know. It is a demon." The corrupter popped another slice of cheese bread into his mouth.

"Okay." The man scowled thoughtfully. "A demon. Does it die if I shoot it?"

"Not permanently, but you might be able to banish it until she calls it again that way."

"What kind of ammunition will work best?"

"Why, Lobo? Are you planning on getting into a fight?" Blighthawk stopped for a moment and looked at him.

"Preparation, as well as improvisation. You never know."

The mastermind resumed his meal. He mumbled, "Blessed copper, believe it or not. Or explosive rounds, if you're going mundane. It is a fire demon, inside that wolf's shell. Cold iron would normally work against demons, but when the demon itself is made of iron, there's no special advantage there."

"Okay. I'll see if I can't find a clip or three." He looked thoughtful and shook his head. "Mmm."

"Mmm, what?"

"They seem nice. Not as stuck up as some hero types. Too bad they're on the opposite side."

"Who? Shee'na and Gayle Force?" Lobo nodded. "I agree. But, they are helping to keep the corrupt order in power. If we can't convince them or avoid them, then we'll have to fight them."

"Yeah." The mutant known as Rio Lobo shrugged. "We do what we gotta do."

"Where is Elf Shot?" Blighthawk was running out of food. He sopped up the marinara sauce with the last slice of bread.

"Still bopping about with her 'preparations.' Did you tell her to do that?"

"No. I told her to turn off her phone and use something else for the next couple of days."

"She doesn't listen." Lobo's voice was full of scorn.

Blighthawk grinned and laughed, "No, you've got that right! As capable as she is, I'm afraid that she's going to get herself caught or killed with this obsession she has." He narrowed his eyes with a thoughtful expression. He drew in a wheezing breath and added, "Speaking of which... Go move Doctor Gardner to our alternate spot. I just realized that she came directly from the hospital with him. She left his electronics behind, but as we were just saying, she's made her own vulnerability."

"Roger that." He stood up and took a step toward the exit. He turned at the corrupter's voice.

"And I wouldn't worry too much about the heroes getting too close. Not just yet. There is another crisis they are going to have to deal with very, very soon."

Lobo hesitated. "Do I need to know?"

"No. Not this time. Our hands are clean of this one."

"All right. I'll see it on the news, afterward."

"Good plan. Go move him, and treat him well. He's just caught up in the middle of all this." As Lobo turned to go again, Blighthawk added, "And thank you again for bringing dinner."

Rio Lobo grunted and left.

"Bits of information have been coming in, and the Feathers we've caught have been unintentionally helpful. Still, you're not going to like this," Agent Schauer told them.

"What now?" Sheena asked with a weary voice.

"The Feathers are already spreading the virus."

"Damn!" Sheena turned and paced back and forth furiously in the FBSA operations room. She stopped and let out a frustrated sigh. "So, what do we do?"

"We are already in the process of activating outbreak response plans, coordinated by the FBSA and the Centers for Disease Control in the United States, and through similar agencies internationally. The vast majority of this happens behind the scenes."

Calderón nodded. "Fortunately, in this case we not only have the disease agent identified, with samples, even, but we also have a known anti-viral treatment for one stage of the virus, thanks to Eric and Dynatech."

Schauer continued. "It will take some time to get that into production and distributed, however, even with the help of advanced civilian and government facilities. The faster we find and shut down the Feathers spreading the virus and any other vectors, the better."

"That's where you and Gayle come in." Calderón explained. "Just keep doing what you're doing. But now, if we can capture this Blighthawk guy—or Kadorsky—we may be able to get information out of either of them that can blunt the outbreak."

Sheena wrinkled her nose. "That's assuming that he doesn't have another doomsday backup plan that we will also have to discover and stop."

"Yes. That's true," Schauer admitted. "There was some hint of that in what the apprehended Feathers were not saying. All the more reason to keep working at this."

"And Eric?"

Calderón shook his head. "Still no word."

Sheena checked her wrist display. "Gayle's still showing 'out of service area.' Meeting with the Curiosity Kilz people, I guess. Sharur is still hunting that truck, too." She looked out the window. It was almost midnight. The Venture City night life went on as if it was a normal Friday night. She supposed that for most people out there, that was true. But for her, the clock was ticking.

Gayle knocked gently and poked her head into the little quiet room at FBSA headquarters where Sheena was trying to get some sleep. "Got it!" She roused Sheena. "Wake up, I got it!"

Sheena sat up and rubbed her face. She stretched and fluttered her wing feathers into place. "Great. What specifically have you got?"

"How about... ta dah!... Elf Shot's cell phone, and a way to track her by cellular towers!"

The winged huntress blinked and then realized what that meant. "All right!" She jumped up, energy restored. "Did you tell Schauer and Calderón?"

"Yep! They're getting the specialist to bring up real time tracking for us. Come on and take a look?"

"This is from... who? Those gray ops guys? Curiosity whatever?"

"Yeah, Curiosity Kilz."

"Weird name," Sheena snorted.

"It makes sense, but it's a long story for another time." Gayle pointed to the situation map. "Here we go. Current location and ping-backs for the past twenty-four hours."

Schauer was studying the map and the time-labeled progression of the villain's location with his arms crossed and one knuckle resting thoughtfully against his chin. Calderón looked about as groggy as Sheena had a minute before, but Schauer remained "perfectly creased," as Sheena described it to herself.

"Well? What do we got?" she asked.

"The phone associated with Elf Shot spent some time at Atlas Southwestern hospital yesterday morning, then suddenly moved eight point eight seven miles almost due east. It stayed there for twenty-one minutes, and then moved seven point three miles northwest. It stayed in that tower area for fifteen minutes, and then moved again, and so on. The longest stay is four hours and eighteen minutes, and counting, for the phone's current location."

"Okay, so she spent the day teleporting from place to place across the city?" Sheena asked.

"Yes, for the most part. There are some parts during the last part of the day when she moved normally by vehicle, from one tower area to another. And part of that time was apparently shopping for additional phones. She forwarded the original number to another phone, and then forwarded that to a third number. Trying to lose or confuse the trail."

"Okay, fine. But the important thing is where are those stops where she could not have taken Eric without being seen? She couldn't do all that with a hostage in tow."

"Correct." Schauer pulled up details on each stop and aerial, satellite, or street camera images to show the surroundings. He swiped at the virtual display with his finger. "Here, here, here, and here. After that, it would not be possible to remain undetected." He keyed in some additional commands and the map was colored with semi-transparent shapes overlaying the street map. "These are the zones where she could have been, based on the accuracy we can get from the cellular towers. Frankly, I'm surprised that she did not just turn off her phone for all of this."

Gayle asked, "Could this be a decoy or misdirection?"

Sheena shook her head. "Not unless there is another teleporting metahuman helping her out. These are nearly instant discontinuities where the signal was lost and then picked up and registered again. We have to assume that she was the one moving the phone at least through any of the jumps like that."

"Good. That's helpful."

"So, where do we start? At the beginning, or where her phone is now, or where the phone that got forwarded to last is now, or what? Add the additional phones to the map, please." Sheena studied the map. Schauer added on the additional numbers to which Elf Shot's number had been forwarded and displayed the locations for those devices since activation. Sheena followed the data trail and pointed. "Okay, phone number two jumped last and most recently, and the original phone did not jump after this intersection point. Number three was turned off, but it will still receive forwarding. Forwarding on phones one and two is on the service, not the device, so they don't need to be on to forward. Hmm… Phone number two is the one she has with her now."

"That's in a different location than any of the first four jumps," Gayle noted. "Do you suppose she is in a different location, and that Eric is stashed somewhere or being guarded by someone else?"

Sheena nodded. "The last move of that phone was a short distance urban transfer between towers, and before that a jump. And she's been there for roughly an hour and a half. I'm betting that's where Elf Shot is now. Eric is…." She looked back across the tracings on the map. She pointed. "Here or here, unless she pushed him into a van that drove him somewhere else."

"Why those two?"

"This is the first jump, and it is into a building in a relatively remote area of the metroplex. She stayed there long enough to get a person secured. The second jump isn't observable, but it was in a park near a school. That would be a good spot to transfer a hostage off to someone else who would drive him away, but she stayed there for fifteen minutes. That's too long for a transfer and that is a fairly public spot for a Friday morning in summer. Even as cloudy as it was then. More likely, she was talking to someone in person or by phone…. Schauer, can you pull calls for these phones, too?"

Schauer brought up more data and added it to the map. Sheena's guess was correct, Elf Shot had made three calls from the second stop on her journey. She had teleported again within thirty seconds of finishing the third call.

Sheena nodded. "My bet is on that first stop, then. Unless someone else moved him, that's where he will be. There is too much time in the open at that second stop. She wouldn't have spent that time there with a hostage, so she had to have dropped him off, first."

Calderón pointed out a possible flaw. "But, remember that she can cast a sort of glamor or charm. If she did that to Eric, he might just follow along willingly."

"I don't think she did, though. Eric was bleeding from a knife wound when they left the hospital. And he was fighting. I think if she could have charmed him, she would have done that at the beginning."

"Maybe she tried, but he resisted or saw through it," Gayle offered. "Besides, if he's not at that first spot, you go to the second and have Sharur sniff about for his scent."

"Right." Sheena stopped and looked at Gayle and the agents. "That second phone is probably with her, and it's at a different location than where Eric might be. The priority is to rescue Eric, first. What preparations should we make?"

Calderón grinned and took a sip from his coffee cup. "You know, Sheena, the perfectly logical thing to do would be to call for your friends in the League of Titans to go in, and for you to stay right here."

Sheena's jaw dropped in disbelief, but she recovered quickly. "Well… yes. That would be the logical thing to do. But, this is my fight and my responsibility."

The shaman laughed. "I knew you were going to say that!"

Schauer was reading another screen on the control panel with a frown. "We have trouble." The others looked at him. "More trouble, that is."

Gayle prompted him, "And…?"

"The Vengeful Earth are attacking the New Land Refinery in Somerset. There is a call out for help. There seems to be quite a bit of damage to the refinery itself and to the surrounding area. They have broken the spill barriers that protect the river."

"Any sign of Ravenger himself?" Gayle asked sharply.

"No. Not at present. It may be that he used the blights in the park reserve as a way to conserve resources and draw attention from this plan. It certainly has caused more destruction already than the walking trees managed to cause over the course of a day."

"Well, that's partly because we stopped it."

Schauer nodded. "Granted."

Sheena was frowning anxiously. "We don't have to help with that, do we? Can we go rescue Eric?"

Calderón sighed and looked at his partner. Schauer glanced through the information on the refinery attack. "This is very convenient timing for the Feathers if they wanted to distract us from a rescue. I recommend making the attempt to rescue your husband now, Sheena."

"All right! Let's get moving!"

"I have a bad feeling about this…," Calderón muttered. "Be careful, you two."

"Sure thing, Dad!" Gayle replied with a grin. "Don't wait up! And we promise that we won't let anything scratch the car, either."

The shaman smirked and rolled his eyes.

Chapter 28 – Classic Heroics 101

"With all due respect to Calderón, though," Sheena said later as they flew southeast across the city, "we have to be careful on this."

"Right! If this is the place she wants to fight, it will be set up to give her an advantage. That means traps, minions, extra ammunition, difficult terrain that she knows and we don't, and so on. If this is just a secure place to hold Eric, then it might have traps to prevent us getting him free." Gayle nodded. "I've been through this before. This is where your stalking and scouting animals will come in very handy."

"Okay, good. We'll get him back. And then, back to Riverhaven. From there, we can keep working on the Feathers. And Elf Shot, too, if she gets away again."

"Unless we hit her hard enough to knock her out or otherwise take her down, she'll probably teleport out again." Gayle laughed ruefully. "She's quick!"

"Like I said earlier, the priority is the rescue. If we can get Elf Shot, too, that's a bonus."

"Right."

They watched the city and the north coast of Buzzard's Bay pass underneath them as they flew further. Most of the narrow peninsula called Sconticut Neck was a residential area with some light commercial offices. Across a causeway from the eastern tip of Sconticut was West Island. Most of it was set aside as a beautiful nature reserve, with scattered park buildings and a sort of private resort on the north end. There was only one way to get to the island by land, and that was across the causeway. Sheena and Gayle were heading for a maintenance garage near the middle of the park. That is where the cellular signal most likely put Elf Shot and Eric after they left the hospital the previous morning.

In the middle of the night, there were few lights, but that did not worry them. Sheena felt that it would actually make it easier when they were ready to scout the place. The maintenance garage was at the end of a dark service road. A single light on a pole was the only source of illumination. The tiny parking area held several types of Park Service vehicles, but nothing else. The south side of the garage roof was covered with solar panels. Sheena landed at the far side of the mowed area inside the park fence.

"There is a light on inside that building," Sheena pointed out. "The blinds are shut, but it's there."

"Okay. Let's go cautiously."

Sheena called Sharur. He greeted her and informed her of his progress in finding the truck she had set him tracking earlier. "Good, thank you, Sharur. That may be helpful later. Can you find your way back to where you left the trail?"

"Yes, I can find it again in the city."

"Good." She explained to him what they were doing now. He made himself hidden and she followed as they approached the building looking for traps or clues.

"There are spirits here, protecting the building," Sharur informed her.

"Toxic spirits?" He nodded. "How many?"

"I think there are six, but it is hard to smell each of them distinctly. Also, I smell the oily feathers again. That person was here earlier today, but I do not think he is here now."

"Elf Shot? Eric?"

The iron wolf sniffed at the ground and the air. "Yes, Eric's scent is here, but probably inside. I do not smell him here outside the place. The woman's scent is present all over the place. Others' too."

"Let's find traps or anything Elf Shot could use against us."

"There is magic, and the spirits watch. I think the magic is to hide this place, but I am not sure. It is very quiet inside the place for humans." He began sniffing about again and made his way closer to the building.

A slight noise atop the roof drew their attention. Something small moved and made a flapping noise for just a second. Sharur snarled softly, "A diseased raven spirit!"

Almost as reflex, Sheena's bow was in her hand and she used it to put a spirit arrow in flight. The arrow caught the raven just as it was taking off from the roof. It dropped to the ground, transfixed, and then dissolved into sulfuric vapor.

"They know we are here," Sharur said.

"Then in we go," responded Sheena. She summoned the rest of her pets while Gayle did the same with her phantom army. "Any smell of live current or explosives on the door?"

"None."

"All right, wolves, first." Sheena tried the door knob just as something hideous came through the door. It was like one of Raven's corpses had been dipped in a pool of acid and brought halfway back to life. It reached for her with hands like melted flesh. Gayle's air bubble prevented it from making physical contact, but the spirit left a slick, slimy feeling where it had attempted to grab her. And then the wolves were on it, tearing it apart.

Sheena hesitated just for a second as her wolves attacked, then turned the knob and threw open the door. The confident growls of her wolves had turned into more desperate, pained cries but they still fought. Gayle's aerial warriors flew in through the door as the wolves finished off the toxic spirit. Gayle followed, bringing up a swirling breeze to dampen the effects of fumes and missiles.

Sheena healed her wolves and went through the door into the garage. There were more of the toxic spirits nearby, already engaged in close combat with Gayle's phantom army. Gayle was hovering a couple of meters off the floor in the center of her defensive breeze and darting about as she looked about the garage for Eric. Sheena's wolves and leopards entered and attacked the spirits she designated. Sharur made a half-growl of surprise as he was blocked at the doorway. He tried again, but could not enter the building.

"This is magic," he said as the other spirit animals bit and clawed at the toxic foes. "It forbids me entrance."

"Okay, take anything that comes out and patrol the outside," Sheena quickly replied.

"No Elf Shot, and no Eric," Gayle reported. "Go ahead and search the offices and smaller areas."

Sheena moved to the interior doors leading to a hallway, but had to pause to heal her spirit animals again. The toxic spirits were grasping, spitting acid, and breathing out clouds of poison on the heroes' pets. The defenses Gayle had created were doing a good job of minimizing the effects of these attacks, but the fight could not be won just by the pets alone, and the wind seemed to have little effect on the insubstantial nature of the spirits. Sharur paced back and forth outside. Sheena called, "Pull them out to where Sharur can help!"

Gayle nodded and looked about, then directed a thin jet of air to push the button that opened the main garage door. Sheena opened the door into the hallway and sniffed. There was nothing conclusive, but she now knew for a fact from the distinctive petroleum smell that Blighthawk had been here recently. She turned back and fired a series of arrows at each of the toxic spirits, one after the other. This was enough to allow the animals to finish off two more and concentrate on the final three.

She flicked on the light switch in the hallway and made a quick search of the office area, bathroom, and storerooms. No Eric, and nobody else, either, though it appeared that they had been here earlier. She ducked back into the maintenance garage. Gayle had made her phantom army withdraw to the open garage doorway. Sheena commanded her animal spirits to do the same, and bathed them all in a burst of golden healing energy. The toxic spirits followed. As soon as they were within a few meters of the entrance, Sharur moved up and opened his mouth. Fire roared forth like billowing dragon's breath, engulfing the toxic spirits, animal spirits, and phantom army, alike. The weakened toxic spirits burned up in a flash, their essences catching fire like the flare atop an oil well. Sheena's wolves and Misty, the gray leopard, also perished in the fire and dissolved into mist. The phantom army was unaffected.

"No one's here, now, but Eric, Elf Shot, and Blighthawk were here earlier. Probably others, too," Sheena informed Gayle. She dismissed the remaining leopard.

"Dang." Gayle looked around the garage a bit more closely. "If this was an ambush for us, it wasn't a very strong one. And those spirits just focused on our pets."

"Mmm. It would have been a lot tougher if the actual villains would have been here. They did manage to fence out Sharur, my strongest defender. And your wind powers weren't doing a lot to them, directly." The iron wolf sat outside the garage, watching and sniffing for further dangers. He glanced at the two heroines when Sheena mentioned his name. "Sharur, Eric is not here. Can you find his scent further from the building, if he was taken away by car, maybe?"

"I will find out." He stood up and padded off away from the garage.

"All right," Sheena said half to herself. "Time to look for trackable clues."

"Right. I'll check and make sure the place is secure, and then let's get out of here, in case they have warning and plan to make a counterattack."

Sheena found recent bloodstains on and near a chair, remnants of some sticky chemical substance on the chair and floor, drippings that she had already come to associate with Blighthawk, the leader of the Feathers, and some other clues. Part of a counter in the office section was cleared off. A cell phone with a bright green sticky note on it had been placed carefully in the center of that cleared area. Sheena looked at the sticky note. Just one word had been written on it: "Shee'na." She took a small plastic zip-close evidence bag from her belt pouch, turned it inside out, picked up the phone with it, and then pulled it right side out with the phone inside, zipping the bag closed.

"I'm pretty sure they left this for me," she told Gayle as her green-clad friend made her own search of the office area.

"Okay, let's take it back to the FBSA. I'm not finding anything else here to tell us where they went." They walked out of the building and Gayle did the same trick to press the button that closed the garage door.

Sharur waited in the parking lot. "Yes, Mistress, I can follow the trail. But it will not be quick. They have tried to mask his scent. Not perfectly, but enough that I will need to go slowly."

"I appreciate it, Sharur. Go ahead. Find me if anything needs my attention along the way."

The demon wolf nodded and disappeared.

Sheena turned to Gayle with a weary look. "I don't know whether to be relieved that Sharur's able to track him, or worried that he's still in danger, or what. I'm just too tired, now."

"Let's get in the air. We can report back to Schauer and Calderón while we fly. Riverhaven is only halfway between here and the FBSA, if you want to crash there."

"No, I have to turn this in and see if there's a message for me on it." She held up the phone. "But I want them to check it, first. Then, I can crash, afterward. I'll survive."

"All right, then. The search continues."

The weekend dragged on slowly and there were dark circles under Sheena's eyes by Sunday afternoon. She had been catching an hour or two of sleep at a time, but couldn't stay asleep for long and didn't feel particularly refreshed when she awakened. Even the persistently cheerful Gayle was becoming irritable with the waiting and worry.

Sharur had followed Eric's trail to an entrance to the Venture City storm and steam tunnel network beneath the North Bank district. When the trail went into the sewers, the smells were so overwhelming that the demon wolf had to admit defeat, albeit temporary. After investigating the end of the trail herself, Sheena suspected that the Feathers had used the toxic spirits to cover their tracks through the underground labyrinth. Smells were too strong and confusing, and traces of passage wiped as clean as the sewer brick and concrete would allow. She and Sharur were more than willing to do an exhaustive search, until Gayle pointed out just how big the maze of tunnels actually was. Sheena was both amazed and irritated to learn that there were multiple levels and more than fifty kilometers of the tunnels winding beneath the city. Only part of the tunnel system was intentionally constructed by the city. Many extensions had been built by private companies for various legitimate purposes and by decades of villains for their own ends. Undoubtedly, there was a map, but neither Gayle nor the Titans' supercomputer could identify with certainty who possessed such a map. As it stood, the tunnels weren't exactly a dead end, but they weren't going to provide quick access to Eric or the villains.

The cell phone was another combination of opportunity and frustration. It was free of anything that would allow it to be tracked back to whoever had left it for Sheena, but when turned on, there was a voice message waiting for her. She and the others had listened to Blighthawk's smoke-damaged voice deliver these words:

> *Hello, Sheena. Your husband is safe for the time being. As you can imagine, Elf Shot intends a contest between you two. A lethal contest, but I will leave the outcome of that to the two of you. I will provide the details of a time and place for that contest Sunday evening, after everything has been arranged. Please know that having moved Doctor Gardner once, it will be inconvenient to do so again. If it seems that you are pursuing us or getting too close to interfering with my plans, I will instead allow Elf Shot to torment your husband as she pleases and to sell him as a slave to the dark fey of the Unseighlie Court. You can verify with your own contacts that getting him free of such a terrifying situation would be difficult, and by no means certain to succeed. As I have suggested to your husband, I recommend that you wait patiently and follow the instructions you are given. Perhaps in the meantime, you could benefit by reading the manifesto and guidelines that the Feathers of the Raven have provided. You may find that your conservation- and justice-oriented aims are not so opposed to ours as you might think. Until later, good-bye.*

The voice message allowed a reply, but that went to an electronic drop box secured by the Broker. It could be hacked with enough time and expertise, but Schauer judged the cost to be more than the benefit. Blighthawk was playing for time, but in return he was offering to keep Eric safe. Schauer had suggested that Sheena prepare for a duel with Elf Shot, assuming the most difficult conditions and worst treachery on the villains' part and preparing to win. He and Calderón would continue to lead the FBSA effort to find and stop the virus carriers and to develop an effective outbreak response.

Gayle engaged North Shore in preparing tactics for herself and Sheena. He did what he could to help, until Sheena's flagging energy prompted him to call a halt to the training. He had sent her to bed to get more rest, pointing out that her own fatigue would be a weapon in her enemy's quiver.

On Sunday morning, Sir Leo had finished the magical compass that would point to the Arama Hallada. Sheena and Gayle spent much of the day taking readings and triangulating the results to find out where Elf Shot was. Unsurprisingly, the compass pointed to the labyrinthine tunnel network beneath the foundations of the city. They provided the results of their work to the FBSA agents and resumed their fretful waiting.

The waiting—or part of it, anyway—came to an end at 7:02 PM as the cell phone rang. Sheena and Gayle were at home in the Riverhaven apartment trying to relax. Most of the Titans were still cleaning up after the Vengeful Earth attack on the refinery. Gayle was strumming her acoustic guitar on the balcony. Sheena waved at her urgently in to come in and listen. Schauer had arranged for any traffic to and from the phone to be monitored and recorded, so she picked up the call. "Hello?"

"Hi, honey," Eric's voice came from the phone. "I love you. I'm doing about as okay as you can expect. I'm sorry for the storm thing. You just tell me what to do, and I'll do it. I have to give the phone back to this Blighthawk guy, now. I love you."

The corrupter's voice came on the line. He coughed for a moment, then caught his breath. "Pardon me. Smoke inhalation. Never really goes away. Anyway... Good evening! I assume that you are with me, Sheena?"

"Yes. Go ahead," she replied numbly. She dried her eyes with the back of her hand. Gayle stood at her side and listened closely

"Let's also assume that our friends in various government agencies and supergroups are monitoring this call, as well. They are welcome to do so. The trace leads back to my Venture City headquarters under the steam tunnels, as I am sure you have discovered." He paused.

"Yes. We've figured that out."

"Right. Elf Shot is eager to get her powers back. Unfortunately, the method required is regrettably violent. Still, if you want us to release Doctor Gardner unharmed, you will choose to participate in this little duel I am arranging. Elf Shot feels confident enough in her own skills to take on this challenge. I hope you feel likewise on your part.

"The site of the challenge will be... Hmm!... the now-ruined New Land refinery. I had nothing to do with that, in case you are wondering. That was purely Ravenger's thing. But the blackened and twisted rubble of the refinery site should provide you both an interesting battleground. The limits of the New Land property form the boundaries of the battleground."

He stopped to cough again before continuing in his raspy voice, "As you are both archers, I encourage you to make the most of the outdoor environment, but if you want to hunt each other through the buildings, have at it. Objects and obstacles—including living ones—on the field of battle may be targeted as desired. As such, I would strongly advise your agency compatriots to clear innocents from the site for the duration of the contest.

"And that will take place as the setting sun touches the horizon tomorrow, let's call it 7:49 PM. You will have a nearly full moon, as well, for your greater enjoyment, if the contest goes on long enough for you to need it. The duel will last until one of you gives up or is unable to fight on. On her side, Elf Shot intends to kill you with the Arama Hallada. What you prefer to do to her is up to you and your own moral and ethical conscience.

"Doctor Gardner will be brought onto the field by Elf Shot and released unharmed at the start of the contest. There is no guarantee that he will remain unharmed once battle begins, so I am advising him to get out of the refinery site by the most expedient means possible.

"This is intended as a contest between you, Sheena, and Elf Shot alone. If others enter the battleground or assist you in any way once the duel begins, we will consider them combatants and I will throw overwhelming force against them and you, assisting Elf Shot. Unless this happens, I, the Feathers of the Raven, and my other associates will remain neutral to the conduct and outcome of the duel.

"That lays out the place, time, and rules of the contest. Do you have any questions?" Blighthawk asked.

"I will be using my pets," Sheena stated flatly.

"Yes, of course. Expected and encouraged. I believe that Elf Shot is particularly looking forward to a rematch with your demon wolf. Expect her to be prepared."

"And this is it? No further demands?"

"No, as long as you adhere to the previous instructions to keep your distance until the duel begins. The disease is already spreading. Whatever you do now, you are too late to stop it. And we both know that you can't really change the past, despite your power over time."

"What does the virus do? Why three stages? We haven't quite figured out why you wanted it that way." Sheena desperately pressed for information as she processed his previous statement. It sounded like he didn't realize her connection to the spirit world. That meant something important, but she wasn't sure what it was.

"Ah, I see," croaked Blighthawk. "Let me explain. Your experts have undoubtedly found the three strains of this polymorphic supervirus. The first is a simple but very spreadable cold virus. It will infect anybody. The second is an influenza variant. It will only infect people who support the current corrupt world order. Ecological and personal liberty patriots will simply not cause the virus to unleash its second or third stage, so the effect of the virus is a matter of personal choice. The third stage is a deadly hemorrhagic virus. It only affects people who have consciously and unrepentantly made decisions to put greed before the environment or individual rights. Lawmakers in Washington and Ottawa, lobbyists, extractive industry executives, most of Wall Street, et cetera.

Again, the effect is a matter of personal choice. Refer to the Feathers' manifesto and recommendations for change to see a treatment of all that."

"So… you are going to kill people because they did legal business practices?"

"Yes. I am going to kill them for seeking benefit for themselves and the few over that of the many and the environment. Current laws and enforcement resources do little to prevent greed and unfairness. Raven greatly prefers that none is greedier than he, and he is *appalled*."

"What do you hope to gain? Justice?"

"Yes, that is part of it. But I also expect to instill an element of fear in people who hold power. Up until now, the consequences for greed have been—by and large—shallow and meaningless. Consider one other thing, Sheena; this virus will remain in circulation long after you and I have passed from this earth! From this day forward, there will be a reason to fear greed! Think of it!"

Sheena shook her head. "It's too much. It isn't justice… it's rule by fear. That's called terrorism, and not free choice."

"Agreed. But nature has no other means than people like me to defend it. Would you prefer Ravenger's vision of the future?"

"No, but…."

"My experience has proven to me that humans will not curb the richest and most powerful among them until it is too late to do so. I am simply adding a consequence of greed to perhaps give people a bit more of a conscience than they have previously demonstrated." He suffered another coughing fit and had to stop to catch his breath.

Sheena shook her head again with a disbelieving look. "I don't agree with you, and I have to do what I can to stop you."

"Yes, I know. We each do what we have to do, and accept the consequences of our actions."

"No more questions, Bryan."

"Ah! You've discovered my past." He sounded amused.

"Yes. But I still don't understand how you went from air force officer to terrorist."

"With difficulty, and after suffering many betrayals both big and little. But that's a topic for another time."

"Can I talk to Eric again? Please?"

Blighthawk paused. "Yes. Please be brief. There are preparations to make."

Eric came back on the line. "Sheena, it's me."

"Eric, I just wanted to say that I love you, too. Whatever happens, keep yourself safe, okay? If she kills me, just get out and stay away. Don't go after her yourself."

"What? I don't think you're going to lose."

"Promise me!"

"Ok, all right. I promise I won't go after her."

"Thanks. I just need to be able to concentrate completely on her. I love you."

"I love you too. Good luck. Uh… good hunting, I guess."

Sheena laughed and started leaking tears again. "Good bye for now. I'll get you back tomorrow night."

The call disconnected. Sheena looked at the display, then turned off the phone. She stared at it numbly until Gayle took it from her hand.

"You can do this," Gayle said. "You're ready."

Sheena shook her head in doubt. "Is anyone ever ready for something like this? A duel to the death, with my husband as the prize?"

Gayle's lip tightened. "No. Not that I know of. Not anyone sane, anyway." She snorted as she thought of something more. "Well, yes... actually, I do know a few people. But half of them are aliens and the other half are like samurai and ready for death at any time, you get the idea. Still, no, not really. But you really are ready to tackle this!"

"Just like a drill," Sheena breathed wearily. "By the numbers, and adapt."

Gayle shrugged. "Yeah, basically. I'd improvise all the way through, you know me, but yeah."

Sheena's regular phone rang. It was Calderón. She answered it. "Hello, Sheena here."

"Hola, Sheena. We heard the whole thing and did trace it back into the sewers. I have an idea, but you tell me, what are you going to do?"

"Prepare for a duel. What else do you suggest?"

"Nothing, yet. We still don't have enough information to try a rescue, so the duel is still best. However, if Blighthawk shows at the refinery, we will try to catch him."

"Okay, as long as we get Eric safe, first."

"Of course. We will want Gayle's help to make sure of that, and then to catch Blighthawk." Gayle nodded enthusiastically.

"She says yes, of course," Sheena relayed.

"Excellent. Have something to eat, then come to the headquarters. We will do some planning. And then you need to get some sleep. I will ask Drake to help, if you need it?"

"Drake? Oh, Josh Swan. He can help me get some rest?"

"Sí. Hypnosis. And he's conveniently located, too!"

She glanced at the ceiling, remembering that Josh and Anathae lived on the floor above Gayle's. "I suppose you're right."

"That happens, sometimes," he joked. "Not often enough, maybe, but sometimes."

"All right, we'll be in soon." She disconnected and looked at the kitchen. So did Gayle. They looked back at each other and said at the same time, "Takeout." With a mutual chuckle, they collected their gear and headed out into the city.

Chapter 29 – Of Elves and Old Gods

Sheena wasn't sure what she had been expecting, but this wasn't it. The New Land Refinery north of Somerset on the far northwestern edge of the metroplex had been almost completely destroyed by the Vengeful Earth less than three days ago. Fortunately for the city, the damage had been largely contained to the company property. The big white storage tanks were gone. Likewise, many kilometers of pipes and towers had been brought down and torn apart. Every fifty meters or so, there was a great pile of metal scrap compressed by heroic powers into tight cubes or bricks. The scrap piles were as much as ten meters high and fifty long. Far from being level and paved over with asphalt, the site looked like an earthquake had hit it. Slabs of earth, stone, and concrete were canted into the air at odd angles. Wherever the ground was almost level, dense shrubs and weeds grew to shoulder height or taller. Some even grew in cracks in the earth.

She had worried about chemical spills, and there were still many of those, but not nearly the number that she thought there would be. The Vengeful Earth had sucked up a lot of the oil and petroleum products to somehow fuel their own growth. Several heroes on the cleanup crew had leveled the earth and used their powers to grow special varieties of plants that captured chemicals in their roots and cells. Most of the shrubs and grasses had come from this metahuman cleanup process. Even with the biological cleanup underway, the place reeked of chemicals.

The office building, five in-ground holding tanks, several warehouses, part of a fractional distillation unit, and one cracking plant with its associated lines still stood, but even these structures had been badly burned and ruined. The only reason they still remained was because the cleanup crew hadn't yet gotten around to tearing them down. There were plenty of places to hide, plenty of places to climb, and a lot of difficult terrain. Sheena snorted to herself. Difficult if she chose to fight on the ground, that was. She expected to leave that to her pets while she moved from cover to cover by air.

She was wearing a new costume for this battle. Most of it was a reinforced, padded, and lightly armored bodysuit of fibermesh. It looked much like a suit of thick, high-tech blue leather from the soles of the integrated boots up to her hips and over her torso and arms. The suit had quilted fibermesh padding in blue and silver trim at flexible points and thicker panels of material over vital areas and across the shoulders. The fibermesh would distribute kinetic energy and seal itself against limited punctures. A thin layer of kelvenite plates between the inner and outer shells of fibermesh provided energy resistance and armor against slashes, cuts, and punctures. Gauntlets of the same material protected the backs of her hands, and she wore very thin gloves of orbitally grown spider silk composite to keep her fingers free for archery and manipulating the time currents. The design of the suit gave her plenty of freedom of movement for her wings while better protecting her shoulder blades. In addition to her circlet, she added eye protection and electronics that looked like a set of bronze-tinted ski goggles with an integrated headset for communications. A matching belt of the same material as the suit had pockets and pouches for her gear. In this costume, she looked more like a sleek motorcycle racer than a pre-Sumerian goddess, but it still fit her style and gave her the protection and comfort she felt she was going to need. For the moment, she had her goggles up on her forehead.

"This little guy will keep your air cushion pumped up," Gayle said as she wove a miniature aerial servant around the back of Sheena's belt. "That will help deflect anything coming at you, and then stop attacks with the shield."

Gayle had switched her own costume, too. Hers was a sky blue version of her normal tights, leaving a circle over her upper chest bare instead of filling it with an aspen tree symbol. Her shoulders and belly were still bare, and there was a similar set of circular cut-outs showing skin on the outside of her thighs. She had a set of sleek impervium armored gauntlets and knee-high boots, and a matching belt, all with sky blue enamel over the metal. She wore the same style of nearly transparent silk cape, but in sky blue and mist gray. For this version of her costume, she wore a close, stick-on mask the same color as her tights over her eyes and the bridge of her nose. Her hands were shaking slightly. Gayle laughed nervously. "Heh. I don't know why I should be so nervous! You're the one going into battle."

Sheena smiled slyly. "You know, it's not like she hasn't been trying to kill me each time we've met before, right?"

"Yeah! Just a normal day at the hero office, right?" She still looked worried but tried to put a good face on it.

Sheena put her hand on Gayle's shoulder. "You're just nervous because you can't jump in and help. It's okay."

"Yeah. You're probably right." The singer took a deep breath. She held it for a count of ten and let it out slowly. "Okay. Check the sun, and let's rock and roll."

Sheena glanced at the sky. The FBSA and backup hero contingent were at the southwest and west borders, near the road entrances. Part of their obvious job was to keep bystanders out of the area. In addition, if Blighthawk showed himself, they were there to apprehend him. She had picked the northeast border of the refinery grounds for her own starting point in order to approach with the wind bringing scents to her and her animals. Sharur stood guard, nose to the wind, back to the river, sniffing attentively. "Just a few minutes."

She called out the rest of her animal spirits. She gave specific instructions to each—wolves to harass the legs and hands, leopards to find the foe and attack from behind and to the left or the right. Sharur would be her primary defense, and she wove a quickening current around him until he was almost four times faster than usual. Her eagle had a special mission. She wanted it to find and snatch the Arama Hallada from Elf Shot, carrying it to Gayle. She sent the bird aloft to circle high above.

It was possible to put an accelerated time stream around herself, but so far in practice she had found it to be confusing and hard to keep going. It was almost no effort at all to slow incoming attacks, however. All she really worried about was being caught by surprise before she could react. And, she reasoned, that's where her pets could give her a second or two to recover. She was counting on Elf Shot using her teleport ability liberally, and on having something that could freeze or take down Sharur in one shot. Sheena was prepared for a lot, but there was still so much uncertain. She shivered and checked the sun again. She adjusted her goggles. "Okay, time to roll. I'm sending him straight back this way."

"Good hunting, my goddess friend!" Gayle offered. Sheena grinned and nodded.

She sent her eagle gliding high over the refinery, looking for the elven villain, and climbed up to the level of the main works. Looking through the eagle's eyes, she spotted a flicker of light—Elf Shot's magical doorway. She had appeared near the center of the complex, in the middle of several giant scrap piles. Eric was with her, his hands tied behind his back, a blindfold over his face. Elf Shot disappeared, leaving Eric to fend for himself. Sheena pulled up a grid map on the heads-up display and marked the location, then passed it electronically to Gayle and the FBSA agents. She added, "Eric is here. Elf Shot came in and vanished. I'm still on the northeast border."

She sent her wolves and leopards in the direction of Elf Shot's last position, telling them to find the villain and follow their instructions. She kept Sharur with her and remained where she was. Then, she checked on the scene through the eagle's eyes again. Eric was slowly making his way toward the east. That was technically the closest border of the refinery, but the farthest from help and the most rugged side of the property, nearest the Taunton River. There was still no movement or shimmer of light that would give away Elf Shot's location. She altered her instructions to the female wolf, Baroness, and had her find Eric and lead him toward Gayle. She informed Gayle of this change in the situation.

"All right, my friend," she said to Sharur, "it's time to go stalking an elf."

Sheena and Sharur faded away and began stalking slowly toward the scrap piles. She continued to make use of cover and concealment, just as if she were visible and hunting poachers back in Wisconsin. Every thirty meters or so she stopped to look through the eagle's eyes again. Still no flickers of teleportation and no giveaways of movement. Elf Shot was being more patient than Sheena had expected. Eric made an irregular movement and Sheena turned her attention to him. He flopped down on the ground and worked his hands down his legs and around his feet to the front. Then, with his hands in front of him, but still bound, he pulled down his blindfold and looked around. Baroness loped toward him. He knelt and greeted her and then followed her as she turned to lead him away.

Sheena let out a sigh of relief. "Baroness has Eric and is leading him northeast. He's got his blindfold off, still tied at the wrists. Gayle?"

"I've got him. And… yeah, I can see him, so I can talk to him. I'll bring him here to me."

"Awesome. Elf Shot is still hidden. I'm going to slide west to come behind Eric as he passes me. Stay alert, everyone." She looked hard for her foe, using the eagle's eyes. The other wolves and the leopards were in the area of the scrap piles now, searching. She switched to her own senses and looked around and behind her. Still nothing, and no alert from Sharur. The wolf shook his head.

An arrow came out of nowhere and struck Eric through the calf. He cried out and fell to the ground. Baroness turned and growled, moving to stand over him protectively. Even with the wind in her favor, Sheena could tell that the wolf had no idea where the villain was. She gritted her teeth and stalked carefully around the puddles and clumps of brush toward the scrap piles. Eric was on a flat area out in the open. Bait. Sheena wondered why Elf Shot was leaving the animals alone. "Tell him I can see him, Gayle. She's using him as bait. I'm on overwatch." She listened through the open channel as Gayle sent a whispering wind to pass her message and encouragement on to Eric. She crept forward again.

Eric examined the wound and then snapped the arrow and pulled it out. He struggled to his feet and hobbled toward Gayle and the fence. Another arrow came out of the sunset, but this time Sheena caught the flicker of movement as Elf Shot fired. She directed all of her animal spirits toward it. The arrow pierced Eric's other calf and he went down again.

Sheena winced for him and told Gayle, "Have him pull it and I will heal him. As soon as he can move, he needs to *run*, and use any available cover." Gayle passed it on. Sheena edged closer. She was on the edge of her healing range from her husband.

"This one's got the bone, he says," Gayle reported, "but he understands. Ready."

The wolves and leopards were right in the area where Sheena had spotted her foe, but they couldn't seem to find her. She shook her head. The elf must have some way of completely fooling their senses. Eric pulled the arrow and cried out. She leaned out and healed him, golden light sparkling in the sunset. Arrows were headed her way. She rolled forward and out of the way. Sharur leaped up and snapped one out of the air, swatted another with his tail, and blew a puff of flame at another. Sheena kept moving and headed for a low scrap pile, only a meter tall and several on each side.

Eric scrambled to his feet and ran. Another flight of arrows was inbound. Sheena accelerated her own time stream for a few seconds and dodged in the opposite direction she had been moving. Noting this, Sharur oriented on the elven archer, instead of going after the arrows, but there was one additional arrow in flight beyond his reach.

The arrow took Eric slightly to the left of the spine and above the center of his back. He tumbled to the ground and didn't move. Sheena screamed, "Nooooo!" She rushed toward him throwing out her arm to heal him. Another arrow was incoming, but not for her. Sharur rushed toward the archer and snapped the arrow from the air. She released another, and then a third immediately following. The iron wolf snapped the first in half and dodged to the right of the second, almost. Another arrow was in the air. This one struck home. With a flash of light and smoke, Sharur tumbled lifeless to the ground.

Eric still breathed, thanks to Sheena's healing. She ripped the arrow out of his back and flooded him with more healing energy. A fresh arrow slid by, pushed out of line by her air cushion. Eric gasped and tried to get to his feet. Sheena whirled and slowed another incoming arrow. She saw Sharur's body and gritted her teeth. She batted away the incoming arrow. The elven archer fired three more arrows. Sheena only managed to slow one of them before they arrived. Eric went down again with an arrow to the left calf and the kidney.

"I can do this all night!" Elf Shot gloated, confident that Sheena could hear her.

"Bitch!" Sheena growled. She set up a bigger slow field between her and the archer, then whirled and healed Eric again. Her animals still searched, anxious but unable to perceive the villain. She called them back to break arrows in the slow field. Another flight of arrows was inbound, and she was being kept busy pulling arrows and healing the wounds.

"This is getting really old!" Eric gasped at the latest shot of healing.

"Darn right." She countershot the arrows out of the slow field as her animals were arriving.

Another arrow, in a high arc. Sheena shot it out of the air and it exploded. Two more were coming through the slow field. The elven archer fired another trio. Sheena accelerated the animals so they would have an advantage in the slow field. One of the slowed arrows exploded when Misty batted it away. Even with the force of the explosion slowed, Sheena was the only one who remained standing. Eric and the animals weren't hurt badly, but were knocked down. *At least that took out the rest of the inbound arrows*, Sheena thought grimly to herself.

Another flight was inbound. Two high and two straight.

"Should I be running?" Eric gasped.

"Get ready. I have to provide some cover."

She doubled the strength of the slow field and defensively slowed the arrows on the high incoming arc. Then, she shot them out of the air. Another exploded, close enough to pepper them with stinging bits of metal. Sheena gasped, "I can't keep doing this!"

One of the arrows made it through the slow field and caught Eric on the outside of his right leg. "Ow, geez!"

Sheena bathed them both in healing energy quickly. "I've had enough of this. She's toying with you and wasting my energy. I'm taking you off the board, Eric. Wish me luck."

"Huh?"

She fired a trio of her own arrows back at Elf Shot, giving her something to dodge for a few seconds. Then, she summoned Sharur again. His corpse disappeared from the other side of the rubble field and he appeared whole and healthy beside her. "Keep the arrows off me. Some are explosive."

"I hear and obey, Mistress." He whirled and began to aid the animal spirits.

Sheena heard a faint curse from her foe. She grinned to herself, guessing that Elf Shot only had one of those arrows that had killed Sharur with one shot. She reached out and looped a spiraling current of time around Eric. Sharur destroyed another flight of incoming arrows. Two exploded, tumbling Baroness and the alpha wolf, Cicero, into a sharp pile of scrap. Both struggled to get up. Sheena had to ignore them for the moment.

"What are you doing?" Eric asked.

"Saving you," she replied. She parted the stream coiling around her husband and flipped it back on itself, as she had done with the ancient tree blight, stopping the flow of time for him. Then, she ducked behind him for extra cover.

"What did you do?" Gayle asked over the radio.

"Time-stopped him. Now, I go after her." She caught her breath and reassessed the situation as Sharur used the slow field to his advantage and kept clearing arrows. With a gesture, she reached out and healed Cicero and Baroness. They jumped back into the arrow-deflecting fray. Sharur had somehow managed to identify the explosive arrows and used his breath on those at a greater distance. They had reached a temporary standoff.

Sheena made sure she was under as much cover as possible and shifted her vision back to the eagle. It had landed on a strut of one of the burned towers closest to where she was fighting Elf Shot. She still couldn't see Elf Shot through the eagle's eyes. She gave the eagle instructions to swoop through the space that the villain was occupying atop the pile of scrap. That might be a distraction. The bird took off and Sheena switched back to her own senses.

The elven archer had slowed her tempo of attack, trying some slower but trickier combinations of shots to keep Sharur and the animals on their toes. Sheena took careful aim and fired a quick series of four spirit arrows at her. Their flight crawled as they hit the slow field, and resumed at full speed on leaving it. The eagle swooped in silently right by the villain's head. She ducked and twisted to the side to cause two of the arrows to miss entirely. The other two puffed into black smoke on touching Elf Shot's rippling armor of darkness.

Elf Shot fired another three arrows: two low, and one arcing high. The first two didn't even reach the slow field. Instead, they exploded right in front of it, sending shrapnel and bits of concrete flying into the field. The arcing arrow split into many more than Sheena could quickly count. Sharur blasted a good lot of them with his furnace breath, but many rained down around Sheena. One hit her squarely on the shoulder, stopped by the armor. Another grazed her wing. Sharur took several hits, and so did most of the animals. The big iron wolf wasn't hurt, but the other animals were. Joker, the beta male wolf, and Bagheera went down and dissolved into mist. When the blast byproducts from the explosive arrows came out the other side of the slow field, they took down Baroness and Misty and made Sheena very glad that she had upgraded her costume armor.

The eagle flew by at Elf Shot's head level again, brushing her with its wing feathers. She batted at it as if it were a mosquito. Sheena took the opportunity to dismiss and summon fresh all of her animal spirits. She made sure to keep the slow field up and slid it another few meters toward her foe.

"Progress?" Gayle asked over the comm channel.

"Not really. I need to let the animals find her or get close enough to her, or something. I think if I press her, though, she'll start teleporting. I don't know what I need to do to get through her armor, though. My last two spirit arrows just went 'poof' against it."

"So use the other arrows. If she goes down, you can heal her to keep her alive."

"Yeah. I suppose."

Another flight of arrows from Elf Shot, nothing fancy or special, this time, and another swoop of the eagle. This time, the bird collided with the elf. Elf Shot cursed in a melodious language Sheena didn't recognize and grabbed the eagle with her drawing hand. Black tendrils looped about the bird and constricted, quickly crushing it. Sheena wasn't wasting any time watching. She loosed another set of her own arrows in rapid succession; three war arrows and a spirit arrow. To her surprise, the entire volley struck the villain. The first arrow bounced off. The second arrow stuck for a fraction of a second and fell to the ground before vanishing. The third arrow sank into the archer's leather tunic just enough to pierce the skin. The spirit arrow affected Sheena's foe like a sledgehammer blow to the rib cage. Elf Shot doubled over and gasped for breath.

Sheena quickly followed up with another flight of two war arrows and two spirit arrows. She re-summoned the eagle, too. As before, the first arrow simply bounced off the join between the archer's shoulder and neck. The second pierced the leather and penetrated a finger's width into her muscle. The third knocked the elf from her feet, causing the final spirit arrow to scrape her shoulder pad with no additional effect.

"Thank heaven for unlimited ammo," Sheena muttered. Her eagle flew directly at Elf Shot's head, clawing at her face. Sheena was confused. "Huh?"

"What?" Gayle asked.

"The eagle is attacking her directly!" She commanded the wolves and leopards. "Get Elf Shot, with original instructions! Go!"

All three wolves and both leopards raced off to attack. "Well, good! Sharur, I'm walking the field forward. Go get her and see if you can catch her before she 'ports."

"Yes, Mistress." The iron wolf took off running as fast as he could. The elven villain was already conjuring a doorway.

Sheena loosed another flight of arrows, anticipating that Elf Shot would move toward the portal. The archer was rolling to the side, however, and all of the arrows missed. Grumbling, Sheena moved her slow field forward as her pets fell upon the elf. As each attacked with tooth or claw, there was a burst of black smoke similar to what had happened to Sheena's first two spirit arrows. With each burst, Elf Shot seemed to recover more from the drubbing she had already taken. She stepped through the doorway before Sharur could arrive.

Sheena had not seen where the villain emerged. "Do you see her? Where did she go?"

"Not in my field of view," Gayle replied.

"Not in view from the southwest," Calderón added.

"Grid T-7, high. On top of the tower, facing west, screened from your position," Agent Schauer reported. He fed it to Sheena's HUD goggles.

"Whatever that armor spell does, it takes direct damage to heal her. It hasn't been doing it with arrow shots, but the claw and bite attacks freshened her up," Sheena explained. "Like it drained life from the critters and passed it to her."

"Could be possible," Calderón said. "Still no sign of Blighthawk on any sensors we have, by the way."

"Fair enough. I wonder how he's supposed to know if we cheat?"

"Spirit observers?" guessed Gayle.

Calderón made a surprised noise. "Oh, almost certainly! I should have known that! That's how he's getting his information, and how he's spreading the virus in big quantities!" He paused. "Crap. I don't know how we can protect public areas against that sort of infection vector. Anyway, Sheena, just focus on Elf Shot. We'll take care of everything else. You've got her on the run, now. Keep it up."

"Heh. This is the battle she's good at, though."

Gayle snorted, "Pfft! You're good at this, too! You can do it!"

"All right. Doing a reset and coming back toward you, Gayle. If she wants me, she's got to come get me." She healed the hurts her pets had taken and renewed their instructions, moving back with them toward where Gayle was hovering outside the fence. She walked the slow field backward with her, shaping it like a shell and orienting its protection toward where Elf Shot was reported. The eagle was back in the sky again, circling. She patted the frozen figure of her husband as she withdrew.

"Target in motion," Schauer reported.

A doorway appeared to Sheena's right next to the easternmost scrap pile, even with where she had been defending before, but now to her right front. She commanded the pets forward to attack. Elf Shot did not step through the portal, but fired an explosive arrow and closed the doorway. The explosion rocked the ground and blasted the clustered pets as they ran forward. All three wolves and Bagheera died and dissolved into mist. Misty tried to drag herself back by her front paws, coughing in pain. Sheena dismissed her. Sharur had escaped significant damage from the arrow, but stopped and sniffed for another trace of the elven archer.

Sheena caught the barest glimpse of something in the air just before another arrow split into dozens and peppered the ground around her. Several arrows struck the dirt around her, deflected by the air cushion. One penetrated the shield and hit her bow arm near the elbow. Another scraped her goggles and left a nasty cut on her right cheek.

She made to heal herself as another door opened between her and the fence behind her. Gayle shouted into the radio, "Sheena! Behind you!" Sheena jumped to her left and turned to see Elf Shot pivot toward Sharur just as the black arrow she had just fired at Sheena sliced a track under her right wing and arm. Confused visions flooded her eyes as she fell to the ground. Another explosive arrow knocked her back and disoriented her further. She shook her head, but it was like seeing two blurry worlds at the same time. She knew Gayle was yelling something in her ear. It didn't make any sense.

Elf Shot fired three white arrows at Sharur as he charged. The demon wolf torched the first with his fiery breath, but the other two hit him squarely in the head. Ice engulfed him and spread down to the ground. The elven archer added another two and froze the wolf inside a solid block of ice. She sidled several meters toward Sheena, continuing to assess the condition of the wolf. Sheena struggled to her feet as Elf Shot switched to explosive arrows and shot one after another into the demon.

Sheena brought up her arm to heal herself, but the elf lunged toward her. Elf Shot kicked Sheena squarely in the chest. The air cushion absorbed most of the impact, but Sheena staggered back into her own slow field. She fell to the ground slowly in the time field. The air cushioned her scraping fall, then dissipated with a soft puff, the little aerial servant's power used up.

Sharur was trying to break free of the ice. He was aided by his internal furnace and Elf Shot's own explosives, but he was looking bad. The archer glanced over her shoulder and decided to finish the job. She turned and shot the wolf again. And again. The demon wolf went limp and dropped to the ground among the shards of ice.

The world was turning slowly around Sheena like the reflections in a mirrored ball. She clenched her eyes shut. A clear picture of Eric melting like ice on a stovetop flashed in front of her eyes. And she had frozen him. She shook her head to try and clear it and opened her eyes. The vision went away. The spinning sensation was slowing.

"Hah! That shows you how elven finesse and skill beats the clunky brute force of some ancient relic gods!" she heard as Elf Shot gloated, standing just outside of the slow field.

"What?" Sheena muttered.

The elven villain laughed and nocked another black arrow. "I win. Is that simple enough for you?"

"But… I thought you… wanted this power. Isn't that… kind of a step down… from elven finesse, then?" Sheena squeezed out the words. Her senses were almost back to normal. Eric was safely frozen, but if she died, he might stay that way forever. Sharur was dead. The animals were dead. All but one.

"When I kill you, I get both, never fear." Elf Shot drew back her bowstring. The black nightmare arrow glittered. "Goodbye, little ranger."

A feathered missile swooped down and grabbed at the elven villain's belt. The eagle flew off toward the fence with the golden eagle-hilted dagger. "I don't think so," Sheena said as Elf Shot whirled in surprise.

Sheena dropped the slow field and rolled quickly and painfully to her right. By the time she completed the roll, her bow was in her hand, a spirit arrow ready to nock. As Elf Shot squawked her surprise and trained her arrow on the bird, Sheena's own arrow was in flight. At less than five meters range and with the villain's attention distracted, the spirit arrow caught her just below the ear. The archer wobbled and shuffled, threw an accusing look at Sheena, then collapsed to the ground.

Sheena struggled to her feet. Groaning, she frowned and fired another spirit arrow at full extension into the supine villain. "Stay that way, bitch," she muttered. She took in a breath and winced as her ribs creaked. She kicked the elf's bow away and summoned Sharur.

"I am here, Mistress." At least he was as good as new.

"Guard her. Keep her helpless."

"You will not kill her, then?" The demon wolf seemed disappointed.

"No." She waved to Gayle and called to the heroes' channel. "Got her. Come and pick up the trash."

"Roger. On our way," Schauer responded. Calderón echoed that, with congratulations.

Gayle swooped down in a flash with a jubilant look on her face. "Yes! You did it!" She summoned her phantom army while Sheena searched the villain and removed weapons and armor.

Sheena took a moment to heal herself, then stretched. That felt a lot better. "I think I earned that one."

"What? Winning, you mean?" Gayle asked. She caught up the unconscious Elf Shot in a column of air to hold her.

"Yeah." She was healed of injury, but very tired. "I'd better release Eric."

"Um, you might want to wait a bit...."

Sheena blinked with confusion. Gayle explained, "Blighthawk is still unaccounted for."

A dull black bird previously unnoticed on the fence nodded its head and hopped to the ground. It quickly took on the shape of a thinly muscled man glistening in places with a tarry sheen of oil. He was neither especially tall nor well-built, but seemed very sure of himself. He settled his dirty black feathers and tucked his wings behind him. Sheena noted the buckskin loincloth, moccasins, and gloves. He cleared his throat as best he could and croaked, "Yes, I am unaccounted for. Well done, Sheena! Congratulations!"

"Blighthawk," she guessed. "Or Bryan John?"

He shook his head sadly. "It might as well stay Blighthawk."

"What now? I don't suppose you're here to surrender peacefully?"

He grinned with a cynical sniff. "I could... After all, everything is well beyond the point where you can stop it. But, no. I can still do more for the cause, and I have no trust in 'the system,' as I'm sure you can understand."

"Then what are you doing here?" Gayle asked suspiciously.

"An autograph, perhaps?" he joked. Gayle snorted and gave him a sour look. "All right, I have been watching to keep the terms of the contest. While you have deprived me of an asset, I expected this outcome, and... to be honest... she has been a hot-headed pain in the ass."

Sheena chuckled. "To you, too, huh?"

The villain smiled. "Yes. As much a problem as an assistant, really, with her obsession with the powers that seem to fit more rightly in you. No, at this point, I am here to give you an opportunity to speak with me, ask questions, and to settle your minds on the fact that you cannot stop or defeat me. I would like to just get this out of the way so that I don't need to make silly threats or waste your time or mine."

"Whoa!" Gayle said. "That's awfully damned confident! I've heard that plenty of times before, you know."

Blighthawk nodded. "I know. You have been very successful, Gayle. But I have enough... 'mojo'... to do what I have to do. In a straight contest, I may not beat you two, but I won't be beaten, either."

Sheena shook her head. "I wish we could have had you as an ally, and not an enemy. But, we can't let you kill thousands of people and sicken millions. That's what you are doing, right?"

"Yes. You could, of course, spend your energy convincing the powers-that-be to make the changes that are needed for the protection of the environment and individual rights. You could save lives more surely, that way, than by trying to... what is the term?... 'bring me to justice.'"

"Democracy works, if you give it a chance," Gayle replied.

Blighthawk shook his head. "If we had the democracy we had twenty years ago and the technology we have today, maybe. Canada and the US, both, have slid too far into the pockets of the moneyed power brokers. We don't have real choices in elections, and both the left and the right are at the service of powerful corporate interests. Corporations have too much money and power and aren't using it for the benefit of society, but for shareholders only, driven by the financial industry that cheats. And so on, and so on. No, democracy... the government and principles I originally swore to protect... has been killed by power. The only way to restore it is to shift the balance of power. That is what I am doing. The shift toward the present state has been achieved at the cost of millions of lives pressed into misery, debt, imprisonment, and death. I think a few thousand deaths of the so-called 'important people' represent a swing of the pendulum back toward justice."

Sheena snorted. "Well, at least *you're* convinced."

He nodded gravely. "If I wasn't, I couldn't and wouldn't do this."

"So, I think now is where we fight you."

"If you must." He seemed unconcerned. He made no move to either attack or defend himself. The FBSA agents and VCPD were approaching across the refinery yard. "You might want to protect yourselves. The police will be shooting at me shortly and ricochets are likely."

Gayle and Sheena backed up. Gayle applied shields.

Schauer and Calderón got out of their vehicle as the VCPD SWAT team landed and poured out of their armored flyer. Schauer drew his sidearm and pointed it at Blighthawk. "You are under arrest. Put your hands on your head and remain where you are."

"No," the toxic shaman replied calmly. "I do not recognize your authority as legitimate."

Schauer's expression remained impassive and he fired at Blighthawk. A crackling blue pulse of lightning struck the shaman and flickered over him for a second, then died out like an ember. Schauer fired twice more. Calderón took cover behind the vehicle and cast some sort of spell. The energy pulses washed over the villain again, and Blighthawk seemed unaffected by them.

Gayle looked impressed. "Sapper charges," she explained to Sheena. "One shot can almost totally drain a metahuman's power—and regular muscular impulse, too—for a good fifteen seconds or more. He's just taken three shots like nothing happened."

"Shields," Sheena replied. "They're splashing off a shield of some sort." She raised her bow and fired a spirit arrow and then a war arrow, aiming the lethal arrow for the shaman's arm, just in case it worked. The spirit arrow illuminated a spherical shell around the shaman for a fraction of a second. The war arrow flew true, but stopped and fell to the ground inches from its target.

Calderón's spell shook the ground underneath the villain violently. Blighthawk grinned in appreciation and flapped his wings to regain his balance. He flapped a bit harder and took up a hover. "Not bad, sir!" He called to Calderón. "You're on the right track, anyway! But, I'm afraid none of this will work. As long as there is corruption on and in the earth, I can ignore these attacks. This is the power that Raven has given me."

The SWAT team opened fire, as well. A volley of several different types of weapons struck Blighthawk's shield. Nothing seemed to have an effect. Gayle had her phantom army beat on him for a few seconds, and then gently push against him. Neither had any effect. A SWAT team psi-officer tried a mental blast, with no effect. Mind control simply slipped off him, too. One of the SWAT sergeants tossed a web grenade and a tear gas canister at him. Blighthawk smiled ruefully. "Those are just going to aid me and do nothing for you." He absorbed the gas and the webbing chemical, somehow.

"Please stand back from your vehicles. I am going to demonstrate a portion of my offensive capability." Blighthawk gave them a three-count to move, then thrust an arm out toward the SWAT flyer. A jet of something sprayed out from his outstretched hand and coated the vehicle. He snapped his fingers, which Sheena thought was no mean feat itself in buckskin gloves, and the stuff coating the flyer burst into flame and started dissolving the protective layer and the armored hull of the vehicle. In ten seconds, the flyer was a ruined shell of melted metal.

Blighthawk looked at the FBSA vehicle and said something in a language Sheena did not recognize. The vehicle was engulfed in a green fireball and a very large, very ominous-looking toxic spirit rose from it. It was similar to the ones she and Gayle had fought at the Park Service maintenance garage, but was easily six meters tall. A wash of strong chemical fumes blew over the area. The villain breathed in deeply and seemed refreshed, but everyone else coughed and backed up. The SWAT officers seemed concerned. They were supposed to be protected from chemical vapors by their masks and helmets, but Sheena got the impression that this had gotten through those filters. She reached out and provided healing energy to each group of law enforcement officers.

Blighthawk gestured at the nearest scrap pile. The giant toxic spirit turned and spat a gob of stuff at it. The fluid hit the metal and both melted it and set it on fire. A big puddle of poisonous, liquid metal spread over the ground as the pile disintegrated.

The villain called out, "I think you get the idea." Even Agent Schauer's forehead was creased with confusion. The corrupter turned back to Sheena. "One more thing, Sheena. On this path you have chosen, there are certain personal costs you must understand. You cannot truly protect your husband. Or anyone else known to be associated with you. This is simply a consequence of having loves, as well as enemies. I wish you better luck dealing with these choices than I have had." He bowed once and transformed himself into a raven again.

The raven croaked, "Go ahead. Shoot me. Convince yourself of my invulnerability in this form, too."

Schauer nodded to the police officers and repeated his attacks. Shrugging, so did they. Calderón merely studied his opponent closely. Sheena could tell that Blighthawk was still shielded, so she just threw a time current around the bird. As expected, it slid off the extraordinary shield.

"Good enough," Blighthawk said as the firing stopped. "Please, do read and consider the Feathers' manifesto and recommendations. That disease will be spreading, and you'll want to give yourselves the best odds. The choice is up to you. Good night." Blighthawk flew directly into the giant toxic spirit and vanished. The spirit collapsed in a shower of pollution immediately afterward.

There was an uneasy silence, and then Sheena said, "Well, get Elf Shot arrested and handled, anyway."

"Hmm… Call for backup transportation," ordered Schauer.

"Okay," Sheena said to Gayle, "*now* I can unfreeze Eric."

Chapter 30 – This Isn't Over

"Whoa, whoa!" Eric protested. "I'm sick! The virus!" He turned his head away from Sheena and held his breath as she hugged him.

She drew back in shock. "They infected you?"

He took a step back himself. He was a sorry sight, with bloodshot eyes short on sleep, a four-day growth of beard, and unbathed, wearing the same clothes he had gone to work in on Thursday, but with bloodstains over most of the material. He sniffed and wiped his nose on the sleeve of his upper arm as best he could. "Yeah, I'm almost positive they did."

Eric blinked again and looked around. "Wait… You won! Oh, Sheena! I…." He almost stepped in and hugged her, but remembered and stopped himself. He clasped his hands to his elbows instead. "Um… Congratulations?"

"Thanks," she replied with a gentle smile. "Let me see if I can fix this."

She closed her eyes and opened herself up to Shanikali's knowledge. This was a more delicate type of healing than rolling back injuries, but it was certainly possible. She nodded and opened her eyes. "Yes, I can do it."

"Ugh, go for it!" Eric encouraged her. "I think I've got a fever, increasing, and I'm all stuffed up, runny nose, sneezing… Stage 1 of that thing, still, but headed into Stage 2. I'm pretty sure I don't meet their definition of 'ecological patriot.'"

Sheena nodded and reached out. The golden motes of energy were smaller, much more like a fine mist than she had done in the past. "Breathe. In and out." He followed her instructions, breathing the mist into his lungs and exhaling again. He felt weak and wobbled on his feet. "Keep going, Eric. It's okay."

Ten more breaths in and out and he was feeling good. Not just better, but really good. Sheena released the effect. "How's that?"

"Wow! Excellent! What did you do?" He looked at his hands. He was all sparkly and tingling as the effect faded away.

She explained, "Just turning your body back to the beginning of the sickness wouldn't be a bad technique, but you would be vulnerable again. Better to push you through the sickness all the way to full recovery, supported every step of the way with extra boosting to your immune system. And cleaning up your body along the way, too."

He chuckled in amazement. "Damn! I should just hang up my shingle entirely!"

"Heh. Don't retire just yet, Doctor Gardner! I can't do this for more than one creature at a time."

Eric grinned ruefully. "Total treatment time, maybe two minutes? I think we could squeeze in a bunch more patients in an hour than we have before. But, whatever you say."

"Let's go home," she said. "I am bone-tired."

"Excellent idea." He gave her the hug he had wanted to and realized that she was in a very different outfit than he remembered. "New costume, too?"

"Yeah. The padding and armored inserts helped."

"Bah, you don't need any padding. You're perfect, as is!" She laughed at that.

They found Eric transportation back to Riverhaven with Calderón, once replacement vehicles arrived. Agent Schauer continued to coordinate the investigation and wanted to get back to the FBSA operations center to analyze the additional data they had on Blighthawk, his abilities, and what he had revealed of his plan. He scheduled time with Eric to capture everything the veterinarian had seen, heard, and experienced, as well. Sheena called Coffee at Dynatech to let her know that they had rescued Eric.

Less than an hour later, Sheena, Gayle, and Eric were back in the Riverhaven apartment. Gayle had taken off her mask, but was still in costume. She went to the kitchen and grabbed a bottle from the rack over the refrigerator. "Okay, so we know this isn't over, but you have achieved a huge victory tonight! Time for a brief celebration!"

Sheena laughed. "Oh, all right! But let's be quick. I really, really want a shower."

"Me, too," added Eric. They looked at each other and grinned.

Gayle laughed. "Okay, okay!" She got the champagne open. Her own personal breeze was blowing a faint sweet scent of champagne around the apartment, too. She took down some glasses and poured for them. After handing them out, she said, "One memory and one toast for each. Here's mine. I want to always remember the eagle grabbing that knife and the expression on Elf Shot's face as she saw victory flying away in its claws. A toast to teamwork, however it may work out in the end!"

"To teamwork!" Sheena and Eric echoed and drank with her.

Sheena nodded and thought for a moment. "All right, I've got it. I want to always remember the way Eric kept going, getting up and pushing on, despite everything she tried to do to him. A toast to determination!"

They drank to that. A thoughtful frown creased Eric's forehead and he looked down at his champagne glass. He looked up and said thoughtfully, "There's not a lot about this whole experience that I really want to remember. Maybe, how good you two are as a team... Yeah, that's something to remember." He lifted his glass and offered, "A toast to friends!"

"To friends!"

"Elf Shot is down, captured and off to prison," Sheena said, reflecting on the situation, "but the real reason I have these powers is still out there."

"Blighthawk," Gayle said.

"Right. And the corruption of Raven." Sheena looked at her champagne glass for a moment, then drained the rest of it. She put the glass aside on the counter. "It really isn't over."

"Yeah, so what will you...," Eric started to ask.

"I have to finish it." She looked up at him. "And I can't do it if I'm constantly worried about you. Gayle knows how badly this whole thing has had me frazzled. I can't make clear-headed decisions when I'm constantly torn between wanting to keep you safe and wanting to take out the villain."

Gayle tentatively offered, "Well, you weren't really that bad, most of the...."

"No, I was only alternating between crying and wanting to fly out there and just charge down into the sewers to get him back! And you know what Blighthawk said there, at the end. 'You can't protect him.' It may not be Blighthawk and the Feathers, but it will be somebody else, some other time."

"So, now what?" Eric asked. "You're a metahuman superhero. I'm just a guy. Is it time for me to go back to Wisconsin and wait this out, or what?"

Sheena shook her head quickly. "I don't know! That's what's messing me up!"

Eric looked sad and gave her a rueful half-smile. "I've had plenty of time to think things over during the past few days. I keep coming up against a couple of big ones: How much I love you and want to be with you, and at the same time how you are now so far beyond me that I can't really do anything to be what you need."

Gayle unconsciously edged back with a concerned look and said nothing. After a moment of shock, Sheena responded with a desperate, pleading expression. "But... I just need you safe!"

"And what else?" Eric frowned with a sigh. "It used to be we were partners, or at least I thought we were. But when I really looked at that, I realized I was wrong. We had a kind of partnership, but it wasn't equal. I was still the man, the head of the household, and in the lead on most of the important decisions. You went along with that. We solved problems together, but you know I always had the final say. It worked well for who we were then. But we're in another place, now. I would like to think we've grown. Maybe in different ways, but still...." He shifted restlessly and gestured as he tried to explain.

"When I was in the hospital after that stupid storm god thing, you said it isn't a competition. But that's not really true for me. It *is* a competition, but it's a team event, and we're on the same team. Us against life, Sheena. Together. Neither one of us can win it alone, and we can't win together if we're not both holding up our ends of it. I can't say what you feel, but I feel that I can't hold up my end of the relationship with the things I can give you right now. I want to give you what you need, but I have to feel good about giving it, too. Hiding out and staying safe? Maybe. So, then I'm supposed to not worry about you at the same time? No, I can't just sit by and do that. I can't be a bystander and you can't just remove me from the board."

Sheena started to say something, but thought about what she had done at the refinery site. She stopped herself and dropped her gaze.

Eric nodded. "I fully, completely acknowledge your power, skill, hero ability, whatever. You are not the game warden anymore. But, you've also taken on an extremely dangerous unpaid volunteer job. Not just dangerous to you, but dangerous to me, too. And maybe there is nothing I can do to help you with that. Okay, I think I can deal with that. But let's not pretend that it doesn't affect both of us."

Sheena looked back up and met his eyes with tears welling in hers. "I don't want anything to happen to you! I couldn't stand it!"

Eric gave her another wry half-smile. "I think you'd get over it better and faster than you would have a couple of months ago."

"What? How could you say that? I still love you!"

"I know, and I'm glad to hear it. But, you're stronger now, and more resilient. Think about this one... Do you need my approval for anything you want to do?"

"Of course I want your approval! I want to...."

"Right." He held up a hand and explained. "You *want* it. You don't *need* it. You value my opinion and want my respect. You are at least an equal, and that is really, really cool. But, you don't need me. Not like you did before."

"I... uh...," she stopped to think that through. After a moment, she nodded with a puzzled expression. It was true. She thought back to the night the source stone had given her Shanikali's powers and how she had been so concerned about how Eric would react. She wouldn't worry like that today.

Eric chuckled to himself and shook his head. "You are one fine woman, and I love you even more than I did before, if that's even possible." He sighed. "Remember our wedding vows when I promised to help you grow, and you said you'd do the same for me?"

She nodded slowly.

"Well, you have certainly helped me, even if you didn't choose this situation. And I am really sorry I didn't realize that before, and that I was such a traditional jerk so much."

"But... but what now?" she asked.

"Honestly, I don't know." He shrugged helplessly. "I don't know how this should work, when there is so much you can do, and I'm just the same, and there are such big, real-life threats like this. I just know that I don't want to lose you, but if that's what's better for you, that's what I'll do."

"I... um...." Sheena felt flustered and confused. In a small voice, she said, "Give me a minute," and hurried off to her bedroom.

Eric sighed and watched her go. Gayle looked pensive. She collected the champagne glasses and tucked them into the dishwasher. She turned to Eric with a wistful half-smile. "She needs you now more than ever, you know."

"Hmm?" Her words broke him out of his own thoughts.

The air had taken on a cinnamon flavor. "No, really. She leans on you for strength to keep her going. For confidence that she's doing the right thing. Even if you aren't a meta yourself, or even able to help with the investigation or anything, you help her."

"But, she can do all of this without me! She doesn't need me to stroke her ego or tell her she's right."

"No, that's not what I'm saying." She sighed and tried to explain. "It's the support she gets from your respect and love that lets her go forward without second-guessing herself. It gives her something to fight for, and not just to fight against."

Eric snorted as thought about that. "That's subtle."

"Sometimes that's the tiny little difference it takes," Gayle insisted. "And most people couldn't even tell you that would mean anything at all. But in those do-or-die moments in this hero business, those are the rock-solid little things that bring out that stubborn resolve to win. We're fighting for something, and that something is what we're really saving when we're out saving the world."

"I see, I think." He nodded slowly. "Uh, if you don't mind me asking... what is that for you?

Gayle nodded and smiled sadly. "For me, it's living up to my mom's legacy. I want to make her proud. I wasn't really paying attention when she was alive, and then suddenly she was gone... and I never got the chance to tell her. I want to be the person that she would be proud of, by being who I really am, and by using my gifts to help others. Even the music, if that makes sense."

"Yeah... it does. That actually makes a lot of sense." He considered that for a long while. He let out a long sigh. "What do you think we should do?"

Gayle leaned her elbows on the counter and swung her hips back and forth as she thought. Eric chuckled. Eventually, she said, "Give it a few days. Don't make any big decisions now. You're safe, and Blighthawk seems like he's above taking cheap shots at innocents, at least in his own way. If you and Sheena really have a partnership, then you can figure it out together."

Eric shook his head appreciatively. "Gayle, I don't care what they say about you. You are definitely not an airhead."

"Nope! I'm a wind controller!" She laughed.

Eric stood on the balcony, looking out at the city and the ocean. He figured he would get his chance at the shower soon enough and he could use the fresh air until then. Somehow, he thought that the city ought to look different, now that the threat that had brought them here was gone. The weather was great and the moon had risen high into the sky in the east, but Venture City looked the same. Eric didn't feel the same, but he supposed multiple near-death experiences would do that. How many times had he died, so far, theoretically speaking? When the SUV exploded, one. Pierced by Elf Shot's nightmare arrow, two. Calling lightning down on himself, three. It could have been another time when the elf grabbed him and carried him off, but they wanted him alive then, so that didn't count. Lethal arrow wounds at the refinery, at least twice more, four and five. Maybe six. He chuckled and shook his head. If he was a cat, he would have to start worrying about running out of lives.

The door to the living room slid open and then closed again. He smelled Sheena, fresh from the shower. He glanced over his shoulder as she walked up beside him. "Hey, there, beautiful."

"Hiya, stud." She leaned on the railing, too. She was wearing her short blue robe, with the modified back that buttoned at the shoulders over her wings.

"Nice moon tonight," he offered.

"Plenty of light to see by, yeah." She sighed and turned toward him. "I've been thinking."

Eric nodded apprehensively.

"Don't leave," she said. She looked at him with a serious expression. "I want you here."

"Then I'll stay." He nodded slightly in acknowledgement, but his shoulders relaxed.

"We'll figure something out."

"Together," Eric agreed.

She grabbed him and hugged him tight. He kissed her forehead and stroked her lower back. Sheena wrapped her wings around him, holding as closely as she could, and replied, "Yes, together."

Chapter 31 – Toxic Overdrive

"Reports of the illness are starting to come in from all over." Calderón looked worried as he brought up incident locators on the map. "They managed to get London, Paris, Amsterdam, and Frankfurt, as well as several major US air hubs. And those people traveled all over the world."

"We haven't issued a specific alert, but the appropriate health authorities have released warnings about a 'travelers' flu' that is spreading. The media have picked it up and are close to making it the story of the day. Conspiracy nuts are also spreading word faster than the virus, which is ironically helpful, in this case," said Schauer.

"We're only going to be able to contain information for another few days, at most. The President and other world leaders have been briefed and are taking precautions," Calderón explained. He added snidely, "Which is appropriate, because almost all of them are primary targets for the Stage 3 hemorrhagic fever."

Sheena leaned back in her chair. She was back in her fantasy ranger costume. Gayle was in her favorite green outfit, as well. "So… It's out in the wild, now. What do we do?"

Calderón pulled up a complex chemical model on the holodisplay. "According to what Eric learned while he was being held, they also created a cure. It's an anti-viral compound designed specifically for this virus."

"Your job will be to apprehend James Kadorsky and get the project and replicator files for that anti-viral drug," Schauer explained. "We have obtained the help of another metahuman who can get you into Blighthawk's hideout in the sewers. She can bypass the security, traps, and dead-end tunnels, taking you right to the source."

Sheena and Gayle exchanged impressed glances. Gayle said, "Nice! Do we get out the same way, or fight our way out, or what?"

"Your partner's name is Melanie Dawson. I believe you know her, Sheena." Sheena nodded with surprise. "She does not do official FBSA hero work, but is on loan from the US Department of Defense as a volunteer. She is not a combat specialist, so you two will need to protect her. She can get the three of you in. You occupy Blighthawk and his followers and find Kadorsky. Ms. Dawson will grab the files and then get herself and Kadorsky out."

"Through the phone or electrical lines," Sheena guessed.

"Exactly," Schauer confirmed.

"And the line we have in is…?"

"The cell phone that Blighthawk left for you."

"Ah, I see," Sheena nodded. "I call him, talk to him long enough for Melanie to find the right pathway, and then she can hop us in when we choose."

"Yes," Calderón nodded. "But, we don't know how and specifically where the line connects. That's why we need Ms. Dawson to scout the path. Otherwise you would be going in blind, and it takes a bit of time to… uh… 'materialize,' I guess you'd call it… out of the phone line."

"And Blighthawk would have several seconds to feel very betrayed and take action against us as we form up. Right. Bad thing." Sheena stood up and stretched. Her wings extended to their full length, then relaxed again. "Let's do it. And, you've been working on that analysis of Blighthawk's defenses for a day. What have you found for us?"

"It's a magic shield," Schauer said calmly. Sheena couldn't tell if he was being sarcastic. "That's almost all that we know."

"That's it?" she asked. "What about all that fancy recording and analysis equipment you guys have? Come on, where are our tax dollars at work?"

"She's got you there!" Gayle laughed. So did Calderón. Schauer remained impassive, as always. "At least give us the power ratings and stuff."

Schauer sighed and brought up the details. "Energy absorption, one hundred percent, all types. Kinetic resilience, one hundred percent, all types. Kinetic reflection, zero, all types. Psionic absorption, one hundred percent. Weakening or stress on the shield in response to attack, zero."

"Umm… zero?" Gayle looked concerned. "You're telling me that thing is a *perfect* shield? That just doesn't happen! Even the best K'rk'ti psi-shields have a bit of a power dip as they adjust to input!"

"You are correct, Gayle." Shauer enlarged the summary panel. Most of the twenty-odd indicator bars stretched all the way across the display to 100%. Three were dark, with no data available. "That does not happen in the great majority of cases. It only occurs in two scenarios we have encountered before."

"And those are?" Sheena asked nervously.

"Complete stasis and so-called 'godlike' powers."

Calderón spoke up. "Translation: Raven is directly powering Blighthawk's shield to protect him from anything that he doesn't want to be affected by. It's a super-magical cheat."

"Is it all around him? Can we attack from below, or shake him up inside the shield, or anything?"

"That's what I tried with the localized earthquake," Calderón replied. "He lost his balance for a moment, but just took off with his wings to compensate. Nothing while he was on the ground or in the air moved his center of mass the slightest bit. Even the gentle pushing by Gayle's constructs did not affect him. He moved under his own power, only. The readings show a field that wraps closely around his body and that makes a spherical shell slightly larger in diameter than his wingspan. I do not think you can get at it from an unusual angle."

"You saw the attempts to drain his power with the sapper bolts," Schauer added. "Those failed, which is very unusual. That would normally work even on a godlike creature."

"He is drawing power directly from Raven when he needs to," Calderón explained. "And I believe that Raven is poisoning the spirit world to provide that power."

Sheena's eyes widened in shock. "That's… he can't…."

"Unfortunately, he can. And, it will have lasting effects on such an eternal place." Calderón looked pained to say it.

"He's sick," Sheena said as she gathered her wits and thought through the problem. "Can we heal him?"

The shaman gave her a wry chuckle and a grin. "You mean, can *you* heal him? I don't know. I think so, but I do not know how. All we have are stories to start from."

"Okay, tell me more."

"In some traditions, the gods are killed all the time, and they always come back for the next story. In other traditions, once a god is killed or hurt, it becomes a defining event for the whole tradition forever afterward. Raven exists in a number of traditions around the world, and so he is going to be very resilient. He has died before. Raven has occasionally been sick, died of sickness, caused sickness, been cured, lost his wings, shed his skin, been female, and many other things."

Sheena listened and nodded. Calderón continued, "I think that it has to be either a very big trick, or the power of an equal—a god or goddess, like you—that turns him back to what he was. But what, specifically, that is? I do not know."

"Okay, fair enough. But let's think through this. If Raven is healed, does Blighthawk lose his powers, or does the shield drop, or do we just not know?"

Calderón shook his head. "We do not know. There are too many possibilities. It is likely, though, that Raven will want to help you repair the damage after he is healed."

"That's a positive. I'll take it." Sheena chuckled grimly.

"So, that's spirit world stuff. For this real-world mission, we just have to protect Melanie long enough for her to get the data and the guy and escape, right?" Gayle asked. "And then, we bust out and play hide and seek in the sewers?"

"Yes, that is the essence of the plan," Schauer confirmed.

"Yay, sewers!" Gayle's voice was dripping with resigned sarcasm. "If I had a song for every time…."

Sheena laughed and flopped a wing over her friend's head. "Stop complaining! All you needed was one song, and you made a hit out of it!"

"Well, yeah…!" Gayle giggled and shrugged apologetically. Her song, *From Sewer to Sky*, about going from a sewer of despair to the heights of hope was still extremely popular with a big segment of her audience six years after its release. Its message of "everyone can be a hero" resonated with many people.

"But it would be helpful to know what he's capable of throwing at us. Is there any data on his attacks or those spirits?" Sheena asked.

"Yes," Schauer responded. "Overall, the burning acid attack is strong, but not out of the ordinary for a threat level 40-50 metahuman. The combustion of fluids in the FBSA vehicle was even simpler. Summoning the toxic spirit seems to either require or benefit from a significant amount of source material. The spirit was composed, in a material sense, of the fluids extracted from the vehicle. As we know from your previous experience with them, the toxic spirits are at least mildly vulnerable to flame and spirit attacks. They are resistant to physical forces, such as blunt force, wind, and bladed weapons, such as arrows. While we have no data on lightning or electrical strikes, Calderón and I believe that they would be vulnerable to those, as well. In addition to the acid and toxic gas attacks with which you are familiar, it is possible that they also emit fumes that have a weakening effect on creatures near them."

"Bottom line," Gayle offered, "they are composed of puddles of toxic goo and are best burned away or spirit-blasted. Try not to breathe the fumes or let them touch you, and don't stand in the fire. Got it. What else do we know?"

"Blighthawk teleported himself by means of a large quantity of liquid pollutant material," Schauer said. "The spirit seemed to have nothing to do with the effect, beyond providing the 'pool' to jump through. Blighthawk just chose it for convenience and visual effect."

"Hmm. Good to know, maybe," Sheena said. "When can we get Melanie here to help with the trace?"

Schauer glanced at a corner of the display. "One PM."

"Then there's time for lunch!" Gayle exclaimed. She looked at Sheena and together they said, "Takeout!"

Melanie Dawson shook Sheena's hand. "It's good to see you under better circumstances."

Sheena smiled politely. "I'm not sure how much better these circumstances are, but it's definitely good to see you. Thank you for your help with this."

"It's in the interest of national security; of course I'll help!" She turned to Agent Schauer. "What gear do you want me to be in, when we jump to the villain?"

"A personal scout suit would be preferable. The Scott Enterprises Mk IV Special Ops version, if you're familiar with it."

Melanie nodded. "Good. I've used the Special Ops Mk III and Raider Mk IV models, so this ought to be fine. You've got my measurements already, but I'll need a little familiarization time."

"Understood." Schauer nodded.

"Uh...," Gayle said as she shot a quick glance at Sheena, "they told us that you weren't a combat specialist."

Melanie looked at the singer and replied matter-of-factly, "I'm not. I'm a tech guru. I can point and shoot, of course, and I usually duck when I'm supposed to, but my abilities really aren't oriented for fighting. I've been along on some missions as a specialist, so I know how to wear the suits."

"That's way more than I know!" Sheena offered with a grin.

Calderón winked at her. "You have other talents, Sheena, not to worry. Besides, they don't make these suits with wing holes!"

"We're talking powersuits like Jet Flash's? No thanks." Gayle made a face. "Couldn't feel the wind anywhere on my body the one time I got into one of those for a UN Vanguard mission. It's almost enough to make you claustrophobic!"

"Still, I like my skin intact, thanks," Melanie replied with an amused look. "I don't have any special resistance while I'm out of the net. I'll be happy relying on you two ladies to keep the bad guys busy while I work."

"Deal." Sheena looked at Schauer. "Let me know when we're ready for me to call him."

The FBSA agent turned to Melanie and gestured to the console. "Ms. Dawson?"

She sat down and put her fingers on the control pads. She nodded. The cell phone Blighthawk had left for Sheena started ringing. With a startled expression, Sheena answered it. "Hello?"

"Just me," Melanie's voice sounded out clearly through the phone connection. Sheena looked over at her. Her lips hadn't moved. "Don't worry, I'm doing this entirely virtually. My specialty." She turned her head toward Schauer and said aloud, "Security on this system and out to the phone and back is standard. Good response time. I'm ready to go."

He nodded to Sheena. The trial call from Melanie disconnected. Sheena hit the redial on the number Blighthawk had used to call her. After seven rings, it connected.

"Hello, Sheena," Blighthawk answered. "I presume your FBSA friends are listening in, as well. Hello, boys! And the lady of the winds, too, I expect. Good afternoon! To what do I owe the pleasure of your call?"

Sheena licked her lips nervously. She had to keep him talking. "I wanted to ask you to call off or delay spreading more of the virus. And, maybe, if you have a cure for it, to share that with us."

Blighthawk chuckled. "I see. You're after the cure. There's a problem there, you know."

"Uh, what's the problem?"

"Think, Sheena! You know who will get that cure if I give it to you... the very people who most need to be held accountable for their greed! If I give it to you, you give it to the FBSA, who give it to the government, who give it to their friends, all of whom are among the powers-that-be that have created the mess that we're all in now."

"Well, who should I give it to, then? I really don't want to see people suffer from this thing! If I understand your system, one bad decision marks a person for death!"

The corrupter snorted. "One bad decision was the trigger for Bhopal, for Agent Orange, for the Exxon Valdez, for the Deepwater Horizon, for any number of chemical and biological disasters. When one bad decision of one person compounds with the one bad decision of other people in similar roles, innocent people die. I strongly suggest that these 'leaders' learn from their collective mistakes and get into the habit of making better decisions."

"True, but does it have to be lethal?"

"Why not? When was the last time any leader of any organization faced serious consequences for destructive negligence? Have we executed any such leaders? Not that I am aware of. Imprisonment is extremely rare, and only when they have hurt other members of the power structure. We rarely even bring criminal charges, and most cases are settled short of prosecution because the perpetrators and their companies are 'too big to fail' or 'might send shocks through the financial community.' If that is supposed to be justice, it falls far, far short!"

She tried another tack. "How will you know when you are done, then? When everyone in power is dead?"

Blighthawk fell silent for a moment. He coughed and answered in a quiet rasp, "No. I wish that this would be so well publicized that people in such positions would have a change of heart. But, I don't really have any hope of that. For someone to make a mistake and own up to it… that puts them out of serious danger. The people who will die are the people who will shout to the very end that it wasn't their fault; that they were only doing what the shareholders, the government, the analysts, the constituents, wanted them to do. The people most calling for personal accountability want it for others, but seldom even try to live up to that ideal themselves. And that is why I will not share the cure with you. But please, if you find innocents who are inadvertently affected by this thing I have created, contact me. Them I would be more than willing to cure."

"I still have to bring you to justice, you know," she said sadly.

"I know, Sheena, and I respect you for what you try to do. I wish you luck in all things, except this. Be well." The call ended.

Melanie shook her head. "That is one unusual villain," she said.

"You got enough?" Sheena asked.

"Yes. That was plenty of time. Let me download and work up the details for you. I should point out that he was in a different place than the last time he called you, but still in the sewer network. And he's not in any kind of lab at all, right now. No one matching Kadorsky's description was nearby. We may have to watch until Kadorsky is in the right place to grab. Blighthawk has his computers nearby, so there is a decent chance that I can get what I need there, but no guarantee."

"Heh," Sheena had an idea. "Could you grab Blighthawk and then dump him into some kind of metahuman containment cell?"

Melanie shook her head. "Too long to materialize, too long to go into the wires with him, too long to escape after re-materializing… and so many seconds for him to kill me or escape. Nuh uh."

"Well, it was worth asking about, I guess," Sheena said. Melanie nodded apologetically.

"What will it take to monitor the area?" Schauer asked Melanie.

"There are some micro cameras nearby that they have set up, but none in the immediate vicinity, so I can't hack anything useful for you there. I'm going to have to watch it manually, myself. Now that I know where it is, I can visit any time, as long as they don't physically tear up the wiring."

Gayle made a low whistle. "Impressive!"

"Thanks. But first things first. I'll scale and render the area he's in. Give me a bit for that and we can look at next steps."

The mutant known as Rio Lobo glanced quickly around the corner of the sewer pipe. He ducked his head back and checked the microcams placed around the tunnel network with his retinal display. There were still no intruders in the area the Feathers called their own.

He continued on his rounds poking into side tunnels and nooks and crannies to make the timing of his patrol unpredictable and to make sure that nothing new had slipped in. Nothing he was likely to encounter could see him when he was on the job, and not much he expected to find could challenge him, anyway. Still, the things he was patrolling for—heroes and rival sewer denizens—made him cautious.

Lobo shook his head as he ducked around another corner and crouched, listening for anything unusual. It was a pretty poor way to make a living, but when you were hunted by people on both sides of the law, there weren't many other options. Four years as a black ops soldier for the shadow government had taken his arm, his optimism, and most of his sense of humor. Curiosity Kilz had made him an offer, got him out of the Organization, and completely cleaned the controlware out his implants. He should have stayed with them, instead of running muscle and takeout food for some crazy, oil-dripping new world order crow wizard in a sewer. The CK crew was another whole kind of crazy, but at least they understood where he was coming from and had comfortable off-duty facilities.

Not that Blighthawk was wrong. He had a certain style, too, but Lobo knew that the kind of op the shaman was running was going to fall on him, and fall hard. If you wanted to take on the powers-that-be, this supervirus deal wasn't a bad start, but there was no way he was going to hurt the people who really ran things with this scheme. The real puppet masters had instant access to healing that would wipe out that superbug with a snap of the fingers. He wondered why he was sticking around. Professional's honor, he supposed.

Lobo finished the main circuit of his patrol. There was nothing in the tunnels that shouldn't be. He wandered back toward the shaman's hall, a cavernous junction in the sewers with all the comforts of a toxic waste dump. At least it had power and connectivity. There were iron platforms suspended over the sloughs that carried muck toward the river culverts, but there was no escaping the fact that this level was a sewer. He missed the clean and comfortable Vengeful Earth lab, but Blighthawk had made sure that they cleared out before the seven day "lease" was up.

Most of the Feathers were topside and out infecting the world now. A few were out waging the information battle. That left Blighthawk, Kadorsky, Lobo, and a DIYer geek nicknamed Jimbo here at the sewer junction. Kadorsky was getting a bit stir-crazy, now that his part in the big plan was done, but he didn't wander too far. Jimbo happily kept the tech running and had his man-crush on Blighthawk continuously reinforced by the shaman's frequent spirit summoning and running philosophical commentary. Blighthawk was just finishing another summon-pack-and-shoot routine preparing one of the freaky spirits to go spread the aerosol virus in a densely-occupied public area. Lobo considered it a kinder, gentler form of terrorism.

"More infectious than an understaffed nursery school that ran out of tissues, huh, boss?" Jimbo joked as Rio Lobo ducked under the central platform and came over to them. Blighthawk was doing his summoning work in the center of the deepest part of the sewer junction. Or, more specifically, he was standing on the concrete walkway beside the pool and was summoning spirits from the toxic muck in the central pool.

"Well, Jim, that would make our work easier," Blighthawk responded absently. He fed the canister of virus mix into the muddy green spirit.

"Oh, here's another one!" the tech crowed. "I dropped by the kindergarten down the street for the annual 'running of the noses.' I couldn't stay because I didn't want to be the pick-a-dor."

Lobo stared at him. "Why is that funny?" he asked with a blank, slightly feral expression.

"Well, uh... runny noses and running of the bulls... picador picking... Never mind." Jimbo shuddered and went back to the power box to check the cables.

"Thank you," the shaman rasped quietly. "That was getting to be a bit much."

"Eh, you Canadians are too nice, sometimes." Lobo found another equipment crate and sat down with his back to the corner.

Blighthawk chuckled wistfully. "And here I just sent out the poisoned corpse of a murdered polluter to spread a lethal disease at a crowded country music performance."

"Country?" He shrugged. "So, you ain't all bad."

The corrupter chuckled and shook his head with amusement. "Nothing new in the tunnels?"

"Nope."

"Stay alert, please. I got a call from Shee'na while you were out. She is looking for the cure. I think we can expect a visit from her and Gayle Force soon."

"Yeah, but you don't have any of that here...."

"She doesn't know that, and I didn't feel it was appropriate to enlighten her." Lobo nodded.

"The virus is moving into the third stage about now in the first victims. We'll have fatalities by the end of the weekend. The media frenzy is beginning, and the 'concerned citizen and lobbyist' letters to government officials are starting to build. Panic is less than a week away."

"Mmm. You do realize that you aren't really going to hurt anyone worth hurting with this virus."

Blighthawk let out a frustrated sigh and nodded. "The real powers-that-be are too well protected. They'll be cured as soon as they get a sniffle. But the real impact of this will be on the masses across the world. This thing is in the wild now, and nothing can stop it. Ever. It will mutate and keep going. There will be a potential consequence of greed, like sexually-transmitted diseases have been a consequence of unbridled lust for millennia. Something to make enough people stop and think before acting. That will tilt the balance."

"Maybe."

"If you can get me close to this Directorate you talk about, by all means, let me know. Until then, I'll shake the game-board and weaken their power base. Besides, Raven is impatient for his corpses."

Lobo shook his head. "Sorry, boss. I could find some operational bases, maybe, if they haven't moved them already. I never had access for the heavy data. The times I saw the Directors, they came to us and sent us out to pull the strings."

Blighthawk grunted. "Well, we're going to be out of the virus matrix soon, anyway. Stay on your toes. We'll be getting out of here before long. Time to burn some bridges."

"Excellent. The longer we stay, the easier it is for unfriendlies to find us."

"Right. And Lobo?"

"Yeah?"

"Could you please bring back a few buckets of spicy extra-crispy on your next run topside? I'm starving again."

Chapter 32 – Overwhelmed!

"Ugh, this is taking forever," Gayle complained softly.

"We do what we have to do," Sheena responded. "Mel will tell us when everything is in place for a jump."

Gayle glanced over at the tech guru sitting at the console, relaxed but still attentive after a good six hours of watching. Melanie Dawson was wearing a stealth model of an armored powersuit, matte finished and so deep a red that it was almost black. The helmet was retracted, but otherwise she was ready to turn on the stealth circuits and go in an instant. Her shoulder-length brown hair was braided and pinned up in a crisp, almost military, style. While Gayle admired her discipline, to the carefree singer it seemed a little excessive.

Sheena checked the clock: 11:46 PM. She shrugged. It had taken some time to get Melanie properly outfitted and used to the suit, and since then she had been watching for the combination of things they needed to start the raid to come together. This was just another stakeout, and she was used to those. The virus technologist, James Kadorsky, hadn't even showed up until after 9 PM. Blighthawk's power and computer tech was present almost constantly, as was the toxic shaman himself. There was another person who appeared at irregular intervals that seemed to fascinate Melanie, apparently a metahuman mercenary working for Blighthawk.

The holodisplay lit up with a green light. Sheena and Gayle sat up sharply and looked over at the board. Melanie had set the system to show a green status when conditions were right. The mercenary had left a couple of minutes ago on a patrol, Blighthawk and the tech were in a distant part of the sewer junction, and Kadorsky was at a computer workstation that was obscured from the view of the others. "This is good," Melanie said. "Let's go."

The heroines jumped up and joined her at her console. "Pardon me," the tech guru said, and then turned Gayle and Sheena slightly so they were oriented at angles from each other. She took her own position next to them, crouched down, and activated the helmet of her suit. It quickly slid into place, the armored plates connecting and sealing around her. The stealth circuits activated and she practically disappeared. "Here we go."

The FBSA operations center faded out of view, and the sewer junction faded in simultaneously. Like the transition Sheena had seen Melanie make before to the hospital, it was a gradual process. Unlike that time, it took much longer. Instead of a three second transition, Sheena was able to count to ten before everything seemed solid and she could move. She was standing on an iron grate and facing down one of the sewer tunnels that exited from the junction. The sounds of dripping and slowly moving liquids came to her ears, along with the clicking of a keyboard nearby. Gayle was facing Kadorsky and made a swooping gesture with her arms, lifting and holding the technologist, and incidentally silencing any sounds he might make. She nodded to Melanie, who just reached over to the mouse and started whatever special work she needed to do to find the Feathers' files on the virus and its cure.

Sheena stalked forward and down to the concrete walkway around the sewer basin, as quiet and invisible as a cat in the night. She listened for the mercenary, but didn't hear anything. It should be anywhere from six to twenty minutes before he returned, unless Blighthawk or the tech could get an alarm to him. Melanie had already spoofed the microcams and security devices that the Feathers had put up in the area.

Blighthawk was resting on an old iron bedframe with an oil-soaked mattress thrown onto the springs. The technician was sitting on a different bed in the same alcove watching something on his tablet with his earbuds in. So far, so good.

A ghastly, transparent form rose from the sewer water in front of Sheena; a toxic spirit on guard. With wide eyes, she quickly raised her bow and fired two spirit arrows into the thing. It popped almost like a giant gas-filled bubble of slime. She looked around carefully and summoned Sharur. It didn't seem like Blighthawk had noticed the dispatch of one of his guards.

Gayle floated into the air and surrounded her part of the cavernous junction with a concealing mist. Melanie seemed to still be working at the computer, though Sheena could not see her clearly. The shaman stirred on his bed, frowning and mumbling something incoherent. Sharur and Sheena had both faded from view and began working their way forward to a place that would keep eyes away from Kadorsky and Melanie.

Two more spirits rose from the muck. One was barely more than arm's reach and the other was near the big alcove where Blighthawk and the tech were resting atop the beds on the suspended iron grates. Sheena realized that each spirit she had seen, including these two, was slightly different, as if they were caricatures of individual people. That was disturbing in its own way. She raised her bow again and fired. As before, two arrows were enough to disrupt the thing. She quickly switched her aim to the more distant spirit.

The shaman was stirring, though, and sat up, sniffing the fetid air. "What?" He blinked and jumped to his feet. "Shee'na! What do… never mind." His gloves and moccasins were by the bedframe, but he was already making casting gestures with goo-covered fingers. By the time he had risen, Sheena had shot and disrupted the second toxic spirit. She felt the now-comforting pressure of Gayle's air cushion shield around her.

"Evening, Blighthawk!" Sheena called out. "If you don't mind, I would like the cure, please. And I'm not particularly happy with you for infecting Eric while he was with you."

A jet of flaming fuel lanced out toward her from the shaman's outstretched hand. She jumped forward and dodged it. The burning gel splashed heavily on the concrete behind her. Sharur became visible and interposed himself between Sheena and the villain. The tech behind Blighthawk in the resting area quickly tucked his tablet and personal items into a sturdy, fireproof box, and then pressed himself back into the corner, making himself as small as he could.

"Everyone can be a carrier. All the better to 'spread the word,'" the corrupter replied. "Where is... ah, that's what I was smelling."

"Hey!" Gayle called out. "I smell good! Way better than this place!"

"Of course! Delightful, even! That's why you are so easy to detect!" He threw a jet of burning gel at the singer. Sheena reached out and slowed it to a crawl. Gayle easily bobbed out of spatter range. The corrupter said, "I don't have the cure here. It's safe. Somewhere else."

"Would you be willing to part with some, now?" Sheena asked.

"Just on principle? No." He held himself ready trying to watch both of the heroines. They had placed themselves at angles that made this difficult. Blighthawk was wary, but did not seem worried at this intrusion.

Gayle tried to scoop up the villain with the air around him, like she had done with Ravenger. It didn't work. The air simply slipped around him without even causing him a quiver of movement. Gayle commented, "Well, your shield is still working, I guess."

"Yes. As I said before, you can't defeat me. Although I'm sure you won't take this offer, if you leave now, I won't attack you further."

Melanie's voice whispered through the communication channel, "I'm done and taking Kadorsky. Keep his attention for another ten seconds."

Sheena responded to Blighthawk's offer. "I really wish I could, but my priority is to save lives from the virus. I can't leave until I get what I came for. And... if you surrendered, that would be a huge bonus, you know. What do you say? We call this whole thing off and go out for a beer or something?"

Blighthawk laughed. "Tempting! You have no idea how tempting that is! But, I'm afraid I can't really rest until people like James' family and mine are avenged. What do you say, James?"

Kadorsky was gone with Melanie. The corrupter scowled and looked around, and over at the computer center to the left of where Gayle was hovering. Gayle said, "James... Kadorsky? The former CDC virus researcher?"

"Yes. He was here not long ago. He is another whose family has been betrayed by the greedy corporations and lawyers, and the government protected the killers, and not the victims or their families."

"Kadorsky was the one who led the work on the virus, wasn't he?" Sheena asked. She tried to play up her mock surprise. "Geez! I thought there was something odd about him being with the Feathers!"

"Don't blame him. The idea was mine. He just implemented it. And came up with the cure." His eyes narrowed suspiciously. "Something's wrong... Enough! Out, now!" With grand sweeping gestures, Blighthawk conjured up a swarm of toxic spirits from the sewer pools.

The spirits surged forward to attack.

Gayle created a miniature cyclone to block the spirits while Sheena fell back to the wall and stretched a slow field in front of her. Sharur breathed a long cone of fire over the spirits and swept it back and forth to ignite and destroy them. Sheena turned her arrows on the spirits pressed by the cyclone. Blighthawk conjured a wall of burning goo out of the sewer like a tidal wave. It started crashing toward them.

"Mistress, we should move," Sharur growled urgently.

"Understood." Sheena put a speed boost on them both and they ran before the toxic tidal wave. She reached out and boosted Gayle as they came up to her. She shouted, "Left!" and ducked down the leftmost tunnel.

Gayle followed, pausing just to throw up her own wall of wind to resist the advance of the wave. The toxic wave lost most of its speed and height crashing through the wind wall. "Hah!" Gayle shouted. The irritated villain threw more burning acid bolts at her. The air cushion deflected the first, mostly splashed the second off of her, but was worn away for the third. "Ahhh!" she yelled, feeling the burning as it sloshed hot acid all over her left shoulder and upper arm. The singer reflexively swooped to the right and flicked at the acid with a gust of air, getting it off quickly, but not quickly enough to escape deep burns. Gritting her teeth, she fled the sewer junction.

Sheena had heard Gayle's cry of pain and stopped running. When her friend came into sight, she immediately bathed her with healing motes. Gayle said, "Thanks. That hurts. A lot."

"Try not to get blasted again, I guess."

"Yeah. Silly me." She looked down the tunnel. "Is he following us?"

Sheena listened. "No, but I don't know where that other mercenary guy is."

"Let's get out of here, then. We still can't beat that shield of his."

"All right, but there's got to be something."

"Pssht! There is! But I have no idea how to do it. That's going to be up to you."

"Later, then." Sheena looked around and chose a direction. One of the passages sloped upward. "Up?"

"Yeah, from here up is good. Look for blue edged doors. That will get us into the mapped section of the city steam tunnels."

Sheena nodded and led the way.

They emerged more than an hour later through a locked access stairway to an alley somewhere in the North Bank. The heroines were glad to be above ground. Sheena called the FBSA agents while Gayle figured out where they were. "I swear that place changes every time I go down into it. It's like magic, or something."

"Maybe it is," Sheena replied. Gayle shrugged. The call connected.

"Hello, Shee'na. This is Agent Schauer. Ms. Dawson was successful. We are now taking further steps to determine what we have. Ms. Dawson herself has departed, leaving kind words for you two."

"That's nice. She seemed very... professional."

"Indeed. It has been a pleasure to work with someone like her. Mister Kadorsky is very agitated, but has not provided a great deal of information, yet. There is something he is not telling us."

Sheena snorted. "I'm not surprised. Any major clues to stopping this thing, yet?"

"Possibly. The files, samples, and Mister Kadorsky's rather limited testimony have verified that the second stage virus is based very closely on the strain for which Dynatech has already developed a vaccine and anti-viral drug. The challenge will be to produce and distribute enough to be useful in this situation."

"Is there anything we should do to help now?"

"You may join us, if you wish, but a complete debriefing will take some time. Rest may be a better choice, at this point."

"And a shower may be the best choice, followed by sleep," Sheena replied. "There's nothing urgent, then?"

"Nothing that won't wait for the morning, no."

"Okay, we'll rejoin you in the morning." She filled in Gayle on her conversation and they headed back through the night sky to Riverhaven.

Sheena looked at the clock on the bedside table. *Only fifteen more minutes until my alarm goes off. It figures.* To the knocking at the door, she called, "What?"

"Need your help!" Gayle called through the door. "Someone is way sick, and I think this is important."

"Ugh, fine." Sheena swung her legs out of bed and stood up, extending her wings for balance. "Come on in."

Gayle opened the door. She had a worried expression. "It's a call for help from Johnny, that homeless guy we helped out a few weeks ago. He's got the flu bad, and from all the stories in the news, he's pretty worried. And, he thinks it might have something to do with Elf Shot's boss."

"You think?" She pulled on her skirt and paused. "Wait… how would he know that?"

"Yeah, that's what I was thinking, but it's not even Blighthawk. He was talking about another boss she was taking money from."

"Huh?" That sounded strange.

"Yeah. But anyway, he's really sick. Can we go there and have you heal him, and see what he knows?"

Sheena slid her arms into her tunic and began adjusting it. "Yeah, sure. I just hope there aren't a horde of people to cure. I don't know how I'm supposed to handle that sort of thing."

"Great. Thanks, Sheena." Gayle tilted her head and asked hesitantly, "Isn't that left shoulder piece supposed to be attached to the other strap?"

Sheena stopped and felt the straps. She groaned. "Yeah. That's what I get for trying to get into my costume before coffee and a splash in the face to wake up." She unbuckled the errant piece and re-adjusted.

Thirty minutes later, they were at the Beachwood Circle Apartments in Fall River on the west side of the metroplex. Johnny Miles had cleaned up well after getting help from the rehabilitation agency, but the flu had really laid him out. He could barely answer the door. After Sheena worked her healing magic on him, he looked and felt much better. Fortunately, he had not been in close contact with many other people before coming down with the flu. Sheena decided not to try to track them down, and crossed her fingers that they would be mild cases, at worst. She had carefully bagged a few specimens of Johnny's used tissues and saliva for the lab before she cured him.

"You said you thought that Elf Shot had something to do with you getting sick?" Gayle asked him.

"Yeah. The elf lady got a big payment to rat out the boss she was working for from some other guy. I'm pretty sure she didn't know I was there, but I was up on that ceiling part in the warehouse, resting. That's when I heard her."

"What did she say?"

"She told the guy on the phone that she had a bunch'a test subjects for the bug that the oilbird was working on, but they didn't know they was test subjects. And she said it was some kinda virus. And later, I was already feeling sick when the stories on the news about this flu epidemic started up, and I thought back to what she said. Gettin' the flu in the summer's pretty unusual. I figured maybe she got me infected as one'a those test subjects."

"Who was she talking to?"

"Sounded kinda like a motorcycle gang leader, maybe. Named Ravage, or something?"

Gayle hesitated and frowned. "Uh… Ravenger, maybe?"

"Yeah, that sounds right. She told that Ravenger guy what the oilbird was working on."

"Have you ever seen the oilbird yourself?" Sheena asked him.

He shook his head. "Nope. But, I didn't want to see anything she didn't want me to see. She paid me to keep watch on who came into the warehouse, that's all."

"Well, I'm glad you got cleaned up. And I'm glad you called," Gayle said. "This is something we need to know, and it might help thousands of people. Thanks, Johnny."

"Whoa! No problem! And thanks for fixing me up. Really, really thanks! I've had it for days, and that stuff sucks, whatever it was."

"You're welcome," Sheena replied. To Gayle she said, "Time to make a call."

The singer nodded. Leaving the apartment building, they started flying back to the city center. Sheena called Agent Schauer to pass on what they had learned. She recommended that he ask Kadorsky what Ravenger had to do with this whole scheme.

Several minutes later, Schauer called her back. "Mister Kadorsky has become very helpful. It appears that he is quite remorseful at the part he has played in this, despite his very intense and simultaneous desire for revenge." The agent paused. "I suspect that he will require quite a bit of therapy."

Sheena snorted and agreed.

Schauer continued. "He said that the virus that the Feathers of the Raven have been spreading was grown in a lab provided by the Vengeful Earth. Mister Kadorsky is almost terrified that the virus the Feathers are spreading will play into Ravenger's plans, instead of their own. He is literally worried sick. Curious."

Sheena thought about the implications of that for a long few seconds. "And what did we learn about stopping it?"

"He said we should make the cure as fast as possible, just in case."

"All right. I have samples of the phlegm that Johhny was coughing up. Should I bring them in to the lab?"

"Yes, please. If this is the same virus, it will be important to compare it to the version that Blighthawk engineered."

"And if Ravenger really did get to it before they started spreading it?"

"Even more reason to check a sample. We need to know what this virus can do."

"All right, we're on our way." She flapped faster toward the FBSA headquarters.

"Finally!" Gayle exclaimed as the videoconference display flickered to life. "What's the diagnosis?"

Sheena had passed the samples on to the lab, and from there it was a matter of waiting. Not much more had come from debriefing Kadorsky. A day later, Friday afternoon, they were back in the FBSA operations center waiting for word from the virus experts.

The crisis management team at Dynatech had been activated the day after Eric put in the warning. That was almost a week ago. Because the Dynatech team had done so much previous work on this, they had quickly become the center of the outbreak response effort. On Wednesday they had finally received live samples of the virus that was affecting people throughout the world. They had finished the verification of results this morning. The specimens that Sheena provided matched those of the virus that Blighthawk and Kadorsky had engineered, lending more weight to Johnny's suspicion that he had been a test subject. More importantly, it did not match the outbreak virus that was spreading so quickly.

"It is not the same virus as the one the Feathers of Raven created," Greg Dawson reported. "It's very similar. It has been artificially mutated, based on the avian H3 variant Eric flagged. There is some good news in this. The hemorrhagic fever component—the Stage 3 effect that Blighthawk designed—is missing entirely. It was removed from the virus. Also, the virus is similar enough to the original that both the Kadorsky cure and the Dynatech formulas will have significant therapeutic effect; the antigen remains effective. The bad news is that the influenza strain involved has been mutated and it will affect anyone affected by Stage 2 with an approximately forty to fifty percent projected mortality rate."

"Forty to fifty percent?" Sheena gasped. "For *anyone* affected by Stage 2?"

"Yes, that is the projection."

"So, this is not limited to the 'greedy' targets that Blighthawk and the Feathers intended?"

"No. There is still a Stage 1 gate, with a custom-designed rhinovirus that enhances the communicability of the overall supervirus. That's why it's spreading so quickly. But the mutated influenza strain will attack anyone 'qualified' for Stage 2. And there is no Stage 3."

"How fast does the disease progress?" she asked nervously.

"Hospitals are already being overwhelmed with patient inflow. Even with treatment, we are expecting fatalities to start mounting by tomorrow. As usual with influenza, it will hit children, elderly, and individuals with weakened immune systems the hardest."

Gayle asked, "So what can we do?"

Greg sighed and rubbed his neck. "Get the anti-viral drugs out as fast as possible and pray."

Chapter 33 – That's Why I Have This Power

Sheena sighed and looked over at Gayle. "You know, I've never been one to leave things solely up to prayer."

"Me, neither. The medical stuff is out of our hands, but the villains are still out there. Any ideas?"

"Time to call Blighthawk again." She waved the agents over.

"Okay, but why?" Gayle asked. "He's been played and this is all out of his hands, now."

"He needs to know what he's caused," Sheena answered with a determined tone. "And maybe he can do something we don't know about."

Schauer nodded. "It's worth an attempt. The line to Blighthawk is still set to monitor and record. Call him whenever you are ready."

She took a deep breath and let it out slowly, then settled her feathers down. She took out the phone and pressed redial. It connected after two rings.

"Good afternoon, Sheena. I'm surprised you are calling. You already have what you wanted." The corrupter's raspy voice seemed to hold a bitter tone.

"Not really."

"You got the files for the cure, and took James."

"And we just learned that his worst fears have been realized."

"Don't toy with me. It doesn't become you."

"The virus is going to kill forty to fifty percent of the people it infects. And, it no longer has a third stage, so it's pretty much a big unguided weapon of mass destruction, now. Ravenger got to it before you released it."

There was silence on the other end of the line.

"Hey, Bryan? Are you there?" she asked.

He started coughing. It was a hard, dry hacking. She waited for him. Eventually he gasped, "Yes, I'm still here."

"Well?" she asked when he didn't say anything else.

"You're sure?"

"Yes. At least, we're sure that the virus in the wild has been artificially mutated from the one you built. Kadorsky insists it must have been Ravenger. And I've got another victim who said he heard Elf Shot explaining your plan to Ravenger, earlier."

She heard a long sigh on the other end of the line that turned into another coughing fit. He recovered more quickly, this time. He really did sound bitter, now. "There's no reason for you to lie, and you have nothing more to gain… so, what do you want from me?"

"Oh, I don't know… help, maybe?!?" she snarled at him. "Saving the millions of people who you insisted weren't supposed to be seriously hurt by this thing? You knew that the virus would mutate over time. And you used one of Ravenger's labs! He is a master of mutation and diabolical strategy, and he wants to destroy human life altogether! Ravenger has already mutated it on purpose! It is killing people, and not just the greedy! How could you take that chance?"

Pain sounded in the shaman's voice. "I had to. There was too much at stake not to take the risk. If...," he sighed. "If I could undo what I have done, believe me, I would. Here... I'm sending you the location of the antiviral drug supply we were able to make before we had to leave Ravenger's lab. You'd better use that cure. Widely. Quickly. I'll publish the antiviral formula online, as well."

"And then what?"

"And then I will go kill the greedy myself. I still have a few canisters of the original virus matrix, and there is a meeting of oil industry finance execs in town that I can visit. After all, Raven still must have his carrion. I'm afraid that will include me, too, in the end, but it is a reasonable price to pay for my mistake. Farewell, Sheena. We may not meet again in this lifetime." He cut the call.

Sheena exclaimed with a frustrated snort, "Geez, what a drama queen! You guys got that?" Gayle and the FBSA agents nodded. She controlled her anger and put the phone down carefully on the table. "Schauer, find that meeting he was talking about. We have to stop him. Or, specifically, Gayle, you have to stop him."

"Huh? Where are you going?" Gayle blinked in surprise.

"I am going to undo what he did. Back to change the time stream. That's why I have this power, and this is the time to use it."

Gayle pumped her fist with enthusiasm. "Yes! You go, Sheena! I'll rescue the mucky-mucks and hold off Blighthawk until you get there! Or... um... or until it's not needed?" She paused and gave Sheena a curious look. "What are you actually going to do?"

Sheena shook her head. "I have no idea. Whatever it takes. But first, I have to visit Eric."

The singer looked puzzled. "Eric?"

"Shanikali said that she has only had about a fifty percent success rate on this sort of thing. Anything I change will create ripples in the time stream. What if I mess it up? I don't want to leave any unfinished business, in case I make mistakes, or if I have to change this reality so much that things are... different... when I get back."

Gayle caught the implications immediately. "Whoa... That's heavy!"

"Right. But, I'm a goddess, right? I'll figure it out." She hoped she sounded more confident than she felt.

Gayle swallowed nervously. "Good luck, Sheena."

"Thanks. And with that luck, I'll be right where you need me, when you need me." She hugged her friend, then turned to the FBSA agents. "Guys, any advice?"

Schauer thought for a moment. "Since you will be out of our time stream while you do this, there's no need to be hasty. Take all the time you need to consider the options. In any event, it has been a pleasure working with you, and you have my full confidence, Shee'na."

Calderón came over and gave her a hug. "Raven is the key to this. Somehow, I think you will find a way to heal his sickness. This is your path, goddess. Travel in beauty!"

Sheena smiled. "You, too, you crazy shaman! Keep the spirits happy with us. I'll need all the aid I can get."

She quickly turned and hurried out, very aware of their eyes on her as she left the operations center.

Sheena climbed the stairs to the roof and turned south, toward Dynatech. The city moved beneath her in its customary patterns as she flew; just another summer day in Venture City. She soared higher. There was a light haze to the sky and a few scattered clouds. The sea beyond the coast to the south was calm. She hoped it would all be the same when she returned.

Flying seemed so natural to her now. Sheena marveled that it was only a few short weeks ago that she had made her first struggling flights along the beach. A lot had changed in that time. Could she go back to her life as a conservation warden in the north woods, now? She shook her head. No, she had changed. She could do that job and enjoy it, if that seemed the best path, but it wouldn't be the same. She wasn't who she used to be. Neither was Eric. This had been a frustrating, humbling and terrifying experience for him. She almost felt sorry for him, but that was the wrong emotion; it wasn't really any kind of pity she was feeling. It was more... sorry that he had to go through what he did, surely, but confident that he was going to be better for it in the end.

She called him to let him know she was coming. Eric met her at the employee break area near the front entrance to the building, by a picnic table under the shade of the trees. He waved as she approached. Sheena backwinged to a stop and gently touched her feet to the ground in front of him.

"Perfect landing, as always!" Eric said with a grin. He gave her a quick hug, but Sheena didn't let go when he did. He put his arms back around her with a bit of confusion and asked, "What's up?"

"I'm going to change the time stream."

Eric's eyebrows shot up and his expression turned to concern, "Oh! It's that serious, then?"

"Yes. Greg didn't tell you?"

"Well, I know about the virus mutation, of course, but I was still thinking that there might be something you two were going to do to stop it."

"There is, if I go back and change the past, but we're out of other options. Elf Shot seems to have betrayed Blighthawk to Ravenger, and now it's snowballed way beyond what he intended. Blighthawk doesn't have any more tricks up his sleeve, so it's up to us to stop this before it kills millions."

"Up to you, you mean." He tilted her chin up and kissed her nose. "This is dangerous, isn't it?"

She nodded solemnly. "Shanikali was very serious about the dangers. She made mistakes she could not correct doing this."

"So, what do you need to do?"

"First, I have to go into the spirit world—to the Cedar Forest and the River of Time—physically; not just a spirit journey."

"Okay, you know how to do that, right?"

"Yes, but going there physically draws the demon guardians of the place. I will probably have to fight them before I can even do anything to the time stream." Eric nodded that he was following. "Then, I have to find exactly the right places to make the smallest possible change or changes that will produce the outcomes I want, and without introducing too many unintended consequences."

He nodded slowly, considering the difficulty of that task. "Okay... you know what you want to change, right?"

"Mostly. I need to do something that will make the virus as harmless as possible or mitigate its effects."

"You can't just turn the whole thing aside as if it never happened?"

She shook her head. "I'll look, but there is already so much power and momentum behind this plot and the outbreak and everything, I doubt I will be able to do that. Shanikali was very specific that I should do no more than absolutely necessary to the time stream. I think I'm going to have to be satisfied with a smaller tweak than that would take."

"Would you like some ideas, then?" he offered tentatively.

"Yes, please! A lot of the virus stuff is so technical that I'm almost afraid to mess with it."

"Well, people have been saying, 'If only we had the drug produced and ready to use!' You know how I noticed the bioterrorism risk from this avian flu strain last year? I was thinking that I should report it then, but I didn't. What would have happened if I did? Could we have vaccinated people against it with last year's flu vaccine? Would we have the anti-viral drug distributed and ready to use now?"

Sheena thought about that.

"The other thing I was thinking is that even an evil genius like Ravenger must make mistakes, now and then. What if his mutation starts off strong, but just fizzles out after a couple of days of symptoms?"

"Can that happen?"

"Yes, especially if you just have one shot at modification. Starts out strong, but has an overly repetitive protein pattern or something that makes it easy for the immune system to adapt and counterattack. And if you need to 'check your work,' so to speak, you can always look at the stats on the whiteboard in our crisis management room. Greg keeps those up to date hourly as more information comes in. Pick a time, slide forward or back in that stream, and see what the data is showing." He frowned as he tried to think through the suggestion. "At least, if that's the way it could work."

"It could, yes. That's very helpful."

"I don't suppose you could go back and stop Blighthawk from corrupting Raven, or whatever happened with that?"

"I don't think so. So much has happened since then that depends on that decision. Even my having the power to make the change. That would probably end up in a paradox, which would be blocked in some way I'm unlikely to see before it happens."

He put his arms around her and held her tightly. "Well, whatever you do, I believe in you. If there is anyone who can do this, it's you."

Sheena responded to his hug by squeezing him tight. "I love you, Eric. I want to do this and fix things and come back to you safely."

"Me, too." He hastily added, "I mean, I love you and want you to come back safe." He grinned shyly. "You're my superhero, you know."

She laughed. "I'll find a way, then!" They kissed for a long time.

Reluctantly, she let him go. "All right, here goes." She closed her eyes and took a few deep breaths. Then, like she was diving off a high riverbank, she launched herself into the air and right out of the real world with a wink of golden light.

Eric blinked in surprise. He stared at the place where she had disappeared for a long moment. Then, he whispered, "Good luck, my beautiful goddess!"

Chapter 34 – A Strong, Strong Wind

"Okay, so I can't defeat him with the shield still up, fine. But I can get those finance people away from him and I can keep him busy until Sheena shows up. Where is the conference?" Gayle asked the agents.

"Sky Plaza, City Center," Calderón replied, looking at the information he was pulling up on the operations center display. "The conference itself is the main event for the Plaza through the weekend. Registration started this morning and most of the execs should be there for the 4 PM opening address. Cocktails follow."

"Great. It's almost 3 PM now. Maybe I can get there before Blighthawk does, and before it really becomes a 'target-rich environment.' The Sky Plaza has metahuman threat plans, if I remember the place correctly. I know the security chief, but what do we need to do to get the management to activate the emergency plans and keep the guests from making targets of themselves?"

Schauer picked up a phone. "A simple set of calls. Maybe ten minutes."

"Awesome! Let's do it!" She grinned cheerfully. "Any advice for me before I head out?"

"We'll send a healer, if we can get one, but most of the metahuman healers are already busy working on the 'flu' outbreak," Calderón explained. "Try not to get hurt."

"Yeah, I'll be careful. One dose of that acid spray was enough to remind me that I'm only human!"

Calderón chuckled. "Hardly! But, I get the point. Good luck, Gayle!"

"Cheerio, guys!" The green-clad heroine followed the path that Sheena had taken shortly before, but headed in the opposite direction once she reached the roof.

The Sky Plaza hotel and conference center was one of the most luxurious and secure buildings in downtown Venture City. It was a soaring structure of white and silver macroplast, reinforced with the best technology that the hotel management corporation could fit into its budget. Because it was such a high-profile venue, it was subject to supervillain attacks every other month or so. The Plaza even had a dedicated metahuman security team on staff. Gayle had worked with them before. They were good, but no match for Blighthawk. She contacted the team leader, a reformed cyber-enhanced bruiser by the name of Scrimmage, as she was flying in and warned him about what was likely to happen. He happily accepted her assistance and told her that he would get the emergency response in motion.

One of the signature features of the Sky Plaza was its expansive conference center at the top of the building. The conference levels spread much wider than the main tower itself, making the hotel look like a giant white and silver flower on the Venture City skyline. She asked herself, *If I was Blighthawk with a load of extra virus to spread, where would I start? The ventilation system!*

Gayle was familiar with ventilation. She liked to freshen the air at places she visited and on airplanes when she traveled long distances, adjusting humidity and clearing away impurities, like airborne viruses and bacteria. She always liked to leave the air in enclosed spaces healthier than she found it. While the Plaza's systems were well-protected from many threats, Gayle was sure that Blighthawk could just burn his way through to gain access. Then, he would try to use the system to spread his virus throughout the hotel. To counter this, she sent a specially-formed aerial servant into the vents and gave it the task of purifying the air from a strategic point within the ductwork. In a modern building like the Sky Plaza, heating, ventilation, and air conditioning was all zoned and controlled by advanced sensors and computer software. She could handle that, but she doubted Blighthawk's attack would be that sophisticated. She figured that while Blighthawk would probably destroy the normal filters, he wouldn't be enough of an HVAC expert to detect her servant's interference. The servant could last for a couple of hours at normal load, or about an hour purifying noxious chemicals. It wasn't perfect, but Gayle was satisfied that it was darned close.

Having finished the defense of the ventilation system, she flew up to the conference center landing deck. She bobbed above the railing and set herself down on the all-weather deck surface, drawing stares and smiles from the guests and staff. She waved pleasantly and strolled around the exterior to refresh her memory of the layout. A young executive tapped her arm as she was doing this. She turned to him.

"Gayle Force?" he asked. "I am a *huge* fan! Are you on some sort of hero business? Is there a problem?" His eyes brightened. "You're not a guest speaker, are you?"

Gayle laughed lightly. "Oh, no, nothing like that! Sorry… um…." She looked at his name tag. "Garry, but I am expecting a very nasty villain to show up any time. He wants to kill all of the people who have made decisions favoring corporate interests over people or the environment. Go figure."

The man blanched. "Oh."

"He probably has a pretty liberal view of what that means, too. It would be a good idea to shelter in your room until this blows over."

"Uh, yeah, right away! Thanks, Gayle!" He stuck his hand out, shaking just a bit with adrenalin beginning to pump. She smiled and shook it, and then he hurried off inside to the elevator.

She switched to a communication channel for the hotel security that Scrimmage had provided. "Hi, guys, Gayle Force here. Any hint of Blighthawk, yet?"

"Hoi, Gayle. This is Scrimmage. Nothing, yet. We're starting to move the guests."

She could see hotel security officers in dark blue suits quietly talking to small groups of guests. The guests appeared alarmed and began moving indoors. "Stairwells clear?" she asked.

"Yeah. We're guarding those to let people get back to their rooms. This guy's not going to try to blow the building, is he?"

"No, he's honorable about innocent casualties, as far as we can tell. But keep an eye on the HVAC system. He uses spirits that are poisonous and has nasty combustible acid powers, too. I have the ventilation system protected, but he may show up there, first. Let me know if you see anything."

"Will do. Thanks."

Gayle went into the big conference hall. The hall itself was mostly a giant half circle, like an amphitheater. The exterior walls were made of clear macroplast that served as extremely tough and resistant windows. The interior walls were made of more normal material, but still constructed with quality. The main structural parts of the building were not going to be easily damaged by Blighthawk's attacks. The hall was filled with round tables covered with black linen tablecloths. Each table had a tasteful but expensive centerpiece. The chairs were padded and more comfortable than a typical hotel's seating. The hall was decorated for the event with banners, hanging images, and holoposters of oil exploration, drilling, and production scenes. Gayle chuckled to herself, "Yeah, that will make him happy... not!"

A tall, very earnest-looking man with carefully windblown hair in a tailored suit of the latest fashion spotted her and gestured her over as if he owned the place. She grinned. Her personal breeze picked up strength and smelled of spicy red peppers. She sauntered toward the fellow and the small knot of other senior executives he had clustered around him. "Afternoon, gents! How can I help you?"

"Good afternoon, miss. You are here about this eco-terrorist threat?" His voice carried an assumption of command.

"Why, yes, I am!" she replied sweetly.

"How long do you think this will take to resolve?"

"That depends. Are you going to comply with the Plaza security instructions?"

"Once we're certain that the threat is serious, we'll move." Not all of the little group seemed quite as blasé about the situation as he did. "Who is this terrorist, and what does he want?"

"He is called Blighthawk, and he is the leader of the Feathers of the Raven group. You may have heard of them, recently."

The man shrugged. "A message or two about them crossed my desk, yes."

"Good. He wants all of you dead. Personally." This got their attention. "He went to elaborate lengths to engineer a supervirus that would kill anyone who put the interests of corporations, shareholders, and profits ahead of environmental protection or individual rights. That plan has spiraled out of control, so he said he would come here to kill you off one by one, instead of wholesale."

"Great. Another liberal tree-hugger nutcase," the man scoffed.

"Yeah, you might say he's planning to 'occupy' this conference." Gayle kept a cheerful face.

He started to say something about how that type never gave anyone credit for the prosperity they enjoyed, but Gayle was getting a call from security. She held up her hand in front of the guy and said, "Hang on. Security."

"Black feathered wings, half-burned, oozing oil, really scrawny-looking? That the guy, Gayle?" Scrimmage asked.

"Yep, that's him! Is he here?" She added the last mostly for the benefit of the execs.

"Yeah, he just did a number on the HVAC defenses on the rooftop of level 26 and wiped out the sensors. I've got him on exterior cams on the bottom of the conference level. He's... yeah, he's headed your way. I think he dumped something into the ventilation system. Filters are showing as out."

"Hah! Sucker!" Gayle laughed.

"Huh?"

"He did exactly what I thought he would do! Yep, my special defense will protect these folks from the deadly virus. He's on his way up here, you say? Okay, keep the evacuation going. I'll take care of it, but it might be a while. I can't beat this guy, but he can't beat me, either, if I play my cards right. That gives the guests the chance to escape." She leveled her gaze on the perfectly coiffed man in front of her. She shifted her position so that she could see the doors to the landing deck.

"Roger that, Gayle. We'll help if we can, otherwise, good luck."

"Thanks, Scrimmage. You're tops!" She caught sight of Blighthawk winging his way onto the deck. She gave the executives a cheerful look. "You guys can stay if you want, but I would strongly advise against it if you have families who want to see you alive again."

That scattered them all, including the leader, for the exits to the hotel interior. Gayle bobbed into the air and shielded herself. She summoned her phantom army and a swirling cyclone around herself for defense. It immediately began pushing away the chairs and tables in the conference hall. She glided forward at a slow hover toward the deck. The scent of her personal breeze had changed to a much stronger, spicy pepper smell.

The corrupter seemed confused that nobody was about on the landing deck. He scowled and summoned two large toxic spirits. Each topped three meters in height and almost two in width. Gayle had her army open the doors. She called out, "Hiya, Blighthawk! You wanna do this out in the open air, or are you dead set on breaking stuff inside?"

The villain's eyes narrowed. "You got here faster than I thought you would." He entered the conference hall with his spirits and looked around. "Where is Sheena?"

"She had something she had to do. You'll have to settle for just me, instead."

He sneered slightly. "I suppose so. You seem a glutton for punishment."

"A girl likes to dream she's learned from her mistakes," Gayle responded cheerfully.

"You've evacuated the greedy sheep," Blighthawk noted. "That's going to make this more tedious."

"Yeah, sorry."

The villain snorted with grim amusement. "Stand aside or be destroyed, Gayle. My quarrel is not with you."

"I know. Still, saving people is my job. I'll stay."

He shrugged. "Had to offer you the chance. It's your funeral, especially without Sheena here to fix those burns." He threw a copy of the triple shot of burning acid bolts that had worked against her last time. This time she immediately responded with a strong gust of wind. This and her cyclone prevented any of the streams of acid from even getting close. Two chairs and a table centerpiece were burned and dissolved, though.

"I guess you have learned," Blighthawk observed. He commanded his spirits to attack and lobbed a ball of noxious goo toward her.

Gayle's phantom army reacted. They couldn't hurt the corrupter, but they could interfere with the spirits and anything Blighthawk chose to throw at her. She dodged to the side and went for distance, assuming the goo to be explosive or sticky or something else big and unpleasant. She wasn't surprised when it hit the floor and burst, spraying flaming acid globules over a wide part of the nearby hall.

"Hey, why don't you shoot down some of these tacky decorations, while you're at it?" Gayle called out. She circled to a point near the exterior wall around to the left of where she had started. She conjured a thunderous air burst near Blighthawk that threw tables and chairs into the villain. As she expected, they simply bounced off him.

"I would monologue, but I'm just too tired," he replied. "But, since you insist...." He fluttered into the air and flapped his wings vigorously. That spattered most of the decorations near him with oily goo. He threw another burning acid blast at her, and followed it up with a rapid fire cone of acid that he thought she might not be able to dodge.

He was partially right. She blew the bulk of the attack away, but a couple of spatters did hit her and flowed off her air cushion. She quickly re-applied the shield. Gayle didn't want to be caught with that down again. She ratcheted up the strength of her cyclone a notch to help deflect the acid.

Gayle conjured a storm cloud and placed it at a strategic distance from the exterior wall where it had the range to cover half of the conference hall with its lightning bolts. She directed it to target the toxic spirits that were having a hard time getting past the phantom army. If the agents' analyses were correct, the lightning might ignite the spirits. Without a large source of toxic base, Blighthawk might run out of spirits. At least Gayle held out the hope, for now.

Blighthawk lobbed another burning acid bolt, but this time at the support beam of the roof over Gayle's head. She dodged aside again, circling to her left as before. The acid mixture ate away at the beam, but slowly. He grimaced. "Good construction."

"Lots of conferences and events, and lots of villains crashing the party. They're trying to protect people."

"Trying to protect their property and profits, you mean," he scoffed.

Gayle muttered a pre-emptive apology to the hotel and created a wide tornado-like windstorm that began pulling in all the loose objects in the hall, centered on Blighthawk. Tables, chairs, boxes, holoposter projectors, anything that would move; it all started converging in the wild wind on the corrupter. Blighthawk stood undisturbed in the middle of it. As the whirlwind started changing the landscape of the hall, a lightning bolt from the storm cloud struck one of the toxic spirits. Gayle grinned. It did set the thing on fire! And, it knocked the spirit back all the way to the wall. The phantom army kept up its interference.

Blighthawk glowered at her for a moment as he was nearly covered with furniture inside his shield. He tossed a bursting acid glob at the junk surrounding him. It burst against a holoprojector and spattered destruction throughout the windstorm. He tossed another. Gayle yelped as the acid was dispersed throughout the entire hall by her windstorm. She tightened the focus of the vortex to suck droplets like that inward. But the air and everything it carried had to go somewhere, and in this case it was up to the ceiling of the hall above Blighthawk.

Gayle swooped to her left again and concentrated, her fist sticking straight out in front of her, targeting the less-damaged toxic spirit. Using the swirling air of the windstorm as a boost, she gathered the electricity in the room and fired it as a lightning bolt at the spirit. It crackled out with a thunderclap and blew a hole through the spirit, which popped like a soap bubble and vanished.

Having been waiting for the singer to focus her attention, Blighthawk flicked a flurry of small flaming acid streams at her. She cried out in surprise and tried to drop beneath them. Dozens of droplets spattered off her shields. This time, she was lucky. The big windstorm, her personal cyclone, and her air cushion kept the acid from reaching her, but it was a near thing. She renewed her shield and launched herself back into the air, this time to the other direction, keeping outside of the edge of the big vortex-powered windstorm.

The acid Blighthawk had tossed at the furniture pile around him had mostly done its job. The pile of junk hemming him in had broken into smaller bits. The corrupter growled in frustration. Unfortunately for him, the smaller bits only obscured his vision more. They couldn't hurt him, but they did make it difficult to see, and to move he had to push through the debris. He summoned a corrosive stream and fed it into the swirling maelstrom around him. The corrosive coated the junk and blasted up against the ceiling, and then down again into the windstorm in a continuous cycle. He smiled grimly to himself. *Time to change the terms of this battle.*

Gayle checked on her phantom army. The aerial servants were still doing well, being immune to the spirit's attacks, and the limited battering they could do was having its effect. Another lightning strike from the storm cloud would finish it off. She glided around the hall further. Blighthawk wouldn't just stay there forever, she knew. Eventually, he would get tired of the distractions and go after the guests. She opened a channel to Scrimmage. "Hiya, Scrimmage. How are we doing on guest safety?"

"Good. The conference center is evacuated, and we're showing no life signs but yours and the Blighthawk guy left up there. Elevators are locked out from those levels and the stairwell doors are sealed. He can get through them, of course, but it will slow him down."

"Yeah, slowing him down is the name of the game, I'm afraid," Gayle replied. "I don't think I can convince him to give up."

"No? What's up with this guy?"

"He's got a god powering his shield, kind of. No way to hurt him."

"Ouch."

"Whoa! There goes the roof!" Gayle dodged another wide-area blast of acid as the melted junk swirling around Blighthawk went up through the roof. The corrupter had done his trick with the corrosive fluid and melted down everything it had covered, including a large patch of the ceiling. The windstorm was now blowing everything up and out of the conference hall. The hall was now a big open space.

"Oops!" Blighthawk shouted in a nasty tone over the roaring wind. He snickered at her. "I broke it!"

Gayle dropped the windstorm and it quickly began to dissipate. "Aw, come on, 'Hawk! Can't you find some other way to fight for justice? It's not like you're wrong, but this isn't the way to do it!"

"I'm sorry, Gayle. Raven demands carrion."

"But that's not the real Raven! He's sick! He needs to be healed!"

The shaman narrowed his eyes suspiciously. "Regardless, these people are monsters. Uncaring monsters so far removed from the effects of their decisions that they have lost their humanity."

"Would you tell that to their families? Their kids? Sure, they may be blind, but it's not from evil intent! Well... mostly. Some of them are fully-complicit scum, I'm sure. But most of them are doing what they think is best!"

Blighthawk grumbled to himself. He threw a series of heavy bolts at Gayle, one after another, forcing her to blow some aside and dodge others. While she was busy, he reached out and summoned another toxic spirit. This one was smaller, barely taller than he was. He frowned, and then gave it instructions. The spirit rushed toward the hovering wind controller.

"Phantom army, to me! Get this thing off me!" she yelled to her aerial servants. She brought her hands together and then flung out her arms and legs in an expansive gesture. A mighty thunderclap resounded across the hall and bolts of lightning shot out from her in all directions. Three of them struck the new spirit. The shockwave rippled through it, pushing it back for a second, but it kept coming.

"What will they tell the families of the people they've killed, I wonder?" the corrupter shouted. "'I was just doing my job' is no excuse! We settled that with the Nazis seventy years ago! And they're all getting paid too much to claim ignorance of what they do!" He threw a flurry of acid bursts at the phantom army as it traveled past him. He snorted and shook his head as much of it hit them but had no effect. His remaining original spirit followed the aerial servants across the hall.

The storm cloud rumbled and crashed. The lightning bolt struck the toxic spirit as it passed by. The spirit popped and dissipated. Blighthawk growled again with frustration. "You know what, Gayle? You're just wasting my time." He walked toward the elevators.

Gayle gritted her teeth. She had delayed him as long as she could. She whispered, "Sheena! Please, I need your help!"

Chapter 35 – Time Huntress

The air in the forest was clear. The sun was shining, the cedars stretched and swayed overhead majestically, and the mist Sheena had seen each time she had visited before was gone. The cedars smelled fresher than fresh, and the breeze was invigorating. She felt energized, recharged. Maybe this really was the home of the gods.

For a moment, she heard something. Eric's voice, like a whisper inside her head, "Good luck, my beautiful goddess!" Strange, but she appreciated it. She listened for more, but that was all. She called Sharur to her.

"Welcome, Mistress. I hear and obey," growled the demon wolf.

"I have to find out how to undo the plague." Strange, she had meant to say "virus," but the word came out differently.

"Then we must go to the river. You must beware, for the guardians will challenge you."

Sheena nodded. "I understand. Is there a way I can prove that I belong here?"

Sharur gave her a wolfish grin and his eyes blazed. "Yes. Gain the recognition of another god."

"Uh… how do I do that?"

Sharur implied a shrug. "I cannot tell you. That is between gods, and I am just a demon."

"Pssht! *Just* a demon, he says!" Sheena laughed. "All right, I'll add that to the long list of things I have to accomplish. For now, let's get to work on fixing the plague." She winged her way into the air while Sharur loped along easily beneath her.

The River of Time was not far. She found Shanikali's campsite, but the goddess was nowhere around. Sheena called out for the goddess, but there was no answer. Sharur just shrugged when she asked him where Shanikali might be. His only comment was a cryptic, "You are Shanikali."

She went down to the water. A great wolf of iron, brother to Sharur, waited for her near the riverbank. "You do not belong here, mortal, and certainly not tampering with things you do not understand. Go now, or be destroyed for eternity."

"No. I belong here and I have a duty to perform." Sheena wrinkled her nose. Again, her words weren't exactly what she had intended, but they were close enough. Maybe English didn't translate directly here in the flesh.

The wolf leaped forward without further warning. Sheena slowed it and its fiery breath as it moved, then stepped to the side, launched herself into the air, and shot it with a spirit arrow. The wolf turned slowly, caught by the effect of her time current, but did not dodge the arrow. It struck deep into its flank and the wolf shuddered. Sheena was reassured that the arrows would work as she hoped, and fired another. This one knocked the wolf to the ground. It struggled to get up.

"Yield," Sheena said. "Your duty is fulfilled. I belong here."

Sharur spoke, hesitantly. "Do you wish me to fight, Mistress?"

"No, Sharur. I think he will see I am not an intruder." *I hope*, she added to herself.

The other wolf stared at her for a long moment and sniffed the wind to catch her scent. She released the slowing current and stared it down. She had plenty of practice at this with both domestic and wild animals in the real world. For this, at least, she know exactly what she was doing. The wolf ducked its head and lowered its tail.

"Very well," she said to the wolf. She reached out and healed its arrow wounds. "I am Shanikali, and I belong here. Please carry the word to the rest of the pack."

The wolf dipped its head in assent and turned to go. It stopped and looked back over its shoulder and said, "Welcome back, goddess," then loped off into the woods.

Sheena looked at Sharur and fluttered down to the ground. He looked back at her with a wide-open grin. "That went about as well as it could have, I think," she said.

"You are the protector of these lands. You *belong* here," he answered in agreement. "But you still may receive challenges. You have not yet gained the recognition of your peers."

"As long as challenges don't come while I'm doing my work, I will be satisfied." She shrugged and went down to the river. While not covered with mist, the River of Time was still filled with half-there currents and it was hard to see anything clearly in the waters. She thought about what she needed. *How about taking a look at the whole scope of the problem, first?* She considered the river from the perspective of events affected by the supervirus.

Her eyes widened. This river was huge! It was almost a kilometer across with many branches and a deep, fast center channel. Okay, so she wasn't going to make the whole virus problem go away—there was way too much temporal momentum behind this. Okay, how about deaths from the virus?

The river shifted and was a shallow, narrow stream. She could jump across it easily. Downstream, not very far, it turned into a raging torrent. That much water simply could not come from the supply where she stood, or from upstream! Apparently, conservation of matter and energy was irrelevant for this purpose. But, she was looking at the impact of events in a time stream, she reminded herself. The character of the river at this point showed her that she was not too late to act and save lives.

"So, I have to keep fatalities from cascading. Let's see how many we actually have at this point." She waded into the river. Sheena felt the metaphorical pressure of the water firmly against her ankles. She studied the river, trying to find the point where she could see Greg Dawson's whiteboard. A pale line caught her eye, stretching back only a few feet from where she stood, and almost in the center of the river. She looked closely. It was the whiteboard. "Huh. That was easy."

She found a point in time and read the whiteboard. There were many statistics on the board, but the important line was:

Fatalities: 12

That was at 8 PM, Friday, the 15th of August… today. She made note of that and looked a bit further upstream. Prior to 6 AM this morning, the number read 0. Okay, that gave her a timeframe, but the people with those cases were in critical condition before they resulted in deaths, so she needed to think a bit further ahead.

She looked for the lifelines of the early fatalities and made herself study each backward from their deaths. All in this group were elderly or immune-compromised travelers who had come through a cloud of the virus in either the Boston or JFK airport on Thursday evening, August 7. As far as Sheena could tell, they were just normal people. There were none of the "powers-that-be" that Blighthawk had targeted. She thought about what she could do to prevent the release of the virus, but quickly discarded that idea. There were just too many places it had been spread, between the toxic spirits and the Feathers' volunteers.

She remembered Eric's suggestions. The message to the authorities that he never sent. She looked back along the river to find that place. Just a year and a half; not very far at all. She walked upstream against the current. This wasn't very hard, but it required more concentration than she thought it would. She was glowing brightly while doing it, too, she noticed. And there it was. Just an ordinary day in Wisconsin, with Eric reading the journal on the couch in their living room. She played it forward, slowly. She could see his expression getting more and more agitated. He finished reading the article, and went back to re-read parts of it. He stood up and headed for his office in the house and sat down at the computer. He looked at the article again with a frustrated and confused expression. He skimmed it again, obviously looking for something specific and not finding it. He set down the journal and ran a few searches on the computer. He shook his head and leaned his chin on his hands. He tried another search and clicked through a few additional links, but shook his head with resignation. Eric leaned back in his chair and then shrugged. He got up and left the office, leaving the journal on the chair beside the desk.

That was it. That was the place where he could have sent the warning, but he couldn't find a place to report what he had realized. Well, that wouldn't require too much poking, even if she had to provide an email address out of thin air for him. She looked at his search terms again and grinned to herself. All she had to do was get Eric to pick one of the suggested search terms and it would show Dynatech's homeland security reporting form! She backed up to time where he made the choice and… reached in… there was no other way to describe it. She nudged his decision to see and choose the suggested option two down from the term he had initially picked. Eric followed this search result and found the reporting form, and then filled it out, picking up the journal to enter the relevant data.

Sheena looked back down the river to see what effect that had on the future and was astounded! The cascade of fatalities had gone from a Niagara-sized waterfall to a small, steady widening of the original stream! Preventing global catastrophe was darned good, she thought. Still, maybe she could do even better and nobody would have to die at all from this thing.

She looked downstream and tried to find the place where the Feathers' virus had been edited. After a couple of subjective minutes of searching, she found it. With corresponding effort, she waded back down the river to that point and looked closely. She wasn't really sure what she was seeing. It looked like clean-suited laboratory workers in a high-tech lab inserting trays of blue material into a machine and running a program on the control panel. She saw Kadorsky behind his hood nod and check items off on a checklist he held on a clipboard. It was the Feathers' production lab. She guessed that the machine must be the bioreactor she had been briefed on. She concentrated on the bioreactor and its controls and followed that backward, but there was nothing to see. Sheena wondered how she would be able to see information or computer software working in the time stream.

Maybe I can look at it with another perspective? She tried to focus on the decisions made in the time stream, instead of the actions people had taken. The people faded to almost two-dimensional simplified images and symbols stood out to her, superimposed over the background images. She was surprised that she could so easily match the decisions with the actors, but that was what she had asked for. And, there was a set of decisions for the bioreactor that were not associated with anyone in that room during that time. She followed the decisions and matched them to their owner… and found the monstrous form of Ravenger standing in front of another computer in a cramped control room elsewhere in the time stream.

The things that Ravenger was considering were technical, complex, and way beyond her understanding of anything having to do with microbiology. If she was going to do this, it might only be by trial and error. She reasoned out her options. If she tried to make Ravenger decide not to tamper with the virus, it would produce the version Blighthawk and Kadorsky wanted. That was unacceptable. Another simple decision would be for Ravenger to leave the Stage 3 portion of the virus intact and to do his modifications to that portion only. That still left a lethal virus for release; again, not acceptable. Eric had suggested causing Ravenger to make a mistake with the second stage mutation that would render it harmless, or at least less dangerous. That would be where she would look more closely.

She tried to find the options the Vengeful Earth leader had considered. The symbols associated with the decisions changed as she studied them, becoming color coded, but still having no real meaning for her. She noticed that Ravenger had picked the option that the associated symbols showed with the deepest shade of green. Around this choice there was a virtual cloud of other options. Some regions in that cloud of possibilities were varying shades of green. Others were yellow, red, or blue, with some shading between them in some cases. She thought for a moment and thought about sorting the options in terms of danger to the people infected. The cloud of possibilities shifted. All options retained their symbols and colors, but were sorted spatially. Interestingly, the red options broke into two categories: choices that Ravenger judged to be too dangerous and choices that weren't dangerous enough.

Just to make sure she was understanding the colors correctly, she mentally re-sorted the cloud by desirability to Ravenger's goals. The cloud resolved into a perfect match spatially with the color coding. She nodded to herself. The blue options appeared to be irrelevant to the villain's goals, while red played against them and green supported them, with yellow in the middle. She re-sorted for danger again.

Here was her first "What if?" trial. She poked Ravenger to choose the virus alteration that was the most undesirable, least dangerous choice. She looked downstream. The river narrowed a bit very near to this point and then widened out slightly more than it had been after her first change. She frowned, wondering why this happened, and studied Ravenger's actions in the time stream. She quickly saw that he had caught and corrected his error.

So, it has to be a smaller thing; one he won't notice. I wonder how I introduce an error? Maybe by changing his judgment of the options, but leaving their real impact the same? She reset Ravenger's decision to its original choice. Then, she touched the symbol associated with the decision and artificially re-colored the choice he had made to be a bright red. She "re-wound" the decision and let him choose again. Ravenger picked a different option—the one he had originally considered next most desirable. *Huh. This is messing with decisions about the decisions. Cool!*

She looked downstream to check her work. There was no significant change on the time stream. About what she expected. She wondered if she could slip by a non-dangerous option with a green color. She touched one of the symbols representing a low-danger option and turned it to become the most desirable option. Just to be safe, she undid her previous change, too. She re-wound the decision and let him choose again, as before. This time, the archvillain picked the option she had forced to be most desirable. She looked downstream. The river was much wider than before. She followed Ravenger's actions to see if could tell what happened. He did not go back to correct his mistake, but let the decision stand.

Puzzled, she looked for Greg Dawson's whiteboard and looked at it. For a while, she couldn't see anything really different, but then she noticed it. The influenza strain had been changed! The decision Ravenger had made wasn't very dangerous, overall, but the preparations Sheena had introduced through Eric's message had been bypassed, with casualty figures increased as a result. She snorted with irritation and reversed her change.

She went back to the decision cloud and asked for an additional sort. This time, she added a tag for the influenza strain used so that she could clearly identify the choices associated not just with desirability to Ravenger and danger to the infected patient, but similarity to the strain that was the basis of the

Dynatech preparations. The cloud sorted itself again. There were fewer options now. She had weeded out a lot of possibilities. Idly, she wondered how the original Shanikali would have handled a situation like this with her ancient understanding of data manipulation. She picked an option with medium-low desirability and medium-low danger that was a near-exact match for the strain Eric had reported, and then colored it to be the most desirable. Ravenger made his choice and let it go into production.

When Sheena glanced downstream she smiled. The stream dried up almost immediately after her original entry point. She checked Greg's whiteboard. The statistics topped out at 2,892 reported infections and 0 fatalities. She breathed a sigh of relief. So, it could be stopped! She reminded herself to check for other unintended consequences.

She altered her perception of the river. This time she limited it to people directly affected by the Feathers' plan and the release of the virus. It was a wide, slow-moving river, more than two hundred meters across, but very shallow across most of it. She oriented herself and looked for Greg's whiteboard. She found it and checked to make sure that the statistics were the same. Satisfied with those outcomes, she hesitated, standing in the river, but decided to chance it. She looked for her own life line. It ran from upriver to slightly downstream of her current spot, where she had most recently entered the Cedar Forest. *Fair enough*, she thought, *I'm outside of time. Now Eric and Gayle.*

She traced Eric's life line and noted with a smile where it intertwined with her own. It continued downriver past her entry point for a good long distance. She noted with satisfaction that it ran down the center of this view of the river, as did her own. She nodded and turned to study Gayle's. She noted with concern that Gayle's line became blurry and disappeared a short time after her entry into the river. She searched her Shanikali memories for what this meant. Shortly, she found it and nodded with understanding: a blurry line was one where the person's fate was closely tied to Shanikali's involvement. That made sense for Gayle's situation. She wondered if there was anything else she should check.

As she was thinking, she heard Gayle's voice whisper in her head, like she had heard Eric before. "Sheena! Please, I need your help!" She looked sharply at the river to see where that had come from. She couldn't be sure, but it seemed to come from the blurry zone of Gayle's life line in her subjective present. Sheena fought the urge to rush out of the river and fly to help. She forced herself to remember, there was plenty of time. All the time in the world, in fact. As she remembered this, her confidence returned. She tried a return message, not really sure how she knew she could do this. "Don't worry, Gayle. Hold on. I will be there when you need me."

With her reply sent, she waded out of the River of Time. As she came up to her/Shanikali's campsite, she felt an angry presence. The air became cloying with the smell of rotting bodies and clouds blotted out the sun. The sound of wingbeats fluttered above her.

"You have robbed me of millions of corpses, Shanikali!" screeched Raven. "And I will have my carrion, whether it comes from them or you!"

Chapter 36 – Raven

Sheena shot a quick glance at Sharur and warned him, "Be ready, and be clever. This may be our opportunity." The iron wolf nodded briefly.

"Cleverness will get you nowhere! I am the trickster! I am the clever one!" croaked Raven. He was the same as they had seen him before, with dripping eyes, shabby feathers, and a hostile, angry aura of decay about him. He settled on a low bough of the tree sheltering Shanikali's campsite. The cedar needles instantly withered and died.

"Greedy, perhaps," Sheena agreed, "but clever? You fell into a trap, oh mighty Raven!"

"A trap? You mean this meeting, or something else?" He looked at her suspiciously.

"When you rescued the man, Bryan John, from the burning pitch, you fell into the pit and were made sick! How is that clever?"

The bird grunted, "Bah! I escaped the pitch, and trained my shaman. He has done well, if a bit too slowly and carefully. You, on the other hand, have only your animals. No worshippers or followers. Bah!" He considered her carefully from his branch.

"If you peck at me, I will shoot you," Sheena warned him.

"Bah! I have other ways to destroy you!"

"But, if you destroy me, you will stay sick. I can heal you. Then you can be as great and clever as you were before."

"I am clever now!" insisted Raven with a screech.

"I don't believe you," Sheena said indifferently. Inwardly, she grinned. Calderón's hints about Raven's foibles were right on target. "Prove it."

Raven dropped to the ground and turned himself into a diseased, rusting copy of Sharur. "Is this not clever, little goddess? I can imitate your servant!"

She shrugged. "Not bad, Raven, but that is just power. That is not cleverness."

He turned himself back into his normal form and fluttered back up to the branch. "I gave Blighthawk a plague that would strike only those who he wants to strike—the ones who are greedier than me. Is that not clever, Shanikali?"

"Well, it would be, but another one outwitted all of your Feathers and switched his own plague for yours. You were tricked and robbed. That's not very clever, I think."

"Oh, yes, Ravenger. He will get his, one day!" Raven croaked in a sulky voice.

"I can change the past and remake the future, Raven. It may be that I am more clever than you. But, I am just a huntress and a protector—not a trickster—and it is not right for me to be more clever than you. I would be happy to heal your sickness, if you wish, and then you will be the best, again."

"No, you will just freeze me in time, like you did to Horgan!" he croaked petulantly.

Sheena wondered what Shanikali had done. It sounded interesting, but she had absolutely no memory of it. "Why would I do that?"

"So you can stop my followers from littering the world with carrion, of course!"

"Ah, yes. I might do that, but if you were not sick, I would not need to freeze you."

"I remain sharp-eyed, and I can see through tricks, Shanikali!"

"Then why do you sit on that branch, out of reach of Sharur's jaws?"

"It is your arrows I watch! Not the jaws of your wolf."

"And right you are to do so, but I thought you could catch arrows. Can't you do that anymore, now that you are sick?"

"Of course I can! That is why I watch, but you mean only to trick me!"

"I think you are too sick to catch arrows, now," Sheena said. An idea was growing in her head.

"I am as sharp as ever!"

"No, that just tells me that you are worried that I will shoot you like a pigeon."

"Bah! I can catch your arrows! That is why you are hesitating. You know you can't hit me!"

"You don't think it is because I like to talk with you, Raven? I am sad! Remember, I said that I would heal your sickness if you would accept it." She had now offered to heal him three times. That seemed important, somehow. Calderón would probably know why.

"I don't want your pity or your help, Shanikali! I am perfectly able to do what I wish, and I can catch arrows, if I wish! Even your arrows!"

"Are you sure?"

"I am sure!"

"Here, then. Try to catch this." In a flash, Sheena drew the golden arrow from her quiver, nocked it, and fired at Raven's breast.

True to his word, the mighty bird spirit fluttered up and caught the arrow in his claws. The golden light swirled around him, sank into him, and washed him from beak to tail feathers with a great sound of rustling wind chimes. Sheena watched in amazement. Raven spun slowly in the air. The sickness and darkness surrounding him was eaten away by the light, the same way she had healed the victims of Elf Shot's nightmare arrows. Some time later—whether seconds or hours it was impossible to say in that place—he settled back on the branch, as healthy, sharp, and alert as Sheena could have hoped for him to be.

He dipped his beak and looked at her with both eyes. She detected a touch of amusement in his voice as he said, "That was a clever trick, goddess."

She bowed to him. "You are welcome, Raven."

He considered for a long moment. "I seem to have created some problems back in the world."

Sheena shrugged and grinned. "Yes. But nothing I couldn't handle, eventually. Still, I would very much appreciate your help cleaning up."

The bird nodded and replied, "Of course! But, a bargain is a bargain. I can't take Bryan's powers away."

"Oh." Sheena was disappointed. "Isn't there some way to get that shield of his down? We have to stop him from killing people."

"Are you sure they don't deserve it?"

"I am sure that there is a different, better way to see justice in my time and place. As Blighthawk, Bryan is not respecting what the people have made for their way of justice."

Raven seemed to think about that, and then he shrugged his wings. "So be it. We can play a trick on him, then. I will tell you how to find the spirit that protects him from wood. You destroy that spirit, and he will be vulnerable to your arrow."

"A spirit? How does that work?"

"The shell of protection I have lent him is very powerful because it is made for many spirits to each hold a part of it. These spirits cannot be found without the eyes to see them. You have the eyes to see spirits, of course, and I will show you how to find just the right one. If a spirit falls, he can summon another to take its place, but this takes some time. I think your friend will be distracting him, and you can shoot him with your arrow."

"But will this stop him?"

"If you use the right arrow, yes."

Sheena thought. "Wood?"

Raven nodded.

Sheena reached into her quiver. The flimsy arrow of spring-green wood was all that she had left. She tried to remember what it did. The memory came creeping back slowly. "Oh! This will make him a child again, with no memory of what he has done!"

"Yes."

"But, he has no more family, and he will have no understanding of what is happening! I can't do that to a child!"

"I will take him under my wing, have no fear."

"Is this the only way?" she asked cautiously.

"No," Raven replied. "You could kill all the spirits, or somehow find the ones that protect him from all of the things that you and your friend of the winds can do. But, that would take time and he will be desperate once he realizes what you are doing. He may decide to use up all of the power he can draw from me to do great harm, ending his life in the process. I think you are better off with a simple trick."

She nodded. "You are probably right. I need to think about this, first, though."

"Take all the time you need, goddess. After all, that is your domain, is it not?" With that acknowledgement, Raven winked and then flapped up off of the branch and winged away to the west. The branch blossomed with new greenery as he flew off.

Sheena sat down at her campsite and studied the spring arrow. Sharur lay down to wait.

Chapter 37 – A Wing and a Prayer

Eric wondered whether he should go back inside or wait by the picnic table. Sheena had brought him out here to talk about how she could defeat Blighthawk, and then she had vanished into the spirit world to fix the time stream. The anti-viral medicine had been stocked up and distributed to regional and international centers for just such a terrorist emergency, so treatment of the victims was going very well. No one really knew whether Ravenger had somehow slipped up or if he had intended the second stage virus to be so easy to fight off. Blighthawk's grand plan had failed miserably due to a combination of luck and Ravenger's interference. All that remained was to catch Blighthawk and prevent him from doing any more damage. He was just about to head inside when a golden light washed over him with the sound of wind chimes. She was back!

Sheena landed gracefully on the Dynatech lawn beside her husband. "Your prayer has been answered and your beautiful goddess has returned!" she said playfully, catching him up in an enthusiastic hug.

Eric blinked in surprise. "Did I say that aloud?"

"No, you didn't! You won't believe this, but I heard it in my head, like a prayer!"

He let her go and stared at her. "Seriously?"

Sheena laughed and nodded enthusiastically. "Yes! I had just arrived in the forest, and I heard you clearly in my head! By the way, what do you remember?"

"Uh…? Well, you only left five minutes ago… right?"

"Oh, never mind. Here." She touched his forehead with two fingers and gave him the memory of the previous time stream.

Eric's head reeled. "Oh my god! I had no idea… I mean, it was never that serious! At least… here, it was never that serious…."

"Specifically because you sent in that warning to the homeland security mailbox? Yes! I could see how that would have unfolded. Submitting that warning was your idea all along, but in the original timeline you didn't know where to send it; you didn't find the form. If I had not altered the timeline, over two million people would have died from this virus, Eric!"

His legs threatened to give way. Eric sat down on the bench of the picnic table. "Died? Two million people?"

"Yes!"

"And you stopped it?"

"Because of your idea and with your help, yes! And you were worried that you couldn't do anything to help me!" She beamed and gave him a kiss. "So, yes, your prayer was answered!"

"Uh… I…!" He was speechless as he processed the difference between what he *knew* for a fact had happened and what would have happened.

"Sending the warning? You made me do that?"

"All I had to do was to help you find the form. You did the rest."

"Ravenger's tampering?"

"Would have been lethal. I made him pick a strain that was less dangerous and subject to the medicine that had been... was going to be... produced."

"Whoa... remind me never to make you angry!" This was a lot to absorb.

"Aw, get angry with me all you want. Just never, ever give up on us. The two of us, together! You're right about that. Together, we're unstoppable!"

Sheena frowned and shook her head. She had just heard Gayle say, "Sheena! Please, I need your help!" inside her head. Then, she heard herself reply, "Don't worry, Gayle. Hold on. I will be there when you need me." She laughed self-consciously.

"What?" asked Eric.

"I just answered another prayer. Or, I need to go answer it... or however that works. I think I got a little bit looped in time, or something. Gayle is in trouble, but I know what to do about it!"

Eric stood up again and gave her a shaky smile. "Go save the day, honey!"

"I'll be back to pick you up later!" She launched herself into the air and flapped her wings for altitude. She returned Eric's wave before she flew out of sight.

As she flew toward the city, she opened a channel to Gayle and the FBSA agents. "Okay, folks, the mission was successful. Raven is healed! And I altered the time stream to reduce the virus threat. I will tell you about that in detail later. Gayle, I got your prayer, as it were, and I'm winging my way to where you are. I just need specifics."

"Huh?" asked Gayle. "You heard that? And I got your answer! That was real? I wasn't just imagining what you would say if you were here? Wow!"

"Yeah! Weird, huh?"

"Uh, yeah! I'm in the Sky Plaza hotel on the conference level, and Blighthawk has just decided that he's done playing with me. He's going to go find and kill the conference guests, and he's not paying attention to me, anymore."

"Okay, one moment while I adjust my GPS." Sheena found the location and banked to her right as she spotted the unique tower on the skyline. "I'm pretty close, actually, but you've got to distract him a bit longer."

"I'll try, but he's ignoring me, now."

"I have another thing for you to try. You remember in the sewer, how he smelled you?"

"Yeah. He said I smelled delightful... Oh! That got through the shield! But how is that gonna help?"

"Don't try to take him down, just keep your defenses up, and SING! Use those pheromones you've been trying to keep under control! He'll inhale the pheromones and that will give you time. I'll take care of the rest when his defenses come down."

"Seriously? You want me to let those pheromones loose? After what happened in Milwaukee?"

"Yes! You can do it! You create moods with those things!"

"But, what mood do you want me to create?" Gayle asked uncertainly.

"Give him something he craves but has not had in years."

Gayle sounded shocked. "Sheena! You don't want me to seduce him, do you?"

Sheena laughed. "No, Gayle! Hope!"

"Ohhhh!" She giggled with relief. "Okay!"

"I'll be right there, but I need to stalk one of his hidden spirits and take it out. Then I need just one clear shot at him. You'll only see me when I'm ready."

"What are you going to do?"

"Roll back time on him. He won't be a threat for long." She was flying over the city center, now. "I'm getting close, on a wing and a prayer. See you soon!"

Chapter 38 – Nature Lover

"Here goes nothing," Gayle muttered. Blighthawk had just dissolved the security doors to the elevator lobby on the conference level. She brought her cyclone back up to speed and made sure that her air cushion was fully charged, but she dismissed her phantom army and the storm cloud.

"Hey, Bryan! Please, give me one more chance!" she called to him.

He ignored her and walked to the elevators. She followed him. A light watermelon scent was blowing in her breeze. She sang out to him a line from one of her songs:

> *At the end of day, don't we want to treat each other*
> *Just the way, that we want for ourselves?*
> *It can be, light up the sky, the darkness gone, but it's up to us*
> *In the end, it's all up to us!*

He turned and looked at her. "That's from *Justice*, isn't it?" he asked.

She glided closer. "Yes, it is. You've heard it?"

"Yes." He clenched his jaw. "I just wish it could really be that way."

"It's more complicated than the song, but it's still possible," she replied. She was hopeful, and she was broadcasting hope. She also hoped he could feel it, or smell it. "You can help! In the end, it's all up to us! Including you, Bryan!"

"I can't," he said bitterly as he shook his head. "I've lost so much. I have to live in the real world, Gayle. All I have left is Raven and this kind of justice."

Gayle sang another verse, putting her soul into it, for him:

> *And every day, we're making choices like we want to live*
> *Can't we stay, and make it all just a little bit better?*
> *It can be, you and me, joining together, but it's up to us*
> *In the end, we'll bring justice!*

"Come on, Bryan!" she sang:

> *You've got so much to live for, so much to give for!*
> *Give it a shot, and let's see what we've got!*

He hesitated. "I don't recognize that last part."

"It's just for you! On the spot!" the singer replied. "You're worth it, and I think there's hope for something better. Just work with me, please!"

He wrinkled his forehead and sniffed at the air. "Is that you? The watermelon?"

"Yeah, that's me, sorry." She grinned. "I can't get rid of the breeze, but I can drop the big wind around me if you promise not to attack me."

"No, no, I like it." He seemed puzzled. "I don't know if I've smelled that since... in a long time. It's nice." He sighed with resignation. "I promise I will not attack you, unless you try to stop me."

"Okay, fair enough!" She let her cyclone go. "With all that tarry stuff, I imagine you'd be kind of sick of smelling oil all the time."

He rolled his eyes gratefully. "You have no idea! This is heavenly!"

She giggled. "See? There is hope! We don't have to be fighting, and we can find other ways to get justice, if we work together." She closed her eyes and bobbed her head in time with the beat:

> *It's been a very long flight*
> *But you don't have to give up the fight*
> *Get yourself a new pair of wings and fly!*
> *And flyyyyy!*
> *You're a new raven-guy, a raven-guy!*

She blushed and laughed, "Okay, that was a bit over the top, sorry!"

Blighthawk laughed, too. "No, that was fine! You just made that up?" he asked in amazement.

"Yep! Inspiration comes when it wants to."

"Well, it seems like a good...." He suddenly frowned and jerked like he had a pain in his side.

Sheena appeared on the other side of the elevator lobby with her bow drawn. "Bryan, please, I want to give you a choice. A very important choice. I healed Raven, and I can help you."

He turned a saddened, betrayed look on Gayle. "You were just distracting me so Sheena could drop my shield!"

Gayle shook her head quickly. "I want to give you hope. There are other endings we can write to this! Listen to her, please! Just take a breath and listen!"

He drew in a deep breath and looked confused. He frowned, trying to figure out what had changed. "Where is the cough?"

Gayle exchanged glances with Sheena and shrugged. Sheena shook her head. "I don't know. I haven't done anything, yet."

He breathed in and out. Then, he did it again, but still there was no coughing or hacking. He could breathe freely. With a puzzled expression, he said, "All right, go ahead. I'll listen."

Sheena explained, "I have a way to turn back time to when you had no powers, no bargain with Raven, before you took the first step on the path of corruption. But, if I did that, I would be forcing it on you and I would be wiping away years of your life. You would have that time to live over, but I couldn't give you back the memories and experiences I would be stripping away. I would rather you accepted hope and healing, instead. Raven is no longer sick, no longer demanding carrion, and he can also help you, if you wish."

He hesitated. "You're giving me the choice?"

"Yes, please. Unless you force my hand by using violence."

Tears welled up in Blighthawk's eyes. "But, I've done such things… I don't know how I can live with all of this…!"

"You can!" Gayle said. "I got through the dark years, with help. You can, too! Trust me, I know despair! There is hope for anyone. Even if you don't think you deserve it, you really do. It's not a matter of deserving or not, it's just a choice to accept the help. Come on, please say yes." She sang the new song verse again for him:

> *It's been a long, long, long flight*
> *But you don't have to give up the fight*
> *Get yourself a new pair of wings and fly!*
> *And flyyyyy!*
> *You're a raven-guy, a brand-new raven-guy!*

Bryan started laughing, the tears running down his cheeks. "All right, I'll do it! That is a little silly, but it's good!"

Gayle grinned. "Most of my songs start off that way. Some of 'em stay that way, too. We'll have to see how this one works itself out!"

Sheena lowered her bow and tucked the spring arrow away in her quiver.

Chapter 39 – Membership has its Rewards

The mid-morning light filtered down gently into the metahuman medical clinic in Riverhaven's north wing. Doctor Amira Grace ran her scanner over Bryan John one more time and nodded with satisfaction. "You are fully functional, Mister John. Burn scars, carcinogen deposits, subcutaneous bitumen glands… all gone. You should still keep on that recovery diet and exercise moderately until you reach a healthy weight, but you get a clean bill of health."

Bryan stretched his arms, ran his palms over his smooth, burn-free cheeks, and relished the ability to pretty much take breathing for granted. His wings were gone, at least until he needed them, and he could even wear normal clothing. He was still on the thin side, but not unnaturally so. He didn't think it would be long before he regained his old muscular physique, if he could keep exercising. It was also nice to brush his hair without oil dripping down his face. It was a nice face. He barely recognized himself when he looked in the mirror. Maybe a few too many lines from worry and things normal people should never have to see, but strong. There was something caring about those dark eyes. He got up from the examination table. "Thanks, Doctor Grace. I really appreciate all of your help."

"Oh, you're welcome. A week is a very fast initial recovery, but not unusual for the team here at Riverhaven, when aided by metahuman healers. And when something like Raven takes a hand… or a wing, or whatever… in the process, we can expect it to work out fairly well."

Bryan made his way out to the lobby where Gayle and Sheena were waiting. He looked a little tentative about his clothes. Sheena figured that it must feel odd to be wearing a polo shirt, slacks, and normal shoes after all this time. She also noticed that he still moved carefully, as if trying not to drip on anything. It would probably take a while to adjust to the changes. After all, it did for her when she changed. Changing "back" would be uncomfortable, too, she imagined.

"So?" she asked him.

"Clean bill of health, according to Doctor Grace!"

"Excellent!" said Gayle.

"So…," Sheena began, "Your legal team's next steps?"

He chuckled ruefully. "I will have a lot of restitution to do, however it works out. Raven has testified that most of what I did was under coercion, even though I have taken responsibility for everything I have done. We were arguing back and forth about who was more to blame! He, of course, wants to take all the blame because he knows they can't do anything to him. Some of the things I have testified about come under whistleblower protections, which is strange, plus there is the war hero status and associated trauma that plays into it, as well. Frankly, I have no idea how this is all going to work out. But, regardless, I will take what I am given, as long as it's fair, and I'll keep working for justice."

"Raven is re-tooling your shaman powers, too," Gayle reminded him. "That includes those healing abilities. He just has to get a chance to teach you how that works. You have a lot of self-healing to do, and the healing of others will go a long way toward making that happen, according to Josh."

"I can believe it." His face fell for a moment and he looked tired and dejected. Then, he took a breath and smiled tentatively. "You make it easier to breathe, Gayle."

She blushed, the watermelon scent was swirling around her again, tinged with strawberry. "Aw, you say the nicest things! I just smell like a fruit salad!"

"Can I see you later?" he asked hopefully.

"Sure! It's not like I need to teach Sheena anything about being a hero, anymore." She grinned at her friend.

"Well, there is still a lot that I have to learn, but at least I've got the basics down, now," Sheena replied. She turned to Bryan. "I think you should go by the name Brighthawk for any hero work you do. That makes it a total turn-around from your previous identity, while still acknowledging who you were."

"I like that," he replied. "Are you and Eric going to stay here in Venture City, or go back to Wisconsin?"

She shook her head. "We don't know yet. We've talked about some options, but haven't come to a decision, yet. That's what we're planning on doing tonight over dinner. That superbug is going to be passing through a lot of populations for a while as it spreads, so he'll have plenty of work to do, if he decides to stay on with Dynatech. Plus, there's the original project, too."

"Well, good luck with whatever decision you both decide to make."

"Thanks, Bryan. You, too, for all of the stuff you're working through."

He paused. "You know, I almost wish I had asked you to shoot me with that arrow. A lot of this would be so much easier if I didn't have these memories, or all this baggage. But, I don't think I would be me if I had gone that way."

She nodded. "We do so much by fighting and conflict, when it should be more about choices. I didn't want it to end by me forcing you to relive your life. That runs against everything we were both fighting for. When I realized that, I had to offer you the choice."

"Well… thank you again, for the choice." He extended his hand to her.

Sheena ignored it and gave him a hug, instead. "You're welcome. I'll keep trying to live up to your ideals."

The FBSA operation center had been turned over to some other crisis. Sheena and Gayle met the agents in one of the second floor conference rooms. She could see the Cedar Swamp Park Reserve out the window in the afternoon sun. It still didn't look right, with so many mature trees gone, but the accelerated growth of the replanted forest mix was showing clearly in the color of the new leaves. Reclamation was easier with metahuman abilities to help. She glanced at Agent Schauer, who was intently examining something on his tablet. Gayle had her eyes closed, nodding and softly humming along with the music in her head.

She had been on a very productive songwriting roll since the end of the "Feathers of the Raven" case, as they had been calling it. As usual, they were waiting for Calderón.

He bustled in. "Hola, sorry. I just passed the remaining source stones on to someone who might be able to do something useful with them."

"Really?" asked Sheena. "Like finding the right people for those powers?"

"Sí, exactly!" He grinned mischievously as he took a seat, but didn't elaborate.

"Good. Let's close out this case. Or, cases, as it happens," Schauer said calmly. "We have file C-1407-126, involving Elf Shot, and B-1408-043, involving Blighthawk and the Feathers of the Raven, and updates to the various ongoing Ravenger incident investigations. Both have resulted in apprehension of the primary suspects and both are now turned over to the judicial system with appropriate details and coordination completed

"I have fully documented your testimony and reports. We have done the after action reviews and passed information on to other case files and agencies, as appropriate. There are just a few remaining items to finish. First, do you have any additional thoughts, questions, or suggestions pertaining to these cases?"

Sheena leaned forward and asked, "Did Johnny Miles' testimony about Elf Shot passing information on to Ravenger get forwarded?"

"Yes," Schauer answered. "To both Elf Shot's case and to the Ravenger ongoing file. Elf Shot verified this, when questioned."

"Did we catch that other mercenary working for Blighthawk?"

"No, but Blighthawk identified him as Rio Lobo. He was substantially uninvolved in the conduct of the Feathers' contagion plot, merely providing security and personal delivery services for Blighthawk. At this point, the only definite new charges for that individual are conspiracy-related. He does, however, have sealed warrants outstanding for other charges. Interesting."

"Is that unusual?" Sheena asked.

"Unusual, yes, but I see it often enough. It's not relevant to these cases. It means that there is something very secret—at least two levels above my normal clearance—that someone very high up has decided requires the apprehension of the individual."

"Hmm...," mused Gayle. She glanced out the window and said nothing more, but Sheena could tell she knew something. She resolved to ask her later.

Sheena had another question. "What will happen to Kadorsky?"

Schauer tapped and scrolled for a moment. "His case has all been remanded to the justice system, with psychiatric evaluation and treatment recommended. He will get appropriate help, though I understand that his prognosis is shaky, at this time."

"And the rest of the Feathers?"

"The great majority have been apprehended. As usual, anti-terror ideological re-orientation will be offered." He shrugged.

"The thief from the museum?"

"At large, real identity unknown, but Elf Shot let slip the name of her associate. Vincent is a known metahuman master thief." He glanced at other notes. "No connection or relation to Sir Vincent Leo."

"And the big one," Sheena began with another glance at Gayle, "What about Ravenger?"

"Yes, that is the big one, isn't it?" Schauer said laconically. He looked to Calderón.

"There is no new word from Ravenger, no claim of responsibility, nothing. He is undoubtedly working on his next 'master plan' already. This is normal. When something fails, he simply moves on to the next thing. But we did learn about his distributed consciousness ability from this case."

Gayle snorted. "I've asked the Titans to figure out how to defeat that. I gathered from PsiKid's response that this might take a while."

"One more thing," Calderón offered. "I made sure that Elf Shot got a look at the analysis of everything we have on Shanikali's power transfer, to convince her that even if she escapes or gets out one day, these powers won't work for her. I'm not sure it convinced her, but it gave her something to think about. And the Arama Hallada has been returned. The item now on display in the Museum is a replica. They intended to create one before, but the knife was stolen too quickly."

"And the Collector?" Sheena asked.

"Still doing what he does," Calderón replied.

"All right, that's all I can think of," she turned to Gayle who shook her head.

"Good. Cases closed," Schauer said as he marked the last box on some checklist he was working from. "Then there are just two more things." He and Calderón stood up. Gayle grinned and did likewise. Sheena looked from one to the other and rose to her feet, as well.

In an even more official tone of voice than usual, Schauer intoned, "By order of the President of the United States of America, Shee'na is awarded the Freedom Cross, gold device, for exceptionally meritorious heroism and service to the citizens of the United States and its allies.

"Your clear thinking, determination, and demonstration of the principles of freedom and service upon which this country was founded in the matter of the 'Feathers of the Raven' incident reflect great credit upon you. Your actions saved millions of lives, upheld the rights of life, liberty, and the pursuit of happiness for millions more, and made the world a brighter place.

"With great thanks and appreciation, the President of the United States."

Calderón grinned and opened a small jewelry box. Inside was a pair of decorations. One was a simple rectangular red and white military uniform ribbon trimmed in gold with a gold cross attached to its center. The other was an actual medal in the same design, red on the left and white on the right, with a circular emblem of the Freedom Cross depending from the ribbon. On the upper arc of the medal was inscribed "Freedom." On the lower arc was "Justice." Calderón gently presented the box to Sheena. "If you decide you would like an official ceremony, we can pin this on you. For now, here. Take this with the thanks and gratitude of the Federal Bureau of Superpowered Affairs."

Sheena was speechless. She took the medal and touched the ribbon, as if assuring herself that it was real. The other three applauded softly for her. Gayle smiled and patted her on the shoulder. "Nice work, Sheena! This is a long, long way from where you were a month and a half ago!"

"Wow…! Thank you, both, and the bureau, too!" She looked at Gayle. "But doesn't Gayle get one? So much of this was because of her. We're partners in this!"

Gayle laughed. "Yep! I've already got one! They added on the 'saved' count to my total, so this boosts me up to the diamond agency award category with more than ten million lives saved, wow! But we wanted this one to be about you, since it's your first award, and it's a big one."

"Thanks!" Sheena hugged her friend, and then Calderón. She grinned and shook hands professionally with Schauer.

Schauer gestured for the group to sit down. He continued, "Appropriate notes and updates will be made to your FBSA official file. There are several other subordinate awards you have earned, as well. I've forwarded the details to you. But, the other matter is this." He activated the tabletop display.

Sheena looked at the virtual document Schauer was pulling up. He rotated the image and slid it toward her. It had the official State of Wisconsin and Department of Natural Resources letterhead. She glanced a question at him. The agent explained, "Your promotion letter. The Wisconsin DNR is promoting you to Senior Special Environmental Warden, effective September 1. The details are described in the letter." He gave her time to read it.

She finished and looked up. Before she could say anything, Schauer continued. "And, there is another option open to you, as well."

Calderón smirked and added in his best game show host voice, "But wait! Don't answer yet! See what else we have to offer!"

Schauer slid another virtual document over to her. "This is an offer for an FBSA Special Agent position. If you decide that you want to remain in law enforcement, but perhaps with a greater scope of responsibility, please give this role serious consideration." He actually smiled for a moment. "We would love to have you on the permanent team."

Sheena was stunned. "Work with you guys full-time? Oh, I would love to! But, I've got to sit down with Eric and think this all through."

Calderón laughed and said, "Of course! But Sheena…?" He gave her a friendly smile.

"Yes?"

"You are too good and you have too much talent and ability to just go back to only doing conservation warden work. Please consider staying on with us. As Tom said, we would *love* to have you on our team."

Gayle added her own thoughts. "The public 'show biz hero' gig isn't for everyone, as you know, Sheena. I think you've got options, now, to go wherever your heart leads you. That's a good place to be."

Sheena reached out and squeezed her friend's hand in thanks. "This is all so much to think about. I will definitely give you answers soon, though. Thank you!"

Schauer nodded. "Excellent. That's all we have for now. Please, ladies, have a good weekend, and call us if anything comes up."

Gayle laughed, "I hope not, but you never know, Agent Schauer! You just never know!"

"So we finally get to eat here?" Eric asked as he looked around at Marty's. They had a corner table close to where Sheena and Gayle had eaten before. Sheena had called ahead to make sure that Tyler was working and that she could get a table in his section.

"Yes. Finally." Sheena smiled. "We could have come here sooner, but after everything that's happened, it seemed better to save it for a private celebration and planning conversation.

Tyler approached the table and introduced himself to Eric. Sheena smiled at him and waved her fingers in greeting. He gave her a warm smile in return. He turned back to Eric. "By the way, Doctor Gardner, I wanted to thank you and the people at Dynatech for all the work on the flu medicine. I didn't get the vaccination last fall, and when that stuff came around, I caught it. I was out for a couple of days, but they said it would have been much worse without the stockpiled anti-viral drugs. So, thank you."

Eric blinked in surprise and responded, "You're welcome."

Sheena added, "Go ahead and put in an order for us." Tyler nodded with a serious little smile and left the table.

"Um... Sheena? We didn't even order drinks!"

"Don't worry. He's almost psychic."

Sheena filled Eric in on the awards, promotion from the DNR, and the FBSA job offer. Something that the agents hadn't mentioned was that some of the secondary awards came with monetary rewards from the agency or insurance cooperatives. This amounted to more than she would usually earn in a year. In addition, the DNR promotion carried a substantial pay increase and the FBSA position was at a combined scale and incentives that was more than three times her previous compensation. He whistled in appreciation.

"So, what do we want to do?" he asked.

"First things first, how are you feeling about the whole hero thing, now?" she asked him.

Eric thought about it for a moment, but he had already been mulling this over for more than a week. "You need to be doing something with your powers and smarts that is more than you could do for the DNR back home. It would feel like a waste of a pretty precious gift not to make full use of that. I've come to terms with it, too. Sure, you're in danger and you're going to be shot at and worse. But, you've got so many friends and allies to help you out that I can't really be too worried. I can handle that."

He grinned self-consciously with a hint of embarrassment. He lowered his voice slightly and added, "And, I have to admit that you are really sexy with all of this. It's not just the costume and those super-sleek curves of yours. I can't even say exactly why, maybe it's partly the confidence, but you are!"

She grinned and squeezed his hand. "What about the risk you get with the deal?"

"I think I'm okay with it." He wrinkled his nose. "The nightmares… and daymares… have faded to just a memory. I am ashamed of them, because they mostly involve me failing you or betraying you in some way, but I think I've gotten the idea into my thick head that those aren't real."

"You are probably going to be targeted again, if we keep this up," Sheena cautioned. "And it won't be just you. It will be our kids, too." She grinned slyly. "I can't imagine that will be too far in the future, you know!"

He smiled at the thought and nodded. "I know. That's why we have to have all those friends and allies around. Having met Steel Magnolia and Warlocke, Fletcher and Autumn Snow, Doctor Graviton, Josh and Anathae, and all the others at Riverhaven, I feel… better, I guess… that there's a community to help us if… when… we get into trouble."

"So, you're leaning toward staying here in Venture City? At Riverhaven?"

"That's what I'm thinking, yeah. I think that the work at Dynatech is taking me far beyond what I would have experienced as a country vet, which is a bit sad, but mostly good. I'm not working with animals at all, now, at least not directly. But, that's okay. And here, with so many opportunities in the city, I can always branch out."

"I don't think you'd really be happy with pet care forever, anyway." She smiled as he admitted she was right with a sideways nod of his head. "I mean, you spotted that virus threat the first time you saw it in the journal."

"And once I got a nudge from you, I did something about it."

"We still make a good team." She leaned over and kissed his cheek.

"Definitely. And if you need suggestions about fixing any more time stream issues, just let me know. I'll at least give you some things to think about."

"Here's what this is all looking like to me," she summarized. Eric nodded for her to go on. "You keep the Dynatech job. I'll take the FBSA job. We can get our own apartment at Riverhaven."

"Yes. I will look into selling the practice back in Sawyer County. But, I still love that area. Would you be open to buying a cabin on the lake?"

She grinned. "Yes! I happen to know of one that's for sale."

He chuckled, guessing where this was headed. "You mean the one across the lake and down the shore a bit? Used to belong to some guy from Chicago who turned out to be a metahuman artifact thief? Had a secret identity and everything? I hear that something really strange and magical happened there, so… Sure, why not!"

"You're right! See, you and I make an awesome partnership!"

Their kiss was only interrupted by Tyler bringing their drinks. They broke for air as the waiter set them down on the table. A custom craft lager for him and a raspberry lemonade, light on the ice, for her.

Sheena and Eric tasted the drinks, and simultaneously exclaimed, "Perfect!" Then, they looked at each other with sparkling eyes and laughed.

Chapter 40 – Epilogue

Sheena walked to the end of the gravel driveway and looked out at the sun setting over the stubble of the cornfield. It had been more than a month since the corn had been harvested, but she still remembered exactly how high the cornstalks had been that evening. It was hard to believe that three months had passed since she had crouched by the wheel of the FBSA agents' rented sedan on the other side of the field, waiting with excitement for something to happen.

"That's where it started," she told Sharur. The iron wolf had stalked up behind her from the cabin where Eric was washing up after dinner. "For me, anyway."

The demon sniffed at the wind. The leaves of the north woods were just past the height of their autumn colors and were drifting down to blanket the ground. "There is a power here," he growled. "Beyond the mark the thief left on this place."

"Really?" Sheena looked about with curiosity. She placed her fingers against the papery bark of a nearby birch tree. The sound that vibrated through her fingers was soft, almost too quiet to hear, but the tree was singing. She strained to hear more. It sounded like a high lilting voice vocalizing without words. A loon out on the lake behind her issued its mournful call and Sheena lost track of the voice. The loon was answered by two others. It took her a moment to find the mysterious voice again. She pressed her ear to the tree, but the sound was no louder.

She closed her eyes and felt for the spirit of the place. Oh, yes, it was singing! It sang in the high lilting voice she heard from the birch, and in many others both lower and higher. It was a glorious chorus of nature. Sheena spread her arms and wings and felt the music as much as heard it. The sound mellowed and softened as the sun sank below the horizon beyond the forest to the west of the cornfield.

Do you hear, goddess? One low voice sang out, almost hidden in the chorus.

"I hear," Sheena replied. She opened her eyes. A slender young man stepped out from a maple tree. It was impossible to describe his features as other than those belonging to a "maple tree man." He was maple colored, with hair the color of autumn maple leaves falling over his shoulders, and eyes deep and rich like maple sap. He was slender and lithe like the maple tree, and neither too short nor stretching too high to the sky. He wore a shirt and leggings of supple fiber in dark reds and muted yellows. He held his hands out and bowed slightly, and even this was reminiscent of the maple tree bowing in the wind.

"Earth's bounty to you, goddess. All forests are one," he said in that same voice that had been joined to the singing moments before.

"Greetings, maple spirit." She relaxed her arms and wings. "I see you and hear you. Do you wish to talk with me?"

"Please." He bowed again.

"I am listening. Is there a name you'd like me to call you?" she asked.

"Aninaatig, if you please."

"Of course, Aninaatig," she nodded. Sharur sat behind her, quietly observing the spirit.

"I bid you welcome, goddess. You have been here among us many times before, but it was not the time for you to hear our song. We are glad that you may hear us now, because a dangerous time is coming."

Sheena's lip curved in a wry smile. "I had a feeling you would say something like that."

"You protect the forest from your place along the river. When the cedars in the east were enchanted and forced to walk, you laid them to rest. This was but one of the things the Dark Ones have done to threaten the forest. When they made Raven sick and he caused the trees of his home to wither and die, this was another. There is more they will do. They have many plans. The sons of Man cannot often hear us, but we of the forest see what the Dark Ones do. One changeling woman with a bow is just the beginning of what they will send to defeat you, so that they may carry out their plans."

"What do these Dark Ones want?"

"There is power in the forest. They want to take that power for their own. Where they succeed, the forest will sicken and become theirs. You have sensed it, perhaps, in your trials with the changeling."

Sheena remembered the sickened, decaying smell of the trees from Elf Shot's portals. She exchanged a glance with Sharur, who inclined his head slightly.

"Yes. I remember this."

"The Dark Ones already master time within their own lands. They will seek to gain more, and when a piece of the forest falls to them, it is beyond your influence. Thus, they threaten life by threatening the forest."

"Which forest do they threaten, Aninaatig?"

Aninaatig bowed again and said with a mournful expression, "*All* forests are one, goddess."

Acknowledgements

This book would not have been written without the influence of a marvelous online game, *City of Heroes*. More than any other MMORPG (massively multiplayer online roleplaying game) I have experienced before or since, the community of players and the development team made it a joy to take on the role of a superpowered hero (or villain) and spend a few hours saving the world, upholding truth and justice, or exploring what a world with metahuman powers would be like. Unlike some other games or genres, *City of Heroes* (and its delightfully evil twin *City of Villains*) attracted a very wide range of players from many different countries, backgrounds, perspectives, and walks of life. The players made the game welcoming, and many truly tried to act as heroes the best that they could. *City of Heroes* was arguably the best creative outlet for superhero play and storytelling available at the time. The game had a good run of eight years and was still profitable when it ended in 2012.

Special thanks for getting me to try the game goes to my longtime friend, Pat Sonnek. One night when he was visiting us out on the prairie in southwest Minnesota, Pat brought up the game and gave us a demo, logged in as his signature character, Sun Man. And there was the orange and gold-suited hero flying over buildings and city streets, fighting bad guys with his own heroic battle cry, "Fire in the Hole!" This was 2004, mind you, and the 3D freedom of flying characters was a pretty novel experience for online games. Pat has been a fan of gold- and silver-age comic book heroes forever, and both Sun Man and PsiKid reflect those noble origins better when he's telling their stories than I can capture. I can simply thank him for allowing me to bring them in to support the Titans in this story.

The next kudos go to my wife, Gretchen, for trying out the game even though she didn't consider herself a big fan of the superhero genre. In a great number of ways, she has facilitated and supported the storytelling captured in this book. I elected to give only one of her characters a minor cameo in "A Wing and a Prayer" mostly because so many of her characters are complex, too interesting to serve in minor supporting roles, and… quite frankly… *hers*. Our thinking meshes well most of the time, but I still have difficulty capturing the essence of many of her characters. Serendipity Blue was the one who got some air time here, and I had Gretchen check her dialog and actions to make sure I got it right. (We will see more of Blue in another story!)

Remember the player community I mentioned a couple of paragraphs above? Foremost for me among that community is the group of players known as the League of Titans. This group assembled on the beta forums two years before the game even launched, much less before I became associated with the game about a year after its launch. The storytelling and roleplaying that the players in this group did was definitely a cut above the vast majority of MMO guilds in other games, and was special even for the *City of Heroes* community. Perhaps more importantly, this group was more than just an in-game guild. It was and remains an extended family of gamers who connected with each other in real life and in other games, as circumstances and interests permitted. When Pat sponsored Gretchen and me to the Titans, there was a special sort of membership process involved. We were interviewed in-character by officers of the group, brought on heroic missions in the game, and evaluated behind the scenes for our fit with the standards of player behavior expected of all members of the league. When we were accepted, joining the League of Titans was an in-character roleplaying experience, as well. Within the group, there was space for action-oriented gameplay, forum-based roleplaying stories, and in-game roleplaying. Styles differed, but respect and support was a common, unifying bond among the Titans. Even though players came and went among different games, and life intervened for many members at different times over the years, the connections and friendships continue for many of us ten (or more) years later. So, to all members of the League of Titans, past, present, and future, a hearty salute!

Signature League of Titans characters who I could find places to include in cameo roles in "A Wing and a Prayer" include: Icelock, Jet Flash, Syngularity, Liberty Girl, Leafchaser, Irish Fury, and Scrimmage. Some others are mentioned: Steel Magnolia, Warlocke, Fletcher, Autumn Sno, and Doctor Graviton. Names I will probably have to save for the next story include: Talus, Tentagil, Bomber, Red Fox Bravo, Spektra, Sovereign Guard, Diamonte, Saldan, Durzo, and Flair. Whether or not the Titan characters got mention in this story, the players behind the heroes' masks have played an enormous role in shaping the kind of stories that get told and the nature of the world in which these stories play out. Thanks to everyone!

Other important influences on the style of the story told in "A Wing and a Prayer" come from some of the people who I have counted as friends over the years. This includes special salutes to friends and gamers in the military: Jerry Noel and Paul Hoeffer from Madison—straight shooters, both of them!—and other fellow officers with whom I worked, played, and laughed over the years: John Zeitler, Al Fortezzo, and Carl Oeschger. Tyson Robinson, Frank Froelich, Rob Cunningham, and a number of other wonderful people whose names have slipped from memories and address books over the years also deserve mention and thanks, especially those with the combination of good luck and fortitude to remain in Alaska for so long! In or from Minnesota, Charlotte Haas, Barb Hively, Even Nelson, Howard Nelson, Doug Cox, Ron Arndt, and the "Mankato Crew" deserve special mention and thanks for putting up with many of my strange ideas over the years. Then there are the "Gamers Wanted" crew in Massachusetts—Larry, Jake, and Scotty—for whom Venture City might strike close to home. I have undoubtedly forgotten some names that should be included. My apologies, if this applies to you!

Additional thanks for the motivation and inspiration to keep writing goes to John Beachem, author of the Lorradda Stone series, Mercedes Lackey, one of the most prolific and consistently wonderful authors I am aware of, and Steve Callender, a professional friend of mine. Steve has two superpowers. One is that he is an idea hamster, finding and applying really neat ideas for lots of different things. The other power is that of authentic, encouraging coaching. Thanks to all three of these motivators!

Many of the places described in this story are taken directly or with creative license from real-world locations. Scenes in northern Wisconsin, for example, are simply re-purposed from real life. Most of the places and districts that found their way into Venture City are based on actual locations in and around New Bedford, Massachusetts. Any aspersions or inaccuracies are mine, of course, tempered by the need (with humorous apologies) to completely level New Bedford in order to create the shining new metahuman-rich center of art and commerce that is the fictional Venture City.

The spirit of *City of Heroes* lives on in this story and other works. While I did not set out specifically to write a superhero story, there is just so much that is possible within this genre that the story—with its blend of situations and characters—quickly dictated the setting. The setting enriched and made possible many of the interactions and options that the heroes and villains had to choose from. For the readers who played the *City of Heroes* game, or who have enjoyed movies or series such as *Arrow*, *The Flash*, *The Avengers*, or *Iron Man*, the flavor of "A Wing and a Prayer" should have a familiar taste.

To those readers for whom this resonates, *remember Atlas Park 33!* For anyone reading through these endnotes, superhero stories are meant to remind us all of something important: that you are (or can be) a hero to somebody. I encourage you to make the choice.

We are heroes. This is what we do.

Author Bio

Steve started by writing fan fiction for Watership Down at the age of 8, and has gone on from there with fantasy and science fiction being his major passions. Early influences ranged from Robert Heinlein, Anne McCaffrey, and Isaac Asimov to the Minneapolis "Scribblies" writers' group (Steven Brust, Emma Bull, Will Shetterly, Pat Wrede, and others). Steve often takes fantasy or science fiction RPGs or MMORPGs as creative inspiration for his stories, and turns them on their sides with "What if...?" questions for those game environments. "A Wing and a Prayer" is his first published novel-length work.

www.ingramcontent.com/pod-product-compliance
Lightning Source LLC
Chambersburg PA
CBHW070223260626
47160CB00002B/670